Katherine Mansfield

STORIES

Katherine Mansfield

STORIES

Introduction by JEFFREY MEYERS

VINTAGE CLASSICS

Vintage Books, A Division of Random House, Inc.

NEW YORK

First Vintage Classics Edition, May 1991

Copyright © 1956 by Alfred A. Knopf, Inc.
Copyright renewed 1984 by Alfred A. Knopf, Inc.
Introduction copyright © 1991 by Jeffrey Meyers

All rights reserved under International and Pan-American Copyright Conventions. Published in the United States by Vintage Books, a division of Random House, Inc., New York, and simultaneously in Canada by Random House of Canada Limited, Toronto. Originally published in hardcover by Alfred A. Knopf, Inc., in 1956.

ISBN: 0-679-73374-4
Library of Congress Catalog Card Number: 90-50474

Book design by Kathleen Carey

Manufactured in the United States of America
10 9 8 7 6 5 4 3 2

CONTENTS

Contents

INTRODUCTION

by Jeffrey Meyers

LIKE THE PAINTER Watteau and the composer Chopin, Katherine Mansfield is an artist whose strength lies in subtle detail, precise phrasing, delicate observation, and concentrated emotion. Her elegant, witty, and sometimes bitterly ironic stories do not emphasize character and plot, the traditional concerns of fiction, but present a quintessential event, a summary of a human life in a few significant scenes. Intensely visual and essentially impressionistic, Mansfield expresses character through the use of symbolic objects and poetic evocations of mood; the fragmentary and casually linked episodes of a Mansfield story tend to convey its theme through suggestion rather than statement.

Mansfield's stories take place in New Zealand, where she was born Kathleen Beauchamp in 1888 and spent her early life, and in England, Germany, and France, where she lived and traveled from 1908 until her early death in 1923. "Prelude," the longest and perhaps most memorable of her stories, was hand printed and stitched by Leonard and Virginia Woolf at their small Hogarth Press in 1918. The first significant achievement of her literary career, "Prelude" begins the family chronicle that continues in "At the Bay," "The Garden Party," and "The Doll's House."

"Prelude" obstensibly concerns a family's move from Wellington to the country village of Karori at Easter 1893, but the title suggests the transition of the autobiographical child, Kezia, from childhood innocence ("Now everything familiar was left behind") to greater awareness of evil in human life. Moreover, like William Wordsworth's long poem of the same title, the story portrays an imaginative awakening and the "growth of a poet's mind."

The most striking aspect of "Prelude" is its vivid portrayal of the Burnell family and their servants: Stanley Burnell, the physical, energetic *paterfamilias* who is completely unaware of his wife's ambiguous feelings; Linda Burnell, the delicate, sensitive invalid who sometimes hates her sexually aggressive husband; Mrs. Fairfield, the gentle, loving grandmother; Beryl Fairfield, vain, restless, and dreamy; the rough Trout cousins; the servant Alice; and the Irish handyman, Pat, who introduces death to Kezia by killing a duck, which leaves "a long spurt of blood [like a tubercular hemorrhage] where the head had been."

The story achieves its effect through symbolic details—the aloe that flowers once every century; Stanley's sensual delicacies; Pat's piratical earrings; Beryl's exotic guitar—and also through an episodic structure that conveys the shifting perspectives of the various characters. A deliberately vague conclusion contributes to the theme of the conflict between the real and the overt self, of the poignant solitude within the complex relationships of the family. In her idealized New Zealand stories, Mansfield burned away the bitterness of her childhood.

Mansfield's moving story of personal betrayal, "Je ne parle pas français" ("I don't speak French"), expresses her profoundest adult fears and settles some personal scores with both her French lover, Francis Carco, and her English husband, John Middleton Murry. The first-person narrator is the loathsome Raoul Duquette (Carco), who is, by his own admission, impudent and cheap, calculating and cynical. Dick Harmon (Murry) has a "dreamy half smile on his lips" that barely disguises his weak and treacherous character. He runs away to Paris with the frail and exquisite, childlike and terribly vulnerable Mouse (Mansfield), and is met at the railway station by Duquette, who escorts them to their hotel. Dick then abandons Mouse, leaving a letter that pathetically explains: "I cannot kill my mother! Not even for you."

When Mouse tells Raoul that is it now impossible for her to go home because all her friends think she is married, he ambiguously promises to come back the next morning to "take care of you a little." But he changes his mind when he realizes that he can gain very little from her. Abandoned by both men and quite helpless, Mouse, a fragile, victimized butterfly who is compared to the tragic heroine in Puccini's opera, is in a desperate state. She may even, it seems, be forced to surrender her virginity to some "dirty old gallant," whose promises of protection would match those of Raoul and Dick.

"Je ne parle pas français," which was privately printed by Mansfield, originally had a deliberately disgusting conclusion (it was deleted from her collection of stories later published by Constable, her English publishers), which hints at Raoul's homosexuality and portrays his revulsion toward the proprietress of a café: "I'd rather like to dine with her. Even to sleep with her afterwards. Would she be pale like that all over? But no. She'd have large moles. They go with that kind of skin. And I can't bear them. They remind me somehow, disgustingly, of mushrooms." The ending in the Constable collection is actually more subtle and effective than the original, which overemphasizes Raoul's cruelty and diminishes the sympathy we feel for the vulnerable Mouse. This story, Mansfield told Murry, is "*a cry against corruption* . . . I mean corruption in the widest sense of the word." It is a protest against moral perversion and betrayal.

"The Daughters of the Late Colonel" is a gentle satire on Mansfield's close friend, Ida Constance Baker, and on Ida's moody and irascible father, a "dried up old stick" who shot himself after World War I. The daughters, Constantia and Josephine, faced with two conflicting alternatives—leading their own lives or sacrificing their lives to their father—chose the latter ("It's much nicer to be weak than to be strong"). The title of the story defines the timid daughters in relation to their authoritarian father, whom they continue to fear after his death. The main event in their lives, the death of the colonel, has already taken place. Yet the daughters feel as though their overbearing father—who had glared at them with one eye just before he died—were still alive, and has not forgiven them for burying him. The story explores the unreality of death, the power of the dead over the living, the sense of lost life and the yearning for fulfillment ("If mother had lived, might they have married?").

Mansfield explained that in the satirical yet sensitive "The

Garden-Party" she tried to convey "the diversity of life and how we try to fit in everything, Death included. That is bewildering for a person of Laura's age." Laura's mother, Mrs. Sheridan, attempts to preserve their innocent Eden by having her elaborate garden party despite the accidental death of her working-class neighbor. Laura, who feels intuitive and imaginative sympathy for the bereaved family and does not want to disturb their mourning, is bribed and distracted by her mother's gift of a new hat that symbolizes the moral corruption of her mother's values and way of life. After the pleasant garden party has ended, Laura is callously urged by Mrs. Sheridan to take a basket of leftover food to the poor family and is then forced by them to see their dead father. Her childishly impossible attempt to synthesize the pleasures of life and the experience of death illuminates the contrast between snobbery and social responsibility. Mrs. Sheridan's inability to respond to Laura's finer feelings and moral awareness illustrates the truth of Blaise Pascal's *pensée:* "Pity for the unfortunate does not clash with our appetites. On the contrary, we are glad to offer this evidence of friendship, and to acquire a reputation for kindness without giving anything."

A group of Mansfield's most important stories—"The Man Without a Temperament," "Bliss," "Marriage à la Mode," and "The Stranger" (all written between 1918 and 1921)—provides a fictional portrait of her marriage to Murry that complements the grim reality of her *Journal* and *Letters*. "The Man Without a Temperament," the most revealing and intimate of the marriage stories, reflects Mansfield's fears about how Murry might have felt if he had given in to her pleas and followed the advice of her doctor, who urged him to live abroad with her for the two years she felt she needed to recover from tuberculosis. The story vividly evokes the boredom and trivial irritations of invalid life in a French Riviera *pension,* and the couple's desperate longing for a more meaningful existence in England. In her *Journal,* Mansfield lamented that Murry seemed to lack a "temperament" and was "not warm, ardent, eager, full of quick response, careless, spendthrift of himself, vividly alive, *high-spirited.*" In this tale, the invalid woman is far more intense and vital than her husband. He is forced to suppress his dissatisfaction beneath an ox-like passivity and obedience, but fails to conceal his resentment about the inevitable sacrifice of his career and independence. Though the couple live in constant intimacy, they are divided by an abyss of unspoken hostility that the wife fears will lead to a dreaded separation. At the end, when she asks, "do you mind awfully being out here with me?," he whispers: "Rot!"—the first expression of his temperament—which suggests both her lung disease and their emotionally crippling life together.

"The Man Without a Temperament" succeeds partly because Mansfield understood Murry's needs and feelings as well as her own, and dramatized the central, insoluble dilemma of their marriage. As she wrote in her *Journal*: "What have you of him now? What is your relationship? He talks to you—sometimes—and then goes off. He thinks of you tenderly. He dreams of a [normal] life with you *some day* when the miracle has happened. You are important to him as a dream. Not as a living reality. For you are not one. What do you share? Almost nothing. . . . Life together, with me ill, is simply torture with happy moments. But it's not life."

"Bliss" describes the destruction of Bertha Young's euphoria about her too-perfect marriage, complete with the baby, money, and home that Mansfield never possessed. The smugness and falsity of the arty guests at her dinner party merely intensify her self-deception. Bertha seems to experience a sexually ambiguous intimacy with her guest Pearl Fulton, a beautiful woman who had "something strange" about her, while at the same time desiring physical relations with her husband for the first time in her life. But the spell is shattered when Bertha discovers that her husband is having an affair with Pearl. This *dénouement,* like the pear tree that symbolizes marital infidelity (as in Chaucer's "Merchant's Tale"), is too obviously ironic. But the story's theme of the worm in the bud, what Mansfield called "the snail under the leaf," and her belief that one can never count on happiness, are basic to Mansfield's life and work; they were nurtured by her profound unhappiness with her lovers as well as her deep-rooted insecurity with Murry.

"Marriage à la Mode" (named after John Dryden's comedy of 1672) portrays a loveless, pretentious marriage in the modern bohemian fashion, after the core of meaning has been lost. William, the rather plodding yet providing husband, disturbed by vague premonitions, comes home, like Ulysses, to a houseful of parasitic suitors and a selfish, indifferent Penelope. He is estranged from his wife, Isabel, and mocked by her phony friends, who eat the fruit he has brought for his children, whom he scarcely manages to see. Unwanted and isolated, William has only the idyllic memories of their earlier life together, when "he hadn't the slightest idea that Isabel wasn't as happy as he." When poor William returns to the city and sends Isabel a sentimental love letter to set things right again, she reads it aloud to her friends, who become hysterical with laughter. Though Isabel suffers a moment of conscience, guilt and self-recrimination—"what a loathsome thing to have done"—she chooses to swim with her friends (who had excluded William from this pleasure) rather than answer his pathetic though well-meaning letter.

In "The Stranger," John Hammond—wealthy, successful, self-important, pompous, yet terribly insecure—waits impatiently for his wife's ship to dock in New Zealand after her ten-month journey to Europe. He is desperately eager to regain and repossess Janey, and childishly jealous of her friends aboard ship, of the doctor and the captain, even of his children's letters to their mother—of anything that distracts her attention from him. Yet, when he finally embraces his wife, "again, as always, he had the feeling that he was holding something that was never quite his—his. Something too delicate, too precious, that would fly away once he let go."

Mansfield subtly conveys the intense strain on Hammond when his wife responds coldly to his caresses. He has great difficulty reestablishing his intimacy with her and "never knew for dead certain that she was as glad as he was." When, in their hotel room, he finally discovers (and all discoveries in these stories are shattering) the reason for the ship's delay and his wife's preoccupation—that a man had died in his wife's arms—he immediately understands that Janey has achieved an emotional connection with a stranger far stronger than she ever had with Hammond; that the memory of the dead is stronger than the love of the living. Despite her half-hearted reassurance, "It's nothing to do with you and me," Hammond is destroyed by this recognition, and the story concludes: "They would never be alone together again."

Hammond's jealousy of the emotional bond between his wife and the dead stranger—which may have been inspired by Murry's jealous rivalry with Mansfield's brother, Leslie, who died in the war—a bond stronger than anything she could feel about a living man, reveals the emotional emptiness of their marriage.

Mansfield defended her technique and clarified her intention in this story in a letter to an editor who had questioned the effectiveness of the final sentence:

> I agree with you that man will forget [the incident of the dead stranger]—almost immediately, really—it certainly won't be true of his future relations with Janey. But in the "keyed up" state he was in, and remembering how it was natural to him to exaggerate everything—to take the most extreme view of everything, and remembering too, his *childishness*—his childish desire for everything to be all right and really his childish grief that it wasn't—I feel that nothing less than such an unqualified statement would fit. There in its glimpse of falsity, too, you had him. . . . It was all up with him, for ever. (Of course, it wasn't!)

Mansfield's marriage stories reflect her own fear of abandonment and betrayal, her self-destructive jealousy, and her guilt about being an invalid. They emphasize the isolated heroine who desperately needs sympathy and love, and the lack of understanding and basic honesty in marital relations. As she told Murry in 1920: "I have hiding places—so have you. They are very different ones. We do though emerge from them strange to each other, and it's only when the strangeness wears off that we are together. This must ever be so."

In February 1922, while Mansfield was enduring a painful and enervating treatment for tuberculosis, she wrote one of her finest stories, "The Fly." The theme and central symbol of this intensely concentrated work derive from Gloucester's bitter statement about the gods' cruelty to mortal men—"As flies to wanton boys are we to the gods; / They kill us for their sport" (*King Lear*, IV.i); from William Blake's poem "The Fly"—"For I dance / And drink, and sing, / Till some blind hand / Shall brush my wing"; from Anton Chekhov's description in his story, "The Duel" (1891), of the heroine who "felt like a fly that kept crawling into an inkwell"; and, more immediately, from Mansfield's use of the fly-in-the-milk-jug metaphor to describe her own exhausted and impotent condition. For both the fly and the tubercular victim suffocate— one in ink, the other in blood. In this autobiographical story, the fly represents Mansfield and her dead brother, Leslie, as well as the fate of all helpless victims.

Mansfield chose the name of Woodifield, a tubercular patient and friend of Ida Baker in a Swiss health resort, because of its similarity to "Fairfield" (the name she used in "Prelude") and to Beauchamp (her real surname). The turning point of the story, which takes place in late autumn, occurs when old Woodifield reminds the prosperous and confident boss (based on Mansfield's father, Harold Beauchamp) of their dead sons in Belgium and complains that the *hôteliers* near the cemetery are "trading on our feelings." When Woodifield leaves, after making this shocking pronouncement, the boss locks himself in his office. He experiences extreme anguish because he can no longer feel grief for his dead son nor shed cathartic tears as he had done at the time of his death six years ago, when (like Woodifield) "he had left the office a broken man, with his life in ruins."

The boss's torture of the fly, a classic example of displaced aggression, is a sadistic attempt to reassert his own omnipotence. The fly's plucky struggle to avoid suffocation symbolizes the destiny of mortals who think they have escaped horrible danger and are "ready for life," but have actually lost divine protection and come under the influence of a malign will. When the boss finally kills the fly with the third ink blot, he drives out the demons of grief and guilt, and once again forgets his dead son. The greatness of this very short story derives from Mansfield's ability to control and then detonate highly compressed emotion and to make the central symbol express a universal theme. Katherine Mansfield, a beautiful woman and immensely talented writer, died tragically at the age of thirty-four, just as she had finally achieved mastery of her art.

Katherine Mansfield

STORIES

The Tiredness of Rosabel

At the corner of Oxford Circus Rosabel bought a bunch of violets, and that was practically the reason why she had so little tea—for a scone and a boiled egg and a cup of cocoa at Lyons are not ample sufficiency after a hard day's work in a millinery establishment. As she swung on to the step of the Atlas 'bus, grabbed her skirt with one hand and clung to the railing with the other, Rosabel thought she would have sacrificed her soul for a good dinner—roast duck and green peas, chestnut stuffing, pudding with brandy sauce—something hot and strong and filling. She sat down next to a girl very much her own age who was reading *Anna Lombard* in a cheap, paper-covered edition, and the rain had tear-spattered the pages. Rosabel looked out of the window; the street was blurred and misty, but light striking on the panes turned their dullness to opal and silver, and the jewellers' shops seen through this, were fairy palaces. Her feet were horribly wet, and she knew the bottom of her skirt and petticoat would be coated with black, greasy mud. There was a sickening smell of warm humanity—it seemed to be oozing out of everybody in the 'bus—and everybody had the same expression, sitting so still, staring in front of them. How many times had she read these advertisements—"Sapolio Saves Time, Saves Labour"—"Heinz's Tomato Sauce"—and the inane, annoying dialogue between doctor and judge concerning the superlative merits of "Lamplough's Pyretic Saline." She glanced at the book which the girl read so earnestly, mouthing the words in a way that Rosabel detested, licking her first finger and thumb each time that she turned the page. She could not see very clearly; it was some-

3

thing about a hot, voluptuous night, a band playing, and a girl with lovely, white shoulders. Oh, Heavens! Rosabel stirred suddenly and unfastened the two top buttons of her coat . . . she felt almost stifled. Through her half-closed eyes the whole row of people on the opposite seat seemed to resolve into one fatuous, staring face. . . .

And this was her corner. She stumbled a little on her way out and lurched against the girl next her. "I beg your pardon," said Rosabel, but the girl did not even look up. Rosabel saw that she was smiling as she read.

Westbourne Grove looked as she had always imagined Venice to look at night, mysterious, dark, even the hansoms were like gondolas dodging up and down, and the lights trailing luridly—tongues of flame licking the wet street—magic fish swimming in the Grand Canal. She was more than glad to reach Richmond Road, but from the corner of the street until she came to No. 26 she thought of those four flights of stairs. Oh, why four flights! It was really criminal to expect people to live so high up. Every house ought to have a lift, something simple and inexpensive, or else an electric staircase like the one at Earl's Court—but four flights! When she stood in the hall and saw the first flight ahead of her and the stuffed albatross head on the landing, glimmering ghost-like in the light of the little gas jet, she almost cried. Well, they had to be faced; it was very like bicycling up a steep hill, but there was not the satisfaction of flying down the other side. . . .

Her own room at last! She closed the door, lit the gas, took off her hat and coat, skirt, blouse, unhooked her old flannel dressing-gown from behind the door, pulled it on, then unlaced her boots—on consideration her stockings were not wet enough to change. She went over to the washstand. The jug had not been filled again to-day. There was just enough water to soak the sponge, and the enamel was coming off the basin—that was the second time she had scratched her chin.

It was just seven o'clock. If she pulled the blind up and put out the gas it was much more restful—Rosabel did not want to read. So she knelt down on the floor, pillowing her arms on the window sill . . . just one little sheet of glass between her and the great wet world outside!

She began to think of all that had happened during the day. Would she ever forget that awful woman in the grey mackintosh who had wanted a trimmed motor-cap—"something purple with something rosy each side"—or the girl who had tried on every hat in the shop and then said she would "call in to-morrow and decide definitely"? Rosabel could not help smiling; the excuse was worn so thin . . .

But there had been one other—a girl with beautiful red hair and a white skin and eyes the colour of that green ribbon shot with gold they had got from Paris last week. Rosabel had seen her electric brougham at the door; a man had come in with her, quite a young man, and so well dressed.

"What is it exactly that I want, Harry?" she had said, as Rosabel took the pins out of her hat, untied her veil, and gave her a hand-mirror.

"You must have a black hat," he had answered, "a black hat with a feather that goes right around it, and then around your neck and ties in a bow under your chin, and the ends tuck into your belt—a decent-sized feather."

The girl glanced at Rosabel laughingly. "Have you any hats like that?"

They had been very hard to please; Harry would demand the impossible, and Rosabel was almost in despair. Then she remembered the big, untouched box upstairs.

"Oh, one moment, Madam," she had said. "I think perhaps I can show you something that will please you better." She had run up, breathlessly, cut the cords, scattered the tissue paper, and yes, there was the very hat—rather large, soft, with a great curled feather, and a black velvet rose, nothing else. They had been charmed. The girl had put it on and then handed it to Rosabel.

"Let me see how it looks on you," she said, frowning a little, very serious indeed.

Rosabel turned to the mirror and placed it on her brown hair, then faced them.

"Oh, Harry, isn't it adorable," the girl cried, "I must have that!" She smiled again at Rosabel. "It suits you, beautifully."

A sudden, ridiculous feeling of anger had seized Rosabel.

She longed to throw the lovely, perishable thing in the girl's face, and bent over the hat, flushing.

"It's exquisitely finished off inside, Madam," she said. The girl swept out to her brougham, and left Harry to pay and bring the box with him.

"I shall go straight home and put it on before I come out to lunch with you," Rosabel heard her say.

The man leant over her as she made out the bill, then, as he counted the money into her hand—"Ever been painted?" he said.

"No," said Rosabel, shortly, realizing the swift change in his voice, the slight tinge of insolence, of familiarity.

"Oh, well you ought to be," said Harry. "You've got such a damned pretty little figure."

Rosabel did not pay the slightest attention. How handsome he had been! She had thought of no one else all day; his face fascinated her; she could see clearly his fine, straight eyebrows, and his hair grew back from his forehead with just the slightest suspicion of crisp curl, his laughing, disdainful mouth. She saw again his slim hands counting the money into hers. . . . Rosabel suddenly pushed the hair back from her face, her forehead was hot . . . if those slim hands could rest one moment . . . the luck of that girl!

Suppose they changed places. Rosabel would drive home with him, of course they were in love with each other, but not engaged, very nearly, and she would say—"I won't be one moment." He would wait in the brougham while her maid took the hat-box up the stairs, following Rosabel. Then the great, white and pink bedroom with roses everywhere in dull silver vases. She would sit down before the mirror and the little French maid would fasten her hat and find her a thin, fine veil and another pair of white suède gloves—a button had come off the gloves she had worn that morning. She had scented her furs and gloves and handkerchief, taken a big muff and run down stairs. The butler opened the door, Harry was waiting, they drove away to-gether. . . . *That* was life, thought Rosabel! On the way to the Carlton they stopped at Gerard's, Harry bought her great sprays of Parma violets, filled her hands with them.

"Oh, they are sweet!" she said, holding them against her face.

"It is as you always should be," said Harry, "with your hands full of violets."

(Rosabel realized that her knees were getting stiff; she sat down on the floor and leant her head against the wall.) Oh, that lunch! The table covered with flowers, a band hidden behind a grove of palms playing music that fired her blood like wine—the soup, and oysters, and pigeons, and creamed potatoes, and champagne, of course, and afterwards coffee and cigarettes. She would lean over the table fingering her glass with one hand, talking with that charming gaiety which Harry so appreciated. Afterwards a matinee, something that gripped them both, and then tea at the "Cottage."

"Sugar? Milk? Cream?" The little homely questions seemed to suggest a joyous intimacy. And then home again in the dusk, and the scent of the Parma violets seemed to drench the air with their sweetness.

"I'll call for you at nine," he said as he left her.

The fire had been lighted in her boudoir, the curtains drawn, there were a great pile of letters waiting her—invitations for the Opera, dinners, balls, a week-end on the river, a motor tour— she glanced through them listlessly as she went upstairs to dress. A fire in her bedroom, too, and her beautiful, shining dress spread on the bed—white tulle over silver, silver shoes, silver scarf, a little silver fan. Rosabel knew that she was the most famous woman at the ball that night; men paid her homage, a foreign Prince desired to be presented to this English wonder. Yes, it was a voluptuous night, a band playing, and *her* lovely white shoulders. . . .

But she became very tired. Harry took her home, and came in with her for just one moment. The fire was out in the drawing-room, but the sleepy maid waited for her in her boudoir. She took off her cloak, dismissed the servant, and went over to the fireplace, and stood peeling off her gloves; the firelight shone on her hair, Harry came across the room and caught her in his arms— "Rosabel, Rosabel, Rosabel" . . . Oh, the haven of those arms, and she was very tired.

(The real Rosabel, the girl crouched on the floor in the dark, laughed aloud, and put her hand up to her hot mouth.)

Of course they rode in the park next morning, the engagement had been announced in the *Court Circular*, all the world knew, all the world was shaking hands with her. . . .

They were married shortly afterwards at St. George's, Hanover Square, and motored down to Harry's old ancestral home for the honeymoon; the peasants in the village curtseyed to them as they passed; under the folds of the rug he pressed her hands convulsively. And that night she wore again her white and silver frock. She was tired after the journey and went upstairs to bed . . . quite early. . . .

The real Rosabel got up from the floor and undressed slowly, folding her clothes over the back of a chair. She slipped over her head her coarse, calico nightdress, and took the pins out of her hair—the soft, brown flood of it fell round her warmly. Then she blew out the candle and groped her way into bed, pulling the blankets and grimy "honeycomb" quilt closely round her neck, cuddling down in the darkness. . . .

So she slept and dreamed, and smiled in her sleep, and once threw out her arm to feel for something which was not there, dreaming still.

And the night passed. Presently the cold fingers of dawn closed over her uncovered hand; grey light flooded the dull room. Rosabel shivered, drew a little gasping breath, sat up. And because her heritage was that tragic optimism, which is all too often the only inheritance of youth, still half asleep, she smiled, with a little nervous tremor round her mouth.

The Baron

Who IS HE?" I said. "And why does he sit always alone, with his back to us, too?"

"Ah!" whispered the Frau Oberregierungsrat, "he is a *Baron*."

She looked at me very solemnly, and yet with the slightest possible contempt—a fancy-not-recognizing-that-at-the-first-glance expression.

"But, poor soul, he cannot help it," I said. "Surely that unfortunate fact ought not to debar him from the pleasures of intellectual intercourse."

If it had not been for her fork I think she would have crossed herself.

"Surely you cannot understand. He is one of the First Barons."

More than a little unnerved, she turned and spoke to the Frau Doktor on her left.

"My omelette is empty—*empty*," she protested, "and this is the third I have tried!"

I looked at the First of the Barons. He was eating salad—taking a whole lettuce leaf on his fork and absorbing it slowly, rabbitwise—a fascinating process to watch.

Small and slight, with scanty black hair and beard and yellow-toned complexion, he invariably wore black serge clothes, a rough linen shirt, black sandals, and the largest black-rimmed spectacles that I had ever seen.

The Herr Oberlehrer, who sat opposite me, smiled benignantly.

"It must be very interesting for you, gnädige Frau, to be able

9

to watch. . . . Of course this is a *very fine house*. There was a lady from the Spanish Court here in the summer; she had a liver. We often spoke together."

I looked gratified and humble.

"Now, in England, in your boarding 'ouse, one does not find the First Class, as in Germany."

"No, indeed," I replied, still hypnotised by the Baron, who looked like a little yellow silk-worm.

"The Baron comes every year," went on the Herr Oberlehrer, "for his nerves. He has never spoken to any of the guests—*yet*." A smile crossed his face. I seemed to see his visions of some splendid upheaval of that silence—a dazzling exchange of courtesies in a dim future, a splendid sacrifice of a newspaper to this Exalted One, a "danke schön" to be handed down to future generations.

At that moment the postman, looking like a German army officer, came in with the mail. He threw my letters into my milk pudding, and then turned to a waitress and whispered. She retired hastily. The manager of the pension came in with a little tray. A picture post card was deposited on it, and reverently bowing his head, the manager of the pension carried it to the Baron.

Myself, I felt disappointed that there was not a salute of twenty-five guns.

At the end of the meal we were served with coffee. I noticed the Baron took three lumps of sugar, putting two in his cup and wrapping up the third in a corner of his pocket-handkerchief. He was always the first to enter the dining-room and the last to leave; and in a vacant chair beside him he placed a little black leather bag.

In the afternoon, leaning from my window, I saw him pass down the street, walking tremulously and carrying the bag. Each time he passed a lamp-post he shrank a little, as though expecting it to strike him, or maybe the sense of plebeian contamination. . . .

I wondered where he was going, and why he carried the bag. Never had I seen him at the Casino or the Bath Establishment. He looked forlorn, his feet slipped in his sandals. I found myself pitying the Baron.

That evening a party of us were gathered in the salon discussing the day's "cure" with feverish animation. The Frau Ober-regierungsrat sat by me knitting a shawl for her youngest of nine daughters, who was in that very interesting, frail condition. . . . "But it is bound to be quite satisfactory," she said to me. "The dear married a banker—the desire of her life."

There must have been eight or ten of us gathered together, we who were married exchanging confidences as to the under-clothing and peculiar characteristics of our husbands, the unmar-ried discussing the overclothing and peculiar fascinations of Possible Ones.

"I knit them myself," I heard the Frau Lehrer cry, "of thick grey wool. He wears one a month, with two soft collars."

"And then," whispered Fräulein Lisa, "he said to me, 'Indeed you please me. I shall, perhaps, write to your mother.' "

Small wonder that we were a little violently excited, a little expostulatory.

Suddenly the door opened and admitted the Baron.

Followed a complete and death-like silence.

He came in slowly, hesitated, took up a toothpick from a dish on the top of the piano, and went out again.

When the door was closed we raised a triumphant cry! It was the first time he had ever been known to enter the salon. Who could tell what the Future held?

Days lengthened into weeks. Still we were together, and still the solitary little figure, head bowed as though under the weight of the spectacles, haunted me. He entered with the black bag, he retired with the black bag—and that was all.

At last the manager of the pension told us the Baron was leaving the next day.

"Oh," I thought, "surely he cannot drift into obscurity—be lost without one word! Surely he will honour the Frau Oberre-gierungsrat or the Frau Feldleutnantswitwe *once* before he goes."

In the evening of that day it rained heavily. I went to the post office, and as I stood on the steps, umbrellaless, hesitating before plunging into the slushy road, a little, hesitating voice seemed to come from under my elbow.

I looked down. It was the First of the Barons with the black bag and an umbrella. Was I mad? Was I sane? He was asking me to share the latter. But I was exceedingly nice, a trifle diffident, appropriately reverential. Together we walked through the mud and slush.

Now, there is something peculiarly intimate in sharing an umbrella.

It is apt to put one on the same footing as brushing a man's coat for him—a little daring, naïve.

I longed to know why he sat alone, why he carried the bag, what he did all day. But he himself volunteered some information.

"I fear," he said, "that my luggage will be damp. I invariably carry it with me in this bag—one requires so little—for servants are untrustworthy."

"A wise idea," I answered. And then: "Why have you denied us the pleasure—"

"I sit alone that I may eat more," said the Baron, peering into the dusk; "my stomach requires a great deal of food. I order double portions, and eat them in peace."

Which sounded finely Baronial.

"And what do you do all day?"

"I imbibe nourishment in my room," he replied, in a voice that closed the conversation and almost repented of the umbrella.

When we arrived at the pension there was very nearly an open riot.

I ran half-way up the stairs, and thanked the Baron audibly from the landing.

He distinctly replied: "Not at all!"

It was very friendly of the Herr Oberlehrer to have sent me a bouquet that evening, and the Frau Oberregierungsrat asked me for my pattern of a baby's bonnet.

Next day the Baron was gone.

Sic transit gloria German mundi.

The Modern Soul

"GOOD-EVENING," said the Herr Professor, squeezing my hand; "wonderful weather! I returned from a party in the wood. I have been making music for them on my trombone. You know, these pine-trees provide most suitable accompaniment for a trombone! They are sighing delicacy against sustained strength, as I remarked once in a lecture on wind instruments in Frankfort. May I be permitted to sit beside you on this bench, gnädige Frau?"

He sat down, tugging at a white-paper package in the tail pocket of his coat.

"Cherries," he said, nodding and smiling. "There is nothing like cherries for producing free saliva after trombone playing, especially after Grieg's 'Iche Liebe Dich.' Those sustained blasts on 'liebe' make my throat as dry as a railway tunnel. Have some?" He shook the bag at me.

"I prefer watching you eat them."

"Ah, ha!" He crossed his legs, sticking the cherry bag between his knees, to leave both hands free. "Psychologically I understood your refusal. It is your innate feminine delicacy in preferring etherealised sensations. . . . Or perhaps you do not care to eat the worms. All cherries contain worms. Once I made a very interesting experiment with a colleague of mine at the university. We bit into four pounds of the best cherries and did not find one specimen without a worm. But what would you? As I remarked to him afterwards—dear friend, it amounts to this: if one wishes to satisfy the desires of nature one must be strong enough to ignore the facts of nature. . . . The conversation is not out of your depth? I

13

have so seldom the time or opportunity to open my heart to a woman that I am apt to forget."

I looked at him brightly.

"See what a fat one!" cried the Herr Professor. "That is almost a mouthful in itself; it is beautiful enough to hang from a watch-chain." He chewed it up and spat the stone an incredible distance—over the garden path into the flower bed. He was proud of the feat. I saw it. "The quantity of fruit I have eaten on this bench," he sighed; "apricots, peaches, and cherries. One day that garden bed will become an orchard grove, and I shall allow you to pick as much as you please, without paying me anything."

I was grateful, without showing undue excitement.

"Which reminds me"—he hit the side of his nose with one finger—"the manager of the pension handed me my weekly bill after dinner this evening. It is almost impossible to credit. I do not expect you to believe me—he has charged me extra for a miserable little glass of milk I drink in bed at night to prevent insomnia. Naturally, I did not pay. But the tragedy of the story is this: I cannot expect the milk to produce somnolence any longer; my peaceful attitude of mind towards it is completely destroyed. I know I shall throw myself into a fever in attempting to plumb this want of generosity in so wealthy a man as the manager of a pension. Think of me to-night"—he ground the empty bag under his heel—"think that the worst is happening to me as your head drops asleep on your pillow."

Two ladies came on the front steps of the pension and stood, arm in arm, looking over the garden. The one, old and scraggy, dressed almost entirely in black bead trimming and a satin reticule; the other, young and thin, in a white gown, her yellow hair tastefully garnished with mauve sweet peas.

The Professor drew in his feet and sat up sharply, pulling down his waistcoat.

"The Godowskas," he murmured. "Do you know them? A mother and daughter from Vienna. The mother has an internal complaint and the daughter is an actress. Fräulein Sonia is a very modern soul. I think you would find her most sympathetic. She is forced to be in attendance on her mother just now. But what a temperament! I have once described her in her autograph album as tigress with a flower in the hair. Will you excuse me? Perhaps I can persuade them to be introduced to you."

I said, "I am going up to my room." But the Professor rose and shook a playful finger at me. "Na," he said, "we are friends, and, therefore, I shall speak quite frankly to you. I think they would consider it a little 'marked' if you immediately retired to the house at their approach, after sitting here alone with me in the twilight. You know this world. Yes, you know it as I do."

I shrugged my shoulders, remarking with one eye that while the Professor had been talking the Godowskas had trailed across the lawn towards us. They confronted the Herr Professor as he stood up.

"Good-evening," quavered Frau Godowska. "Wonderful weather! It has given me quite a touch of hay fever!" Fräulein Godowska said nothing. She swooped over a rose growing in the embryo orchard, then stretched out her hand with a magnificent gesture to the Herr Professor. He presented me.

"This is my little English friend of whom I have spoken. She is the stranger in our midst. We have been eating cherries together."

"How delightful," sighed Frau Godowska. "My daughter and I have often observed you through the bedroom window. Haven't we, Sonia?"

Sonia absorbed my outward and visible form with an inward and spiritual glance, then repeated the magnificent gesture for my benefit. The four of us sat on the bench, with that faint air of excitement of passengers established in a railway carriage on the qui vive for the train whistle. Frau Godowska sneezed. "I wonder if it is hay fever," she remarked, worrying the satin reticule for her handkerchief, "or would it be the dew? Sonia, dear, is the dew falling?"

Fräulein Sonia raised her face to the sky, and half closed her eyes. "No, mamma, my face is quite warm. Oh, look, Herr Professor, there are swallows in flight; they are like a little flock of Japanese thoughts—nicht wahr?"

"Where?" cried the Herr Professor. "Oh yes, I see, by the kitchen chimney. But why do you say 'Japanese'? Could you not compare them with equal veracity to a little flock of German thoughts in flight?" He rounded on me. "Have you swallows in England?"

"I believe there are some at certain seasons. But doubtless they have not the same symbolical value for the English. In Germany—"

"I have never been to England," interrupted Fräulein Sonia, "but I have many English acquaintances. They are so cold!" She shivered.

"Fish-blooded," snapped Frau Godowska. "Without soul, without heart, without grace. But you cannot equal their dress materials. I spent a week in Brighton twenty years ago, and the travelling cape I bought there is not yet worn out—the one you wrap the hot-water bottle in, Sonia. My lamented husband, your father, Sonia, knew a great deal about England. But the more he knew about it the oftener he remarked to me, 'England is merely an island of beef flesh swimming in a warm gulf stream of gravy.' Such a brilliant way of putting things. Do you remember, Sonia?"

"I forget nothing, mamma," answered Sonia.

Said the Herr Professor: "That is the proof of your calling, gnädige Fräulein. Now I wonder—and this is a very interesting speculation—is memory a blessing or—excuse the word—a curse?"

Frau Godowska looked into the distance, then the corners of her mouth dropped and her skin puckered. She began to shed tears.

"Ach Gott! Gracious lady, what have I said?" exclaimed the Herr Professor.

Sonia took her mother's hand. "Do you know," she said, "to-night it is stewed carrots and nut tart for supper. Suppose we go in and take our places," her sidelong, tragic stare accusing the Professor and me the while.

I followed them across the lawn and up the steps. Frau Godowska was murmuring, "Such a wonderful, beloved man"; with her disengaged hand Fräulein Sonia was arranging the sweet-pea garniture.

"A concert for the benefit of afflicted Catholic infants will take place in the salon at eight-thirty P.M. Artists: Fräulein Sonia

Godowska, from Vienna; Herr Professor Windberg and his trombone; Frau Oberlehrer Weidel, and others."

This notice was tied round the neck of the melancholy stag's head in the dining-room. It graced him like a red and white dinner bib for days before the event, causing the Herr Professor to bow before it and say "good appetite" until we sickened of his pleasantry and left the smiling to be done by the waiter, who was paid to be pleasing to the guests.

On the appointed day the married ladies sailed about the pension dressed like upholstered chairs, and the unmarried ladies like draped muslin dressing-table covers. Frau Godowska pinned a rose in the centre of her reticule; another blossom was tucked in the mazy folds of a white antimacassar thrown across her breast. The gentlemen wore black coats, white silk ties and ferny buttonholes tickling the chin.

The floor of the salon was freshly polished, chairs and benches arranged, and a row of little flags strung across the ceiling—they flew and jigged in the draught with all the enthusiasm of family washing. It was arranged that I should sit beside Frau Godowska, and that the Herr Professor and Sonia should join us when their share of the concert was over.

"That will make you feel quite one of the performers," said the Herr Professor genially. "It is a great pity that the English nation is so unmusical. Never mind! To-night you shall hear something—we have discovered a nest of talent during the rehearsals."

"What do you intend to recite, Fräulein Sonia?"

She shook back her hair. "I never know until the last moment. When I come on the stage I wait for one moment and then I have the sensation as though something struck me here,"—she placed her hand upon her collar brooch—"and . . . words come!"

"Bend down a moment," whispered her mother. "Sonia, love, your skirt safety-pin is showing at the back. Shall I come outside and fasten it properly for you, or will you do it yourself?"

"Oh, mamma, please don't say such things," Sonia flushed and grew very angry. "You know how sensitive I am to the slightest unsympathetic impression at a time like this. . . . I would rather my skirt dropped off my body—"

"Sonia—my heart!"

A bell tinkled.

The waiter came in and opened the piano. In the heated excitement of the moment he entirely forgot what was fitting, and flicked the keys with the grimy table napkin he carried over his arm. The Frau Oberlehrer tripped on the platform followed by a very young gentleman, who blew his nose twice before he hurled his handkerchief into the bosom of the piano.

> "Yes, I know you have no love for me,
> And no forget-me-not.
> No love, no heart, and no forget-me-not."

sang the Frau Oberlehrer, in a voice that seemed to issue from her forgotten thimble and have nothing to do with her.

"Ach, how sweet, how delicate," we cried, clapping her soothingly. She bowed as though to say, "Yes, isn't it?" and retired, the very young gentleman dodging her train and scowling.

The piano was closed, an arm-chair was placed in the centre of the platform. Fräulein Sonia drifted towards it. A breathless pause. Then, presumably, the winged shaft struck her collar brooch. She implored us not to go into the woods in trained dresses, but rather as lightly draped as possible, and bed with her among the pine needles. Her loud, slightly harsh voice filled the salon. She dropped her arms over the back of the chair, moving her lean hands from the wrists. We were thrilled and silent. The Herr Professor, beside me, abnormally serious, his eyes bulging, pulled at his moustache ends. Frau Godowska adopted that peculiarly detached attitude of the proud parent. The only soul who remained untouched by her appeal was the waiter, who leaned idly against the wall of the salon and cleaned his nails with the edge of a programme. He was off duty and intended to show it.

"What did I say?" shouted the Herr Professor under cover of tumultuous applause, "tem-per-ament! There you have it. She is a flame in the heart of a lily. I know I am going to play well. It is my turn now. I am inspired. Fräulein Sonia"—as the lady returned to us, pale and draped in a large shawl—"you are my inspiration. To-night you shall be the soul of my trombone. Wait only."

To right and left of us people bent over and whispered admiration down Fräulein Sonia's neck. She bowed in the grand style.

"I am always successful," she said to me. "You see, when I act I *am*. In Vienna, in the plays of Ibsen we had so many bouquets that the cook had three in the kitchen. But it is difficult here. There is so little magic. Do you not feel it? There is none of that mysterious perfume which floats almost as a visible thing from the souls of the Viennese audiences. My spirit starves for want of that." She leaned forward, chin on hand. "Starves," she repeated.

The Professor appeared with his trombone, blew into it, held it up to one eye, tucked back his shirt cuffs and wallowed in the soul of Sonia Godowska. Such a sensation did he create that he was recalled to play a Bavarian dance, which he acknowledged was to be taken as a breathing exercise rather than an artistic achievement. Frau Godowska kept time to it with a fan.

Followed the very young gentleman who piped in a tenor voice that he loved somebody, "with blood in his heart and a thousand pains." Fräulein Sonia acted a poison scene with the assistance of her mother's pill vial and the armchair replaced by a chaise longue; a young girl scratched a lullaby on a young fiddle; and the Herr Professor performed the last sacrificial rites on the altar of the afflicted children by playing the National Anthem.

"Now I must put mamma to bed," whispered Fräulein Sonia. "But afterwards I must take a walk. It is imperative that I free my spirit in the open air for a moment. Would you come with me, as far as the railway station and back?"

"Very well, then, knock on my door when you're ready."

Thus the modern soul and I found ourselves together under the stars.

"What a night!" she said. "Do you know that poem of Sappho about her hands in the stars? . . . I am furiously sapphic. And this is so remarkable—not only am I sapphic, I find in all the works of all the greatest writers, especially in their unedited letters, some touch, some sign of myself—some resemblance, some part of myself, like a thousand reflections of my own hands in a dark mirror."

"But what a bother," said I.

"I do not know what you mean by 'bother'; is it rather the curse of my genius. . . ." She paused suddenly, staring at me. "Do you know my tragedy?" she asked.

I shook my head.

"My tragedy is my mother. Living with her I live with the coffin of my unborn aspirations. You heard that about the safety-pin to-night. It may seem to you a little thing, but it ruined my three first gestures. They were—"

"Impaled on a safety-pin," I suggested.

"Yes, exactly that. And when we are in Vienna I am the victim of moods, you know. I long to do wild, passionate things. And mamma says, 'Please pour out my mixture first.' Once I remember I flew into a rage and threw a washstand jug out of the window. Do you know what she said? 'Sonia, it is not so much throwing things out of windows, if only you would—' "

"Choose something smaller?" said I.

"No . . . 'tell me about it beforehand.' Humiliating! And I do not see any possible light out of this darkness."

"Why don't you join a touring company and leave your mother in Vienna?"

"What! Leave my poor, little, sick widowed mother in Vienna! Sooner than that I would drown myself. I love my mother as I love nobody else in the world—nobody and nothing! Do you think it is impossible to love one's tragedy? 'Out of my great sorrows I make my little songs,' that is Heine or myself."

"Oh, well, that's all right," I said cheerfully.

"But it is not all right!"

I suggested we should turn back. We turned.

"Sometimes I think the solution lies in marriage," said Fräulein Sonia. "If I find a simple, peaceful man who adores me and will look after mamma—a man who would be for me a pillow—for genius cannot hope to mate—I shall marry him. . . . You know the Herr Professor has paid me very marked attentions."

"Oh, Fräulein Sonia," I said, very pleased with myself, "why not marry him to your mother?" We were passing the hairdresser's shop at the moment. Fräulein Sonia clutched my arm.

"You, you," she stammered. "The cruelty. I am going to faint.

Mamma to marry again before I marry—the indignity. I am going to faint here and now."

I was frightened.

"You can't," I said, shaking her. "Come back to the pension and faint as much as you please. But you can't faint here. All the shops are closed. There is nobody about. Please don't be so foolish."

"Here and here only!" She indicated the exact spot and dropped quite beautifully, lying motionless.

"Very well," I said, "faint away; but please hurry over it."

She did not move. I began to walk home, but each time I looked behind me I saw the dark form of the modern soul prone before the hairdresser's window. Finally I ran, and rooted out the Herr Professor from his room. "Fräulein Sonia has fainted," I said crossly.

"Du lieber Gott! Where? How?"

"Outside the hairdresser's shop in the Station Road."

"Jesus and Maria! Has she no water with her?"—he seized his carafe—"nobody beside her?"

"Nothing."

"Where is my coat? No matter, I shall catch a cold on the chest. Willingly, I shall catch one. . . . You are ready to come with me?"

"No," I said; "you can take the waiter."

"But she must have a woman. I cannot be so indelicate as to attempt to loosen her stays."

"Modern souls oughtn't to wear them," said I. He pushed past me and clattered down the stairs.

When I came down to breakfast next morning there were two places vacant at table. Fräulein Sonia and the Herr Professsor had gone off for a day's excursion in the woods.

I wondered.

The Woman at the Store

ALL THAT DAY the heat was terrible. The wind blew close to the ground; it rooted among the tussock grass, slithered along the road, so that the white pumice dust swirled in our faces, settled and sifted over us and was like a dry-skin itching for growth on our bodies. The horses stumbled along, coughing and chuffing. The pack horse was sick—with a big, open sore rubbed under the belly. Now and again she stopped short, threw back her head, looked at us as though she were going to cry, and whinnied. Hundreds of larks shrilled; the sky was slate colour, and the sound of the larks reminded me of slate pencils scraping over its surface. There was nothing to be seen but wave after wave of tussock grass, patched with purple orchids and manuka bushes covered with thick spider webs.

Jo rode ahead. He wore a blue galatea shirt, corduroy trousers and riding boots. A white handkerchief, spotted with red—it looked as though his nose had been bleeding on it—was knotted round his throat. Wisps of white hair straggled from under his wideawake—his moustache and eyebrows were called white—he slouched in the saddle, grunting. Not once that day had he sung

"I don't care, for don't you see,
My wife's mother was in front of me!"

It was the first day we had been without it for a month, and now there seemed something uncanny in his silence. Jim rode beside me, white as a clown; his black eyes glittered, and he kept shooting out his tongue and moistening his lips. He was dressed in a Jaeger vest, and a pair of blue duck trousers, fastened round the waist with a plaited leather belt. We had hardly spoken since dawn. At noon we had lunched off fly biscuits and apricots by the side of a swampy creek.

"My stomach feels like the crop of a hen," said Jo. "Now then, Jim, you're the bright boy of the party—where's this 'ere store you kep' on talking about? 'Oh, yes,' you says, 'I know a fine store, with a paddock for the horses and a creek runnin' through, owned by a friend of mine who'll give yer a bottle of whisky before 'e shakes hands with yer.' I'd like ter see that place— merely as a matter of curiosity—not that I'd ever doubt yer word—as yer know very well—but . . ."

Jim laughed. "Don't forget there's a woman too, Jo, with blue eyes and yellow hair, who'll promise you something else before she shakes hands with you. Put that in your pipe and smoke it."

"The heat's making you balmy," said Jo. But he dug his knees into the horse. We shambled on. I half fell asleep, and had a sort of uneasy dream that the horses were not moving forward at all— then that I was on a rocking-horse, and my old mother was scolding me for raising such a fearful dust from the drawing-room carpet. "You've entirely worn off the pattern of the carpet," I heard her saying, and she gave the reins a tug. I snivelled and woke to find Jim leaning over me, maliciously smiling.

"That was a case of all but," said he. "I just caught you. What's up? Been bye-bye?"

"No!" I raised my head. "Thank the Lord we're arriving somewhere."

We were on the brow of the hill, and below us there was a whare roofed with corrugated iron. It stood in a garden, rather far back from the road—a big paddock opposite, and a creek and a clump of young willow trees. A thin line of blue smoke stood up straight from the chimney of the whare; and as I looked a woman came out, followed by a child and a sheep dog—the woman carrying what appeared to me a black stick. She made gestures at us. The horses put on a final spurt, Jo took off his wideawake, shouted, threw out his chest, and began singing, "I don't care, for don't you see. . . ." The sun pushed through the pale clouds and shed a vivid light over the scene. It gleamed on

23

the woman's yellow hair, over her flapping pinafore and the rifle she was carrying. The child hid behind her, and the yellow dog, a mangy beast, scuttled back into the whare, his tail between his legs. We drew rein and dismounted.

"Hallo," screamed the woman. "I thought you was three 'awks. My kid comes runnin' in ter me. 'Mumma,' says she, 'there's three brown things comin' over the 'ill,' says she. An' I comes out smart, I can tell yer. 'They'll be 'awks,' I says to her. Oh, the 'awks about 'ere yer wouldn't believe."

The "kid" gave us the benefit of one eye from behind the woman's pinafore—then retired again.

"Where's your old man?" asked Jim.

The woman blinked rapidly, screwing up her face.

"Away shearin'. Bin away a month. I suppose yer not goin' to stop, are yer? There's a storm comin' up."

"You bet we are," said Jo. "So you're on your lonely, missus?"

She stood, pleating the frills of her pinafore, and glancing from one to the other of us, like a hungry bird. I smiled at the thought of how Jim had pulled Jo's leg about her. Certainly her eyes were blue, and what hair she had was yellow, but ugly. She was a figure of fun. Looking at her, you felt there was nothing but sticks and wires under that pinafore—her front teeth were knocked out, she had red pulpy hands, and she wore on her feet a pair of dirty Bluchers.

"I'll go and turn out the horses," said Jim. "Got any embrocation? Poi's rubbed herself to hell!"

" 'Arf a mo!" The woman stood silent for a moment, her nostrils expanding as she breathed. Then she shouted violently. "I'd rather you didn't stop. . . . You *can't,* and there's the end of it. I don't let out that paddock any more. You'll have to go on; I ain't got nothing!"

"Well, I'm blest!" said Jo, heavily. He pulled me aside. "Gone a bit off 'er dot," he whispered. "Too much alone, *you know,*" very significantly. "Turn the sympathetic tap on 'er, she'll come round all right."

But there was no need—she had come round by herself.

"Stop if yer like!" she muttered shrugging her shoulders. To me—"I'll give yer the embrocation if yer come along."

"Right-o, I'll take it down to them." We walked together up the garden path. It was planted on both sides with cabbages. They smelled like stale dish-water. Of flowers there were double poppies and sweet-williams. One little patch was divided off by pawa shells—presumably it belonged to the child—for she ran from her mother and began to grub in it with a broken clothes-peg. The yellow dog lay across the doorstep, biting fleas; the woman kicked him away.

"Gar-r, get away, you beast . . . the place ain't tidy. I 'aven't 'ad time ter fix things to-day—been ironing. Come right in."

It was a large room, the walls plastered with old pages of English periodicals. Queen Victoria's Jubilee appeared to be the most recent number. A table with an ironing board and wash tub on it, some wooden forms, a black horsehair sofa, and some broken cane chairs pushed against the walls. The mantelpiece above the stove was draped in pink paper, further ornamented with dried grasses and ferns and a coloured print of Richard Seddon. There were four doors—one, judging from the smell, let into the "Store," one on to the "back yard," through a third I saw the bedroom. Flies buzzed in circles round the ceiling, and treacle papers and bundles of dried clover were pinned to the window curtains.

I was alone in the room; she had gone into the store for the embrocation. I heard her stamping about and muttering to herself: "I got some, now where did I put that bottle? . . . It's behind the pickles . . . no, it ain't." I cleared a place on the table and sat there, swinging my legs. Down in the paddock I could hear Jo singing and the sound of hammer strokes as Jim drove in the tent pegs. It was sunset. There is no twilight in our New Zealand days, but a curious half-hour when everything appears grotesque—it frightens—as though the savage spirit of the country walked abroad and sneered at what it saw. Sitting alone in the hideous room I grew afraid. The woman next door was a long time finding that stuff. What was she doing in there? Once I thought I heard her bang her hands down on the counter, and once she half moaned, turning it into a cough and clearing her throat. I wanted to shout "Buck up!" but I kept silent.

"Good Lord, what a life!" I thought. "Imagine being here

day in, day out, with that rat of a child and a mangy dog. Imagine bothering about ironing. *Mad,* of course she's mad! Wonder how long she's been here—wonder if I could get her to talk."

At that moment she poked her head round the door.

"Wot was it yer wanted?" she asked.

"Embrocation."

"Oh, I forgot. I got it, it was in front of the pickle jars."

She handed me the bottle.

"My, you do look tired, you do! Shall I knock yer up a few scones for supper! There's some tongue in the store, too, and I'll cook yer a cabbage if you fancy it."

"Right-o." I smiled at her. "Come down to the paddock and bring the kid for tea."

She shook her head, pursing up her mouth.

"Oh, no. I don't fancy it. I'll send the kid down with the things and a billy of milk. Shall I knock up a few extry scones to take with yer ter-morrow?"

"Thanks."

She came and stood by the door.

"How old is the kid?"

"Six—come next Christmas. I 'ad a bit of trouble with 'er one way an' another. I 'adn't any milk till a month after she was born and she sickened like a cow."

"She's not like you—takes after her father?" Just as the woman had shouted her refusal at us before, she shouted at me then.

"No, she don't! She's the dead spit of me. Any fool could see that. Come on in now, Else, you stop messing in the dirt."

I met Jo climbing over the paddock fence.

"What's the old bitch got in the store?" he asked.

"Don't know—didn't look."

"Well, of all the fools. Jim's slanging you. What have you been doing all this time?"

"She couldn't find this stuff. Oh, my shakes, you are smart!"

Jo had washed, combed his wet hair in a line across his forehead, and buttoned a coat over his shirt. He grinned.

Jim snatched the embrocation from me. I went to the end of the paddock where the willows grew and bathed in the creek.

The water was clear and soft as oil. Along the edges held by the grass and rushes, white foam tumbled and bubbled. I lay in the water and looked up at the trees that were still a moment, then quivered lightly, and again were still. The air smelt of rain. I forgot about the woman and the kid until I came back to the tent. Jim lay by the fire, watching the billy boil.

I asked where Jo was, and if the kid had brought our supper.

"Pooh," said Jim, rolling over and looking up at the sky. "Didn't you see how Jo had been titivating? He said to me before he went up to the whare, 'Dang it! she'll look better by night light—at any rate, my buck, she's female flesh!' "

"You had Jo about her looks—you had me, too."

"No—look here. I can't make it out. It's four years since I came past this way, and I stopped here two days. The husband was a pal of mine once, down the West Coast—a fine, big chap, with a voice on him like a trombone. She'd been barmaid down the Coast—as pretty as a wax doll. The coach used to come this way then once a fortnight, that was before they opened the railway up Napier way, and she had no end of a time! Told me once in a confidential moment that she knew one hundred and twenty-five different ways of kissing!"

"Oh, go on, Jim! She isn't the same woman!"

"Course she is. . . . I can't make it out. What I think is the old man's cleared out and left her: that's all my eye about shearing. Sweet life! The only people who come through now are Maoris and sundowners!"

Through the dark we saw the gleam of the kid's pinafore. She trailed over to us with a basket in her hand, the milk billy in the other. I unpacked the basket, the child standing by.

"Come over here," said Jim, snapping his fingers at her.

She went, the lamp from the inside of the tent cast a bright light over her. A mean, undersized brat, with whitish hair, and weak eyes. She stood, legs wide apart and her stomach protruding.

"What do you do all day?" asked Jim.

She scraped out one ear with her little finger, looked at the result and said, "Draw."

"Huh! What do you draw? Leave your ears alone!"

"Pictures."

"What on?"

"Bits of butter paper an' a pencil of my Mumma's."

"Boh! What a lot of words at one time!" Jim rolled his eyes at her. "Baa-lambs and moo-cows?"

"No, everything. I'll draw all of you when you're gone, and your horses and the tent, and that one"—she pointed to me—"with no clothes on in the creek I looked at her where she couldn't see me from."

"Thanks very much. How ripping of you," said Jim. "Where's Dad?"

The kid pouted. "I won't tell you because I don't like yer face!" She started operations on the other ear.

"Here," I said. "Take the basket, get along home and tell the other man supper's ready."

"I don't want to."

"I'll give you a box on the ear if you don't," said Jim, savagely.

"Hie! I'll tell Mumma. I'll tell Mumma." The kid fled.

We ate until we were full, and had arrived at the smoke stage before Jo came back, very flushed and jaunty, a whisky bottle in his hand.

" 'Ave a drink—you two!" he shouted, carrying off matters with a high hand. " 'Ere, shove along the cups."

"One hundred and twenty-five different ways," I murmured to Jim.

"What's that? Oh! stow it!" said Jo. "Why 'ave you always got your knife into me? You gas like a kid at a Sunday School beano. She wants us to go up there to-night, and have a comfortable chat. I'—he waved his hand airily—"I got 'er round."

"Trust you for that," laughed Jim. "But did she tell you where the old man's got to?"

Jo looked up. "Shearing! You 'eard 'er, you fool!"

The woman had fixed up the room, even to a light bouquet of sweet-williams on the table. She and I sat one side of the table, Jo and Jim the other. An oil lamp was set between us, the whisky bottle and glasses, and a jug of water. The kid knelt against one of the forms, drawing on butter paper. I wondered, grimly, if she was attempting the creek episode. But Jo had been right about night time. The woman's hair was tumbled—two red spots burned in her cheeks—her eyes shone—and we knew that they were kissing feet under the table. She had changed the blue pinafore for a white calico dressing jacket and a black skirt—the kid was decorated to the extent of a blue sateen hair ribbon. In the stifling room, with the flies buzzing against the ceiling and dropping on to the table, we got slowly drunk.

"Now listen to me," shouted the woman, banging her fist on the table. "It's six years since I was married, and four miscarriages. I says to 'im, I says, what do you think I'm doin' up 'ere? If you was back at the coast, I'd 'ave you lynched for child murder. Over and over I tells 'im—you've broken my spirit and spoiled my looks, and wot for—that's wot I'm driving at." She clutched her head with her hands and stared round at us. Speaking rapidly, "Oh, some days—an' months of them—I 'ear them two words knockin' inside me all the time—'Wot for!' but sometimes I'll be cooking the spuds an' I lifts the lid off to give 'em a prong and I 'ears, quite sudden again, 'Wot for!' Oh! I don't mean only the spuds and the kid—I mean—I mean," she hiccoughed—"you know what I mean, Mr. Jo."

"I know," said Jo, scratching his head.

"Trouble with me is," she leaned across the table, "he left me too much alone. When the coach stopped coming, sometimes he'd go away days, sometimes he'd go away weeks, and leave me ter look after the store. Back 'e'd come—pleased as Punch. 'Oh, 'allo,' 'e'd say. ' 'Ow are you gettin' on. Come and give us a kiss.' Sometimes I'd turn a bit nasty, and then 'e'd go off again, and if I took it all right, 'e'd wait till 'e could twist me round 'is finger, then 'e'd say, 'Well, so long, I'm off,' and do you think I could keep 'im?—not me!"

"Mumma," bleated the kid, "I made a picture of them on the 'ill, an' you an' me, an' the dog down below."

"Shut your mouth!" said the woman.

A vivid flash of lightning played over the room—we heard the mutter of thunder.

"Good thing that's broke loose," said Jo. "I've 'ad it in me 'ead for three days."

"Where's your old man now?" asked Jim, slowly.

The woman blubbered and dropped her head on to the table. "Jim, 'e's gone shearin' and left me alone again," she wailed.

" 'Ere, look out for the glasses," said Jo. "Cheer-o, 'ave another drop. No good cryin' over spilt 'usbands! You Jim, you blasted cuckoo!"

"Mr. Jo," said the woman, drying her eyes on her jacket frill, "you're a gent, an' if I was a secret woman, I'd place any confidence in your 'ands. I don't mind if I do 'ave a glass on that."

Every moment the lightning grew more vivid and the thunder sounded nearer. Jim and I were silent—the kid never moved from her bench. She poked her tongue out and blew on her paper as she drew.

"It's the loneliness," said the woman, addressing Jo—he made sheep's eyes at her—"and bein' shut up 'ere like a broody 'en." He reached his hand across the table and held hers, and though the position looked most uncomfortable when they wanted to pass the water and whisky, their hands stuck together as though glued. I pushed back my chair and went over to the kid, who immediately sat flat down on her artistic achievements and made a face at me.

"You're not to look," said she.

"Oh, come on, don't be nasty!" Jim came over to us, and we were just drunk enough to wheedle the kid into showing us. And those drawings of hers were extraordinary and repulsively vulgar. The creations of a lunatic with a lunatic's cleverness. There was no doubt about it, the kid's mind was diseased. While she showed them to us, she worked herself up into a mad excitement, laughing and trembling, and shooting out her arms.

"Mumma," she yelled. "Now I'm going to draw them what you told me I never was to—now I am."

The woman rushed from the table and beat the child's head with the flat of her hand.

"I'll smack you with yer clothes turned up if yer dare say that again," she bawled.

Jo was too drunk to notice, but Jim caught her by the arm. The kid did not utter a cry. She drifted over to the window and began picking flies from the treacle paper.

We returned to the table—Jim and I sitting one side, the woman and Jo, touching shoulders, the other. We listened to the thunder, saying stupidly, "That was a near one," "There it goes again," and Jo, at a heavy hit, "Now we're off," "Steady on the brake," until rain began to fall, sharp as cannon shot on the iron roof.

"You'd better doss here for the night," said the woman.

"That's right," assented Jo, evidently in the know about this move.

"Bring up yer things from the tent. You two can doss in the store along with the kid—she's used to sleep in there and won't mind you."

"Oh Mumma, I never did," interrupted the kid.

"Shut yer lies! An' Mr. Jo can 'ave this room."

It sounded a ridiculous arrangement, but it was useless to attempt to cross them, they were too far gone. While the woman sketched the plan of action, Jo sat, abnormally solemn and red, his eyes bulging, and pulling at his moustache.

"Give us a lantern," said Jim. "I'll go down to the paddock." We two went together. Rain whipped in our faces, the land was light as though a bush fire was raging. We behaved like two children let loose in the thick of an adventure, laughed and shouted to each other, and came back to the whare to find the kid already bedded in the counter of the store. The woman brought us a lamp. Jo took his bundle from Jim, the door was shut.

"Good-night all," shouted Jo.

Jim and I sat on two sacks of potatoes. For the life of us we could not stop laughing. Strings of onions and half-hams dangled from the ceiling—wherever we looked there were advertisements for "Camp Coffee" and tinned meats. We pointed at them, tried to read them aloud—overcome with laughter and hiccoughs. The kid in the counter stared at us. She threw off her blanket and scrambled to the floor, where she stood in her grey flannel nightgown, rubbing one leg against the other. We paid no attention to her.

"Wot are you laughing at?" she said, uneasily.

"You!" shouted Jim. "The red tribe of you, my child."

She flew into a rage and beat herself with her hands. "I won't

31

be laughed at, you curs—you." He swooped down upon the child and swung her on to the counter.

"Go to sleep, Miss Smarty—or make a drawing—here's a pencil—you can use Mumma's account book."

Through the rain we heard Jo creak over the boarding of the next room—the sound of a door being opened—then shut to.

"It's the loneliness," whispered Jim.

"One hundred and twenty-five different ways—alas! my poor brother!"

The kid tore out a page and flung it at me.

"There you are," she said. "Now I done it ter spite Mumma for shutting me up 'ere with you two. I done the one she told me I never ought to. I done the one she told me she'd shoot me if I did. Don't care! Don't care!"

The kid had drawn the picture of the woman shooting at a man with a rook rifle and then digging a hole to bury him in.

She jumped off the counter and squirmed about on the floor biting her nails.

Jim and I sat till dawn with the drawing beside us. The rain ceased, the little kid fell asleep, breathing loudly. We got up, stole out of the whare, down into the paddock. White clouds floated over a pink sky—a chill wind blew; the air smelled of wet grass. Just as we swung into the saddle Jo came out of the whare—he motioned to us to ride on.

"I'll pick you up later," he shouted.

A bend in the road, and the whole place disappeared.

Ole Underwood

To Anne Estelle Rice

Down the windy hill stalked Ole Underwood. He carried a black umbrella in one hand, in the other a red and white spotted handkerchief knotted into a lump. He wore a black peaked cap like a pilot; gold rings gleamed in his ears and his little eyes snapped like two sparks. Like two sparks they glowed in the smoulder of his bearded face. On one side of the hill grew a forest of pines from the road right down to the sea. On the other side short tufted grass and little bushes of white manuka flower. The pine-trees roared like waves in their topmost branches, their stems creaked like the timber of ships; in the windy air flew the white manuka flower. "Ah-k!" shouted Ole Underwood, shaking his umbrella at the wind bearing down upon him, beating him, half strangling him with his black cape. "Ah-k!" shouted the wind a hundred times as loud, and filled his mouth and nostrils with dust. Something inside Ole Underwood's breast beat like a hammer. One, two—one, two—never stopping, never changing. He couldn't do anything. It wasn't loud. No, it didn't make a noise—only a thud. One, two—one, two—like some one beating on an iron in a prison, some one in a secret place—bang—bang—bang—trying to get free. Do what he would, fumble at his coat, throw his arms about, spit, swear, he couldn't stop the noise. Stop! Stop! Stop! Stop! Ole Underwood began to shuffle and run.

Away below, the sea heaving against the stone walls, and the little town just out of its reach close packed together, the better to face the grey water. And up on the other side of the hill the prison with high red walls. Over all bulged the grey sky with black weblike clouds streaming.

33

Ole Underwood slackened his pace as he neared the town, and when he came to the first house he flourished his umbrella like a herald's staff and threw out his chest, his head glancing quickly from right to left. They were ugly little houses leading into the town, built of wood—two windows and a door, a stumpy verandah and a green mat of grass before. Under one verandah yellow hens huddled out of the wind. "Shoo!" shouted Ole Underwood, and laughed to see them fly, and laughed again at the woman who came to the door and shook a red soapy fist at him. A little girl stood in another yard untwisting some rags from a clothes-line. When she saw Ole Underwood she let the clothes-prop fall and rushed screaming to the door, beating it, screaming "Mumma—Mumma!" That started the hammer in Ole Underwood's heart. Mum-ma—Mum-ma! He saw an old face with a trembling chin and grey hair nodding out of the window as they dragged him past. Mumma—Mum-ma! He looked up at the big red prison perched on the hill and he pulled a face as if he wanted to cry.

At the corner in front of the pub some carts were pulled up, and some men sat in the porch of the pub drinking and talking. Ole Underwood wanted a drink. He slouched into the bar. It was half full of old and young men in big coats and top boots with stock whips in their hands. Behind the counter a big girl with red hair pulled the beer handles and cheeked the men. Ole Underwood sneaked to one side, like a cat. Nobody looked at him, only the men looked at each other, one or two of them nudged. The girl nodded and winked at the fellow she was serving. He took some money out of his knotted handkerchief and slipped it on to the counter. His hand shook. He didn't speak. The girl took no notice; she served everybody, went on with her talk, and then as if by accident shoved a mug towards him. A great big jar of red pinks stood on the bar counter. Ole Underwood stared at them as he drank and frowned at them. Red—red—red—red! beat the hammer. It was very warm in the bar and quiet as a pond, except for the talk and the girl. She kept on laughing. Ha! Ha! That was what the men liked to see, for she threw back her head and her great breasts lifted and shook to her laughter.

In one corner sat a stranger. He pointed at Ole Underwood.

"Cracked!" said one of the men. "When he was a young fellow, thirty years ago, a man 'ere done in 'is woman, and 'e foun' out an' killed 'er. Got twenty years in quod up on the 'ill. Came out cracked!"

"Oo done 'er in?" asked the man.

"Dunno. 'E dunno, nor nobody. 'E was a sailor till 'e marrid 'er. Cracked!" The man spat and smeared the spittle on the floor, shrugging his shoulders. "'E's 'armless enough."

Ole Underwood heard; he did not turn, but he shot out an old claw and crushed up the red pinks. "Uh-Uh! You ole beast! Uh! You ole swine!" screamed the girl, leaning across the counter and banging him with a tin jug. "Get art! Get art! Don' you never come 'ere no more!" Somebody kicked him: he scuttled like a rat.

He walked past the Chinamen's shops. The fruit and vegetables were all piled up against the windows. Bits of wooden cases, straw, and old newspapers were strewn over the pavement. A woman flounced out of a shop and slushed a pail of slops over his feet. He peered in at the windows, at the Chinamen sitting in little groups on old barrels playing cards. They made him smile. He looked and looked, pressing his face against the glass and sniggering. They sat still with their long pigtails bound round their heads and their faces yellow as lemons. Some of them had knives in their belts, and one old man sat by himself on the floor plaiting his long crooked toes together. The Chinamen didn't mind Ole Underwood. When they saw him they nodded. He went to the door of a shop and cautiously opened it. In rushed the wind with him, scattering the cards. "Ya-Ya! Ya-Ya!" screamed the Chinamen, and Ole Underwood rushed off, the hammer beating quick and hard. Ya-Ya! He turned a corner out of sight. He thought he heard one of the Chinks after him, and he slipped into a timberyard. There he lay panting. . . .

Close by him, under another stack there was a heap of yellow shavings. As he watched them they moved and a little grey cat unfolded herself and came out waving her tail. She trod delicately over to Ole Underwood and rubbed against his sleeve. The hammer in Ole Underwood's heart beat madly. It pounded up into his throat, and then it seemed to half stop and beat very, very faintly. "Kit! Kit! Kit!" That was what she used to call the little

35

cat he brought her off the ship—"Kit! Kit! Kit!"—and stoop down with the saucer in her hands.

"Ah! my God! my Lord!" Ole Underwood sat up and took the kitten in his arms and rocked to and fro, crushing it against his face. It was warm and soft, and it mewed faintly. He buried his eyes in its fur. My God! My Lord! He tucked the little cat in his coat and stole out of the woodyard, and slouched down towards the wharves. As he came near the sea, Ole Underwood's nostrils expanded. The mad wind smelled of tar and ropes and slime and salt. He crossed the railway line, he crept behind the wharf-sheds and along a little cinder path that threaded through a patch of rank fennel to some stone drain pipes carrying the sewage into the sea. And he stared up at the wharves and at the ships with flags flying, and suddenly the old, old lust swept over Ole Underwood. "I will! I will! I will!" he muttered.

He tore the little cat out of his coat and swung it by its tail and flung it out to the sewer opening. The hammer beat loud and strong. He tossed his head, he was young again. He walked on to the wharves, past the wool-bales, past the loungers and the loafers to the extreme end of the wharves. The sea sucked against the wharf-poles as though it drank something from the land. One ship was loading wool. He heard a crane rattle and the shriek of a whistle. So he came to the little ship lying by herself with a bit of a plank for a gangway, and no sign of anybody—anybody at all. Ole Underwood looked once back at the town, at the prison perched like a red bird, at the black webby clouds trailing. Then he went up the gangway and on to the slippery deck. He grinned, and rolled in his walk, carrying high in his hand the red and white handkerchief. His ship! Mine! Mine! Mine! beat the hammer. There was a door latched open on the lee-side, labelled "State-room." He peered in. A man lay sleeping on a bunk—his bunk— a great big man in a seaman's coat with a long fair beard and hair on the red pillow. And looking down upon him from the wall there shone her picture—his woman's picture—smiling and smiling at the big sleeping man.

The Little Governess

O H , D E A R , how she wished that it wasn't night-time. She'd have much rather travelled by day, much much rather. But the lady at the Governess Bureau had said: "You had better take an evening boat and then if you get into a compartment for 'Ladies Only' in the train you will be far safer than sleeping in a foreign hotel. Don't go out of the carriage; don't walk about the corridors and *be sure* to lock the lavatory door if you go there. The train arrives at Munich at eight o'clock, and Frau Arnholdt says that the Hotel Grunewald is only one minute away. A porter can take you there. She will arrive at six the same evening, so you will have a nice quiet day to rest after the journey and rub up your German. And when you want anything to eat I would advise you to pop into the nearest baker's and get a bun and some coffee. You haven't been abroad before, have you?" "No." "Well, I always tell my girls that it's better to mistrust people at first rather than trust them, and it's safer to suspect people of evil intentions rather than good ones. . . . It sounds rather hard but we've got to be women of the world, haven't we?"

It had been nice in the Ladies' Cabin. The stewardess was so kind and changed her money for her and tucked up her feet. She lay on one of the hard pink-sprigged couches and watched the other passengers, friendly and natural, pinning their hats to the bolsters, taking off their boots and skirts, opening dressing-cases and arranging mysterious rustling little packages, tying their heads up in veils before lying down. *Thud, thud, thud,* went the steady screw of the steamer. The stewardess pulled a green shade over the light and sat down by the stove, her skirt turned back

37

over her knees, a long piece of knitting on her lap. On a shelf above her head there was a water-bottle with a tight bunch of flowers stuck in it. "I like travelling very much," thought the little governess. She smiled and yielded to the warm rocking.

But when the boat stopped and she went up on deck, her dress-basket in one hand, her rug and umbrella in the other, a cold, strange wind flew under her hat. She lookd up at the masts and spars of the ship black against a green glittering sky and down to the dark landing stage where strange muffled figures lounged, waiting; she moved forward with the sleepy flock, all knowing where to go to and what to do except her, and she felt afraid. Just a little—just enough to wish—oh, to wish that it was daytime and that one of those women who had smiled at her in the glass, when they both did their hair in the Ladies' Cabin, was somewhere near now. "Tickets, please. Show your tickets. Have your tickets ready." She went down the gangway balancing herself carefully on her heels. Then a man in a black leather cap came forward and touched her on the arm. "Where for, Miss?" He spoke English— he must be a guard or a stationmaster with a cap like that. She had scarcely answered when he pounced on her dress-basket. "This way," he shouted, in a rude, determined voice, and elbowing his way he strode past the people. "But I don't want a porter." What a horrible man! "I don't want a porter. I want to carry it myself." She had to run to keep up with him, and her anger, far stronger than she, ran before her and snatched the bag out of the wretch's hand. He paid no attention at all, but swung on down the long dark platform, and across a railway line. "He is a robber." She was sure he was a robber as she stepped between the silvery rails and felt the cinders crunch under her shoes. On the other side— oh, thank goodness!—there was a train with Munich written on it. The man stopped by the huge lighted carriages. "Second class?" asked the insolent voice. "Yes, a Ladies' compartment." She was quite out of breath. She opened her little purse to find something small enough to give this horrible man while he tossed her dress-basket into the rack of an empty carriage that had a ticket, *Dames Seules*, gummed on the window. She got into the train and handed him twenty centimes. "What's this?" shouted the man, glaring at the money and then at her, holding it up to his nose, sniffing at it as though he had never in his life seen, much less held, such a sum. "It's a franc. You know that, don't you? It's a franc. That's my fare!" A franc! Did he imagine that she was going to give him a franc for playing a trick like that just because she was a girl and travelling alone at night? Never, never! She squeezed her purse in her hand and simply did not see him—she looked at a view of St. Malo on the wall opposite and simply did not hear him. "Ah, no. Ah, no. Four sous. You make a mistake. Here, take it. It's a franc I want." He leapt on to the step of the train and threw the money on to her lap. Trembling with terror she screwed herself tight, tight, and put out an icy hand and took the money—stowed it away in her hand. "That's all you're going to get," she said. For a minute or two she felt his sharp eyes pricking her all over, while he nodded slowly, pulling down his mouth: "Ve-ry well. *Trrrès bien*." He shrugged his shoulders and disappeared into the dark. Oh, the relief! How simply terrible that had been! As she stood up to feel if the dress-basket was firm she caught sight of herself in the mirror, quite white, with big round eyes. She untied her "motor veil" and unbuttoned her green cape. "But it's all over now," she said to the mirror face, feeling in some way that it was more frightened than she.

People began to assemble on the platform. They stood together in little groups talking; a strange light from the station lamps painted their faces almost green. A little boy in red clattered up with a huge tea wagon and leaned against it, whistling and flicking his boots with a serviette. A woman in a black alpaca apron pushed a barrow with pillows for hire. Dreamy and vacant she looked—like a woman wheeling a perambulator—up and down, up and down—with a sleeping baby inside it. Wreaths of white smoke floated up from somewhere and hung below the roof like misty vines. "How strange it all is," thought the little governess, "and the middle of the night, too." She looked out from her safe corner, frightened no longer but proud that she had not given that franc. "I can look after myself—of course I can. The great thing is not to—" Suddenly from the corridor there came a stamping of feet and men's voices, high and broken with snatches of loud laughter. They were coming her way. The little governess shrank into her corner as four young men in bowler hats passed, staring through the door and window. One of them, bursting with the joke, pointed to the notice *Dames Seules* and the four bent down the better to see the one little girl in the corner. Oh dear, they were in the carriage next door. She heard them tramping about and then a sudden hush followed by a tall thin fellow with a tiny black moustache who flung her door open. "If mademoiselle cares to come in with us," he said, in French. She saw the others crowding behind him, peeping under his arm and over his shoulder, and she sat very straight and still. "If mademoiselle will do us the honour," mocked the tall man. One of them could be quiet no longer; his laughter went off in a loud crack. "Mademoiselle is serious," persisted the young man, bowing and grimacing. He took off his hat with a flourish, and she was alone again.

"En voiture. En voi-ture!" Some one ran up and down beside the train. "I wish it wasn't night-time. I wish there was another woman in the carriage. I'm frightened of the men next door." The little governess looked out to see her porter coming back again—the same man making for her carriage with his arms full of luggage. But—but what *was* he doing? He put his thumb nail under the label *Dames Seules* and tore it right off and then stood aside squinting at her while an old man wrapped in a plaid cape climbed up the high step. "But this is a Ladies' compartment." "Oh, no, Mademoiselle, you make a mistake. No, no, I assure you. Merci. Monsieur." *"En voi-turre!"* A shrill whistle. The porter stepped off triumphant and the train started. For a moment or two big tears brimmed her eyes and through them she saw the old man unwinding a scarf from his neck and untying the flaps of his Jaeger cap. He looked very old. Ninety at least. He had a white moustache and big gold-rimmed spectacles with little blue eyes behind them and pink wrinkled cheeks. A nice face—and charming the way he bent forward and said in halting French: "Do I disturb you, Mademoiselle? Would you rather I took all these things out of the rack and found another carriage?" What! that old man have to move all those heavy things just because she . . . "No, it's quite all right. You don't disturb me at all." "Ah, a thousand thanks." He sat down opposite her and unbuttoned the cape of his enormous coat and flung it off his shoulders.

The train seemed glad to have left the station. With a long

leap it sprang into the dark. She rubbed a place in the window with her glove but she could see nothing—just a tree outspread like a black fan or a scatter of lights, or the line of a hill, solemn and huge. In the carriage next door the young men started singing, "*Un, deux, trois.*" They sang the same song over and over at the tops of their voices.

"I never could have dared to go to sleep if I had been alone," she decided. "*I couldn't* have put my feet up or even taken off my hat." The singing gave her a queer little tremble in her stomach and, hugging herself to stop it, with her arms crossed under her cape, she felt really glad to have the old man in the carriage with her. Careful to see that he was not looking she peered at him through her long lashes. He sat extremely upright, the chest thrown out, the chin well in, knees pressed together, reading a German paper. That was why he spoke French so funnily. He was a German. Something in the army, she supposed—a Colonel or a General—once, of course, not now; he was too old for that now. How spick and span he looked for an old man. He wore a pearl pin stuck in his black tie and a ring with a dark red stone on his little finger; the tip of a white silk handkerchief showed in the pocket of his double-breasted jacket. Somehow, altogether, he was really nice to look at. Most old men were so horrid. She couldn't bear them doddery—or they had a disgusting cough or something. But not having a beard—that made all the difference—and then his cheeks were so pink and his moustache so very white. Down went the German paper and the old man leaned forward with the same delightful courtesy: "Do you speak German, Mademoiselle?" "*Ja, ein wenig, mehr als Französisch,*" said the little governess, blushing a deep pink colour that spread slowly over her cheeks and made her blue eyes look almost black. "Ach, so!" The old man bowed graciously. "Then perhaps you would care to look at some illustrated papers." He slipped a rubber band from a little roll of them and handed them across. "Thank you very much." She was very fond of looking at pictures, but first she would take off her hat and gloves. So she stood up, unpinned the brown straw and put it neatly in the rack beside the dress-basket, stripped off her brown kid gloves, paired them in a tight roll and put them in the crown of the hat for safety, and then sat down again, more comfortably this time, her feet crossed, the papers on her lap. How kindly the old man in the corner watched her bare little hand turning over the big white pages, watched her lips moving as she pronounced the long words to herself, rested upon her hair that fairly blazed under the light. Alas! how tragic for a little governess to possess hair that made one think of tangerines and marigolds, of apricots and tortoiseshell cats and champagne! Perhaps that was what the old man was thinking as he gazed and gazed, and that not even the dark ugly clothes could disguise her soft beauty. Perhaps the flush that licked his cheeks and lips was a flush of rage that anyone so young and tender should have to travel alone and unprotected through the night. Who knows he was not murmuring in his sentimental German fashion: "*Ja, es ist eine Tragödie!* Would to God I were the child's grandpapa!"

"Thank you very much. They were very interesting." She smiled prettily handing back the papers. "But you speak German extremely well," said the old man. "You have been in Germany before, of course?" "Oh no, this is the first time"—a little pause then—"this is the first time that I have ever been abroad at all." "Really! I am surprised. You gave me the impression, if I may say so, that you were accustomed to travelling." "Oh, well—I have been about a good deal in England, and to Scotland, once." "So. I myself have been in England once, but I could not learn English." He raised one hand and shook his head, laughing. "No, it was too difficult for me. . . . 'Ow-do-you-do. Please vich is ze vay to Leicestaire Squaare.' " She laughed too. "Foreigners always say . . ." They had quite a little talk about it. "But you will like Munich," said the old man. "Munich is a wonderful city. Museums, pictures, galleries, fine buildings and shops, concerts, theatres, restaurants—all are in Munich. I have travelled all over Europe many, many times in my life, but it is always to Munich that I return. You will enjoy yourself there." "I am not going to *stay* in Munich," said the little governess, and she added shyly, "I am going to a post as governess to a doctor's family in Augsburg." "Ah, that was it." Augsburg he knew. Augsburg—well—was not beautiful. A solid manufacturing town. But if Germany was new to her he hoped she would find something interesting there too.

"I am sure I shall." "But what a pity not to see Munich before you go. You ought to take a little holiday on your way"—he smiled—"and store up some pleasant memories." "I am afraid I could not do *that*," said the little governess, shaking her head, suddenly important and serious. "And also, if one is alone . . ." He quite understood. He bowed, serious too. They were silent after that. The train shattered on, baring its dark, flaming breast to the hills and to the valleys. It was warm in the carriage. She seemed to lean against the dark rushing and to be carried away and away. Little sounds made themselves heard; steps in the corridor, doors opening and shutting—a murmur of voices—whistling. . . . Then the window was pricked with long needles of rain. . . . But it did not matter . . . it was outside . . . and she had her umbrella . . . she pouted, sighed, opened and shut her hands once and fell fast asleep.

"Pardon! Pardon!" The sliding back of the carriage door woke her with a start. What had happened? Some one had come in and gone out again. The old man sat in his corner, more upright than ever, his hands in the pockets of his coat, frowning heavily. "Ha! ha! ha!" came from the carriage next door. Still half asleep, she put her hands to her hair to make sure it wasn't a dream. "Disgraceful!" muttered the old man more to himself than to her. "Common, vulgar fellows! I am afraid they disturbed you, gracious Fräulein, blundering in here like that." No, not really. She was just going to wake up, and she took out her silver watch to look at the time. Half-past four. A cold blue light filled the window panes. Now when she rubbed a place she could see bright patches of fields, a clump of white houses like mushrooms, a road "like a picture" with poplar trees on either side, a thread of river. How pretty it was! How pretty and how different! Even those pink clouds in the sky looked foreign. It was cold, but she pretended that it was far colder and rubbed her hands together and shivered, pulling at the collar of her coat because she was so happy.

The train began to slow down. The engine gave a long shrill whistle. They were coming to a town. Taller houses, pink and yellow, glided by, fast asleep behind their green eyelids, and

43

guarded by the poplar trees that quivered in the blue air as if on tiptoe, listening. In one house a woman opened the shutters, flung a red and white mattress across the window frame and stood staring at the train. A pale woman with black hair and a white woolen shawl over her shoulders. More women appeared at the doors and at the windows of the sleeping houses. There came a flock of sheep. The shepherd wore a blue blouse and pointed wooden shoes. Look! look what flowers—and by the railway station too! Standard roses like bridesmaids' bouquets, white geraniums, waxy pink ones that you would *never* see out of a greenhouse at home. Slower and slower. A man with a watering-can was spraying the platform. "A-a-a-ah!" Somebody came running and waving his arms. A huge fat woman waddled through the glass doors of the station with a tray of strawberries. Oh, she was thirsty! She was very thirsty! "A-a-a-ah!" The same somebody ran back again. The train stopped.

The old man pulled his coat round him and got up, smiling at her. He murmured something she didn't quite catch, but she smiled back at him as he left the carriage. While he was away the little governess looked at herself again in the glass, shook and patted herself with the precise practical care of a girl who is old enough to travel by herself and has nobody else to assure her that she is "quite all right behind." Thirsty and thirsty! The air tasted of water. She let down the window and the fat woman with the strawberries passed as if on purpose; holding up the tray to her. "*Nein, danke,*" said the little governess, looking at the big berries on their gleaming leaves. "*Wie viel?*" she asked as the fat woman moved away. "Two marks fifty, Fräulein." "Good gracious!" She came in from the window and sat down in the corner, very sobered for a minute. Half a crown! "H-o-o-o-o-o-e-e-e!" shrieked the train, gathering itself together to be off again. She hoped the old man wouldn't be left behind. Oh, it was daylight—everything was lovely if only she hadn't been so thirsty. Where *was* the old man—oh, here he was—she dimpled at him as though he were an old accepted friend as he closed the door and, turning, took from under his cape a basket of the strawberries. "If Fräulein would honour me by accepting these . . ." "What, for me?" But she drew back and raised her hands as though he were about to put a wild little kitten on her lap.

"Certainly, for you," said the old man. "For myself it is twenty years since I was brave enough to eat strawberries." "Oh, thank you very much. *Danke bestens,*" she stammered, *"sie sind so sehr schön!"* "Eat them and see," said the old man looking pleased and friendly. "You won't have even one?" "No, no, no." Timidly and charmingly her hand hovered. They were so big and juicy she had to take two bites to them—the juice ran all down her fingers— and it was while she munched the berries that she first thought of the old man as a grandfather. What a perfect grandfather he would make! Just like one out of a book!

The sun came out, the pink clouds in the sky, the strawberry clouds were eaten by the blue. "Are they good?" asked the old man. "As good as they look?"

When she had eaten them she felt she had known him for years. She told him about Frau Arnholdt and how she had got the place. Did he know the Hotel Grunewald? Frau Arnholdt would not arrive until the evening. He listened, listened until he knew as much about the affair as she did, until he said—not looking at her—but smoothing the palms of his brown suède gloves together: "I wonder if you would let me show you a little of Munich to-day. Nothing much—but just perhaps a picture gallery and the Englischer Garten. It seems such a pity that you should have to spend the day at the hotel, and also a little un-comfortable . . . in a strange place. *Nicht wahr?* You would be back there by the early afternoon or whenever you wish, of course, and you would give an old man a great deal of pleasure."

It was not until long after she had said "Yes"—because the moment she had said it and he had thanked her he began telling her about his travels in Turkey and attar of roses—that she won-dered whether she had done wrong. After all, she really did not know him. But he was so old and he had been so very kind— not to mention the strawberries. . . . And she couldn't have ex-plained the reason why she said "No," and it was her *last* day in a way, her last day to really enjoy herself in. "Was I wrong? Was I?" A drop of sunlight fell into her hands and lay there, warm and quivering. "If I might accompany you as far as the hotel," he suggested, "and call for you again at about ten o'clock." He took out his pocket-book and handed her a card. "Herr Regierungs-rat. . . ." He had a title! Well, it was *bound* to be all right! So after that the little governess gave herself up to the excitement of being really abroad, to looking out and reading the foreign advertise-ment signs, to being told about the places they came to—having her attention and enjoyment looked after by the charming old grandfather—until they reached Munich and the Hauptbahnhof. "Porter! Porter!" He found her a porter, disposed of his own luggage in a few words, guided her through the bewildering crowd out of the station down the clean white steps into the white road to the hotel. He explained who she was to the manager as though all this had been bound to happen, and then for one moment her little hand lost itself in the big brown suède ones. "I will call for you at ten o'clock." He was gone.

"This way, Fräulein," said a waiter, who had been dodging behind the manager's back, all eyes and ears for the strange couple. She followed him up two flights of stairs into a dark bedroom. He dashed down her dress-basket and pulled up a clattering, dusty blind. Ugh! What an ugly, cold room—what enormous furniture! Fancy spending the day in here! "Is this the room Frau Arnholdt ordered?" asked the little governess. The waiter had a curious way of staring as if there was something *funny* about her. He pursed up his lips about to whistle, and then changed his mind. "*Gewiss*," he said. Well, why didn't he go? Why did he stare so?" "*Gehen Sie*," said the little governess, with frigid English simplicity. His little eyes, like currants, nearly popped out of his doughy cheeks. "*Gehen Sie sofort*," she repeated icily. At the door he turned. "And the gentleman," said he, "shall I show the gentleman upstairs when he comes?"

Over the white streets big white clouds fringed with silver—and sunshine everywhere. Fat, fat coachmen driving fat cabs; funny women with little round hats cleaning the tramway lines; people laughing and pushing against one another; trees on both

sides of the streets and everywhere you looked almost, immense
fountains; a noise of laughing from the footpaths or the middle
of the streets or the open windows. And beside her, more beautifully brushed than ever, with a rolled umbrella in one hand and
yellow gloves instead of brown ones, her grandfather who had
asked her to spend the day. She wanted to run, she wanted to
hang on his arm, she wanted to cry every minute, "Oh, I am so
frightfully happy!" He guided her across the roads, stood still
while she "looked," and his kind eyes beamed on her and he said
"just whatever you wish." She ate two white sausages and two
little rolls of fresh bread at eleven o'clock in the morning and she
drank some beer, which he told her wasn't intoxicating, wasn't
at all like English beer, out of a glass like a flower vase. And then
they took a cab and really she must have seen thousands and
thousands of wonderful classical pictures in about a quarter of an
hour! "I shall have to think them over when I am alone." . . . But
when they came out of the picture gallery it was raining. The
grandfather unfurled his umbrella and held it over the little governess. They started to walk to the restaurant for lunch. She, very
close beside him so that he should have some of the umbrella,
too. "It goes easier," he remarked in a detached way, "if you take
my arm, Fräulein. And besides it is the custom in Germany." So
she took his arm and walked beside him while he pointed out the
famous statues, so interested that he quite forgot to put down
the umbrella even when the rain was long over.

After lunch they went to a café to hear a gipsy band, but she
did not like that at all. Ugh! such horrible men were there with
heads like eggs and cuts on their faces, so she turned her chair
and cupped her burning cheeks in her hands and watched her old
friend instead. . . . Then they went to the Englischer Garten.

"I wonder what the time is," asked the little governess. "My
watch has stopped. I forgot to wind it in the train last night.
We've seen such a lot of things that I feel it must be quite late."
"Late!" He stopped in front of her laughing and shaking his head
in a way she had begun to know. "Then you have not really
enjoyed yourself. Late! Why, we have not had any ice cream yet!"
"Oh, but I have enjoyed myself," she cried, distressed, "more than

I can possibly say. It has been wonderful! Only Frau Arnholdt is to be at the hotel at six and I ought to be there by five." "So you shall. After the ice cream I shall put you into a cab and you can go there comfortably." She was happy again. The chocolate ice cream melted—melted in little sips a long way down. The shadows of the trees danced on the table cloths, and she sat with her back safely turned to the ornamental clock that pointed to twenty-five minutes to seven. "Really and truly," said the little governess earnestly, "this has been the happiest day of my life. I've never even imagined such a day." In spite of her ice cream her grateful baby heart glowed with love for the fairy grandfather.

So they walked out of the garden down a long alley. The day was nearly over. "You see those big buildings opposite," said the old man. "The third storey—that is where I live. I and the old housekeeper who looks after me." She was very interested. "Now just before I find a cab for you, will you come and see my little 'home' and let me give you a bottle of the attar of roses I told you about in the train? For remembrance?" She would love to. "I've never seen a bachelor's flat in my life," laughed the little governess.

The passage was quite dark. "Ah, I suppose my old woman has gone out to buy me a chicken. One moment." He opened a door and stood aside for her to pass, a little shy but curious, into a strange room. She did not know quite what to say. It wasn't pretty. In a way it was very ugly—but neat, and, she supposed, comfortable for such an old man. "Well, what do you think of it?" He knelt down and took from a cupboard a round tray with two pink glasses and a tall pink bottle. "Two little bedrooms beyond," he said gaily, "and a kitchen. It's enough, eh?" "Oh, quite enough." "And if ever you should be in Munich and care to spend a day or two—why there is always a little nest—a wing of a chicken, and a salad, and an old man delighted to be your host once more and many many times, dear little Fräulein!" He took the stopper out of the bottle and poured some wine into the two pink glasses. His hand shook and the wine spilled over the tray. It was very quiet in the room. She said: "I think I ought to go now." "But you will have a tiny glass of wine with me—

just one before you go?" said the old man. "No, really no. I never drink wine. I—I have promised never to touch wine or anything like that." And though he pleaded and though she felt dreadfully rude, especially when he seemed to take it to heart so, she was quite determined. "No, *really,* please." "Well, will you just sit down on the sofa for five minutes and let me drink your health?" The little governess sat down on the edge of the red velvet couch and he sat down beside her and drank her health at a gulp. "Have you really been happy today?" asked the old man, turning round, so close beside her that she felt his knee twitching against hers. Before she could answer he held her hands. "And are you going to give me one little kiss before you go?" he asked, drawing her closer still.

It was a dream! It wasn't true! It wasn't the same old man at all. Ah, how horrible! The little governess stared at him in terror. "No, no, no!" she stammered, struggling out of his hands. "One little kiss. A kiss. What is it? Just a kiss, dear little Fräulein. A kiss." He pushed his face forward, his lips smiling broadly; and how his little blue eyes gleamed behind the spectacles! "Never— never. How can you!" She sprang up, but he was too quick and he held her against the wall, pressed against her his hard old body and his twitching knee and, though she shook her head from side to side, distracted, kissed her on the mouth. On the mouth! Where not a soul who wasn't a near relation had ever kissed her before. . . .

She ran, ran down the street until she found a broad road with tram lines and a policeman standing in the middle like a clockwork doll. "I want to get a tram to the Hauptbahnhof," sobbed the little governess. "Fräulein?" She wrung her hands at him. "The Hauptbahnhof. There—there's one now," and while he watched very much surprised, the little girl with her hat on one side, crying without a handkerchief, sprang on to the tram— not seeing the conductor's eyebrows, nor hearing the *hochwohl-gebildete Dame* talking her over with a scandalized friend. She rocked herself and cried out loud and said "Ah, ah!" pressing her hands to her mouth. "She has been to the dentist," shrilled a fat old woman, too stupid to be uncharitable. "*Na, sagen Sie 'mal,* what toothache! The child hasn't one left in her mouth." While the tram swung and jangled through a world full of old men with twitching knees.

When the little governess reached the hall of the Hotel Grunewald the same waiter who had come into her room in the morning was standing by a table, polishing a tray of glasses. The sight of the little governess seemed to fill him out with some inexplicable important content. He was ready for her question; his answer came pat and suave. "Yes, Fräulein, the lady has been here. I told her that you had arrived and gone out again immediately with a gentleman. She asked me when you were coming back again— but of course I could not say. And then she went to the manager." He took up a glass from the table, held it up to the light, looked at it with one eye closed, and started polishing it with a corner of his apron.". . ." "Pardon, Fräulein? Ach, no, Fräulein. The manager could tell her nothing—nothing." He shook his head and smiled at the brilliant glass. "Where is the lady now?" asked the little governess, shuddering so violently that she had to hold her handkerchief up to her mouth. "How should I know?" cried the waiter, and as he swooped past her to pounce upon a new arrival his heart beat so hard against his ribs that he nearly chuckled aloud. "That's it! that's it!" he thought. "That will show her." And as he swung the new arrival's box on to his shoulders— hoop!—as though he were a giant and the box a feather, he minced over again the little governess's words, "*Gehen Sie. Gehen Sie sofort*. Shall I! Shall I!" he shouted to himself.

Prelude

I

T HERE WAS NOT an inch of room for Lottie and Kezia
in the buggy. When Pat swung them on top of the luggage they
wobbled; the grandmother's lap was full and Linda Burnell could
not possibly have held a lump of a child on hers for any distance.
Isabel, very superior, was perched beside the new handy-man on
the driver's seat. Hold-alls, bags and boxes were piled upon the
floor. "These are absolute necessities that I will not let out of my
sight for one instant," said Linda Burnell, her voice trembling
with fatigue and excitement.

Lottie and Kezia stood on the patch of lawn just inside the
gate all ready for the fray in their coats with brass anchor buttons
and little round caps with battleship ribbons. Hand in hand, they
stared with round solemn eyes first at the absolute necessities and
then at their mother.

"We shall simply have to leave them. That is all. We shall
simply have to cast them off," said Linda Burnell. A strange little
laugh flew from her lips; she leaned back against the buttoned
leather cushions and shut her eyes, her lips trembling with laughter. Happily at that moment Mrs. Samuel Josephs, who had been
watching the scene from behind her drawing-room blind, waddled
down the garden path.

"Why nod leave the chudren with be for the afterdoon, Brs.
Burnell? They could go on the dray with the storeban when he

comes in the eveding. Those thigs on the path have to go, dod't they?"

"Yes, everything outside the house is supposed to go," said Linda Burnell, and she waved a white hand at the tables and chairs standing on their heads on the front lawn. How absurd they looked! Either they ought to be the other way up, or Lottie and Kezia ought to stand on their heads, too. And she longed to say: "Stand on your heads, children, and wait for the storeman." It seemed to her that would be so exquisitely funny that she could not attend to Mrs. Samuel Josephs.

The fat creaking body leaned across the gate, and the big jelly of a face smiled. "Dod't you worry, Brs. Burnell. Loddie and Kezia can have tea with by chudren in the dursery, and I'll see theb on the dray afterwards."

The grandmother considered. "Yes, it really is quite the best plan. We are very obliged to you, Mrs. Samuel Josephs. Children, say 'thank you' to Mrs. Samuel Josephs."

Two subdued chirrups: "Thank you, Mrs. Samuel Josephs."

"And be good little girls, and—come closer—" they advanced, "don't forget to tell Mrs. Samuel Josephs when you want to . . ."

"No, granma."

"Dod't worry, Brs. Burnell."

At the last moment Kezia let go Lottie's hand and darted towards the buggy.

"I want to kiss my granma good-bye again."

But she was too late. The buggy rolled off up the road, Isabel bursting with pride, her nose turned up at all the world, Linda Burnell prostrated, and the grandmother rummaging among the very curious oddments she had had put in her black silk reticule at the last moment, for something to give her daughter. The buggy twinkled away in the sunlight and fine golden dust up the hill and over. Kezia bit her lip, but Lottie, carefully finding her handkerchief first, set up a wail.

"Mother! Granma!"

Mrs. Samuel Josephs, like a huge warm black silk tea cosy, enveloped her.

"It's all right, by dear. Be a brave child. You come and blay in the dursery!"

She put her arm round weeping Lottie and led her away. Kezia followed, making a face at Mrs. Samuel Josephs' placket, which was undone as usual, with two long pink corset laces hanging out of it. . . .

Lottie's weeping died down as she mounted the stairs, but the sight of her at the nursery door with swollen eyes and a blob of a nose gave great satisfaction to the S. J.'s, who sat on two benches before a long table covered with American cloth and set out with immense plates of bread and dripping and two brown jugs that faintly steamed.

"Hullo! You've been crying!"

"Ooh! Your eyes have gone right in."

"Doesn't her nose look funny."

"You're all red-and-patchy."

Lottie was quite a success. She felt it and swelled, smiling timidly.

"Go and sit by Zaidee, ducky," said Mrs. Samuel Josephs, "and Kezia, you sid ad the end by Boses."

Moses grinned and gave her a nip as she sat down; but she pretended not to notice. She did hate boys.

"Which will you have?" asked Stanley, leaning across the table very politely, and smiling at her. "Which will you have to begin with—strawberries and cream or bread and dripping?"

"Strawberries and cream, please," said she.

"Ah-h-h-h." How they all laughed and beat the table with their teaspoons. Wasn't that a take in! Wasn't it now! Didn't he fox her! Good old Stan!

"Ma! She thought it was real."

Even Mrs. Samuel Josephs, pouring out the milk and water, could not help smiling. "You bustn't tease theb on their last day," she wheezed.

But Kezia bit a big piece out of her bread and dripping, and then stood the piece up on her plate. With the bite out it made a dear little sort of a gate. Pooh! She didn't care! A tear rolled down her cheek, but she wasn't crying. She couldn't have cried

53

in front of those awful Samuel Josephs. She sat with her head bent, and as the tear dripped slowly down, she caught it with a neat little whisk of her tongue and ate it before any of them had seen.

2

After tea Kezia wandered back to their own house. Slowly she walked up the back steps, and through the scullery into the kitchen. Nothing was left in it but a lump of gritty yellow soap in one corner of the kitchen window sill and a piece of flannel stained with a blue bag in another. The fireplace was choked up with rubbish. She poked among it but found nothing except a hair-tidy with a heart painted on it that had belonged to the servant girl. Even that she left lying, and she trailed through the narrow passage into the drawing-room. The Venetian blind was pulled down but not drawn close. Long pencil rays of sunlight shone through and the wavy shadow of a bush outside danced on the gold lines. Now it was still, now it began to flutter again, and now it came almost as far as her feet. Zoom! Zoom! a blue-bottle knocked against the ceiling; the carpet-tacks had little bits of red fluff sticking to them.

The dining-room window had a square of coloured glass at each corner. One was blue and one was yellow. Kezia bent down to have one more look at a blue lawn with blue arum lilies growing at the gate, and then at a yellow lawn with yellow lilies and a yellow fence. As she looked a little Chinese Lottie came out on to the lawn and began to dust the tables and chairs with a corner of her pinafore. Was that really Lottie? Kezia was not quite sure until she had looked through the ordinary window.

Upstairs in her father's and mother's room she found a pill box black and shiny outside and red in, holding a blob of cotton wool.

"I could keep a bird's egg in that," she decided.

In the servant girl's room there was a stay-button stuck in a crack of the floor, and in another crack some beads and a long needle. She knew there was nothing in her grandmother's room; she had watched her pack. She went over to the window and leaned against it, pressing her hands against the pane.

Kezia liked to stand so before the window. She liked the feeling of the cold shining glass against her hot palms, and she liked to watch the funny white tops that came on her fingers when she pressed them hard against the pane. As she stood there, the day flickered out and dark came. With the dark crept the wind snuffling and howling. The windows of the empty house shook, a creaking came from the walls and floors, a piece of loose iron on the roof banged forlornly. Kezia was suddenly quite, quite still, with wide open eyes and knees pressed together. She was frightened. She wanted to call Lottie and to go on calling all the while she ran downstairs and out of the house. But IT was just behind her, waiting at the door, at the head of the stairs, at the bottom of the stairs, hiding in the passage, ready to dart out at the back door. But Lottie was at the back door, too.

"Kezia!" she called cheerfully. "The storeman's here. Everything is on the dray and three horses, Kezia. Mrs. Samuel Josephs has given us a big shawl to wear round us, and she says to button up your coat. She won't come out because of asthma."

Lottie was very important.

"Now then, you kids," called the storeman. He hooked his big thumbs under their arms and up they swung. Lottie arranged the shawl "most beautifully" and the storeman tucked up their feet in a piece of old blanket.

"Lift up. Easy does it."

They might have been a couple of young ponies. The storeman felt over the cords holding his load, unhooked the brakechain from the wheel, and whistling, he swung up beside them.

"Keep close to me," said Lottie, "because otherwise you pull the shawl away from my side, Kezia."

But Kezia edged up to the storeman. He towered beside her big as a giant and he smelled of nuts and new wooden boxes.

3

It was the first time that Lottie and Kezia had ever been out so late. Everything looked different—the painted wooden houses far smaller than they did by day, the gardens far bigger and wilder. Bright stars speckled the sky and the moon hung over the harbour dabbling the waves with gold. They could see the lighthouse shining on Quarantine Island, and the green lights on the old coal hulks.

"There comes the Picton boat," said the storeman, pointing to a little steamer all hung with bright beads.

But when they reached the top of the hill and began to go down the other side the harbour disappeared, and although they were still in the town they were quite lost. Other carts rattled past. Everybody knew the storeman.

"Night, Fred."

"Night O," he shouted.

Kezia liked very much to hear him. Whenever a cart appeared in the distance she looked up and waited for his voice. He was an old friend; and she and her grandmother had often been to his place to buy grapes. The storeman lived alone in a cottage that had a glasshouse against one wall built by himself. All the glasshouse was spanned and arched over with one beautiful vine. He took her brown basket from her, lined it with three large leaves, and then he felt in his belt for a little horn knife, reached up and snapped off a big blue cluster and laid it on the leaves so tenderly that Kezia held her breath to watch. He was a very big man. He wore brown velvet trousers, and he had a long brown beard. But he never wore a collar, not even on Sunday. The back of his neck was burnt bright red.

"Where are we now?" Every few minutes one of the children asked him the question.

"Why, this is Hawk Street, or Charlotte Crescent."

"Of course it is," Lottie pricked up her ears at the last name; she always felt that Charlotte Crescent belonged specially to her. Very few people had streets with the same name as theirs.

"Look, Kezia, there is Charlotte Crescent. Doesn't it look

different?" Now everything familiar was left behind. Now the big dray rattled into unknown country, along new roads with high clay banks on either side, up steep, steep hills, down into bushy valleys, through wide shallow rivers. Further and further. Lottie's head wagged; she drooped, she slipped half into Kezia's lap and lay there. But Kezia could not open her eyes wide enough. The wind blew and she shivered; but her cheeks and ears burned.

"Do stars ever blow about?" she asked.

"Not to notice," said the storeman.

"We've got a nuncle and a naunt living near our new house," said Kezia. "They have got two children, Pip, the eldest is called, and the youngest's name is Rags. He's got a ram. He has to feed it with a nenamuel teapot and a glove top over the spout. He's going to show us. What is the difference between a ram and a sheep?"

"Well, a ram has horns and runs for you."

Kezia considered. "I don't want to see it frightfully," she said. "I hate rushing animals like dogs and parrots. I often dream that animals rush at me—even camels—and while they are rushing, their heads swell e-enormous."

The storeman said nothing. Kezia peered up at him, screwing up her eyes. Then she put her finger out and stroked his sleeve; if felt hairy. "Are we near?" she asked.

"Not far off, now," answered the storeman. "Getting tired?"

"Well, I'm not an atom bit sleepy," said Kezia. "But my eyes keep curling up in such a funny sort of way." She gave a long sigh, and to stop her eyes from curling she shut them. . . . When she opened them again they were clanking through a drive that cut through the garden like a whip lash, looping suddenly an island of green, and behind the island, but out of sight until you came upon it, was the house. It was long and low built, with a pillared verandah and balcony all the way round. The soft white bulk of it lay stretched upon the green garden like a sleeping beast. And now one and now another of the windows leaped into light. Someone was walking through the empty rooms carrying a lamp. From a window downstairs the light of a fire flickered. A strange beautiful excitement seemed to stream from the house in quivering ripples.

"Where are we?" said Lottie, sitting up. Her reefer cap was all on one side and on her cheek there was the print of an anchor button she had pressed against while sleeping. Tenderly the storeman lifted her, set her cap straight, and pulled down her crumpled clothes. She stood blinking on the lowest verandah step watching Kezia who seemed to come flying through the air to her feet.

"Ooh!" cried Kezia, flinging up her arms. The grandmother came out of the dark hall carrying a lamp. She was smiling.

"You found your way in the dark?" said she.

"Perfectly well."

But Lottie staggered on the lowest verandah step like a bird fallen out of the nest. If she stood still for a moment she fell asleep, if she leaned against anything her eyes closed. She could not walk another step.

"Kezia," said the grandmother, "can I trust you to carry the lamp?"

"Yes, my granma."

The old woman bent down and gave the bright breathing thing into her hands and then she caught up drunken Lottie. "This way."

Through a square hall filled with bales and hundreds of parrots (but the parrots were only on the wall-paper) down a narrow passage where the parrots persisted in flying past Kezia with her lamp.

"Be very quiet," warned the grandmother, putting down Lottie and opening the dining-room door. "Poor little mother has got such a headache."

Linda Burnell, in a long cane chair, with her feet on a hassock, and a plaid over her knees, lay before a crackling fire. Burnell and Beryl sat at the table in the middle of the room eating a dish of fried chops and drinking tea out of a brown china teapot. Over the back of her mother's chair leaned Isabel. She had a comb in her fingers and in a gentle absorbed fashion she was combing the curls from her mother's forehead. Outside the pool of lamp and firelight the room stretched dark and bare to the hollow windows.

"Are those the children?" But Linda did not really care; she did not even open her eyes to see.

"Put down the lamp, Kezia," said Aunt Beryl, "or we shall have the house on fire before we are out of the packing cases. More tea, Stanley?"

"Well, you might just give me five-eighths of a cup," said Burnell, leaning across the table. "Have another chop, Beryl. Tip-top meat, isn't it? Not too lean and not too fat." He turned to his wife. "You're sure you won't change your mind, Linda darling?"

"The very thought of it is enough." She raised one eyebrow in the way she had. The grandmother brought the children bread and milk and they sat up to table, flushed and sleepy behind the wavy steam.

"I had meat for my supper," said Isabel, still combing gently.

"I had a whole chop for my supper, the bone and all and Worcester sauce. Didn't I, father?"

"Oh, don't boast, Isabel," said Aunt Beryl.

Isabel looked astounded. "I wasn't boasting, was I, Mummy? I never thought of boasting. I thought they would like to know. I only meant to tell them."

"Very well. That's enough," said Burnell. He pushed back his plate, took a tooth-pick out of his pocket and began picking his strong white teeth.

"You might see that Fred has a bite of something in the kitchen before he goes, will you, mother?"

"Yes, Stanley." The old woman turned to go.

"Oh, hold on half a jiffy. I suppose nobody knows where my slippers were put? I suppose I shall not be able to get at them for a month or two—what?"

"Yes," came from Linda. "In the top of the canvas holdall marked 'urgent necessities.' "

"Well you might get them for me will you, mother?"

"Yes, Stanley."

Burnell got up, stretched himself, and going over to the fire he turned his back to it and lifted up his coat tails.

"By Jove, this is a pretty pickle. Eh, Beryl?"

Beryl, sipping tea, her elbows on the table, smiled over the cup at him. She wore an unfamiliar pink pinafore; the sleeves of her blouse were rolled up to her shoulders showing her lovely freckled arms, and she had let her hair fall down her back in a long pig-tail.

"How long do you think it will take to get straight—couple of weeks—eh?" he chaffed.

"Good heavens, no," said Beryl airily. "The worst is over already. The servant girl and I have simply slaved all day, and ever since mother came she has worked like a horse, too. We have never sat down for a moment. We have had a day."

Stanley scented a rebuke.

"Well, I suppose you did not expect me to rush away from the office and nail carpets—did you?"

"Certainly not," laughed Beryl. She put down her cup and ran out of the dining-room.

"What the hell does she expect us to do?" asked Stanley. "Sit down and fan herself with a palm leaf fan while I have a gang of professionals to do the job? By Jove, if she can't do a hand's turn occasionally without shouting about it in return for . . ."

And he gloomed as the chops began to fight the tea in his sensitive stomach. But Linda put up a hand and dragged him down to the side of her long chair.

"This is a wretched time for you, old boy," she said. Her cheeks were very white but she smiled and curled her fingers into the big red hand she held. Burnell became quiet. Suddenly he began to whistle "Pure as a lily, joyous and free"—a good sign.

"Think you're going to like it?" he asked.

"I don't want to tell you, but I think I ought to, mother," said Isabel. "Kezia is drinking tea out of Aunt Beryl's cup."

4

They were taken off to bed by the grandmother. She went first with a candle; the stairs rang to their climbing feet. Isabel and Lottie lay in a room to themselves, Kezia curled in her grandmother's soft bed.

"Aren't there going to be any sheets, my granma?"

"No, not to-night."

"It's tickly," said Kezia, "but it's like Indians." She dragged her grandmother down to her and kissed her under the chin. "Come to bed soon and be my Indian brave."

"What a silly you are," said the old woman, tucking her in as she loved to be tucked.

"Aren't you going to leave me a candle?"

"No. Sh—h. Go to sleep."

"Well, can I have the door left open?"

She rolled herself up into a round but she did not go to sleep. From all over the house came the sound of steps. The house itself creaked and popped. Loud whispering voices came from downstairs. Once she heard Aunt Beryl's rush of high laughter, and once she heard a loud trumpeting from Burnell blowing his nose. Outside the window hundreds of black cats with yellow eyes sat in the sky watching her—but she was not frightened. Lottie was saying to Isabel

"I'm going to say my prayers in bed to-night."

"No you can't, Lottie." Isabel was very firm. "God only excuses you saying your prayers in bed if you've got a temperature." So Lottie yielded:

> Gentle Jesus meek anmile,
> Look pon a little chile.
> Pity me, simple Lizzie
> Suffer me to come to thee.

And then they lay down back to back, their little behinds just touching, and fell asleep.

Standing in a pool of moonlight Beryl Fairfield undressed herself. She was tired, but she pretended to be more tired than she really was—letting her clothes fall, pushing back with a languid gesture her warm, heavy hair.

"Oh, how tired I am—very tired."

She shut her eyes a moment, but her lips smiled. Her breath rose and fell in her breast like two fanning wings. The window was wide open; it was warm, and somewhere out there in the garden a young man, dark and slender, with mocking eyes, tiptoed among the bushes, and gathered the flowers into a big bouquet, and slipped under her window and held it up to her. She saw herself bending forward. He thrust his head among the bright waxy flowers, sly and laughing. "No, no," said Beryl. She turned from the window and dropped her nightgown over her head.

"How frightfully unreasonable Stanley is sometimes," she thought, buttoning. And then, as she lay down, there came the old thought, the cruel thought—ah, if only she had money of her own.

A young man, immensely rich, has just arrived from England. He meets her quite by chance. . . . The new governor is unmarried. . . . There is a ball at Government house. . . . Who is that exquisite creature in *eau de nil* satin? Beryl Fairfield. . . .

"The thing that pleases me," said Stanley, leaning against the side of the bed and giving himself a good scratch on his shoulders and back before turning in, "is that I've got the place dirt cheap, Linda. I was talking about it to little Wally Bell to-day and he said he simply could not understand why they had accepted my figure. You see land about here is bound to become more and more valuable . . . in about ten years' time . . . of course we shall have to go very slow and cut down expenses as fine as possible. Not asleep—are you?"

"No, dear, I've heard every word," said Linda.

He sprang into bed, leaned over her and blew out the candle.

"Good night, Mr. Business Man," said she, and she took hold of his head by the ears and gave him a quick kiss. Her faint faraway voice seemed to come from a deep well.

"Good night, darling." He slipped his arm under her neck and drew her to him.

"Yes, clasp me," said the faint voice from the deep well.

Pat the handy-man sprawled in his little room behind the kitchen. His sponge-bag coat and trousers hung from the door-peg like a hanged man. From the edge of the blanket his twisted toes protruded, and on the floor beside him there was an empty cane bird-cage. He looked like a comic picture.

"Honk, honk," came from the servant girl. She had adenoids. Last to go to bed was the grandmother.

"What! Not asleep yet?"

"No, I'm waiting for you," said Kezia. The old woman sighed and lay down beside her. Kezia thrust her head under the grand-mother's arm and gave a little squeak. But the old woman only pressed her faintly, and sighed again, took out her teeth, and put them in a glass of water beside her on the floor.

In the garden some tiny owls, perched on the branches of a lace-bark tree, called: "More pork; more pork." And far away in the bush there sounded a harsh rapid chatter: "Ha-ha-ha . . . Ha-ha-ha."

5

Dawn came sharp and chill with red clouds on a faint green sky and drops of water on every leaf and blade. A breeze blew over the garden, dropping dew and dropping petals, shivered over the drenched paddocks, and was lost in the sombre bush. In the sky some tiny stars floated for a moment and then they were gone—they were dissolved like bubbles. And plain to be heard in the early quiet was the sound of the creek in the paddock running over the brown stones, running in and out of the sandy hollows, hiding under clumps of dark berry bushes, spilling into a swamp of yellow water flowers and cresses.

And then at the first beam of sun the birds began. Big cheeky birds, starlings and mynahs, whistled on the lawns, the little birds, the goldfinches and linnets and fan-tails flicked from bough to bough. A lovely kingfisher perched on the paddock fence preening his rich beauty, and a *tui* sang his three notes and laughed and sang them again.

"How loud the birds are," said Linda in her dream. She was

walking with her father through a green paddock sprinkled with daisies. Suddenly he bent down and parted the grasses and showed her a tiny ball of fluff just at her feet. "Oh, Papa, the darling." She made a cup of her hands and caught the tiny bird and stroked its head with her finger. It was quite tame. But a funny thing happened. As she stroked it began to swell, it ruffled and pouched, it grew bigger and bigger and its round eyes seemed to smile knowingly at her. Now her arms were hardly wide enough to hold it and she dropped it into her apron. It had become a baby with a big naked head and a gaping bird-mouth, opening and shutting. Her father broke into a loud clattering laugh and she woke to see Burnell standing up by the windows rattling the Venetian blind up to the very top.

"Hullo," he said. "Didn't wake you, did I? Nothing much wrong with the weather this morning."

He was enormously pleased. Weather like this set a final seal on his bargain. He felt, somehow, that he had bought the lovely day, too—got it chucked in dirt cheap with the house and ground. He dashed off to his bath and Linda turned over and raised herself on one elbow to see the room by daylight. All the furniture had found a place—all the old paraphernalia—as she expressed it. Even the photographs were on the mantelpiece and the medicine bottles on the shelf above the washstand. Her clothes lay across a chair—her outdoor things, a purple cape and a round hat with a plume in it. Looking at them she wished that she was going away from this house, too. And she saw herself driving away from them all in a little buggy, driving away from everybody and not even waving.

Back came Stanley girt with a towel, glowing and slapping his thighs. He pitched the wet towel on top of her hat and cape, and standing firm in the exact centre of a square of sunlight he began to do his exercises. Deep breathing, bending and squatting like a frog and shooting out his legs. He was so delighted with his firm, obedient body that he hit himself on the chest and gave a loud "Ah." But this amazing vigour seemed to set him worlds away from Linda. She lay on the white tumbled bed and watched him as if from the clouds.

"Oh, damn! Oh, blast!" said Stanley, who had butted into a

crisp white shirt only to find that some idiot had fastened the neckband and he was caught. He stalked over to Linda waving his arms.

"You look like a big fat turkey," said she.

"Fat. I like that," said Stanley. "I haven't a square inch of fat on me. Feel that."

"It's rock—it's iron," mocked she.

"You'd be surprised," said Stanley, as though this were intensely interesting, "at the number of chaps at the club who have got a corporation. Young chaps, you know—men of my age." He began parting his bushy ginger hair, his blue eyes fixed and round in the glass, his knees bent, because the dressing table was always—confound it—a bit too low for him. "Little Wally Bell, for instance," and he straightened, describing upon himself an enormous curve with the hairbrush. "I must say I've a perfect horror . . ."

"My dear, don't worry. You'll never be fat. You are far too energetic."

"Yes, yes, I suppose that's true," said he, comforted for the hundredth time, and taking a pearl pen-knife out of his pocket he began to pare his nails.

"Breakfast, Stanley." Beryl was at the door. "Oh, Linda, mother says you are not to get up yet." She popped her head in at the door. She had a big piece of syringa stuck through her hair.

"Everything we left on the verandah last night is simply sopping this morning. You should see poor dear mother wringing out the tables and the chairs. However, there is no harm done—" this with the faintest glance at Stanley.

"Have you told Pat to have the buggy round in time? It's a good six and a half miles to the office."

"I can imagine what this early start for the office will be like," thought Linda. "It will be very high pressure indeed."

"Pat, Pat." She heard the servant girl calling. But Pat was evidently hard to find; the silly voice went baa-baaing through the garden.

Linda did not rest again until the final slam of the front door told her that Stanley was really gone.

Later she heard her children playing in the garden. Lottie's stolid, compact little voice cried: "Ke-zia. Isa-bel." She was always getting lost or losing people only to find them again, to her great surprise, round the next tree or the next corner. "Oh, there you are after all." They had been turned out after breakfast and told not to come back to the house until they were called. Isabel wheeled a neat pramload of prim dolls and Lottie was allowed for a great treat to walk beside her holding the doll's parasol over the face of the wax one.

"Where are you going to, Kezia?" asked Isabel, who longed to find some light and menial duty that Kezia might perform and so be roped in under her government.

"Oh, just away," said Kezia. . . .

Then, she did not hear them any more. What a glare there was in the room. She hated blinds pulled up to the top at any time, but in the morning it was intolerable. She turned over to the wall and idly, with one finger, she traced a poppy on the wallpaper with a leaf and a stem and a fat bursting bud. In the quiet, and under her tracing finger, the poppy seemed to come alive. She could feel the sticky, silky petals, the stem, hairy like a gooseberry skin, the rough leaf and the tight glazed bud. Things had a habit of coming alive like that. Not only large substantial things like furniture, but curtains and the patterns of stuffs and fringes of quilts and cushions. How often she had seen the tassel fringe of her quilt change into a funny procession of dancers with priests attending. . . . For there were some tassels that did not dance at all but walked stately, bent forward as if praying or chanting. How often the medicine bottles had turned into a row of little men with brown top-hats on; and the washstand jug had a way of sitting in the basin like a fat bird in a round nest.

"I dreamed about birds last night," thought Linda. What was it? She had forgotten. But the strangest part of this coming alive of things was what they did. They listened, they seemed to swell out with some myterious important content, and when they were full she felt that they smiled. But it was not for her, only, their sly secret smile; they were members of a secret society and they smiled among themselves. Sometimes, when she had fallen asleep in the daytime, she woke and could not lift a finger, could not even turn her eyes to left or right because THEY were there; some-

times when she went out of a room and left it empty, ↕
as she clicked the door to that THEY were filling it. ↕
were times in the evenings when she was upstairs, per↕
everybody else was down, when she could hardly escape from
them. Then she could not hurry, she could not hum a tune; if
she tried to say ever so carelessly—"Bother that old thimble"—
THEY were not deceived. THEY knew how frightened she was;
THEY saw how she turned her head away as she passed the mirror.
What Linda always felt was that THEY wanted something of her,
and she knew that if she gave herself up and was quiet, more than
quiet, silent, motionless, something would really happen.

"It's very quiet now," she thought. She opened her eyes wide,
and she heard the silence spinning its soft endless web. How
lightly she breathed; she scarcely had to breathe at all.

Yes, everything had come alive down to the minutest, tiniest
particle, and she did not feel her bed, she floated, held up in the
air. Only she seemed to be listening with her wide open watchful
eyes, waiting for someone to come who just did not come, watching for something to happen that just did not happen.

6

In the kitchen at the long deal table under the two windows
old Mrs. Fairfield was washing the breakfast dishes. The kitchen
window looked out on to a big grass patch that led down to the
vegetable garden and the rhubarb beds. On one side the grass
patch was bordered by the scullery and washhouse and over this
whitewashed lean-to there grew a knotted vine. She had noticed
yesterday that a few tiny corkscrew tendrils had come right
through some cracks in the scullery ceiling and all the windows
of the lean-to had a thick frill of ruffled green.

"I am very fond of a grape vine," declared Mrs. Fairfield,
"but I do not think that the grapes will ripen here. It takes Australian sun." And she remembered how Beryl when she was a
baby had been picking some white grapes from the vine on the

back verandah of their Tasmanian house and she had been stung on the leg by a huge red ant. She saw Beryl in a little plaid dress with red ribbon tie-ups on the shoulders screaming so dreadfully that half the street rushed in. And how the child's leg had swelled! "T-t-t-t!" Mrs. Fairfield caught her breath remembering. "Poor child, how terrifying it was." And she set her lips tight and went over to the stove for some more hot water. The water frothed up in the big soapy bowl with pink and blue bubbles on top of the foam. Old Mrs. Fairfield's arms were bare to the elbow and stained a bright pink. She wore a grey foulard dress patterned with large purple pansies, a white linen apron and a high cap shaped like a jelly mould of white muslin. At her throat there was a silver crescent moon with five little owls seated on it, and round her neck she wore a watchguard made of black beads.

It was hard to believe that she had not been in that kitchen for years; she was so much a part of it. She put the crocks away with a sure, precise touch, moving leisurely and ample from the stove to the dresser, looking into the pantry and the larder as though there were not an unfamiliar corner. When she had finished, everything in the kitchen had become part of a series of patterns. She stood in the middle of the room wiping her hands on a check cloth; a smile beamed on her lips; she thought it looked very nice, very satisfactory.

"Mother! Mother! Are you there?" called Beryl.

"Yes, dear. Do you want me?"

"No. I'm coming," and Beryl rushed in, very flushed, dragging with her two big pictures.

"Mother, whatever can I do with these awful hideous Chinese paintings that Chung Wah gave Stanley when he went bankrupt? It's absurd to say that they are valuable, because they were hanging in Chung Wah's fruit shop for months before. I can't make out why Stanley wants them kept. I'm sure he thinks them just as hideous as we do, but it's because of the frames," she said spitefully. "I suppose he thinks the frames might fetch something some day or other."

"Why don't you hang them in the passage?" suggested Mrs. Fairfield; "they would not be much seen there."

"I can't. There is no room. I've hung all the photographs of his office there before and after building, and the signed photos of his business friends, and that awful enlargement of Isabel lying on the mat in her singlet." Her angry glance swept the placid kitchen. "I know what I'll do. I'll hang them here. I will tell Stanley they got a little damp in the moving so I have put them in here for the time being."

She dragged a chair forward, jumped on it, took a hammer and a big nail out of her pinafore pocket and banged away.

"There! That is enough! Hand me the picture, mother."

"One moment, child." Her mother was wiping over the carved ebony frame.

"Oh, mother, really you need not dust them. It would take years to dust all those little holes." And she frowned at the top of her mother's head and bit her lip with impatience. Mother's deliberate way of doing things was simply maddening. It was old age, she supposed, loftily.

At last the two pictures were hung side by side. She jumped off the chair, stowing away the little hammer.

"They don't look so bad there, do they?" said she. "And at any rate nobody need gaze at them except Pat and the servant girl—have I got a spider's web on my face, mother? I've been poking into that cupboard under the stairs and now something keeps tickling my nose."

But before Mrs. Fairfield had time to look Beryl had turned away. Someone tapped on the window: Linda was there, nodding and smiling. They heard the latch of the scullery door lift and she came in. She had no hat on; her hair stood up on her head in curling rings and she was wrapped up in an old cashmere shawl.

"I'm so hungry," said Linda: "where can I get something to eat, mother? This is the first time I've been in the kitchen. It says 'mother' all over; everything is in pairs."

"I will make you some tea," said Mrs. Fairfield, spreading a clean napkin over a corner of the table, "and Beryl can have a cup with you."

"Beryl, do you want half my gingerbread?" Linda waved the knife at her. "Beryl, do you like the house now that we are here?"

"Oh yes, I like the house immensely and the garden is beautiful, but it feels very far away from everything to me. I can't

69

imagine people coming out from town to see us in that dreadful jolting bus, and I am sure there is not anyone here to come and call. Of course it does not matter to you because—"

"But there's the buggy," said Linda. "Pat can drive you into town whenever you like."

That was a consolation, certainly, but there was something at the back of Beryl's mind, something she did not even put into words for herself.

"Oh, well, at any rate it won't kill us," she said dryly, putting down her empty cup and standing up and stretching. "I am going to hang curtains." And she ran away singing:

> How many thousand birds I see
> That sing aloud from every tree . . .

". . . birds I see That sing aloud from every tree. . . ." But when she reached the dining-room she stopped singing, her face changed; it became gloomy and sullen.

"One may as well rot here as anywhere else," she muttered savagely, digging the stiff brass safety-pins into the red serge curtains.

The two left in the kitchen were quiet for a little. Linda leaned her cheek on her fingers and watched her mother. She thought her mother looked wonderfully beautiful with her back to the leafy window. There was something comforting in the sight of her that Linda felt she could never do without. She needed the sweet smell of her flesh, and the soft feel of her cheeks and her arms and shoulders still softer. She loved the way her hair curled, silver at her forehead, lighter at her neck, and bright brown still in the big coil under the muslin cap. Exquisite were her mother's hands, and the two rings she wore seemed to melt into her creamy skin. And she was always so fresh, so delicious. The old woman could bear nothing but linen next to her body and she bathed in cold water winter and summer.

"Isn't there anything for me to do?" asked Linda.

"No, darling. I wish you would go into the garden and give an eye to your children; but that I know you will not do."

"Of course I will, but you know Isabel is much more grown up than any of us."

"Yes, but Kezia is not," said Mrs. Fairfield.

"Oh, Kezia has been tossed by a bull hours ago," said Linda, winding herself up in her shawl again.

But no, Kezia had seen a bull through a hole in a knot of wood in the paling that separated the tennis lawn from the paddock. But she had not liked the bull frightfully, so she had walked away back through the orchard, up the grassy slope, along the path by the lace-bark tree and so into the spread tangled garden. She did not believe that she would ever not get lost in this garden. Twice she had found her way back to the big iron gates they had driven through the night before, and then had turned to walk up the drive that led to the house, but there were so many little paths on either side. On one side they all led into a tangle of tall dark trees and strange bushes with flat velvet leaves and feathery cream flowers that buzzed with flies when you shook them—this was the frightening side, and no garden at all. The little paths here were wet and clayey with tree roots spanned across them like the marks of big fowls' feet.

But on the other side of the drive there was a high box border and the paths had box edges and all of them led into a deeper and deeper tangle of flowers. The camellias were in bloom, white and crimson and pink and white striped with flashing leaves. You could not see a leaf on the syringa bushes for the white clusters. The roses were in flower—gentlemen's button-hole roses, little white ones, but far too full of insects to hold under anyone's nose, pink monthly roses with a ring of fallen petals round the bushes, cabbage roses on thick stalks, moss roses, always in bud, pink smooth beauties opening curl on curl, red ones so dark they seemed to turn black as they fell, and a certain exquisite cream kind with a slender red stem and bright scarlet leaves.

There were clumps of fairy bells, and all kinds of geraniums, and there were little trees of verbena and bluish lavender bushes and a bed of pelagoniums with velvet eyes and leaves like moths' wings. There was a bed of nothing but mignonette and another of nothing but pansies—borders of double and single daisies and all kinds of little tufty plants she had never seen before.

The red-hot pokers were taller than she; the Japanese sunflowers grew in a tiny jungle. She sat down on one of the box borders. By pressing hard at first it made a nice seat. But how dusty it was inside! Kezia bent down to look and sneezed and rubbed her nose.

And then she found herself at the top of the rolling grassy slope that led down to the orchard. . . . She looked down at the slope a moment; then she lay down on her back, gave a squeak and rolled over and over into the thick flowery orchard grass. As she lay waiting for things to stop spinning, she decided to go up to the house and ask the servant girl for an empty match-box. She wanted to make a surprise for the grandmother. . . . First she would put a leaf inside with a big violet lying on it, then she would put a very small white picotee, perhaps, on each side of the violet, and then she would sprinkle some lavender on the top, but not to cover their heads.

She often made these surprises for the grandmother, and they were always most successful.

"Do you want a match, my granny?"

"Why, yes, child, I believe a match is just what I'm looking for."

The grandmother slowly opened the box and came upon the picture inside.

"Good gracious, child! How you astonished me!"

"I can make her one every day here," she thought, scrambling up the grass on her slippery shoes.

But on her way back to the house she came to that island that lay in the middle of the drive, dividing the drive into two arms that met in front of the house. The island was made of grass banked up high. Nothing grew on the top except one huge plant with thick, grey-green, thorny leaves, and out of the middle there sprang up a tall stout stem. Some of the leaves of the plant were so old that they curled up in the air no longer; they turned back, they were split and broken; some of them lay flat and withered on the ground.

Whatever could it be? She had never seen anything like it before. She stood and stared. And then she saw her mother coming down the path.

"Mother, what is it?" asked Kezia.

Linda looked up at the fat swelling plant with its cruel leaves and fleshy stem. High above them, as though becalmed in the air, and yet holding so fast to the earth it grew from, it might have had claws instead of roots. The curving leaves seemed to be hiding something; the blind stem cut into the air as if no wind could ever shake it.

"That is an aloe, Kezia," said her mother.

"Does it ever have any flowers?"

"Yes, Kezia," and Linda smiled down at her, and half shut her eyes. "Once every hundred years."

7

On his way home from the office Stanley Burnell stopped the buggy at the Bodega, got out and bought a large bottle of oysters. At the Chinaman's shop next door he bought a pineapple in the pink of condition, and noticing a basket of fresh black cherries he told John to put him a pound of those as well. The oysters and the pine he stowed away in the box under the front seat, but the cherries he kept in his hand.

Pat, the handy-man, leapt off the box and tucked him up again in the brown rug.

"Lift yer feet, Mr. Burnell, while I give yer a fold under," said he.

"Right! Right! First-rate!" said Stanley. "You can make straight for home now."

Pat gave the grey mare a touch and the buggy sprang forward.

"I believe this man is a first-rate chap," thought Stanley. He liked the look of him sitting up there in his neat brown coat and brown bowler. He liked the way Pat had tucked him in, and he liked his eyes. There was nothing servile about him—and if there was one thing he hated more than another it was servility. And he looked as if he was pleased with his job—happy and contented already.

The grey mare went very well; Burnell was impatient to be out of the town. He wanted to be home. Ah, it was splendid to live in the country—to get right out of that hole of a town once the office was closed; and this drive in the fresh warm air, knowing all the while that his own house was at the other end, with its garden and paddocks, its three tip-top cows and enough fowls and ducks to keep them in poultry, was splendid too.

As they left the town finally and bowled away up the deserted road his heart beat hard for joy. He rooted in the bag and began to eat the cherries, three or four at a time, chucking the stones over the side of the buggy. They were delicious, so plump and cold, without a spot or a bruise on them.

Look at those two, now—black one side and white the other—perfect! A perfect little pair of Siamese twins. And he stuck them in his button-hole. . . . By Jove, he wouldn't mind giving that chap up there a handful—but no, better not. Better wait until he had been with him a bit longer.

He began to plan what he would do with his Saturday afternoons and his Sundays. He wouldn't go to the club for lunch on Saturday. No, cut away from the office as soon as possible and get them to give him a couple of slices of cold meat and half a lettuce when he got home. And then he'd get a few chaps out from town to play tennis in the afternoon. Not too many—three at most. Beryl was a good player, too. . . . He stretched out his right arm and slowly bent it, feeling the muscle. . . . A bath, a good rubdown, a cigar on the verandah after dinner. . . .

On Sunday morning they would go to church—children and all. Which reminded him that he must hire a pew, in the sun if possible and well forward so as to be out of the draught from the door. In fancy he heard himself intoning extremely well: "When thou didst overcome the *Sharp*ness of Death Thou didst open the *King*dom of Heaven to *all* Believers." And he saw the neat brass-edged card on the corner of the pew—Mr. Stanley Burnell and family. . . . The rest of the day he'd loaf about with Linda. . . . Now they were walking about the garden; she was on his arm, and he was explaining to her at length what he intended doing at the office the week following. He heard her saying: "My dear, I think that is most wise.". . . Talking things over with Linda was a wonderful help even though they were apt to drift away from the point.

Hang it all! They weren't getting along very fast. Pat had put the brake on again. Ugh! What a brute of a thing it was. He could feel it in the pit of his stomach.

A sort of panic overtook Burnell whenever he approached near home. Before he was well inside the gate he would shout to anyone within sight: "Is everything all right?" And then he did not believe it was until he heard Linda say: "Hullo! Are you home again?" That was the worst of living in the country—it took the deuce of a long time to get back. . . . But now they weren't far off. They were on the top of the last hill; it was a gentle slope all the way now and not more than half a mile.

Pat trailed the whip over the mare's back and he coaxed her: "Goop now. Goop now."

It wanted a few minutes to sunset. Everything stood motionless bathed in bright, metallic light and from the paddocks' on either side there steamed the milky scent of ripe grass. The iron gates were open. They dashed through and up the drive and round the island, stopping at the exact middle of the verandah.

"Did she satisfy yer, Sir?" said Pat, getting off the box and grinning at his master.

"Very well indeed, Pat," said Stanley.

Linda came out of the glass door; her voice rang in the shadowy quiet. "Hullo! Are you home again?"

At the sound of her his heart beat so hard that he could hardly stop himself dashing up the steps and catching her in his arms.

"Yes, I'm home again. Is everything all right?"

Pat began to lead the buggy round to the side gate that opened into the courtyard.

"Here, half a moment," said Burnell. "Hand me those two parcels." And he said to Linda, "I've brought you back a bottle of oysters and a pineapple," as though he had brought her back all the harvest of the earth.

They went into the hall; Linda carried the oysters in one hand and the pineapple in the other. Burnell shut the glass door, threw his hat down, put his arms round her and strained her to him, kissing the top of her head, her ears, her lips, her eyes.

"Oh, dear! Oh, dear!" said she. "Wait a moment. Let me put

down these silly things," and she put the bottle of oysters and the pine on a little carved chair. "What have you got in your button-hole—cherries?" She took them out and hung them over his ear.

"Don't do that, darling. They are for you."

So she took them off his ear again. "You don't mind if I save them. They'd spoil my appetite for dinner. Come and see your children. They are having tea."

The lamp was lighted on the nursery table. Mrs. Fairfield was cutting and spreading bread and butter. The three little girls sat up to table wearing large bibs embroidered with their names. They wiped their mouths as their father came in ready to be kissed. The windows were open; a jar of wild flowers stood on the mantelpiece, and the lamp made a big soft bubble of light on the ceiling.

"You seem pretty snug, mother," said Burnell, blinking at the light. Isabel and Lottie sat one on either side of the table, Kezia at the bottom—the place at the top was empty.

"That's where my boy ought to sit," thought Stanley. He tightened his arm round Linda's shoulder. By God, he was a perfect fool to feel as happy as this!

"We are, Stanley. We are very snug," said Mrs. Fairfield, cutting Kezia's bread into fingers.

"Like it better than town—eh, children?" asked Burnell.

"Oh, yes," said the three little girls, and Isabel added as an after-thought: "Thank you very much indeed, father dear."

"Come upstairs," said Linda. "I'll bring your slippers."

But the stairs were too narrow for them to go up arm in arm. It was quite dark in the room. He heard her ring tapping on the marble mantelpiece as she felt for the matches.

"I've got some, darling. I'll light the candles."

But instead he came up behind her and again he put his arms round her and pressed her head into his shoulder.

"I'm so confoundedly happy," he said.

"Are you?" She turned and put her hands on his breast and looked up at him.

"I don't know what has come over me," he protested.

It was quite dark outside now and heavy dew was falling. When Linda shut the window the cold dew touched her finger tips. Far away a dog barked. "I believe there is going to moon," she said.

At the words, and with the cold wet dew on her fingers, she felt as though the moon had risen—that she was being strangely discovered in a flood of cold light. She shivered; she came away from the window and sat down upon the box ottoman beside Stanley.

In the dining-room, by the flicker of a wood fire, Beryl sat on a hassock playing the guitar. She had bathed and changed all her clothes. Now she wore a white muslin dress with black spots on it and in her hair she had pinned a black silk rose.

> Nature has gone to her rest, love,
>   See, we are alone.
> Give me your hand to press, love,
>   Lightly within my own.

She played and sang half to herself, for she was watching herself playing and singing. The firelight gleamed on her shoes, on the ruddy belly of the guitar, and on her white fingers. . . .

"If I were outside the window and looked in and saw myself I really would be rather struck," thought she. Still more softly she played the accompaniment—not singing now but listening.

. . . "The first time that I ever saw you, little girl—oh, you had no idea that you were not alone—you were sitting with your little feet upon a hassock, playing the guitar. God, I can never forget. . . ." Beryl flung up her head and began to sing again:

> Even the moon is aweary . . .

But there came a loud bang at the door. The servant girl's crimson face popped through.

"Please, Miss Beryl, I've got to come and lay."

"Certainly, Alice," said Beryl, in a voice of ice. She put the guitar in a corner. Alice lunged in with a heavy black iron tray.

"Well, I have had a job with that oving," said she. "I can't get nothing to brown."

"Really!" said Beryl.

But no, she could not stand that fool of a girl. She ran into the dark drawing-room and began walking up and down. . . . Oh, she was restless, restless. There was a mirror over the mantel. She leaned her arms along and looked at her pale shadow in it. How beautiful she looked, but there was nobody to see, nobody.

"Why must you suffer so?" said the face in the mirror. "You were not made for suffering. . . . Smile!"

Beryl smiled, and really her smile *was* so adorable that she smiled again—but this time because she could not help it.

8

"Good morning, Mrs. Jones."

"Oh, good morning, Mrs. Smith. I'm so glad to see you. Have you brought your children?"

"Yes, I've brought both my twins. I have had another baby since I saw you last, but she came so suddenly that I haven't had time to make her any clothes, yet. So I left her. . . . How is your husband?"

"Oh, he is very well, thank you. At least he had a nawful cold but Queen Victoria—she's my godmother, you know—sent him a case of pineapples and that cured it im—immediately. Is that your new servant?"

"Yes, her name's Gwen. I've only had her two days. Oh, Gwen, this is my friend, Mrs. Smith."

"Good morning, Mrs. Smith. Dinner won't be ready for about ten minutes."

"I don't think you ought to introduce me to the servant. I think I ought to just begin talking to her."

"Well, she's more of a lady-help than a servant and you do introduce lady-helps, I know, because Mrs. Samuel Josephs had one."

"Oh, well, it doesn't matter," said the servant, carelessly, beating up a chocolate custard with half a broken clothes peg. The dinner was baking beautifully on a concrete step. She began to lay the cloth on a pink garden seat. In front of each person she put two geranium leaf plates, a pine needle fork and a twig knife. There were three daisy heads on a laurel leaf for poached eggs, some slices of fuchsia petal cold beef, some lovely little rissoles made of earth and water and dandelion seeds, and the chocolate custard which she had decided to serve in the pawa shell she had cooked it in.

"You needn't trouble about my children," said Mrs. Smith graciously. "If you'll take this bottle and fill it at the tap—I mean at the dairy."

"Oh, all right," said Gwen, and she whispered to Mrs. Jones: "Shall I go and ask Alice for a little bit of real milk?"

But someone called from the front of the house and the luncheon party melted away, leaving the charming table, leaving the rissoles and the poached eggs to the ants and to an old snail who pushed his quivering horns over the edge of the garden seat and began to nibble a geranium plate.

"Come round to the front, children. Pip and Rags have come."

The Trout boys were the cousins Kezia had mentioned to the storeman. They lived about a mile away in a house called Monkey Tree Cottage. Pip was tall for his age, with lank black hair and a white face, but Rags was very small and so thin that when he was undressed his shoulder blades stuck out like two little wings. They had a mongrel dog with pale blue eyes and a long tail turned up at the end who followed them everywhere; he was called Snooker. They spent half their time combing and brushing Snooker and dosing him with various awful mixtures concocted by Pip, and kept secretly by him in a broken jug covered with an old kettle lid. Even faithful little Rags was not allowed to know the full secret of these mixtures. . . . Take some carbolic tooth powder and a pinch of sulphur powdered up fine, and perhaps a bit of starch to stiffen up Snooker's coat. . . . But that was not all; Rags privately thought that the rest was gunpowder. . . . And he never was allowed to help with the mixing because of the danger. . . . "Why if a spot of this flew in your eye, you would be blinded for life," Pip would say, stirring the mixture with an iron spoon. "And there's always the chance—just the chance, mind you—of it exploding if you whack it hard enough. . . . Two spoons of this in a kerosene tin will be enough to kill thousands of fleas." But Snooker spent all his spare time biting and snuffling, and he stank abominably.

"It's because he is such a grand fighting dog," Pip would say. "All fighting dogs smell."

The Trout boys had often spent the day with the Burnells in town, but now that they lived in this fine house and boncer garden they were inclined to be very friendly. Besides, both of them liked playing with girls—Pip, because he could fox them so, and because Lottie was so easily frightened, and Rags for a shameful reason. He adored dolls. How he would look at a doll as it lay asleep, speaking in a whisper and smiling timidly, and what a treat it was to him to be allowed to hold one. . . .

"Curve your arms round her. Don't keep them stiff like that. You'll drop her," Isabel would say sternly.

Now they were standing on the verandah and holding back Snooker who wanted to go into the house but wasn't allowed to because Aunt Linda hated decent dogs.

"We came over in the bus with Mum," they said, "and we're going to spend the afternoon with you. We brought over a batch of our gingerbread for Aunt Linda. Our Minnie made it. It's all over nuts."

"I skinned the almonds," said Pip. "I just stuck my hand into a saucepan of boiling water and grabbed them out and gave them a kind of pinch and the nuts flew out of the skins, some of them as high as the ceiling. Didn't they, Rags?"

Rags nodded. "When they make cakes at our place," said Pip, "we always stay in the kitchen, Rags and me, and I get the bowl and he gets the spoon and the egg beater. Sponge cake's best. It's all frothy stuff, then."

He ran down the verandah steps to the lawn, planted his hands on the grass, bent forward, and just did not stand on his head.

"That lawn's all bumpy," he said. "You have to have a flat place for standing on your head. I can walk round the monkey tree on my head at our place. Can't I, Rags?"

"Nearly," said Rags faintly.

"Stand on your head on the verandah. That's quite flat," said Kezia.

"No, smarty," said Pip. "You have to do it on something soft. Because if you give a jerk and fall over, something in your neck goes click, and it breaks off. Dad told me."

"Oh, do let's play something," said Kezia.

"Very well," said Isabel quickly, "we'll play hospitals. I will be the nurse and Pip can be the doctor and you and Lottie and Rags can be the sick people."

Lottie didn't want to play that, because last time Pip had squeezed something down her throat and it hurt awfully.

"Pooh," scoffed Pip. "It was only the juice out of a bit of mandarin peel."

"Well, let's play ladies," said Isabel. "Pip can be the father and you can be all our dear little children."

"I hate playing ladies," said Kezia. "You always make us go to church hand in hand and come home and go to bed."

Suddenly Pip took a filthy handkerchief out of his pocket. "Snooker! Here, sir," he called. But Snooker, as usual, tried to sneak away, his tail between his legs. Pip leapt on top of him, and pressed him between his knees.

"Keep his head firm, Rags," he said, and he tied the handkerchief round Snooker's head with a funny knot sticking up at the top.

"Whatever is that for?" asked Lottie.

"It's to train his ears to grow more close to his head—see?" said Pip. "All fighting dogs have ears that lie back. But Snooker's ears are a bit too soft."

"I know," said Kezia. "They are always turning inside out. I hate that."

Snooker lay down, made one feeble effort with his paw to get the handkerchief off, but finding he could not, trailed after the children, shivering with misery.

Pat came swinging along; in his hand he held a little toma-hawk that winked in the sun.

"Come with me," he said to the children, "and I'll show you how the kings of Ireland chop the head off a duck."

They drew back—they didn't believe him, and besides, the Trout boys had never seen Pat before.

"Come on now," he coaxed, smiling and holding out his hand to Kezia.

"Is it a real duck's head? One from the paddock?"

"It is," said Pat. She put her hand in his hard dry one, and he stuck the tomahawk in his belt and held out the other to Rags. He loved little children.

"I'd better keep hold of Snooker's head if there's going to be any blood about," said Pip, "because the sight of blood makes him awfully wild." He ran ahead dragging Snooker by the hand-kerchief.

"Do you think we ought to go?" whispered Isabel. "We haven't asked or anything. Have we?"

At the bottom of the orchard a gate was set in the paling fence. On the other side a steep bank led down to a bridge that spanned the creek, and once up the bank on the other side you were on the fringe of the paddocks. A little old stable in the first paddock had been turned into a fowl-house. The fowls had strayed far away across the paddock down to a dumping ground in a hollow, but the ducks kept close to that part of the creek that flowed under the bridge.

Tall bushes overhung the stream with red leaves and yellow flowers and clusters of blackberries. At some places the stream was wide and shallow, but at others it tumbled into deep little pools with foam at the edges and quivering bubbles. It was in these pools that the big white ducks had made themselves at home, swimming and guzzling along the weedy banks.

Up and down they swam, preening their dazzling breasts, and other ducks with the same dazzling breasts and yellow bills swam upside down with them.

"There is the little Irish navy," said Pat, "and look at the old admiral there with the green neck and the grand little flagstaff on his tail."

He pulled a handful of grain from his pocket and began to walk towards the fowl-house, lazy, his straw hat with the broken crown pulled over his eyes.

"Lid. Lid—lid—lid—lid—" he called.

"Qua. Qua—qua—qua—qua—" answered the ducks, making for land, and flapping and scrambling up the bank they streamed after him in a long waddling line. He coaxed them, pretending to throw the grain, shaking it in his hands and calling to them until they swept round him in a white ring.

From far away the fowls heard the clamour and they too came running across the paddock, their heads thrust forward, their wings spread, turning in their feet in the silly way fowls run and scolding as they came.

Then Pat scattered the grain and the greedy ducks began to gobble. Quickly he stooped, seized two, one under each arm, and strode across to the children. Their darting heads and round eyes frightened the children—all except Pip.

"Come on, sillies," he cried, "they can't bite. They haven't any teeth. They've only got those two little holes in their beaks for breathing through."

"Will you hold one while I finish with the other?" asked Pat. Pip let go of Snooker. "Won't I? Won't I? Give us one. I don't mind how much he kicks."

He nearly sobbed with delight when Pat gave the white lump into his arms.

There was an old stump beside the door of the fowl-house. Pat grabbed the duck by the legs, laid it flat across the stump, and almost at the same moment down came the little tomahawk and the duck's head flew off the stump. Up the blood spurted over the white feathers and over his hand.

When the children saw the blood they were frightened no longer. They crowded round him and began to scream. Even Isabel leaped about crying: "The blood! The blood!" Pip forgot all about his duck. He simply threw it away from him and shouted, "I saw it. I saw it," and jumped round the wood block.

Rags, with cheeks as white as paper, ran up to the little head, put out a finger as if he wanted to touch it, shrank back again and then again put out a finger. He was shivering all over.

Even Lottie, frightened little Lottie, began to laugh and pointed at the duck and shrieked: "Look, Kezia, look."

"Watch it!" shouted Pat. He put down the body and it began to waddle—with only a long spurt of blood where the head had been; it began to pad away without a sound towards the steep bank that led to the stream. . . . That was the crowning wonder.

"Do you see that? Do you see that?" yelled Pip. He ran among the little girls tugging at their pinafores.

"It's like a little engine. It's like a funny little railway engine," squealed Isabel.

But Kezia suddenly rushed at Pat and flung her arms round his legs and butted her head as hard as she could against his knees.

"Put head back! Put head back!" she screamed.

When he stooped to move her she would not let go or take her head away. She held on as hard as she could and sobbed: "Head back! Head back!" until it sounded like a loud strange hiccup.

"It's stopped. It's tumbled over. It's dead," said Pip.

Pat dragged Kezia up into his arms. Her sunbonnet had fallen back, but she would not let him look at her face. No, she pressed her face into a bone in his shoulder and clasped her arms round his neck.

The children stopped screaming as suddenly as they had begun. They stood round the dead duck. Rags was not frightened of the head any more. He knelt down and stroked it, now.

"I don't think the head is quite dead yet," he said. "Do you think it would keep alive if I gave it something to drink?"

But Pip got very cross: "Bah! You baby." He whistled to Snooker and went off.

When Isabel went up to Lottie, Lottie snatched away.

"What are you always touching me for, Isabel?"

"There now," said Pat to Kezia. "There's the grand little girl."

She put up her hands and touched his ears. She felt something. Slowly she raised her quivering face and looked. Pat wore little round gold ear-rings. She never knew that men wore ear-rings. She was very much surprised.

"Do they come on and off?" she asked huskily.

10

Up in the house, in the warm tidy kitchen, Alice, the servant girl, was getting the afternoon tea. She was "dressed." She had on a black stuff dress that smelt under the arms, a white apron like a large sheet of paper, and a lace bow pinned on to her hair with two jetty pins. Also her comfortable carpet slippers were changed for a pair of black leather ones that pinched her corn on her little toe something dreadful. . . .

It was warm in the kitchen. A blow-fly buzzed, a fan of whity steam came out of the kettle, and the lid kept up a rattling jig as the water bubbled. The clock ticked in the warm air, slow and deliberate, like the click of an old woman's knitting needle, and sometimes—for no reason at all, for there wasn't any breeze—the blind swung out and back, tapping the window.

Alice was making water-cress sandwiches. She had a lump of butter on the table, a barracouta loaf, and the cresses tumbled in a white cloth.

But propped against the butter dish there was a dirty, greasy little book, half unstitched, with curled edges, and while she mashed the butter she read:

"To dream of black-beetles drawing a hearse is bad. Signifies death of one you hold near or dear, either father, husband, brother, son, or intended. If beetles crawl backwards as you watch them it means death from fire or from great height such as flight of stairs, scaffolding, etc.

"Spiders. To dream of spiders creeping over you is good. Signifies large sum of money in near future. Should party be in family way an easy confinement may be expected. But care should be taken in sixth month to avoid eating of probable present of shell fish. . . ."

How many thousand birds I see.

Oh, life. There was Miss Beryl. Alice dropped the knife and slipped the *Dream Book* under the butter dish. But she hadn't time to hide it quite, for Beryl ran into the kitchen and up to the table, and the first thing her eye lighted on were those greasy edges. Alice saw Miss Beryl's meaning little smile and the way she raised her eyebrows and screwed up her eyes as though she were not quite sure what that could be. She decided to answer if Miss Beryl should ask her: "Nothing as belongs to you, Miss." But she knew Miss Beryl would not ask her.

Alice was a mild creature in reality, but she had the most marvellous retorts ready for questions that she knew would never be put to her. The composing of them and the turning of them over and over in her mind comforted her just as much as if they'd been expressed. Really, they kept her alive in places where she'd been that chivvied she'd been afraid to go to bed at night with a box of matches on the chair in case she bit the tops off in her sleep, as you might say.

"Oh, Alice," said Miss Beryl. "There's one extra to tea, so heat a plate of yesterday's scones, please. And put on the Victoria sandwich as well as the coffee cake. And don't forget to put little doyleys under the plates—will you? You did yesterday, you know, and the tea looked so ugly and common. And, Alice, don't put that dreadful old pink and green cosy on the afternoon teapot again. That is only for the mornings. Really, I think it ought to be kept for the kitchen—it's so shabby, and quite smelly. Put on the Japanese one. You quite understand, don't you?"

Miss Beryl had finished.

That sing aloud from every tree . . .

she sang as she left the kitchen, very pleased with her firm handling of Alice.

Oh, Alice was wild. She wasn't one to mind being told, but there was something in the way Miss Beryl had of speaking to her that she couldn't stand. Oh, that she couldn't. It made her curl up inside, as you might say, and she fair trembled. But what Alice really hated Miss Beryl for was that she made her feel low.

86

She talked to Alice in a special voice as though she wasn't quite all there; and she never lost her temper with her—never. Even when Alice dropped anything or forgot anything important Miss Beryl seemed to have expected it to happen.

"If you please, Mrs. Burnell," said an imaginary Alice, as she buttered the scones, "I'd rather not take my orders from Miss Beryl. I may be only a common servant girl as doesn't know how to play the guitar, but . . ."

This last thrust pleased her so much that she quite recovered her temper.

"The only thing to do," she heard, as she opened the dining-room door, "is to cut the sleeves out entirely and just have a broad band of black velvet over the shoulders instead. . . ."

II

The white duck did not look as if it had ever had a head when Alice placed it in front of Stanley Burnell that night. It lay, in beautifully basted resignation, on a blue dish—its legs tied together with a piece of string and a wreath of little balls of stuffing round it.

It was hard to say which of the two, Alice or the duck, looked the better basted; they were both such a rich colour and they both had the same air of gloss and strain. But Alice was fiery red and the duck a Spanish mahogany.

Burnell ran his eye along the edge of the carving knife. He prided himself very much upon his carving, upon making a first-class job of it. He hated seeing a woman carve; they were always too slow and they never seemed to care what the meat looked like afterwards. Now he did; he took a real pride in cutting delicate shaves of cold beef, little wads of mutton, just the right thickness, and in dividing a chicken or a duck with nice precision. . . .

"Is this the first of the home products?" he asked, knowing perfectly well that it was.

"Yes, the butcher did not come. We have found out that he only calls twice a week."

But there was no need to apologise. It was a superb bird. It wasn't meat at all, but a kind of very superior jelly. "My father would say," said Burnell, "this must have been one of those birds whose mother played to it in infancy upon the German flute. And the sweet strains of the dulcet instrument acted with such effect upon the infant mind. . . . Have some more, Beryl? You and I are the only ones in this house with a real feeling for food. I'm perfectly willing to state, in a court of law, if necessary, that I love good food."

Tea was served in the drawing-room, and Beryl, who for some reason had been very charming to Stanley ever since he came home, suggested a game of crib. They sat at a little table near one of the open windows. Mrs. Fairfield disappeared, and Linda lay in a rocking-chair, her arms above her head, rocking to and fro.

"You don't want the light—do you, Linda?" said Beryl. She moved the lamp so that she sat under its soft light.

How remote they looked, those two, from where Linda sat and rocked. The green table, the polished cards, Stanley's big hands and Beryl's tiny ones, all seemed to be part of one mysterious movement. Stanley himself, big and solid, in his dark suit, took his ease, and Beryl tossed her bright head and pouted. Round her throat she wore an unfamiliar velvet ribbon. It changed her, some-how—altered the shape of her face—but it was charming, Linda decided. The room smelled of lilies; there were two big jars of arums in the fire-place.

"Fifteen two—fifteen four—and a pair is six and a run of three is nine," said Stanley, so deliberately, he might have been counting sheep.

"I've nothing but two pairs," said Beryl, exaggerating her woe because she knew how he loved winning.

The cribbage pegs were like two little people going up the road together, turning round the sharp corner, and coming down the road again. They were pursuing each other. They did not so much want to get ahead as to keep near enough to talk—to keep near, perhaps that was all.

But no, there was always one who was impatient and hopped away as the other came up, and would not listen. Perhaps the white peg was frightened of the red one, or perhaps he was cruel and would not give the red one a chance to speak. . . .

In the front of her dress Beryl wore a bunch of pansies, and once when the little pegs were side by side, she bent over and the pansies dropped out and covered them.

"What a shame," said she, picking up the pansies. "Just as they had a chance to fly into each other's arms."

"Farewell, my girl," laughed Stanley, and away the red peg hopped.

The drawing-room was long and narrow with glass doors that gave on to the verandah. It had a cream paper with a pattern of gilt roses, and the furniture, which had belonged to old Mrs. Fairfield, was dark and plain. A little piano stood against the wall with yellow pleated silk let into the carved front. Above it hung an oil painting by Beryl of a large cluster of surprised looking clematis. Each flower was the size of a small saucer, with a centre like an astonished eye fringed in black. But the room was not finished yet. Stanley had set his heart on a Chesterfield and two decent chairs. Linda liked it best as it was. . . .

Two big moths flew in through the window and round and round the circle of lamplight.

"Fly away before it is too late. Fly out again."

Round and round they flew; they seemed to bring the silence and the moonlight in with them on their silent wings. . . .

"I've two kings," said Stanley. "Any good?"

"Quite good," said Beryl.

Linda stopped rocking and got up. Stanley looked across. "Anything the matter, darling?"

"No, nothing. I'm going to find mother."

She went out of the room and standing at the foot of the stairs she called, but her mother's voice answered her from the verandah.

The moon that Lottie and Kezia had seen from the storeman's wagon was full, and the house, the garden, the old woman and Linda—all were bathed in dazzling light.

"I have been looking at the aloe," said Mrs. Fairfield. "I believe it is going to flower this year. Look at the top there. Are those buds, or is it only an effect of light?"

As they stood on the steps, the high grassy bank on which the aloe rested rose up like a wave, and the aloe seemed to ride upon it like a ship with the oars lifted. Bright moonlight hung upon the lifted oars like water, and on the green wave glittered the dew.

"Do you feel it, too," said Linda, and she spoke to her mother with the special voice that women use at night to each other as though they spoke in their sleep or from some hollow cave— "Don't you feel that it is coming towards us?"

She dreamed that she was caught up out of the cold water into the ship with the lifted oars and the budding mast. Now the oars fell striking quickly, quickly. They rowed far away over the top of the garden trees, the paddocks and the dark bush beyond. Ah, she heard herself cry: "Faster! Faster!" to those who were rowing.

How much more real this dream was than that they should go back to the house where the sleeping children lay and where Stanley and Beryl played cribbage.

"I believe those are buds," said she. "Let us go down into the garden, mother. I like that aloe. I like it more than anything here. And I am sure I shall remember it long after I've forgotten all the other things."

She put her hand on her mother's arm and they walked down the steps, round the island and on to the main drive that led to the front gates.

Looking at it from below she could see the long sharp thorns that edged the aloe leaves, and at the sight of them her heart grew hard. . . . She particularly liked the long sharp thorns. . . . Nobody would dare to come near the ship or to follow after.

"Not even my Newfoundland dog," thought she, "that I'm so fond of in the daytime."

For she really was fond of him; she loved and admired and respected him tremendously. Oh, better than anyone else in the world. She knew him through and through. He was the soul of truth and decency, and for all his practical experience he was awfully simple, easily pleased and easily hurt. . . .

If only he wouldn't jump at her so, and bark so loudly, and watch her with such eager, loving eyes. He was too strong for her; she had always hated things that rush at her, from a child. There were times when he was frightening—really frightening. When she just had not screamed at the top of her voice: "You are killing me." And at those times she had longed to say the most coarse, hateful things. . . .

"You know I'm very delicate. You know as well as I do that my heart is affected, and the doctor has told you I may die any moment. I have had three great lumps of children already. . . ."

Yes, yes, it was true. Linda snatched her hand from her mother's arm. For all her love and respect and admiration she hated him. And how tender he always was after times like those, how submissive, how thoughtful. He would do anything for her; he longed to serve her. . . . Linda heard herself saying in a weak voice:

"Stanley, would you light a candle?"

And she heard his joyful voice answer: "Of course I will my darling." And he leapt out of bed as though he were going to leap at the moon for her.

It had never been so plain to her as it was at this moment. There were all her feelings for him, sharp and defined, one as true as the other. And there was this other, this hatred, just as real as the rest. She could have done her feelings up in little packets and given them to Stanley. She longed to hand him that last one, for a surprise. She could see his eyes as he opened that . . .

She hugged her folded arms and began to laugh silently. How absurd life was—it was laughable, simply laughable. And why this mania of hers to keep alive at all? For it really was a mania, she thought, mocking and laughing.

"What am I guarding myself for so preciously? I shall go on having children and Stanley will go on making money and the children and the gardens will grow bigger and bigger, with whole fleets of aloes in them for me to choose from."

She had been walking with her head bent, looking at nothing.

Now she looked up and about her. They were standing by the red and white camellia trees. Beautiful were the rich dark leaves spangled with light and the round flowers that perch among them like red and white birds. Linda pulled a piece of verbena and crumpled it, and held her hands to her mother.

"Delicious," said the old woman. "Are you cold, child? Are you trembling? Yes, your hands are cold. We had better go back to the house."

"What have you been thinking about?" said Linda. "Tell me."

"I haven't really been thinking of anything. I wondered as we passed the orchard what the fruit trees were like and whether we should be able to make much jam this autumn. There are splendid healthy currant bushes in the vegetable garden. I noticed them to-day. I should like to see those pantry shelves thoroughly well stocked with our own jam. . . ."

12

M Y DARLING NAN,

Don't think me a piggy wig because I haven't written before. I haven't had a moment, dear, and even now I feel so exhausted that I can hardly hold a pen.

Well, the dreadful deed is done. We have actually left the giddy whirl of town, and I can't see how we shall ever go back again, for my brother-in-law has bought this house 'lock, stock and barrel,' to use his own words.

In a way, of course, it is an awful relief, for he has been threatening to take a place in the country ever since I've lived with them—and I must say the house and garden are awfully nice—a million times better than that awful cubby-hole in town.

But buried, my dear. Buried isn't the word.

We have got neighbours, but they are only farmers—big louts of boys who seem to be milking all day, and two dreadful females with rabbit teeth who brought us some scones when we were moving and said they would be pleased to help. But my sister who lives a mile away doesn't know a soul here, so I am sure we never shall. It's pretty certain nobody will ever come out from town to see us, because though there is a bus it's an awful old rattling thing with black leather sides that any decent person would rather die than ride in for six miles.

Such is life. It's a sad ending for poor little B. I'll get to be a most awful frump in a year or two and come and see you in a mackintosh and a sailor hat tied on with a white china silk motor veil. So pretty.

Stanley says that now we are settled—for after the most awful week of my life we really are settled—he is going to bring out a couple of men from the club on Saturday afternoons for tennis. In fact, two are promised as a great treat to-day. But, my dear, if you could see Stanley's men from the club . . . rather fattish, the type who look frightfully indecent without waistcoats—always with toes that turn in rather—so conspicuous when you are walking about a court in white shoes. And they are pulling up their trousers every minute—don't you know—and whacking at imaginary things with their rackets.

I used to play with them at the club last summer, and I am sure you will know the type when I tell you that after I'd been there about three times they all called me Miss Beryl. It's a weary world. Of course mother simply loves the place, but then I suppose when I am mother's age I shall be content to sit in the sun and shell peas into a basin. But I'm not—not—not.

What Linda thinks about the whole affair, per usual, I haven't the slightest idea. Mysterious as ever. . . .

My dear, you know that white satin dress of mine. I have taken the sleeves out entirely, put bands of black velvet across the shoulders and two big red poppies off my dear sister's *chapeau*. It is a great success, though when I shall wear it I do not know."

Beryl sat writing this letter at a little table in her room. In a way, of course, it was all perfectly true, but in another way it was all the greatest rubbish and she didn't believe a word of it. No, that wasn't true. She felt all those things, but she didn't really feel them like that.

It was her other self who had written that letter. It not only bored, it rather disgusted her real self.

"Flippant and silly," said her real self. Yet she knew that she'd send it and she'd always write that kind of twaddle to Nan Pym. In fact, it was a very mild example of the kind of letter she generally wrote.

Beryl leaned her elbows on the table and read it through again. The voice of the letter seemed to come up to her from the page. It was faint already, like a voice heard over the telephone, high, gushing, with something bitter in the sound. Oh, she detested it to-day.

"You've always got so much animation," said Nan Pym. "That's why men are so keen on you." And she had added, rather mournfully, for men were not at all keen on Nan, who was a solid kind of girl, with fat hips and a high colour—"I can't understand how you can keep it up. But it is your nature, I suppose."

What rot. What nonsense. It wasn't her nature at all. Good heavens, if she had ever been her real self with Nan Pym, Nannie would have jumped out of the window with surprise. . . . My dear, you know that white satin of mine. . . . Beryl slammed the letter-case to.

She jumped up and half unconsciously, half consciously she drifted over to the looking-glass.

There stood a slim girl in white—a white serge skirt, a white silk blouse, and a leather belt drawn in very tightly at her tiny waist.

Her face was heart-shaped, wide at the brows and with a pointed chin—but not too pointed. Her eyes, her eyes were perhaps her best feature; they were such a strange uncommon colour—greeny blue with little gold points in them.

She had fine black eyebrows and long lashes—so long, that when they lay on her cheeks you positively caught the light in them, someone or other had told her.

Her mouth was rather large. Too large? No, not really. Her underlip protruded a little; she had a way of sucking it in that somebody else had told her was awfully fascinating.

Her nose was her least satisfactory feature. Not that it was really ugly. But it was not half as fine as Linda's. Linda really had a perfect little nose. Hers spread rather—not badly. And in all probability she exaggerated the spreadiness of it just because it was her nose, and she was so awfully critical of herself. She pinched it with a thumb and first finger and made a little face. . . .

Lovely, lovely hair. And such a mass of it. It had the colour of fresh fallen leaves, brown and red with a glint of yellow. When she did it in a long plait she felt it on her backbone like a long snake. She loved to feel the weight of it dragging her head back, and she loved to feel it loose, covering her bare arms. "Yes, my dear, there is no doubt about it, you really are a lovely little thing."

At the words her bosom lifted; she took a long breath of delight, half closing her eyes.

But even as she looked the smile faded from her lips and eyes. Oh God, there she was, back again, playing the same old game. False—false as ever. False as when she'd written to Nan Pym. False even when she was alone with herself, now.

What had that creature in the glass to do with her, and why was she staring? She dropped down to one side of her bed and buried her face in her arms.

"Oh," she cried, "I am so miserable—so frightfully miserable. I know that I'm silly and spiteful and vain; I'm always acting a part. I'm never my real self for a moment." And plainly, plainly, she saw her false self running up and down the stairs, laughing a special trilling laugh if they had visitors, standing under the lamp if a man came to dinner, so that he should see the light on her hair, pouting and pretending to be a little girl when she was asked to play the guitar. Why? She even kept it up for Stanley's benefit. Only last night when he was reading the paper her false self had stood beside him and leaned against his shoulder on purpose. Hadn't she put her hand over his, pointing out something so that he should see how white her hand was beside his brown one.

How despicable! Despicable! Her heart was cold with rage. "It's marvellous how you keep it up," said she to the false self. But then it was only because she was so miserable—so miserable. If she had been happy and leading her own life, her false life would cease to be. She saw the real Beryl—a shadow . . . a shadow. Faint and unsubstantial she shone. What was there of her except the radiance? And for what tiny moments she was really she. Beryl could almost remember every one of them. At those times she had felt: "Life is rich and mysterious and good, and I

95

am rich and mysterious and good, too." Shall I ever be that Beryl for ever? Shall I? How can I? And was there ever a time when I did not have a false self? . . . But just as she had got that far she heard the sound of little steps running along the passage; the door handle rattled. Kezia came in.

"Aunt Beryl, mother says will you please come down? Father is home with a man and lunch is ready."

Botheration! How she had crumpled her skirt, kneeling in that idiotic way.

"Very well, Kezia." She went over to the dressing table and powdered her nose.

Kezia crossed too, and unscrewed a little pot of cream and sniffed it. Under her arm she carried a very dirty calico cat.

When Aunt Beryl ran out of the room she sat the cat up on the dressing table and stuck the top of the cream jar over its ear.

"Now look at yourself," said she sternly.

The calico cat was so overcome by the sight that it toppled over backwards and bumped and bumped on to the floor. And the top of the cream jar flew through the air and rolled like a penny in a round on the linoleum—and did not break.

But for Kezia it had broken the moment it flew through the air, and she picked it up, hot all over, and put it back on the dressing table.

Then she tip-toed away, far too quickly and airily. . . .

At the Bay

I

Very early morning. The sun was not yet risen, and the whole of Crescent Bay was hidden under a white sea-mist. The big bush-covered hills at the back were smothered. You could not see where they ended and the paddocks and bungalows began. The sandy road was gone and the paddocks and bungalows the other side of it; there were no white dunes covered with reddish grass beyond them; there was nothing to mark which was beach and where was the sea. A heavy dew had fallen. The grass was blue. Big drops hung on the bushes and just did not fall; the silvery, fluffy toi-toi was limp on its long stalks, and all the marigolds and the pinks in the bungalow gardens were bowed to the earth with wetness. Drenched were the cold fuchsias, round pearls of dew lay on the flat nasturtium leaves. It looked as though the sea had beaten up softly in the darkness, as though one immense wave had come rippling, rippling—how far? Perhaps if you had waked up in the middle of the night you might have seen a big fish flicking in at the window and gone again. . . .

Ah-Aah! sounded the sleepy sea. And from the bush there came the sound of little streams flowing, quickly, lightly, slipping between the smooth stones, gushing into ferny basins and out again; and there was the splashing of big drops on large leaves, and something else—what was it?—a faint stirring and shaking, the snapping of a twig and then such silence that it seemed some one was listening.

Round the corner of Crescent Bay, between the piled-up masses of broken rock, a flock of sheep came pattering. They were huddled, together, a small, tossing, woolly mass, and their thin, stick-like legs trotted along quickly as if the cold and the quiet had frightened them. Behind them an old sheep-dog, his soaking paws covered with sand, ran along with his nose to the ground, but carelessly, as if thinking of something else. And then in the rocky gateway the shepherd himself appeared. He was a lean, upright old man, in a frieze coat that was covered with a web of tiny drops, velvet trousers tied under the knee, and a wideawake with a folded blue handkerchief round the brim. One hand was crammed into his belt, the other grasped a beautifully smooth yellow stick. And as he walked, taking his time, he kept up a very soft light whistling, an airy, far-away fluting that sounded mournful and tender. The old dog cut an ancient caper or two and then drew up sharp, ashamed of his levity, and walked a few dignified paces by his master's side. The sheep ran forward in little pattering rushes; they began to bleat, and ghostly flocks and herds answered them from under the sea. "Baa! Baaa!" For a time they seemed to be always on the same piece of ground. There ahead was stretched the sandy road with shallow puddles; the same soaking bushes showed on either side and the same shadowy palings. Then something immense came into view; an enormous shock-haired giant with his arms stretched out. It was the big gum-tree outside Mrs. Stubbs's shop, and as they passed by there was a strong whiff of eucalyptus. And now big spots of light gleamed in the mist. The shepherd stopped whistling; he rubbed his red nose and wet beard on his wet sleeve and, screwing up his eyes, glanced in the direction of the sea. The sun was rising. It was marvellous how quickly the mist thinned, sped away, dissolved from the shallow plain, rolled up from the bush and was gone as if in a hurry to escape; big twists and curls jostled and shouldered each other as the silvery beams broadened. The far-away sky—a bright, pure blue—was reflected in the puddles, and the drops, swimming along the telegraph poles, flashed into points of light. Now the leaping, glittering sea was so bright it made one's eyes ache to look at it. The shepherd drew a pipe, the bowl as small as an acorn, out of his breast pocket, fumbled for a chunk of speckled tobacco, pared off a few shavings and stuffed the bowl. He was a grave, fine-looking old man. As he lit up and the blue smoke wreathed his head, the dog, watching, looked proud of him.

"Baa! Baaa!" The sheep spread out into a fan. They were just clear of the summer colony before the first sleeper turned over and lifted a drowsy head; their cry sounded in the dreams of little children . . . who lifted their arms to drag down, to cuddle the darling little woolly lambs of sleep. Then the first inhabitant appeared; it was the Burnells' cat Florrie, sitting on the gatepost, far too early as usual, looking for their milk-girl. When she saw the old sheep-dog she sprang up quickly, arched her back, drew in her tabby head, and seemed to give a little fastidious shiver. "Ugh! What a coarse, revolting creature!" said Florrie. But the old sheep-dog, not looking up, waggled past, flinging out his legs from side to side. Only one of his ears twitched to prove that he saw, and thought her a silly young female.

The breeze of morning lifted in the bush and the smell of leaves and wet black earth mingled with the sharp smell of the sea. Myriads of birds were singing. A goldfinch flew over the shepherd's head and, perching on the tiptop of a spray, it turned to the sun, ruffling its small breast feathers. And now they had passed the fisherman's hut, passed the charred-looking little whare where Leila the milk-girl lived with her old Gran. The sheep strayed over a yellow swamp and Wag, the sheep-dog, padded after, rounded them up and headed them for the steeper, narrower rocky pass that led out of Crescent Bay and towards Daylight Cove. "Baa! Baa!" Faint the cry came as they rocked along the fast-drying road. The shepherd put away his pipe, dropping it into his breast pocket so that the little bowl hung over. And straightway the soft airy whistling began again. Wag ran out along a ledge of rock after something that smelled, and ran back again disgusted. Then pushing, nudging, hurrying, the sheep rounded the bend and the shepherd followed after out of sight.

A few months later the back door of one of the bungalows opened, and a figure in a broad-striped bathing suit flung down the paddock, cleared the stile, rushed through the tussock grass into the hollow, staggered up the sandy hillock, and raced for dear life over the big porous stones, over the cold, wet pebbles, on to the hard sand that gleamed like oil. Splish-splosh! Splish-splosh! The water bubbled round his legs as Stanley Burnell waded out exulting. First man in as usual! He'd beaten them all again. And he swooped down to souse his head and neck.

"Hail, brother! All hail, Thou Mighty One!" A velvety bass voice came booming over the water.

Great Scott! Damnation take it! Stanley lifted up to see a dark head bobbing far out and an arm lifted. It was Jonathan Trout—there before him! "Glorious morning!" sang the voice.

"Yes, very fine!" said Stanley briefly. Why the dickens didn't the fellow stick to his part of the sea? Why should he come barging over to this exact spot? Stanley gave a kick, a lunge and struck out, swimming overarm. But Jonathan was a match for him. Up he came, his black hair sleek on his forehead, his short beard sleek.

"I had an extraordinary dream last night!" he shouted.

What was the matter with the man? This mania for conversation irritated Stanley beyond words. And it was always the same—always some piffle about a dream he'd had, or some cranky idea he'd got hold of, or some rot he'd been reading. Stanley turned over on his back and kicked with his legs till he was a living waterspout. But even then . . . "I dreamed I was hanging over a terrifically high cliff, shouting to some one below." You would be! thought Stanley. He could stick no more of it. He stopped splashing. "Look here, Trout," he said, "I'm in rather a hurry this morning."

"You're WHAT?" Jonathan was so surprised—or pretended to be—that he sank under the water, then appeared again blowing.

"All I mean is," said Stanley, "I've no time to—to—to fool about. I want to get this over. I'm in a hurry. I've work to do this morning—see?"

Jonathan was gone before Stanley had finished. "Pass, friend!" said the bass voice gently, and he slid away through the water with scarcely a ripple. . . . But curse the fellow! He'd ruined Stanley's bathe. What an unpractical idiot the man was! Stanley struck out to sea again, and then as quickly swam in again, and away he rushed up the beach. He felt cheated.

Jonathan stayed a little longer in the water. He floated, gently moving his hands like fins, and letting the sea rock his long, skinny body. It was curious, but in spite of everything he was fond of Stanley Burnell. True, he had a fiendish desire to tease him sometimes, to poke fun at him, but at bottom he was sorry for the fellow. There was something pathetic in his determination to make a job of everything. You couldn't help feeling he'd be caught out one day, and then what an almighty cropper he'd come! At that moment an immense wave lifted Jonathan, rode past him, and broke along the beach with a joyful sound. What a beauty! And now there came another. That was the way to live—carelessly, recklessly, spending oneself. He got on to his feet and began to wade towards the shore, pressing his toes into the firm, wrinkled sand. To take things easy, not to fight against the ebb and flow of life, but to give way to it—that was what was needed. It was this tension that was all wrong. To live—to live! And the perfect morning, so fresh and fair, basking in the light, as though laughing at its own beauty, seemed to whisper, "Why not?"

But now he was out of the water Jonathan turned blue with cold. He ached all over; it was as though some one was wringing the blood out of him. And stalking up the beach, shivering, all his muscles tight, he too felt his bathe was spoilt. He'd stayed in too long.

3

Beryl was alone in the living-room when Stanley appeared, wearing a blue serge suit, a stiff collar and a spotted tie. He looked almost uncannily clean and brushed; he was going to town for the day. Dropping into his chair, he pulled out his watch and put it beside his plate.

"I've just got twenty-five minutes," he said. "You might go and see if the porridge is ready, Beryl?"

"Mother's just gone for it," said Beryl. She sat down at the table and poured out his tea.

"Thanks!" Stanley took a sip. "Hallo!" he said in an astonished voice, "you've forgotten the sugar."

"Oh, sorry!" But even then Beryl didn't help him; she pushed the basin across. What did this mean? As Stanley helped himself his blue eyes widened; they seemed to quiver. He shot a quick glance at his sister-in-law and leaned back.

"Nothing wrong, is there?" he asked carelessly, fingering his collar.

Beryl's head was bent; she turned her plate in her fingers.

"Nothing," said her light voice. Then she too looked up, and smiled at Stanley. "Why should there be?"

"O-oh! No reason at all as far as I know. I thought you seemed rather—"

At that moment the door opened and the three little girls appeared, each carrying a porridge plate. They were dressed alike in blue jerseys and knickers; their brown legs were bare, and each had her hair plaited and pinned up in what was called a horse's tail. Behind them came Mrs. Fairfield with the tray.

"Carefully, children," she warned. But they were taking the very greatest care. They loved being allowed to carry things. "Have you said good morning to your father?"

"Yes, grandma." They settled themselves on the bench opposite Stanley and Beryl.

"Good morning, Stanley!" Old Mrs. Fairfield gave him his plate.

"Morning, mother! How's the boy?"

"Splendid! He only woke up once last night. What a perfect morning!" The old woman paused, her hand on the loaf of bread, to gaze out of the open door into the garden. The sea sounded. Through the wide-open window streamed the sun on to the yellow varnished walls and bare floor. Everything on the table flashed and glittered. In the middle there was an old salad bowl filled with yellow and red nasturtiums. She smiled, and a look of deep content shone in her eyes.

"You might *cut* me a slice of that bread, mother," said Stanley. "I've only twelve and a half minutes before the coach passes. Has any one given my shoes to the servant girl?"

"Yes, they're ready for you." Mrs. Fairfield was quite unruffled.

"Oh, Kezia! Why are you such a messy child!" cried Beryl despairingly.

"Me, Aunt Beryl?" Kezia stared at her. What had she done now? She had only dug a river down the middle of her porridge, filled it, and was eating the banks away. But she did that every single morning, and no one had said a word up till now.

"Why can't you eat your food properly like Isabel and Lottie?" How unfair grown-ups are!

"But Lottie always makes a floating island, don't you, Lottie?"

"I don't," said Isabel smartly. "I just sprinkle mine with sugar and put on the milk and finish it. Only babies play with their food."

Stanley pushed back his chair and got up.

"Would you get me those shoes, mother? And, Beryl, if you've finished, I wish you'd cut down to the gate and stop the coach. Run in to your mother, Isabel, and ask her where my bowler hat's been put. Wait a minute—have you children been playing with my stick?"

"No, father!"

"But I put it here." Stanley began to bluster. "I remember distinctly putting it in this corner. Now, who's had it? There's no time to lose. Look sharp! The stick's got to be found."

Even Alice, the servant-girl, was drawn into the chase. "You haven't been using it to poke the kitchen fire with by any chance?"

Stanley dashed into the bedroom where Linda was lying. "Most extraordinary thing. I can't keep a single possession to myself. They've made away with my stick, now!"

"Stick, dear? What stick?" Linda's vagueness on these occasions could not be real, Stanley decided. Would nobody sympathize with him?

"Coach! Coach, Stanley!" Beryl's voice cried from the gate.

Stanley waved his arm to Linda. "No time to say good-bye!" he cried. And he meant that as a punishment to her.

He snatched his bowler hat, dashed out of the house, and swung down the garden path. Yes, the coach was there waiting, and Beryl, leaning over the open gate, was laughing up at somebody or other just as if nothing had happened. The heartlessness of women! The way they took it for granted it was your job to slave away for them while they didn't even take the trouble to see that your walking-stick wasn't lost. Kelly trailed his whip across the horses.

"Good-bye, Stanley," called Beryl, sweetly and gaily. It was easy enough to say good-bye! And there she stood, idle, shading her eyes with her hand. The worst of it was Stanley had to shout good-bye too, for the sake of appearances. Then he saw her turn, give a little skip and run back to the house. She was glad to be rid of him!

Yes, she was thankful. Into the living-room she ran and called "He's gone!" Linda cried from her room: "Beryl! Has Stanley gone?" Old Mrs. Fairfield appeared, carrying the boy in his little flannel coatee.

"Gone?"

"Gone!"

Oh, the relief, the difference it made to have the man out of the house. Their very voices were changed as they called to one another; they sounded warm and loving and as if they shared a secret. Beryl went over to the table. "Have another cup of tea, mother. It's still hot." She wanted, somehow, to celebrate the fact that they could do what they liked now. There was no man to disturb them; the whole perfect day was theirs.

"No, thank you, child," said old Mrs. Fairfield, but the way at that moment she tossed the boy up and said "a-goos-a-goos-a-ga!" to him meant that she felt the same. The little girls ran into the paddock like chickens let out of a coop.

Even Alice, the servant-girl, washing up the dishes in the kitchen, caught the infection and used the precious tank water in a perfectly reckless fashion.

"Oh, these men!" she said, and she plunged the teapot into

the bowl and held it under the water even after it had stopped bubbling, as if it too was a man and drowning was too good for them.

4

"Wait for me, Isa-bel! Kezia, wait for me!"

There was poor little Lottie, left behind again, because she found it so fearfully hard to get over the stile by herself. When she stood on the first step her knees began to wobble; she grasped the post. Then you had to put one leg over. But which leg? She never could decide. And when she did finally put one leg over with a sort of stamp of despair—then the feeling was awful. She was half in the paddock still and half in the tussock grass. She clutched the post desperately and lifted up her voice. "Wait for me!"

"No, don't you wait for her, Kezia!" said Isabel. "She's such a little silly. She's always making a fuss. Come on!" And she tugged Kezia's jersey. "You can use my bucket if you come with me," she said kindly. "It's bigger than yours." But Kezia couldn't leave Lottie all by herself. She ran back to her. By this time Lottie was very red in the face and breathing heavily.

"Here, put your other foot over," said Kezia.

"Where?"

Lottie looked down at Kezia as if from a mountain height.

"Here where my hand is." Kezia patted the place.

"Oh, *there* do you mean!" Lottie gave a deep sigh and put the second foot over.

"Now—sort of turn round and sit down and slide," said Kezia.

"But there's nothing to sit down *on*, Kezia," said Lottie.

She managed it at last, and once it was over she shook herself and began to beam.

"I'm getting better at climbing over stiles, aren't I, Kezia?"

Lottie's was a very hopeful nature.

The pink and the blue sunbonnet followed Isabel's bright red sunbonnet up that sliding, slipping hill. At the top they paused to decide where to go and to have a good stare at who was there already. Seen from behind, standing against the skyline, gesticulating largely with their spades, they looked like minute puzzled explorers.

The whole family of Samuel Josephs was there already with their lady-help, who sat on a camp-stool and kept order with a whistle that she wore tied round her neck, and a small cane with which she directed operations. The Samuel Josephs never played by themselves or managed their own game. If they did, it ended in the boys pouring water down the girls' necks or the girls trying to put little black crabs into the boys' pockets. So Mrs. S. J. and the poor lady-help drew up what she called a "brogramme" every morning to keep them "abused and out of bischief." It was all competitions or races or round games. Everything began with a piercing blast of the lady-help's whistle and ended with another. There were even prizes—large, rather dirty paper parcels which the lady-help with a sour little smile drew out of a bulging string kit. The Samuel Josephs fought fearfully for the prizes and cheated and pinched one another's arms—they were all expert pinchers. The only time the Burnell children ever played with them Kezia had got a prize, and when she undid three bits of paper she found a very small rusty button-hook. She couldn't understand why they made such a fuss. . . .

But they never played with the Samuel Josephs now or even went to their parties. The Samuel Josephs were always giving children's parties at the Bay and there was always the same food. A big washhand basin of very brown fruit-salad, buns cut into four and a washhand jug full of something the lady-help called "Limonadear." And you went away in the evening with half the frill torn off your frock or something spilled all down the front of your open-work pinafore, leaving the Samuel Josephs leaping like savages on their lawn. No! They were too awful.

On the other side of the beach, close down to the water, two little boys, their knickers rolled up, twinkled like spiders. One was digging, the other pattered in and out of the water, filling a small bucket. They were the Trout boys, Pip and Rags. But Pip was so busy digging and Rags was so busy helping that they didn't see their little cousins until they were quite close.

"Look!" said Pip. "Look what I've discovered." And he showed them an old, wet, squashed-looking boot. The three little girls stared.

"Whatever are you going to do with it?" asked Kezia.

"Keep it, of course!" Pip was very scornful. "It's a find—see?"

Yes, Kezia saw that. All the same . . .

"There's lots of things buried in the sand," explained Pip. "They get chucked up from wrecks. Treasure. Why—you might find—"

"But why does Rags have to keep on pouring water in?" asked Lottie.

"Oh, that's to moisten it," said Pip, "to make the work a bit easier. Keep it up, Rags."

And good little Rags ran up and down, pouring in the water that turned brown like cocoa.

"Here, shall I show you what I found yesterday?" said Pip mysteriously, and he stuck his spade into the sand. "Promise not to tell."

They promised.

"Say, cross my heart straight dinkum."

The little girls said it.

Pip took something out of his pocket, rubbed it a long time on the front of his jersey, then breathed on it and rubbed it again.

"Now turn round!" he ordered.

They turned round.

"All look the same way! Keep still! Now!"

And his hand opened; he held up to the light something that flashed, that winked, that was a most lovely green.

"It's a nemeral," said Pip solemnly.

"Is it really, Pip?" Even Isabel was impressed.

The lovely green thing seemed to dance in Pip's fingers. Aunt Beryl had a nemeral in a ring, but it was a very small one. This one was as big as a star and far more beautiful.

As the morning lengthened whole parties appeared over the sand-hills and came down on the beach to bathe. It was understood that at eleven o'clock the women and children of the summer colony had the sea to themselves. First the women undressed, pulled on their bathing dresses and covered their heads in hideous caps like sponge bags; then the children were unbuttoned. The beach was strewn with little heaps of clothes and shoes; the big summer hats, with stones on them to keep them from blowing away, looked like immense shells. It was strange that even the sea seemed to sound differently when all those leaping, laughing figures ran into the waves. Old Mrs. Fairfield, in a lilac cotton dress and a black hat tied under the chin, gathered her little brood and got them ready. The little Trout boys whipped their shirts over their heads, and away the five sped, while their grandma sat with one hand in her knitting-bag ready to draw out the ball of wool when she was satisfied they were safely in.

The firm compact little girls were not half so brave as the tender, delicate-looking little boys. Pip and Rags, shivering, crouching down, slapping the water, never hesitated. But Isabel, who could swim twelve strokes, and Kezia, who could nearly swim eight, only followed on the strict understanding they were not to be splashed. As for Lottie, she didn't follow at all. She liked to be left to go in her own way, please. And that way was to sit down at the edge of the water, her legs straight, her knees pressed together, and to make vague motions with her arms as if she expected to be wafted out to sea. But when a bigger wave than usual, an old whiskery one, came lolloping along in her direction, she scrambled to her feet with a face of horror and flew up the beach again.

"Here, mother, keep those for me, will you?"

Two rings and a thin gold chain were dropped into Mrs. Fairfield's lap.

"Yes, dear. But aren't you going to bathe here?"

"No-o," Beryl drawled. She sounded vague. "I'm undressing farther along. I'm going to bathe with Mrs. Harry Kember."

"Very well." But Mrs. Fairfield's lips set. She disapproved of Mrs. Harry Kember. Beryl knew it.

Poor old mother, she smiled, as she skimmed over the stones. Poor old mother! Old! Oh, what joy, what bliss it was to be young. . . .

"You look very pleased," said Mrs. Harry Kember. She sat hunched up on the stones, her arms round her knees, smoking.

"It's such a lovely day," said Beryl, smiling down at her.

"Oh, my *dear!*" Mrs. Harry Kember's voice sounded as though she knew better than that. But then her voice always sounded as though she knew something better about you than you did yourself. She was a long, strange-looking woman with narrow hands and feet. Her face, too, was long and narrow and exhausted-looking; even her fair curled fringe looked burnt out and withered. She was the only woman at the Bay who smoked, and she smoked incessantly, keeping the cigarette between her lips while she talked, and only taking it out when the ash was so long you could not understand why it did not fall. When she was not playing bridge—she played bridge every day of her life—she spent her time lying in the full glare of the sun. She could stand any amount of it; she never had enough. All the same, it did not seem to warm her. Parched, withered, cold, she lay stretched on the stones like a piece of tossed-up driftwood. The women at the Bay thought she was very, very fast. Her lack of vanity, her slang, the way she treated men as though she was one of them, and the fact that she didn't care twopence about her house and called the servant Gladys "Glad-eyes," was disgraceful. Standing on the ver-andah steps Mrs. Kember would call in her indifferent, tired voice, "I say, Glad-eyes, you might heave me a handkerchief if I've got one, will you?" And Glad-eyes, a red bow in her hair instead of a cap, and white shoes, came running with an impudent smile. It was an absolute scandal! True, she had no children, and her hus-band. . . . Here the voices were always raised; they became fer-vent. How can he have married her? How can he, how can he? It must have been money, of course, but even then!

Mrs. Kember's husband was at least ten years younger than she was, and so incredibly handsome that he looked like a mask or a most perfect illustration in an American novel rather than a man. Black hair, dark blue eyes, red lips, a slow sleepy smile, a fine tennis player, a perfect dancer, and with it all a mystery. Harry Kember was like a man walking in his sleep. Men couldn't stand him, they couldn't get a word out of the chap; he ignored his wife just as she ignored him. How did he live? Of course there were stories, but such stories! They simply couldn't be told. The women he'd been seen with, the places he'd been seen in . . . but nothing was ever certain, nothing definite. Some of the women at the Bay privately thought he'd commit a murder one day. Yes, even while they talked to Mrs. Kember and took in the awful concoction she was wearing, they saw her, stretched as she lay on the beach; but cold, bloody, and still with a cigarette stuck in the corner of her mouth.

Mrs. Kember rose, yawned, unsnapped her belt buckle, and tugged at the tape of her blouse. And Beryl stepped out of her skirt and shed her jersey, and stood up in her short white petticoat, and her camisole with ribbon bows on the shoulders.

"Mercy on us," said Mrs. Harry Kember, "what a little beauty you are!"

"Don't!" said Beryl softly; but, drawing off one stocking and then the other, she felt a little beauty.

"My dear—why not?" said Mrs. Harry Kember, stamping on her own petticoat. Really—her underclothes! A pair of blue cotton knickers and a linen bodice that reminded one somehow of a pillow-case. . . . "And you don't wear stays, do you?" She touched Beryl's waist, and Beryl sprang away with a small affected cry. Then "Never!" she said firmly.

"Lucky little creature," sighed Mrs. Kember, unfastening her own.

Beryl turned her back and began the complicated movements of some one who is trying to take off her clothes and to pull on her bathing-dress all at one and the same time.

"Oh, my dear—don't mind me," said Mrs. Harry Kember. "Why be shy? I shan't eat you. I shan't be shocked like those other ninnies." And she gave her strange neighing laugh and grimaced at the other women.

But Beryl was shy. She never undressed in front of anybody. Was that silly? Mrs. Harry Kember made her feel it was silly, even something to be ashamed of. Why be shy indeed! She glanced quickly at her friend standing so boldly in her torn chemise and lighting a fresh cigarette; and a quick, bold, evil feeling started up in her breast. Laughing recklessly, she drew on the limp, sandy-feeling bathing-dress that was not quite dry and fastened the twisted buttons.

"That's better," said Mrs. Harry Kember. They began to go down the beach together. "Really, it's a sin for you to wear clothes, my dear. Somebody's got to tell you some day."

The water was quite warm. It was that marvellous transparent blue, flecked with silver, but the sand at the bottom looked gold; when you kicked with your toes there rose a little puff of gold-dust. Now the waves just reached her breast. Beryl stood, her arms outstretched, gazing out, and as each wave came she gave the slightest little jump, so that it seemed it was the wave which lifted her so gently.

"I believe in pretty girls having a good time," said Mrs. Harry Kember. "Why not? Don't you make a mistake, my dear. Enjoy yourself." And suddenly she turned turtle, disappeared, and swam away quickly, quickly, like a rat. Then she flicked round and began swimming back. She was going to say something else. Beryl felt that she was being poisoned by this cold woman, but she longed to hear. But oh, how strange, how horrible! As Mrs. Harry Kember came up close she looked, in her black waterproof bathing-cap, with her sleepy face lifted above the water, just her chin touching, like a horrible caricature of her husband.

6

In a steamer chair, under a manuka tree that grew in the middle of the front grass patch, Linda Burnell dreamed the morning away. She did nothing. She looked up at the dark, close, dry leaves of the manuka, at the chinks of blue between, and now and again a tiny yellowish flower dropped on her. Pretty—yes, if you held one of those flowers on the palm of your hand and looked at it closely, it was an exquisite small thing. Each pale yellow petal shone as if each was the careful work of a loving hand. The tiny tongue in the centre gave it the shape of a bell. And when you turned it over the outside was a deep bronze colour. But as soon as they flowered, they fell and were scattered. You brushed them off your frock as you talked; the horrid little things got caught in one's hair. Why, then, flower at all? Who takes the trouble— or the joy—to make all these things that are wasted, wasted. . . . It was uncanny.

On the grass beside her, lying between two pillows, was the boy. Sound asleep he lay, his head turned away from his mother. His fine dark hair looked more like a shadow than like real hair, but his ear was a bright, deep coral. Linda clasped her hands above her head and crossed her feet. It was very pleasant to know that all these bungalows were empty, that everybody was down on the beach, out of sight, out of hearing. She had the garden to herself; she was alone.

Dazzling white the picotees shone; the golden-eyed marigolds glittered; the nasturtiums wreathed the verandah poles in green and gold flame. If only one had time to look at these flowers long enough, time to get over the sense of novelty and strangeness, time to know them! But as soon as one paused to part the petals, to discover the underside of the leaf, along came Life and one was swept away. And, lying in her cane chair, Linda felt so light; she felt like a leaf. Along came Life like a wind and she was seized and shaken; she had to go. Oh dear, would it always be so? Was there no escape?

. . . Now she sat on the verandah of their Tasmanian home, leaning against her father's knee. And he promised, "As soon as you and I are old enough, Linny, we'll cut off somewhere, we'll escape. Two boys together. I have a fancy I'd like to sail up a river in China." Linda saw that river, very wide, covered with little rafts and boats. She saw the yellow hats of the boatmen and she heard their high, thin voices as they called . . .

"Yes, papa."

But just then a very broad young man with bright ginger hair walked slowly past their house, and slowly, solemnly even, uncovered. Linda's father pulled her ear teasingly, in the way he had.

"Linny's beau," he whispered.

"Oh, papa, fancy being married to Stanley Burnell!"

Well, she was married to him. And what was more she loved him. Not the Stanley whom every one saw, not the everyday one; but a timid, sensitive, innocent Stanley who knelt down every night to say his prayers, and who longed to be good. Stanley was simple. If he believed in people—as he believed in her, for instance—it was with his whole heart. He could not be disloyal; he could not tell a lie. And how terribly he suffered if he thought any one—she—was not being dead straight, dead sincere with him! "This is too subtle for me!" He flung out the words, but his open, quivering, distraught look was like the look of a trapped beast.

But the trouble was—here Linda felt almost inclined to laugh, though Heaven knows it was no laughing matter—she saw *her* Stanley so seldom. There were glimpses, moments, breathing spaces of calm, but all the rest of the time it was like living in a house that couldn't be cured of the habit of catching on fire, on a ship that got wrecked every day. And it was always Stanley who was in the thick of the danger. Her whole time was spent in rescuing him, and restoring him, and calming him down, and listening to his story. And what was left of her time was spent in the dread of having children.

Linda frowned; she sat up quickly in her steamer chair and clasped her ankles. Yes, that was her real grudge against life; that was what she could not understand. That was the question she asked and asked, and listened in vain for the answer. It was all very well to say it was the common lot of women to bear children. It wasn't true. She, for one, could prove that wrong. She was broken, made weak, her courage was gone, through childbearing. And what made it doubly hard to bear was, she did not love her children. It was useless pretending. Even if she had had the strength she never would have nursed and played with the little girls. No, it was as though a cold breath had chilled her through and through on each of those awful journeys; she had no warmth left to give them. As to the boy—well, thank Heaven, mother had taken him; he was mother's, or Beryl's, or anybody's who wanted him. She had hardly held him in her arms. She was so indifferent about him that as he lay there . . . Linda glanced down.

The boy had turned over. He lay facing her, and he was no longer asleep. His dark-blue, baby eyes were open; he looked as though he was peeping at his mother. And suddenly his face dimpled; it broke into a wide, toothless smile, a perfect beam, no less.

"I'm here!" that happy smile seemed to say. "Why don't you like me?"

There was something so quaint, so unexpected about that smile that Linda smiled herself. But she checked herself and said to the boy coldly, "I don't like babies."

"Don't like babies?" The boy couldn't believe her. "Don't like *me*?" He waved his arms foolishly at his mother.

Linda dropped off her chair on to the grass.

"Why do you keep on smiling?" she said severely. "If you knew what I was thinking about, you wouldn't."

But he only squeezed up his eyes, slyly, and rolled his head on the pillow. He didn't believe a word she said.

"We know all about that!" smiled the boy.

Linda was so astonished at the confidence of this little creature. . . . Ah no, be sincere. That was not what she felt; it was something far different, it was something so new, so . . . The tears danced in her eyes; she breathed in a small whisper to the boy, "Hallo, my funny!"

But by now the boy had forgotten his mother. He was serious again. Something pink, something soft waved in front of him. He made a grab at it and it immediately disappeared. But when he lay back, another, like the first, appeared. This time he determined to catch it. He made a tremendous effort and rolled right over.

The tide was out; the beach was deserted; lazily flopped the warm sea. The sun beat down, beat down hot and fiery on the fine sand, baking the grey and blue and black and white-veined pebbles. It sucked up the little drop of water that lay in the hollow of the curved shells; it bleached the pink convolvulus that threaded through and through the sand-hills. Nothing seemed to move but the small sand-hoppers. Pit-pit-pit! They were never still.

Over there on the weed-hung rocks that looked at low tide like shaggy beasts come down to the water to drink, the sunlight seemed to spin like a silver coin dropped into each of the small rock pools. They danced, they quivered, and minute ripples laved the porous shores. Looking down, bending over, each pool was like a lake with pink and blue houses clustered on the shores; and oh! the vast mountainous country behind those houses—the ravines, the passes, the dangerous creeks and fearful tracks that led to the water's edge. Underneath waved the sea-forest—pink thread-like trees, velvet anemones, and orange berry-spotted weeds. Now a stone on the bottom moved, rocked, and there was a glimpse of a black feeler; now a thread-like creature wavered by and was lost. Something was happening to the pink, waving trees; they were changing to a cold moonlight blue. And now there sounded the faintest "plop." Who made that sound? What was going on down there? And how strong, how damp the seaweed smelt in the hot sun. . . .

The green blinds were drawn in the bungalows of the summer colony. Over the verandahs, prone on the paddock, flung over the fences, there were exhausted-looking bathing-dresses and rough striped towels. Each back window seemed to have a pair of sand-shoes on the sill and some lumps of rock or a bucket or a collection of pawa shells. The bush quivered in a haze of heat; the sandy road was empty except for the Trouts' dog Snooker, who lay stretched in the very middle of it. His blue eye was turned up, his legs stuck out stiffly, and he gave an occasional desperate-sounding puff, as much as to say he had decided to make an end of it and was only waiting for some kind cart to come along.

"What are you looking at, my grandma? Why do you keep stopping and sort of staring at the wall?"

Kezia and her grandmother were taking their siesta together. The little girl, wearing only her short drawers and her underbodice, her arms and legs bare, lay on one of the puffed-up pillows of her grandma's bed, and the old woman, in a white ruffled dressing-gown, sat in a rocker at the window, with a long piece of pink knitting in her lap. This room that they shared, like the other rooms of the bungalow, was of light varnished wood and the floor was bare. The furniture was of the shabbiest, the simplest. The dressing table, for instance, was a packing-case in a sprigged muslin petticoat, and the mirror above was very strange; it was as though a little piece of forked lightning was imprisoned in it. On the table there stood a jar of sea-pinks, pressed so tightly together they looked more like a velvet pincushion, and a special shell which Kezia had given her grandma for a pin-tray, and another even more special which she had thought would make a very nice place for a watch to curl up in.

"Tell me, grandma," said Kezia.

The old woman sighed, whipped the wool twice round her thumb, and drew the bone needle through. She was casting on.

"I was thinking of your Uncle William, darling," she said quietly.

"My Australian Uncle William?" said Kezia. She had another.

"Yes, of course."

"The one I never saw?"

"That was the one."

"Well, what happened to him?" Kezia knew perfectly well, but she wanted to be told again.

"He went to the mines, and he got a sunstroke there and died," said old Mrs. Fairfield.

Kezia blinked and considered the picture again . . . a little man fallen over like a tin soldier by the side of a big black hole.

"Does it make you sad to think about him, grandma?" She hated her grandma to be sad.

It was the old woman's turn to consider. Did it make her sad? To look back, back. To stare down the years, as Kezia had seen her doing. To look after *them* as a woman does, long after *they* were out of sight. Did it make her sad? No, life was like that.

"No, Kezia."

"But why?" asked Kezia. She lifted one bare arm and began to draw things in the air. "Why did Uncle William have to die? He wasn't old."

Mrs. Fairfield began counting the stitches in threes. "It just happened," she said in an absorbed voice.

"Does everybody have to die?" asked Kezia.

"Everybody!"

"*Me?*" Kezia sounded fearfully incredulous.

"Some day, my darling."

"But, grandma." Kezia waved her left leg and waggled the toes. They felt sandy. "What if I just won't?"

The old woman sighed again and drew a long thread from the ball.

"We're not asked, Kezia," she said sadly. "It happens to all of us sooner or later."

Kezia lay still thinking this over. She didn't want to die. It meant she would have to leave here, leave everywhere, for ever, leave—leave her grandma. She rolled over quickly.

"Grandma," she said in a startled voice.

"What, my pet!"

"*You're* not to die." Kezia was very decided.

"Ah, Kezia"—her grandma looked up and smiled and shook her head—"don't let's talk about it."

"But you're not to. You couldn't leave me. You couldn't not be there." This was awful. "Promise me you won't ever do it, grandma," pleaded Kezia.

The old woman went on knitting.

"Promise me! Say never!"

But still her grandma was silent.

Kezia rolled off the bed; she couldn't bear it any longer, and lightly she leapt on to her grandma's knees, clasped her hands round the old woman's throat and began kissing her, under the chin, behind the ear, and blowing down her neck.

"Say never . . . say never . . . say never—" She gasped between the kisses. And then she began, very softly and lightly, to tickle her grandma.

"Kezia!" The old woman dropped her knitting. She swung back in the rocker. She began to tickle Kezia. "Say never, say never, say never," gurgled Kezia, while they lay there laughing in each other's arms. "Come, that's enough, my squirrel! That's enough, my wild pony!" said old Mrs. Fairfield, setting her cap straight. "Pick up my knitting."

Both of them had forgotten what the "never" was about.

8

The sun was still full on the garden when the back door of the Burnells' shut with a bang, and a very gay figure walked down the path to the gate. It was Alice, the servant-girl, dressed for her afternoon out. She wore a white cotton dress with such large red spots on it and so many that they made you shudder, white shoes and a leghorn turned up under the brim with poppies. Of course she wore gloves, white ones, stained at the fastenings with iron-mould, and in one hand she carried a very dashed-looking sun-shade which she referred to as her *perishall*.

Beryl, sitting in the window, fanning her freshly-washed hair, thought she had never seen such a guy. If Alice had only blacked her face with a piece of cork before she started out, the picture would have been complete. And where did a girl like that go to in a place like this? The heart-shaped Fijian fan beat scornfully at that lovely bright mane. She supposed Alice had picked up some horrible common larrikin and they'd go off into the bush together. Pity to make herself so conspicuous; they'd have hard work to hide with Alice in that rig-out.

But no, Beryl was unfair. Alice was going to tea with Mrs. Stubbs, who'd sent her an "invite" by the little boy who called for orders. She had taken ever such a liking to Mrs. Stubbs ever since the first time she went to the shop to get something for her mosquitoes.

"Dear heart!" Mrs. Stubbs had clapped her hand to her side.

"I never seen any one so eaten. You might have been attacked by canningbals."

Alice did wish there'd been a bit of life on the road though. Made her feel so queer, having nobody behind her. Made her feel all weak in the spine. She couldn't believe that some one wasn't watching her. And yet it was silly to turn round; it gave you away. She pulled up her gloves, hummed to herself and said to the distant gumtree, "Shan't be long now." But that was hardly company.

Mrs. Stubbs's shop was perched on a little hillock just off the road. It had two big windows for eyes, a broad verandah for a hat, and the sign on the roof, scrawled MRS. STUBBS'S, was like a little card stuck rakishly in the hat crown.

On the verandah there hung a long string of bathing-dresses, clinging together as though they'd just been rescued from the sea rather than waiting to go in, and beside them there hung a cluster of sand-shoes so extraordinarily mixed that to get at one pair you had to tear apart and forcibly separate at least fifty. Even then it was the rarest thing to find the left that belonged to the right. So many people had lost patience and gone off with one shoe that fitted and one that was a little too big. . . . Mrs. Stubbs prided herself on keeping something of everything. The two windows, arranged in the form of precarious pyramids, were crammed so tight, piled so high, that it seemed only a conjuror could prevent them from toppling over. In the left-hand corner of one window, glued to the pane by four gelatine lozenges, there was—and there had been from time immemorial—a notice.

LOST! HANDSOME GOLE BROOCH

SOLID GOLD

ON OR NEAR BEACH

REWARD OFFERED

Alice pressed open the door. The bell jangled, the red serge curtains parted, and Mrs. Stubbs appeared. With her broad smile and the long bacon knife in her hand, she looked like a friendly brigand. Alice was welcomed so warmly that she found it quite difficult to keep up her "manners." They consisted of persistent little coughs and hems, pulls at her gloves, tweaks at her skirt, and a curious difficulty in seeing what was set before her or understanding what was said.

Tea was laid on the parlour table—ham, sardines, a whole pound of butter, and such a large johnny cake that it looked like an advertisement for somebody's baking-powder. But the Primus stove roared so loudly that it was useless to try to talk above it. Alice sat down on the edge of a basket-chair while Mrs. Stubbs pumped the stove still higher. Suddenly Mrs. Stubbs whipped the cushion off a chair and disclosed a large brown-paper parcel.

"I've just had some new photers taken, my dear," she shouted cheerfully to Alice. "Tell me what you think of them."

In a very dainty, refined way Alice wet her finger and put the tissue back from the first one. Life! How many there were! There were three dozzing at least. And she held it up to the light.

Mrs. Stubbs sat in an arm-chair, leaning very much to one side. There was a look of mild astonishment on her large face, and well there might be. For though the arm-chair stood on a carpet, to the left of it, miraculously skirting the carpet-border, there was a dashing water-fall. On her right stood a Grecian pillar with a giant fern-tree on either side of it, and in the background towered a gaunt mountain, pale with snow.

"It is a nice style, isn't it?" shouted Mrs. Stubbs; and Alice had just screamed "Sweetly" when the roaring of the Primus stove died down, fizzled out, ceased, and she said "Pretty" in a silence that was frightening.

"Draw up your chair, my dear," said Mrs. Stubbs, beginning to pour out. "Yes," she said thoughtfully, as she handed the tea, "but I don't care about the size. I'm having an enlargemint. All very well for Christmas cards, but I never was the one for small photers myself. You get no comfort out of them. To say the truth, I find them dis'eartening."

Alice quite saw what she meant.

"Size," said Mrs. Stubbs. "Give me size. That was what my poor dear husband was always saying. He couldn't stand anything

small. Gave him the creeps. And, strange as it may
dear"—here Mrs. Stubbs creaked and seemed to exp:
at the memory—"it was dropsy that carried him off
Many's the time they drawn one and a half pints from 'im at the
'ospital. . . . It seemed like a judgmint."

Alice burned to know exactly what it was that was drawn
from him. She ventured, "I suppose it was water."

But Mrs. Stubbs fixed Alice with her eyes and replied meaningly, "It was *liquid,* my dear."

Liquid! Alice jumped away from the word like a cat and came
back to it, nosing and wary.

"That's 'im!" said Mrs. Stubbs, and she pointed dramatically
to the life-size head and shoulders of a burly man with a dead
white rose in the button-hole of his coat that made you think of
a curl of cold mutting fat. Just below, in silver letters on a red
cardboard ground, were the words, "Be not afraid, it is I."

"It's ever such a fine face," said Alice faintly.

The pale-blue bow on the top of Mrs. Stubb's fair frizzy hair
quivered. She arched her plump neck. What a neck she had! It
was bright pink where it began and then it changed to warm
apricot, and that faded to the colour of a brown egg and then to
a deep creamy.

"All the same, my dear," she said surprisingly, "freedom's
best!" Her soft, fat chuckle sounded like a purr. "Freedom's best,"
said Mrs. Stubbs again.

Freedom! Alice gave a loud, silly little titter. She felt awkward. Her mind flew back to her own kitching. Ever so queer!
She wanted to be back in it again.

9

A strange company assembled in the Burnells' washhouse
after tea. Round the table there sat a bull, a rooster, a donkey
that kept forgetting it was a donkey, a sheep and a bee. The
washhouse was the perfect place for such a meeting because they

could make as much noise as they liked, and nobody ever interrupted. It was a small tin shed standing apart from the bungalow. Against the wall there was a deep trough and in the corner a copper with a basket of clothes-pegs on top of it. The little window, spun over with cobwebs, had a piece of candle and a mousetrap on the dusty sill. There were clotheslines crisscrossed overhead and, hanging from a peg on the wall, a very big, a huge, rusty horseshoe. The table was in the middle with a form at either side.

"You can't be a bee, Kezia. A bee's not an animal. It's a ninseck."

"Oh, but I do want to be a bee frightfully," wailed Kezia. . . . A tiny bee, all yellow-furry, with striped legs. She drew her legs up under her and leaned over the table. She felt she was a bee.

"A ninseck must be an animal," she said stoutly. "It makes a noise. It's not like a fish."

"I'm a bull, I'm a bull!" cried Pip. And he gave such a tremendous bellow—how did he make that noise?—that Lottie looked quite alarmed.

"I'll be a sheep," said little Rags. "A whole lot of sheep went past this morning."

"How do you know?"

"Dad heard them. Baa!" He sounded like the little lamb that trots behind and seems to wait to be carried.

"Cock-a-doodle-do!" shrilled Isabel. With her red cheeks and bright eyes she looked like a rooster.

"What'll I be?" Lottie asked everybody, and she sat there smiling, waiting for them to decide for her. It had to be an easy one.

"Be a donkey, Lottie." It was Kezia's suggestion. "Hee-haw! You can't forget that."

"Hee-haw!" said Lottie solemnly. "When do I have to say it?"

"I'll explain, I'll explain," said the bull. It was he who had the cards. He waved them round his head. "All be quiet! All listen!" And he waited for them. "Look here, Lottie." He turned up a card. "It's got two spots on it—see? Now, if you put that card in the middle and somebody else has one with two spots as well, you say 'Hee-haw,' and the card's yours."

"Mine?" Lottie was round-eyed. "To keep?"

"No, silly. Just for the game, see? Just while we're playing." The bull was very cross with her.

"Oh, Lottie, you *are* a little silly," said the proud rooster.

Lottie looked at both of them. Then she hung her head; her lip quivered. "I don't not want to play," she whispered. The others glanced at one another like conspirators. All of them knew what that meant. She would go away and be discovered somewhere standing with her pinny thrown over her head, in a corner, or against a wall, or even behind a chair.

"Yes, you *do*, Lottie. It's quite easy," said Kezia.

And Isabel, repentant, said exactly like a grown-up, "Watch *me*, Lottie, and you'll soon learn."

"Cheer up, Lot," said Pip. "There, I know what I'll do. I'll give you the first one. It's mine, really, but I'll give it to you. Here you are." And he slammed the card down in front of Lottie.

Lottie revived at that. But now she was in another difficulty. "I haven't got a hanky," she said; "I want one badly, too."

"Here, Lottie, you can use mine." Rags dipped into his sailor blouse and brought up a very wet-looking one, knotted together. "Be very careful," he warned her. "Only use that corner. Don't undo it. I've got a little starfish inside I'm going to try and tame."

"Oh, come on, you girls," said the bull. "And mind—you're not to look at your cards. You've got to keep your hands under the table till I say 'Go.'"

Smack went the cards round the table. They tried with all their might to see, but Pip was too quick for them. It was very exciting, sitting there in the washhouse; it was all they could do not to burst into a little chorus of animals before Pip had finished dealing.

"Now, Lottie, you begin."

Timidly Lottie stretched out a hand, took the top card off her pack, had a good look at it—it was plain she was counting the spots—and put it down.

"No, Lottie, you can't do that. You mustn't look first. You must turn it the other way over."

"But then everybody will see it the same time as me," said Lottie.

The game proceeded. Mooe-ooo-er! The bull was terrible. He charged over the table and seemed to eat the cards up.

Bss-ss! said the bee.

Cock-a-doodle-do! Isabel stood up in her excitement and moved her elbows like wings.

Baa! Little Rags put down the King of Diamonds and Lottie put down the one they called the King of Spain. She had hardly any cards left.

"Why don't you call out, Lottie?"

"I've forgotten what I am," said the donkey woefully.

"Well, change! Be a dog instead! Bow-wow!"

"Oh yes. That's *much* easier." Lottie smiled again. But when she and Kezia both had a one Kezia waited on purpose. The others made signs to Lottie and pointed. Lottie turned very red; she looked bewildered, and at last she said, "Hee-haw! Ke-zia."

"Ss! Wait a minute!" They were in the very thick of it when the bull stopped them, holding up his hand. "What's that? What's that noise?"

"What noise? What do you mean?" asked the rooster.

"Ss! Shut up! Listen!" They were mouse-still. "I thought I heard a—a sort of knocking," said the bull.

"What was it like?" asked the sheep faintly.

No answer.

The bee gave a shudder. "Whatever did we shut the door for?" she said softly. Oh, why, why had they shut the door?

While they were playing, the day had faded; the gorgeous sunset had blazed and died. And now the quick dark came racing over the sea, over the sand-hills, up the paddock. You were frightened to look in the corners of the washhouse, and yet you had to look with all your might. And somewhere, far away, grandma was lighting a lamp. The blinds were being pulled down; the kitchen fire leapt in the tins on the mantelpiece.

"It would be awful now," said the bull, "if a spider was to fall from the ceiling on to the table, wouldn't it?"

"Spiders don't fall from ceilings."

"Yes, they do. Our Min told us she'd seen a spider as big as a saucer, with long hairs on it like a gooseberry."

Quickly all the little heads were jerked up; all the little bodies drew together, pressed together.

"Why doesn't somebody come and call us?" cried the rooster.

Oh, those grown-ups, laughing and snug, sitting in the lamp-light, drinking out of cups! They'd forgotten about them. No, not really forgotten. That was what their smile meant. They had decided to leave them there all by themselves.

Suddenly Lottie gave such a piercing scream that all of them jumped off the forms, all of them screamed too. "A face—a face looking!" shrieked Lottie.

It was true, it was real. Pressed against the window was a pale face, black eyes, a black beard.

"Grandma! Mother! Somebody!"

But they had not got to the door, tumbling over one another, before it opened for Uncle Jonathan. He had come to take the little boys home.

10

He had meant to be there before, but in the front garden he had come upon Linda walking up and down the grass, stopping to pick off a dead pink or give a top-heavy carnation something to lean against, or to take a deep breath of something, and then walking on again, with her little air of remoteness. Over her white frock she wore a yellow, pink-fringed shawl from the Chinaman's shop.

"Hallo, Jonathan!" called Linda. And Jonathan whipped off his shabby panama, pressed it against his breast, dropped on one knee, and kissed Linda's hand.

"Greeting, my Fair One! Greeting, my Celestial Peach Blossom!" boomed the bass voice gently. "Where are the other noble dames?"

"Beryl's out playing bridge and mother's giving the boy his bath. . . . Have you come to borrow something?"

The Trouts were for ever running out of things and sending across to the Burnells' at the last moment.

But Jonathan only answered, "A little love, a little kindness"; and he walked by his sister-in-law's side.

Linda dropped into Beryl's hammock under the manuka tree, and Jonathan stretched himself on the grass beside her, pulled a long stalk and began chewing it. They knew each other well. The voices of children cried from the other gardens. A fisherman's light cart shook along the sandy road, and from far away they heard a dog barking; it was muffled as though the dog had its head in a sack. If you listened you could just hear the soft swish of the sea at full tide sweeping the pebbles. The sun was sinking.

"And so you go back to the office on Monday, do you, Jonathan?" asked Linda.

"On Monday the cage door opens and clangs to upon the victim for another eleven months and a week," answered Jonathan.

Linda swung a little. "It must be awful," she said slowly.

"Would ye have me laugh, my fair sister? Would ye have me weep?"

Linda was so accustomed to Jonathan's way of talking that she paid no attention to it.

"I suppose," she said vaguely, "one gets used to it. One gets used to anything."

"Does one? Hum!" The "Hum" was so deep it seemed to boom from underneath the ground. "I wonder how it's done," brooded Jonathan; "I've never managed it."

Looking at him as he lay there, Linda thought again how attractive he was. It was strange to think that he was only an ordinary clerk, that Stanley earned twice as much money as he. What was the matter with Jonathan? He had no ambition; she supposed that was it. And yet one felt he was gifted, exceptional. He was passionately fond of music; every spare penny he had went on books. He was always full of new ideas, schemes, plans. But nothing came of it all. The new fire blazed in Jonathan; you almost heard it roaring softly as he explained, described and dilated on the new thing; but a moment later it had fallen in and there was nothing but ashes, and Jonathan went about with a look like hunger in his black eyes. At these times he exaggerated his absurd manner of speaking, and he sang in church—he was the leader of the choir—with such fearful dramatic intensity that the meanest hymn put on an unholy splendour.

"It seems to me just as imbecile, just as infernal, to have to go to the office on Monday," said Jonathan, "as it always has done and always will do. To spend all the best years of one's life sitting on a stool from nine to five, scratching in somebody's ledger! It's a queer use to make of one's . . . one and only life, isn't it? Or do I fondly dream?" He rolled over on the grass and looked up at Linda. "Tell me, what is the difference between my life and that of an ordinary prisoner? The only difference I can see is that I put myself in jail and nobody's ever going to let me out. That's a more intolerable situation than the other. For if I'd been—pushed in, against my will—kicking, even—once the door was locked, or at any rate in five years or so, I might have accepted the fact and begun to take an interest in the flight of flies or counting the warder's steps along the passage with particular attention to variations of tread and so on. But as it is, I'm like an insect that's flown into a room of its own accord. I dash against the walls, dash against the windows, flop against the ceiling, do everything on God's earth, in fact, except fly out again. And all the while I'm thinking, like that moth, or that butterfly, or whatever it is, 'The shortness of life! The shortness of life!' I've only one night or one day, and there's this vast dangerous garden, waiting out there, undiscovered, unexplored."

"But, if you feel like that, why—" began Linda quickly.

"*Ah!*" cried Jonathan. And that "ah!" was somehow almost exultant. "There you have me. Why? Why indeed? There's the maddening, mysterious question. Why don't I fly out again? There's the window or the door or whatever it was I came in by. It's not hopelessly shut—is it? Why don't I find it and be off? Answer me that, little sister." But he gave her no time to answer.

"I'm exactly like that insect again. For some reason"—Jonathan paused between the words—"it's not allowed, it's forbidden, it's against the insect law, to stop banging and flopping and crawling up the pane even for an instant. Why don't I leave the office? Why don't I seriously consider, this moment, for instance, what it is that prevents me leaving? It's not as though I'm tremendously tied. I've two boys to provide for, but, after all, they're boys. I could cut off to sea, or get a job up-country, or—" Suddenly he smiled at Linda and said in a changed voice, as if he were confiding a secret, "Weak . . . weak. No stamina. No anchor. No guiding principle, let us call it." But then the dark velvety voice rolled out:

> Would ye hear the story
> How it unfolds itself . . .

and they were silent.

The sun had set. In the western sky there were great masses of crushed-up rose-coloured clouds. Broad beams of light shone through the clouds and beyond them as if they would cover the whole sky. Overhead the blue faded; it turned a pale gold, and the bush outlined against it gleamed dark and brilliant like metal. Sometimes when those beams of light show in the sky they are very awful. They remind you that up there sits Jehovah, the jealous God, the Almighty, Whose eye is upon you, ever watchful, never weary. You remember that at his coming the whole earth will shake into one ruined graveyard; the cold, bright angels will drive you this way and that, and there will be no time to explain what could be explained so simply. . . . But to-night it seemed to Linda there was something infinitely joyful and loving in those silver beams. And now no sound came from the sea. It breathed softly as if it would draw that tender, joyful beauty into its own bosom.

"It's all wrong, it's all wrong," came the shadowy voice of Jonathan. "It's not the scene, it's not the setting for . . . three stools, three desks, three inkpots and a wire blind."

Linda knew that he would never change, but she said, "Is it too late, even now?"

"I'm old—I'm old," intoned Jonathan. He bent towards her, he passed his hand over his head. "Look!" His black hair was speckled all over with silver, like the breast plumage of a black fowl.

Linda was surprised. She had no idea that he was grey. And yet, as he stood up beside her and sighed and stretched, she saw him, for the first time, not resolute, not gallant, not careless, but touched already with age. He looked very tall on the darkening grass, and the thought crossed her mind, "He is like a weed."

Jonathan stooped again and kissed her fingers.

"Heaven reward thy sweet patience, lady mine," he murmured. "I must go seek those heirs to my fame and fortune. . . ." He was gone.

II

Light shone in the windows of the bungalow. Two square patches of gold fell upon the pinks and the peaked marigolds. Florrie, the cat, came out on to the verandah, and sat on the top step, her white paws close together, her tail curled round. She looked content, as though she had been waiting for this moment all day.

"Thank goodness, it's getting late," said Florrie. "Thank goodness, the long day is over." Her greengage eyes opened.

Presently there sounded the rumble of the coach, the crack of Kelly's whip. It came near enough for one to hear the voices of the men from town, talking loudly together. It stopped at the Burnells' gate.

Stanley was half-way up the path before he saw Linda. "Is that you, darling?"

"Yes, Stanley."

He leapt across the flower-bed and seized her in his arms. She was enfolded in that familiar, eager, strong embrace.

"Forgive me, darling, forgive me," stammered Stanley, and he put his hand under her chin and lifted her face to him.

"Forgive you?" smiled Linda. "But whatever for?"

"Good God! You can't have forgotten," cried Stanley Burnell. "I've thought of nothing else all day. I've had the hell of a day. I made up my mind to dash out and telegraph, and then I thought the wire mightn't reach you before I did. I've been in tortures, Linda."

But Stanley," said Linda, "what must I forgive you for?"

"Linda!"—Stanley was very hurt—"didn't you realize—you must have realized—I went away without saying good-bye to you this morning? I can't imagine how I can have done such a thing. My confounded temper, of course. But—well"—and he sighed and took her in his arms again—"I've suffered for it enough to-day."

"What's that you've got in your hand?" asked Linda. "New gloves? Let me see."

"Oh, just a cheap pair of wash-leather ones," said Stanley. "I noticed Bell was wearing some in the coach this morning, so, as I was passing the shop, I dashed in and got myself a pair. What are you smiling at? You don't think it was wrong of me, do you?"

"On the *con*-trary, darling," said Linda. "I think it was most sensible."

She pulled one of the large, pale gloves on her own fingers and looked at her hand, turning it this way and that. She was still smiling.

Stanley wanted to say, "I was thinking of you the whole time I bought them." It was true, but for some reason he couldn't say it. "Let's go in," said he.

12

Why does one feel so different at night? Why is it so exciting to be awake when everybody else is asleep? Late—it is very late! And yet every moment you feel more and more wakeful, as though you were slowly, almost with every breath, waking up into a new, wonderful, far more thrilling and exciting world than the daylight one. And what is this queer sensation that you're a conspirator? Lightly, stealthily you move about your room. You take something off the dressing table and put it down again without a sound. And everything, even the bed-post, knows you, responds, shares your secret. . . .

You're not very fond of your room by day. You never think about it. You're in and out, the door opens and slams, the cupboard creaks. You sit down on the side of your bed, change your shoes and dash out again. A dive down to the glass, two pins in your hair, powder your nose and off again. But now—it's suddenly dear to you. It's a darling little funny room. It's yours. Oh, what a joy it is to own things! Mine—my own!

"My very own for ever?"

"Yes." Their lips met.

No, of course, that had nothing to do with it. That was all nonsense and rubbish. But, in spite of herself, Beryl saw so plainly two people standing in the middle of her room. Her arms were round his neck; he held her. And now he whispered, "My beauty, my little beauty!" She jumped off her bed, ran over to the window and kneeled on the window-seat, with her elbows on the sill. But the beautiful night, the garden, every bush, every leaf, even the white palings, even the stars, were conspirators too. So bright was the moon that the flowers were bright as by day; the shadow of the nasturtiums, exquisite lilylike leaves and wide-open flowers, lay across the silvery verandah. The manuka tree, bent by the southerly winds, was like a bird on one leg stretching out a wing.

But when Beryl looked at the bush, it seemed to her the bush was sad.

"We are dumb trees, reaching up in the night, imploring we know not what," said the sorrowful bush.

It is true when you are by yourself and you think about life, it is always sad. All that excitement and so on has a way of suddenly leaving you, and it's as though, in the silence, somebody called your name, and you heard your name for the first time. "Beryl!"

"Yes, I'm here. I'm Beryl. Who wants me?"

"Beryl!"

"Let me come."

It is lonely living by oneself. Of course, there are relations, friends, heaps of them; but that's not what she means. She wants some one who will find the Beryl they none of them know, who will expect her to be that Beryl always. She wants a lover.

"Take me away from all these other people, my love. Let us

go far away. Let us live our life, all new, all ours, from the very beginning. Let us make our fire. Let us sit down to eat together. Let us have long talks at night."

And the thought was almost, "Save me, my love. Save me!"

. . . "Oh, go on! Don't be a prude, my dear. You enjoy yourself while you're young. That's my advice." And a high rush of silly laughter joined Mrs. Harry Kember's loud, indifferent neigh.

You see, it's so frightfully difficult when you've nobody. You're so at the mercy of things. You can't just be rude. And you've always this horror of seeming inexperienced and stuffy like the other ninnies at the Bay. And—and it's fascinating to know you've power over people. Yes, that is fascinating. . . .

Oh why, oh why doesn't "he" come soon?

If I go on living here, thought Beryl, anything may happen to me.

"But how do you know he is coming at all?" mocked a small voice within her.

But Beryl dismissed it. She couldn't be left. Other people, perhaps, but not she. It wasn't possible to think that Beryl Fairfield never married, that lovely fascinating girl.

"Do you remember Beryl Fairfield?"

"Remember her! As if I could forget her! It was one summer at the Bay that I saw her. She was standing on the beach in a blue"—no, pink—"muslin frock, holding on a big cream"—no, black—"straw hat. But it's years ago now."

"She's as lovely as ever, more so if anything."

Beryl smiled, bit her lip, and gazed over the garden. As she gazed, she saw somebody, a man, leave the road, step along the paddock beside their palings as if he was coming straight towards her. Her heart beat. Who was it? Who could it be? It couldn't be a burglar, certainly not a burglar, for he was smoking and he strolled lightly. Beryl's heart leapt; it seemed to turn right over, and then to stop. She recognized him.

"Good evening, Miss Beryl," said the voice softly.

"Good evening."

"Won't you come for a little walk?" it drawled.

Come for a walk—at that time of night! "I couldn't. Everybody's in bed. Everybody's asleep."

"Oh," said the voice lightly, and a whiff of sweet smoke reached her. "What does everybody matter? Do come! It's such a fine night. There's not a soul about."

Beryl shook her head. But already something stirred in her, something reared its head.

The voice said, "Frightened?" It mocked, "Poor little girl!"

"Not in the least," said she. As she spoke that weak thing within her seemed to uncoil, to grow suddenly tremendously strong; she longed to go!

And just as if this was quite understood by the other, the voice said, gently and softly, but finally, "Come along!"

Beryl stepped over her low window, crossed the verandah, ran down the grass to the gate. He was there before her.

"That's right," breathed the voice, and it teased, "You're not frightened, are you? You're not frightened?"

She was; now she was here she was terrified, and it seemed to her everything was different. The moonlight stared and glittered; the shadows were like bars of iron. Her hand was taken.

"Not in the least," she said lightly. "Why should I be?"

Her hand was pulled gently, tugged. She held back.

"No, I'm not coming any farther," said Beryl.

"Oh, rot!" Harry Kember didn't believe her. "Come along! We'll just go as far as that fuchsia bush. Come along!"

The fuchsia bush was tall. It fell over the fence in a shower. There was a little pit of darkness beneath.

"No, really, I don't want to," said Beryl.

For a moment Harry Kember didn't answer. Then he came close to her, turned to her, smiled and said quickly, "Don't be silly! Don't be silly!"

His smile was something she'd never seen before. Was he drunk? That bright, blind, terrifying smile froze her with horror. What was she doing? How had she got here? the stern garden asked her as the gate pushed open, and quick as a cat Harry Kember came through and snatched her to him.

"Cold little devil! Cold little devil!" said the hateful voice.

But Beryl was strong. She slipped, ducked, wrenched free.

"You are vile, vile," said she.

"Then why in God's name did you come?" stammered Harry Kember.

Nobody answered him.

13

A cloud, small, serene, floated across the moon. In that moment of darkness the sea sounded deep, troubled. Then the cloud sailed away, and the sound of the sea was a vague murmur, as though it waked out of a dark dream. All was still.

Psychology

W~H E N S H E O P E N E D~ the door and saw him standing there she was more pleased than ever before, and he, too, as he followed her into the studio, seemed very very happy to have come.

"Not busy?"

"No. Just going to have tea."

"And you are not expecting anybody?"

"Nobody at all."

"Ah! That's good."

He laid aside his coat and hat gently, lingeringly, as though he had time and to spare for everything, or as though he were taking leave of them for ever, and came over to the fire and held out his hands to the quick, leaping flame.

Just for a moment both of them stood silent in that leaping light. Still, as it were, they tasted on their smiling lips the sweet shock of their greeting. Their secret selves whispered:

"Why should we speak? Isn't this enough?"

"More than enough. I never realized until this moment . . ."

"How good it is just to be with you. . . ."

"Like this. . . ."

"It's more than enough."

But suddenly he turned and looked at her and she moved quickly away.

"Have a cigarette? I'll put the kettle on. Are you longing for tea?"

"No. Not longing."

"Well, I am."

"Oh, you." He thumped the Armenian cushion and flung on to the *sommier*. "You're a perfect little Chinee."

"Yes, I am," she laughed. "I long for tea as strong men long for wine."

She lighted the lamp under its broad orange shade, pulled the curtains and drew up the tea table. Two birds sang in the kettle; the fire fluttered. He sat up clasping his knees. It was delightful—this business of having tea—and she always had delicious things to eat—little sharp sandwiches, short sweet almond fingers, and a dark, rich cake tasting of rum—but it was an interruption. He wanted it over, the table pushed away, their two chairs drawn up to the light, and the moment came when he took out his pipe, filled it, and said, pressing the tobacco tight into the bowl: "I have been thinking over what you said last time and it seems to me . . ."

Yes, that was what he waited for and so did she. Yes, while she shook the teapot hot and dry over the spirit flame she saw those other two, him, leaning back, taking his ease among the cushions, and her, curled up *en escargot* in the blue shell armchair. The picture was so clear and so minute it might have been painted on the blue teapot lid. And yet she couldn't hurry. She could almost have cried: "Give me time." She must have time in which to grow calm. She wanted time in which to free herself from all these familiar things with which she lived so vividly. For all these gay things round her were part of her—her offspring—and they knew it and made the largest, most vehement claims. But now they must go. They must be swept away, shooed away—like children, sent up the shadowy stairs, packed into bed and commanded to go to sleep—at once—without a murmur!

For the special thrilling quality of their friendship was in their complete surrender. Like two open cities in the midst of some vast plain their two minds lay open to each other. And it wasn't as if he rode into hers like a conqueror, armed to the eyebrows and seeing nothing but a gay silken flutter—nor did she enter his like a queen walking soft on petals. No, they were eager, serious travellers, absorbed in understanding what was to be seen and discovering what was hidden—making the most of this extraordinary absolute chance which made it possible for him to be utterly truthful to her and for her to be utterly sincere with him.

And the best of it was they were both of them old enough to enjoy their adventure to the full without any stupid emotional complication. Passion would have ruined everything; they quite saw that. Besides, all that sort of thing was over and done with for both of them—he was thirty-one, she was thirty—they had had their experiences, and very rich and varied they had been, but now was the time for harvest—harvest. Weren't his novels to be very big novels indeed? And her plays. Who else had her exquisite sense of real English Comedy? . . .

Carefully she cut the cake into thick little wads and he reached across for a piece.

"Do you realize how good it is," she implored. "Eat it imaginatively. Roll your eyes if you can and taste it on the breath. It's not a sandwich from the hatter's bag—it's the kind of cake that might have been mentioned in the Book of Genesis. . . . And God said: 'Let there be cake. And there was cake. And God saw that it was good.' "

"You needn't entreat me," said he. "Really you needn't. It's a queer thing but I always do notice what I eat here and never anywhere else. I suppose it comes of living alone so long and always reading while I feed . . . my habit of looking upon food as just food . . . something that's there, at certain times . . . to be devoured . . . to be . . . not there." He laughed. "That shocks you. Doesn't it?"

"To the bone," she said.

"But—look here—" He pushed away his cup and began to speak very fast. "I simply haven't got any external life at all. I don't know the names of things a bit—trees and so on—and I never notice places or furniture or what people look like. One room is just like another to me—a place to sit and read or talk in—except," and here he paused, smiled in a strange naive way, and said, "except this studio." He looked round him and then at her; he laughed in his astonishment and pleasure. He was like a man who wakes up in a train to find that he has arrived, already, at the journey's end.

"Here's another queer thing. If I shut my eyes I can see this

137

place down to every detail—every detail. . . . Now I come to think of it—I've never realized this consciously before. Often when I am away from here I revisit it in spirit—wander about among your red chairs, stare at the bowl of fruit on the black table—and just touch, very lightly, that marvel of a sleeping boy's head."

He looked at it as he spoke. It stood on the corner of the mantelpiece; the head to one side down-drooping, the lips parted, as though in his sleep the little boy listened to some sweet sound. . . .

"I love that little boy," he murmured. And then they both were silent.

A new silence came between them. Nothing in the least like the satisfactory pause that had followed their greetings—the "Well, here we are together again, and there's no reason why we shouldn't go on from just where we left off last time." That silence could be contained in the circle of warm, delightful fire and lamp-light. How many times hadn't they flung something into it just for the fun of watching the ripples break on the easy shores. But into this unfamiliar pool the head of the little boy sleeping his timeless sleep dropped—and the ripples flowed away, away—boundlessly far—into deep glittering darkness.

And then both of them broke it. She said: "I must make up the fire," and he said: "I have been trying a new . . ." Both of them escaped. She made up the fire and put the table back, the blue chair was wheeled forward, she curled up and he lay back among the cushions. Quickly! Quickly! They must stop it from happening again.

"Well, I read the book you left last time."

"Oh, what do you think of it?"

They were off and all was as usual. But was it? Weren't they just a little too quick, too prompt with their replies, too ready to take each other up? Was this really anything more than a won-derfully good imitation of other occasions? His heart beat; her cheek burned and the stupid thing was she could not discover where exactly they were or what exactly was happening. She hadn't time to glance back. And just as she had got so far it happened again. They faltered, wavered, broke down, were silent. Again they were conscious of the boundless, questioning dark. Again, there they were—two hunters, bending over their fire, but hearing suddenly from the jungle beyond a shake of wind and a loud, questioning cry. . . .

She lifted her head. "It's raining," she murmured. And her voice was like his when he had said "I love that little boy."

Well. Why didn't they just give way to it—yield—and see what will happen then? But no. Vague and troubled though they were, they knew enough to realize their precious friendship was in danger. She was the one who would be destroyed—not they—and they'd be no party to that.

He got up, knocked out his pipe, ran his hand through his hair and said: "I have been wondering very much lately whether the novel of the future will be a psychological novel or not. How sure are you that psychology *qua* psychology has got anything to do with literature at all?"

"Do you mean you feel there's quite a chance that the mysterious non-existent creatures—the young writers of to-day—are trying simply to jump the psycho-analyst's claim?"

"Yes, I do. And I think it's because this generation is just wise enough to know that it is sick and to realize that its only chance of recovery is by going into its symptoms—making an exhaustive study of them—tracking them down—trying to get at the root of the trouble."

"But oh," she wailed. "What a dreadfully dismal outlook."

"Not at all," said he. "Look here . . ." On the talk went. And now it seemed they really had succeeded. She turned in her chair to look at him while she answered. Her smile said: "We have won." And he smiled back, confident: "Absolutely."

But the smile undid them. It lasted too long; it became a grin. They saw themselves as two little grinning puppets jigging away in nothingness.

"What have we been talking about?" thought he. He was so utterly bored he almost groaned.

"What a spectacle we have made of ourselves," thought she. And she saw him laboriously—oh, laboriously—laying out the grounds and herself running after, putting here a tree and there a flowery shrub and here a handful of glittering fish in a pool. They were silent this time from sheer dismay.

The clock struck six merry little pings and the fire made a soft flutter. What fools they were—heavy, stodgy, elderly—with positively upholstered minds.

And now the silence put a spell upon them like solemn music. It was anguish—anguish for her to bear it and he would die— he'd die if it were broken. . . . And yet he longed to break it. Not by speech. At any rate not by their ordinary maddening chatter. There was another way for them to speak to each other, and in the new way he wanted to murmur: "Do you feel this too? Do you understand it at all?" . . .

Instead, to his horror, he heard himself say: "I must be off; I'm meeting Brand at six."

What devil made him say that instead of the other? She jumped—simply jumped out of her chair, and he heard her crying: "You must rush, then. He's so punctual. Why didn't you say so before?"

"You've hurt me; you've hurt me! We've failed!" said her secret self while she handed him his hat and stick, smiling gaily. She wouldn't give him a moment for another word, but ran along the passage and opened the big outer door.

Could they leave each other like this? How could they? He stood on the step and she just inside holding the door. It was not raining now.

"You've hurt me—hurt me," said her heart. "Why don't you go? No, don't go. Stay. No—go!" And she looked out upon the night.

She saw the beautiful fall of the steps, the dark garden ringed with glittering ivy, on the other side of the road the huge bare willows and above them the sky big and bright with stars. But of course he would see nothing of all this. He was superior to it all. He—with his wonderful "spiritual" vision!

She was right. He did see nothing at all. Misery! He'd missed it. It was too late to do anything now. Was it too late? Yes, it was. A cold snatch of hateful wind blew into the garden. Curse life! He heard her cry "au revoir" and the door slammed.

Running back into the studio she behaved so strangely. She ran up and down lifting her arms and crying: "Oh! Oh! How stupid! How imbecile! How stupid!" And then she flung herself down on the *sommier* thinking of nothing—just lying there in her rage. All was over. What was over? Oh—something was. And she'd never see him again—never. After a long long time (or perhaps ten minutes) had passed in that black gulf her bell rang a sharp quick jingle. It was he, of course. And equally, of course, she oughtn't to have paid the slightest attention to it but just let it go on ringing and ringing. She flew to answer.

On the doorstep there stood an elderly virgin, a pathetic creature who simply idolized her (heaven knows why) and had this habit of turning up and ringing the bell and then saying, when she opened the door: "My dear, send me away!" She never did. As a rule she asked her in and let her admire everything and accepted the bunch of slightly soiled looking flowers—more than graciously. But to-day . . .

"Oh, I am so sorry," she cried. "But I've got someone with me. We are working on some wood-cuts. I'm hopelessly busy all evening."

"It doesn't matter. It doesn't matter at all, darling," said the good friend. "I was just passing and I thought I'd leave you some violets." She fumbled down among the ribs of a large old umbrella. "I put them down here. Such a good place to keep flowers out of the wind. Here they are," she said, shaking out a little dead bunch.

For a moment she did not take the violets. But while she stood just inside, holding the door, a strange thing happened. . . . Again she saw the beautiful fall of the steps, the dark garden ringed with glittering ivy, the willows, the big bright sky. Again she felt the silence that was like a question. But this time she did not hesitate. She moved forward. Very softly and gently, as though fearful of making a ripple in that boundless pool of quiet she put her arms round her friend.

"My dear," murmured her happy friend, quite overcome by this gratitude. "They are really nothing. Just the simplest little thrippeny bunch."

But as she spoke she was enfolded—more tenderly, more beautifully embraced, held by such a sweet pressure and for so long that the poor dear's mind positively reeled and she just had the strength to quaver: "Then you really don't mind me too much?"

"Good night, my friend," whispered the other. "Come again soon."

"Oh, I will. I will."

This time she walked back to the studio slowly, and standing in the middle of the room with half-shut eyes she felt so light, so rested, as if she had woken up out of a childish sleep. Even the act of breathing was a joy. . . .

The *sommier* was very untidy. All the cushions "like furious mountains" as she said; she put them in order before going over to the writing-table.

"I have been thinking over our talk about the psychological novel," she dashed off, "it really is intensely interesting." . . . And so on and so on.

At the end she wrote: "Good night, my friend. Come again soon."

Bliss

ALTHOUGH Bertha Young was thirty she still had moments like this when she wanted to run instead of walk, to take dancing steps on and off the pavement, to bowl a hoop, to throw something up in the air and catch it again, or to stand still and laugh at—nothing—at nothing, simply.

What can you do if you are thirty and, turning the corner of your own street, you are overcome, suddenly, by a feeling of bliss—absolute bliss!—as though you'd suddenly swallowed a bright piece of that late afternoon sun and it burned in your bosom, sending out a little shower of sparks into every particle, into every finger and toe? . . .

Oh, is there no way you can express it without being "drunk and disorderly?" How idiotic civilization is! Why be given a body if you have to keep it shut up in a case like a rare, rare fiddle?

"No, that about the fiddle is not quite what I mean," she thought, running up the steps and feeling in her bag for the key—she'd forgotten it, as usual—and rattling the letter-box. "It's not what I mean, because—Thank you, Mary"—she went into the hall. "Is nurse back?"

"Yes, M'm."

"And has the fruit come?"

"Yes, M'm. Everything's come."

"Bring the fruit up to the dining-room, will you? I'll arrange it before I go upstairs."

It was dusky in the dining-room and quite chilly. But all the same Bertha threw off her coat; she could not bear the tight clasp of it another moment, and the cold air fell on her arms.

But in her bosom there was still that bright glowing place—that shower of little sparks coming from it. It was almost unbearable. She hardly dared to breathe for fear of fanning it higher, and yet she breathed deeply, deeply. She hardly dared to look into the cold mirror—but she did look, and it gave her back a woman, radiant, with smiling, trembling lips, with big, dark eyes and an air of listening, waiting for something ... divine to happen ... that she knew must happen ... infallibly.

Mary brought in the fruit on a tray and with it a glass bowl, and a blue dish, very lovely, with a strange sheen on it as though it had been dipped in milk.

"Shall I turn on the light, M'm?"

"No, thank you. I can see quite well."

There were tangerines and apples stained with strawberry pink. Some yellow pears, smooth as silk, some white grapes covered with a silver bloom and a big cluster of purple ones. These last she had bought to tone in with the new dining-room carpet. Yes, that did sound rather far-fetched and absurd, but it was really why she had bought them. She had thought in the shop: "I must have some purple ones to bring the carpet up to the table." And it had seemed quite sense at the time.

When she had finished with them and had made two pyramids of these bright round shapes, she stood away from the table to get the effect—and it really was most curious. For the dark table seemed to melt into the dusky light and the glass dish and the blue bowl to float in the air. This, of course in her present mood, was so incredibly beautiful. . . . She began to laugh.

"No, no. I'm getting hysterical." And she seized her bag and coat and ran upstairs to the nursery.

Nurse sat at a low table giving Little B her supper after her bath. The baby had on a white flannel gown and a blue woollen jacket, and her dark, fine hair was brushed up into a funny little peak. She looked up when she saw her mother and began to jump.

"Now, my lovey, eat it up like a good girl," said Nurse, getting her lips in a way that Bertha knew, and that meant she had come into the nursery at another wrong moment.

"Has she been good, Nanny?"

"She's been a little sweet all the afternoon," whispered Nanny. "We went to the park and I sat down on a chair and took her out of the pram and a big dog came along and put its head on my knee and she clutched its ear, tugged it. Oh, you should have seen her."

Bertha wanted to ask if it wasn't rather dangerous to let her clutch at a strange dog's ear. But she did not dare to. She stood watching them, her hands by her side, like the poor little girl in front of the rich little girl with the doll.

The baby looked up at her again, stared, and then smiled so charmingly that Bertha couldn't help crying:

"Oh, Nanny, do let me finish giving her her supper while you put the bath things away."

"Well, M'm, she oughtn't to be changed hands while she's eating," said Nanny, still whispering. "It unsettles her; it's very likely to upset her."

How absurd it was. Why have a baby if it has to be kept— not in a case like a rare, rare fiddle—but in another woman's arms?

"Oh, I must!" said she.

Very offended, Nanny handed her over.

"Now, don't excite her after her supper. You know you do, M'm. And I have such a time with her after!"

Thank heaven! Nanny went out of the room with the bath towels.

"Now I've got you to myself, my little precious," said Bertha, as the baby leaned against her.

She ate delightfully, holding up her lips for the spoon and then waving her hands. Sometimes she wouldn't let the spoon go; and sometimes, just as Bertha had filled it, she waved it away to the four winds.

When the soup was finished Bertha turned round to the fire.

"You're nice—you're very nice!" said she, kissing her warm baby. "I'm fond of you. I like you."

And, indeed, she loved Little B so much—her neck as she bent forward, her exquisite toes as they shone transparent in the

145

firelight—that all her feeling of bliss came back again, and again she didn't know how to express it—what to do with it.

"You're wanted on the telephone," said Nanny, coming back in triumph and seizing *her* Little B.

Down she flew. It was Harry.

"Oh, is that you, Ber? Look here. I'll be late. I'll take a taxi and come along as quickly as I can, but get dinner put back ten minutes—will you? All right?"

"Yes, perfectly. Oh, Harry!"

"Yes?"

What had she to say? She'd nothing to say. She only wanted to get in touch with him for a moment. She couldn't absurdly cry: "Hasn't it been a divine day!"

"What is it?" rapped out the little voice.

"Nothing. *Entendu*," said Bertha, and hung up the receiver, thinking how more than idiotic civilization was.

They had people coming to dinner. The Norman Knights— a very sound couple—he was about to start a theatre, and she was awfully keen on interior decoration, a young man, Eddie Warren, who had just published a little book of poems and whom everybody was asking to dine, and a "find" of Bertha's called Pearl Fulton. What Miss Fulton did, Bertha didn't know. They had met at the club and Bertha had fallen in love with her, as she always did fall in love with beautiful women who had something strange about them.

The provoking thing was that, though they had been about together and met a number of times and really talked, Bertha couldn't yet make her out. Up to a certain point Miss Fulton was rarely, wonderfully frank, but the certain point was there, and beyond that she would not go.

Was there anything beyond it? Harry said "No." Voted her dullish, and "cold like all blond women, with a touch, perhaps, of anæmia of the brain." But Bertha wouldn't agree with him; not yet, at any rate.

"No, the way she has of sitting with her head a little on one side, and smiling, has something behind it, Harry, and I must find out what that something is."

"Most likely it's a good stomach," answered Harry.

He made a point of catching Bertha's heels with replies of that kind . . . "liver frozen, my dear girl," or "pure flatulence," or "kidney disease," . . . and so on. For some strange reason Bertha liked this, and almost admired it in him very much.

She went into the drawing-room and lighted the fire; then, picking up the cushions, one by one, that Mary had disposed so carefully, she threw them back on to the chairs and the couches. That made all the difference; the room came alive at once. As she was about to throw the last one she surprised herself by suddenly hugging it to her, passionately, passionately. But it did not put out the fire in her bosom. Oh, on the contrary!

The windows of the drawing-room opened on to a balcony overlooking the garden. At the far end, against the wall, there was a tall, slender pear tree in fullest, richest bloom; it stood perfect, as though becalmed against the jade-green sky. Bertha couldn't help feeling, even from this distance, that it had not a single bud or a faded petal. Down below, in the garden beds, the red and yellow tulips, heavy with flowers, seemed to lean upon the dusk. A grey cat, dragging its belly, crept across the lawn, and a black one, its shadow, trailed after. The sight of them, so intent and so quick, gave Bertha a curious shiver.

"What creepy things cats are!" she stammered, and she turned away from the window and began walking up and down. . . .

How strong the jonquils smelled in the warm room. Too strong? Oh, no. And yet, as though overcome, she flung down on a couch and pressed her hands to her eyes.

"I'm too happy—too happy!" she murmured.

And she seemed to see on her eyelids the lovely pear tree with its wide open blossoms as a symbol of her own life.

Really—really—she had everything. She was young. Harry and she were as much in love as ever, and they got on together splendidly and were really good pals. She had an adorable baby. They didn't have to worry about money. They had this absolutely satisfactory house and garden. And friends—modern, thrilling friends, writers and painters and poets or people keen on social questions—just the kind of friends they wanted. And then there were books, and there was music, and she had found a wonderful little dressmaker, and they were going abroad in the summer, and their new cook made the most superb omelettes. . . .

"I'm absurd. Absurd!" She sat up; but she felt quite dizzy, quite drunk. It must have been the spring.

Yes, it was the spring. Now she was so tired she could not drag herself upstairs to dress.

A white dress, a string of jade beads, green shoes and stockings. It wasn't intentional. She had thought of this scheme hours before she stood at the drawing-room window.

Her petals rustled softly into the hall, and she kissed Mrs. Norman Knight, who was taking off the most amusing orange coat with a procession of black monkeys round the hem and up the fronts.

". . . Why! Why! Why is the middle-class so stodgy—so utterly without a sense of humour! My dear, it's only by a fluke that I am here at all—Norman being the protective fluke. For my darling monkeys so upset the train that it rose to a man and simply ate me with its eyes. Didn't laugh—wasn't amused—that I should have loved. No, just stared—and bored me through and through."

"But the cream of it was," said Norman, pressing a large tortoiseshell-rimmed monocle into his eye, "you don't mind me telling this, Face, do you?" (In their house and among their friends they called each other Face and Mug.) "The cream of it was when she, being full fed, turned to the woman beside her and said: 'Haven't you ever seen a monkey before?' "

"Oh, yes!" Mrs. Norman Knight joined in the laughter. "Wasn't that too absolutely creamy?"

And a funnier thing still was that now her coat was off she did look like a very intelligent monkey—who had even made that yellow silk dress out of scraped banana skins. And her amber earrings; they were like little dangling nuts.

"This is a sad, sad fall!" said Mug, pausing in front of Little B's perambulator. "When the perambulator comes into the hall—" and he waved the rest of the quotation away.

The bell rang. It was lean, pale Eddie Warren (as usual) in a state of acute distress.

"It *is* the right house, *isn't* it?" he pleaded.

"Oh, I think so—I hope so," said Bertha brightly.

"I have had such a *dreadful* experience with a taximan; he was *most* sinister. I couldn't get him to *stop*. The *more* I knocked and called the *faster* he went. And *in* the moonlight this *bizarre* figure with the *flattened* head *crouching* over the *lit-tle* wheel. . . ."

He shuddered, taking off an immense white silk scarf. Bertha noticed that his socks were white, too—most charming.

"But how dreadful!" she cried.

"Yes, it really was," said Eddie, following her into the drawing-room. "I saw myself *driving* through Eternity in a *timeless* taxi."

He knew the Norman Knights. In fact, he was going to write a play for N.K. when the theatre scheme came off.

"Well, Warren, how's the play?" said Norman Knight, dropping his monocle and giving his eye a moment in which to rise to the surface before it was screwed down again.

And Mrs. Norman Knight: "Oh, Mr. Warren, what happy socks!"

"I *am* so glad you like them," said he, staring at his feet. "They seem to have got so *much* whiter since the moon rose." And he turned his lean sorrowful young face to Bertha. "There *is* a moon, you know."

She wanted to cry: "I am sure there is—often—often!"

He really was a most attractive person. But so was Face, crouched before the fire in her banana skins, and so was Mug, smoking a cigarette and saying as he flicked the ash: "Why doth the bridegroom tarry?"

"There he is, now."

Bang went the front door open and shut. Harry shouted: "Hullo, you people. Down in five minutes." And they heard him swarm up the stairs. Bertha couldn't help smiling; she knew how he loved doing things at high pressure. What, after all, did an extra five minutes matter? But he would pretend to himself that they mattered beyond measure. And then he would make a great point of coming into the drawing-room, extravagantly cool and collected.

Harry had such a zest for life. Oh, how she appreciated it in him. And his passion for fighting—for seeking in everything that came up against him another test of his power and of his courage—that, too, she understood. Even when it made him just occasionally, to other people, who didn't know him well, a little ridiculous perhaps. . . . For there were moments when he rushed into battle where no battle was. . . . She talked and laughed and positively forgot until he had come in (just as she had imagined) that Pearl Fulton had not turned up.

"I wonder if Miss Fulton has forgotten?"

"I expect so," said Harry. "Is she on the 'phone?"

"Ah! There's a taxi, now." And Bertha smiled with that little air of proprietorship that she always assumed while her women finds were new and mysterious. "She lives in taxis."

"She'll run to fat if she does," said Harry coolly, ringing the bell for dinner. "Frightful danger for blond women."

"Harry—don't," warned Bertha, laughing up at him.

Came another tiny moment, while they waited, laughing and talking, just a trifle too much at their ease, a trifle too unaware. And then Miss Fulton, all in silver, with a silver fillet binding her pale blond hair, came in smiling, her head a little on one side.

"Am I late?"

"No, not at all," said Bertha. "Come along." And she took her arm and they moved into the dining-room.

What was there in the touch of that cool arm that could fan— fan—start blazing—blazing—the fire of bliss that Bertha did not know what to do with?

Miss Fulton did not look at her; but then she seldom did look at people directly. Her heavy eyelids lay upon her eyes and the strange half smile came and went upon her lips as though she lived by listening rather than seeing. But Bertha knew, suddenly, as if the longest, most intimate look had passed between them— as if they had said to each other: "You, too?"—that Pearl Fulton, stirring the beautiful red soup in the grey plate, was feeling just what she was feeling.

And the others? Face and Mug, Eddie and Harry, their

150

spoons rising and falling—dabbing their lips with their napkins, crumbling bread, fiddling with the forks and glasses and talking.

"I met her at the Alpha show—the weirdest little person. She'd not only cut off her hair, but she seemed to have taken a dreadfully good snip off her legs and arms and her neck and her poor little nose as well."

"Isn't she very *liée* with Michael Oat?"

"The man who wrote *Love in False Teeth?*"

"He wants to write a play for me. One act. One man. Decides to commit suicide. Gives all the reasons why he should and why he shouldn't. And just as he has made up his mind either to do it or not to do it—curtain. Not half a bad idea."

"What's he going to call it—'Stomach Trouble'?"

"I *think* I've come across the *same* idea in a lit-tle French review, *quite* unknown in England."

No, they didn't share it. They were dears—dears—and she loved having them there, at her table, and giving them delicious food and wine. In fact, she longed to tell them how delightful they were, and what a decorative group they made, how they seemed to set one another off and how they reminded her of a play by Chekhov!

Harry was enjoying his dinner. It was part of his—well, not his nature, exactly, and certainly not his pose—his—something or other—to talk about food and to glory in his "shameless passion for the white flesh of the lobster" and "the green of pistachio ices—green and cold like the eyelids of Egyptian dancers."

When he looked up at her and said: "Bertha, this is a very admirable *soufflée!*" she almost could have wept with child-like pleasure.

Oh, why did she feel so tender towards the whole world tonight? Everything was good—was right. All that happened seemed to fill again her brimming cup of bliss.

And still, in the back of her mind, there was the pear tree. It would be silver now, in the light of poor dear Eddie's moon, silver as Miss Fulton, who sat there turning a tangerine in her slender fingers that were so pale a light seemed to come from them.

What she simply couldn't make out—what was miraculous—

151

was how she should have guessed Miss Fulton's mood so exactly and so instantly. For she never doubted for a moment that she was right, and yet what had she to go on? Less than nothing.

"I believe this does happen very, very rarely between women. Never between men," thought Bertha. "But while I am making the coffee in the drawing-room perhaps she will 'give a sign.'"

What she meant by that she did not know, and what would happen after that she could not imagine.

While she thought like this she saw herself talking and laughing. She had to talk because of her desire to laugh.

"I must laugh or die."

But when she noticed Face's funny little habit of tucking something down the front of her bodice—as if she kept a tiny, secret hoard of nuts there, too—Bertha had to dig her nails into her hands—so as not to laugh too much.

It was over at last. And: "Come and see my new coffee machine," said Bertha.

"We only have a new coffee machine once a fortnight," said Harry. Face took her arm this time; Miss Fulton bent her head and followed after.

The fire had died down in the drawing-room to a red, flickering "nest of baby phœnixes," said Face.

"Don't turn up the light for a moment. It is so lovely." And down she crouched by the fire again. She was always cold . . . "without her little red flannel jacket, of course," thought Bertha.

At that moment Miss Fulton "gave the sign."

"Have you a garden?" said the cool, sleepy voice.

This was so exquisite on her part that all Bertha could do was to obey. She crossed the room, pulled the curtains apart, and opened those long windows.

"There!" she breathed.

And the two women stood side by side looking at the slender, flowering tree. Although it was so still it seemed, like the flame of a candle, to stretch up, to point, to quiver in the bright air, to grow taller and taller as they gazed—almost to touch the rim of the round, silver moon.

How long did they stand there? Both, as it were, caught in that circle of unearthly light, understanding each other perfectly, creatures of another world, and wondering what they were to do in this one with all this blissful treasure that burned in their bosoms and dropped, in silver flowers, from their hair and hands?

For ever—for a moment? And did Miss Fulton murmur: "Yes. Just *that*." Or did Bertha dream it?

Then the light was snapped on and Face made the coffee and Harry said: "My dear Mrs. Knight, don't ask me about my baby. I never see her. I shan't feel the slightest interest in her until she has a lover," and Mug took his eye out of the conservatory for a moment and then put it under glass again and Eddie Warren drank his coffee and set down the cup with a face of anguish as though he had drunk and seen the spider.

"What I want to do is to give the young men a show. I believe London is simply teeming with first-chop, unwritten plays. What I want to say to 'em is: 'Here's the theatre. Fire ahead.'"

"You know, my dear, I am going to decorate a room for the Jacob Nathans. Oh, I am so tempted to do a fried-fish scheme, with the backs of the chairs shaped like frying pans and lovely chip potatoes embroidered all over the curtains."

"The trouble with our young writing men is that they are still too romantic. You can't put out to sea without being seasick and wanting a basin. Well, why won't they have the courage of those basins?"

"A *dreadful* poem about a *girl* who was *violated* by a beggar *without* a nose in a lit-tle wood. . . ."

Miss Fulton sank into the lowest, deepest chair and Harry handed round the cigarettes.

From the way he stood in front of her shaking the silver box and saying abruptly: "Egyptian? Turkish? Virginian? They're all mixed up," Bertha realized that she not only bored him; he really disliked her. And she decided from the way Miss Fulton said: "No, thank you, I won't smoke," that she felt it, too, and was hurt.

"Oh, Harry, don't dislike her. You are quite wrong about her. She's wonderful, wonderful. And, besides, how can you feel so differently about someone who means so much to me. I shall try to tell you when we are in bed to-night what has been happening. What she and I have shared."

At those last words something strange and almost terrifying darted into Bertha's mind. And this something blind and smiling whispered to her: "Soon these people will go. The house will be quiet—quiet. The lights will be out. And you and he will be alone together in the dark room—the warm bed. . . ."

She jumped up from her chair and ran over to the piano.

"What a pity someone does not play!" she cried. "What a pity somebody does not play."

For the first time in her life Bertha Young desired her husband.

Oh, she'd loved him—she'd been in love with him, of course, in every other way, but just not in that way. And, equally, of course, she'd understood that he was different. They'd discussed it so often. It had worried her dreadfully at first to find that she was so cold, but after a time it had not seemed to matter. They were so frank with each other—such good pals. That was the best of being modern.

But now—ardently! ardently! The word ached in her ardent body! Was this what that feeling of bliss had been leading up to? But then then—

"My dear," said Mrs. Norman Knight, "you know our shame. We are the victims of time and train. We live in Hampstead. It's been so nice."

"I'll come with you into the hall," said Bertha. "I loved having you. But you must not miss the last train. That's so awful, isn't it?"

"Have a whisky, Knight, before you go?" called Harry.

"No, thanks, old chap."

Bertha squeezed his hand for that as she shook it.

"Good night, good-bye," she cried from the top step, feeling that this self of hers was taking leave of them for ever.

When she got back into the drawing-room the others were on the move.

". . . Then you can come part of the way in my taxi."

"I shall be *so* thankful *not* to have to face *another* drive *alone* after my *dreadful* experience."

"You can get a taxi at the rank just at the end of the street. You won't have to walk more than a few yards."

"That's a comfort. I'll go and put on my coat."

Miss Fulton moved towards the hall and Bertha was following when Harry almost pushed past.

"Let me help you."

Bertha knew that he was repenting his rudeness—she let him go. What a boy he was in some ways—so impulsive—so—simple.

And Eddie and she were left by the fire.

"I *wonder* if you have seen Bilks' *new* poem called 'Table d'Hôte,'" said Eddie softly. "It's *so* wonderful. In the last Anthology. Have you got a copy? I'd *so* like to *show* it to you. It begins with an *incredibly* beautiful line: 'Why Must it Always be Tomato Soup?'"

"Yes," said Bertha. And she moved noiselessly to a table opposite the drawing-room door and Eddie glided noiselessly after her. She picked up the little book and gave it to him; they had not made a sound.

While he looked it up she turned her head towards the hall. And she saw . . . Harry with Miss Fulton's coat in his arms and Miss Fulton with her back turned to him and her head bent. He tossed the coat away, put his hands on her shoulders and turned her violently to him. His lips said: "I adore you," and Miss Fulton laid her moonbeam fingers on his cheeks and smiled her sleepy smile. Harry's nostrils quivered; his lips curled back in a hideous grin while he whispered: "To-morrow," and with her eyelids Miss Fulton said: "Yes."

"Here it is," said Eddie. "'Why Must it Always be Tomato Soup?' It's so *deeply* true, don't you feel? Tomato soup is so *dreadfully* eternal."

"If you prefer," said Harry's voice, very loud, from the hall, "I can phone you a cab to come to the door."

"Oh, no. It's not necessary," said Miss Fulton, and she came up to Bertha and gave her the slender fingers to hold.

"Good-bye. Thank you so much."

"Good-bye," said Bertha.

Miss Fulton held her hand a moment longer.

"Your lovely pear tree!" she murmured.

And then she was gone, with Eddie following, like the black cat following the grey cat.

"I'll shut up shop," said Harry, extravagantly cool and collected.

"Your lovely pear tree—pear tree—pear tree!"

Bertha simply ran over to the long windows.

"Oh, what is going to happen now?" she cried.

But the pear tree was as lovely as ever and as full of flower and as still.

[handwritten marginalia: love triangle - she is jealous and her husband and affair with pearl]

[handwritten marginalia: profound realization about realization sexuality, and discovery]

[handwritten marginalia: had none before]

Je Ne Parle Pas Français

I DO NOT KNOW why I have such a fancy for this little café. It's dirty and sad, sad. It's not as if it had anything to distinguish it from a hundred others—it hasn't; or as if the same strange types came here every day, whom one could watch from one's corner and recognize and more or less (with a strong accent on the less) get the hang of.

But pray don't imagine that those brackets are a confession of my humility before the mystery of the human soul. Not at all; I don't believe in the human soul. I never have. I believe that people are like portmanteaux—packed with certain things, started going, thrown about, tossed away, dumped down, lost and found, half emptied suddenly, or squeezed fatter than ever, until finally the Ultimate Porter swings them on to the Ultimate Train and away they rattle. . . .

Not but what these portmanteaux can be very fascinating. Oh, but very! I see myself standing in front of them, don't you know, like a Customs official.

"Have you anything to declare? Any wines, spirits, cigars, perfumes, silks?"

And the moment of hesitation as to whether I am going to be fooled just before I chalk that squiggle, and then the other moment of hesitation just after, as to whether I have been, are perhaps the two most thrilling instants in life. Yes, they are, to me.

But before I started that long and rather far-fetched and not frightfully original digression, what I meant to say quite simply was that there are no portmanteaux to be examined here because the clientele of this café, ladies and gentlemen, does not sit down. No, it stands at the counter, and it consists of a handful of workmen who come up from the river, all powdered over with white flour, lime or something, and a few soldiers, bringing with them thin, dark girls with silver rings in their ears and market baskets on their arms.

Madame is thin and dark, too, with white cheeks and white hands. In certain lights she looks quite transparent, shining out of her black shawl with an extraordinary effect. When she is not serving she sits on a stool with her face turned, always, to the window. Her dark-ringed eyes search among and follow after the people passing, but not as if she was looking for somebody. Perhaps, fifteen years ago, she was; but now the pose has become a habit. You can tell from her air of fatigue and hopelessness that she must have given them up for the last ten years, at least. . . .

And then there is the waiter. Not pathetic—decidedly not comic. Never making one of those perfectly insignificant remarks which amaze you so coming from a waiter (as though the poor wretch were a sort of cross between a coffee-pot and a wine bottle and not expected to hold so much as a drop of anything else). He is grey, flat-footed and withered, with long, brittle nails that set your nerves on edge while he scrapes up your two sous. When he is not smearing over the table or flicking at a dead fly or two, he stands with one hand on the back of a chair, in his far too long apron, and over his other arm the three-cornered dip of dirty napkin, waiting to be photographed in connection with some wretched murder. "Interior of Café where Body was Found." You've seen him hundreds of times.

Do you believe that every place has its hour of the day when it really does come alive? That's not exactly what I mean. It's more like this. There does seem to be a moment when you realize that, quite by accident, you happen to have come on to the stage at exactly the moment you were expected. Everything is arranged for you—waiting for you. Ah, master of the situation! You fill with important breath. And at the same time you smile, secretly, slyly, because Life seems to be opposed to granting you these entrances, seems indeed to be engaged in snatching them from you and making them impossible, keeping you in the wings until it is too late, in fact. . . . Just for once you've beaten the old hag.

I enjoyed one of these moments the first time I ever came in here. That's why I keep coming back, I suppose. Revisiting the scene of my triumph, or the scene of the crime where I had the old bitch by the throat for once and did what I pleased with her.

Query: Why am I so bitter against Life? And why do I see her as a rag-picker on the American cinema, shuffling along wrapped in a filthy shawl with her old claws crooked over a stick?

Answer: The direct result of the American cinema acting upon a weak mind.

Anyhow, the "short winter afternoon was drawing to a close," as they say, and I was drifting along, either going home or not going home, when I found myself in here, walking over to this seat in the corner.

I hung up my English overcoat and grey felt hat on that same peg behind me, and after I had allowed the waiter time for at least twenty photographers to snap their fill of him, I ordered a coffee.

He poured me out a glass of the familiar, purplish stuff with a green wandering light playing over it, and shuffled off, and I sat pressing my hands against the glass because it was bitterly cold outside.

Suddenly I realized that quite apart from myself, I was smiling. Slowly I raised my head and saw myself in the mirror opposite. Yes, there I sat, leaning on the table, smiling my deep, sly smile, the glass of coffee with its vague plume of steam before me and beside it the ring of white saucer with two pieces of sugar.

I opened my eyes very wide. There I had been for all eternity, as it were, and now at last I was coming to life. . . .

It was very quiet in the café. Outside, one could just see through the dusk that it had begun to snow. One could just see the shapes of horses and carts and people, soft and white, moving through the feathery air. The waiter disappeared and reappeared with an armful of straw. He strewed it over the floor from the door to the counter and round about the stove with humble, almost adoring gestures. One would not have been surprised if the door had opened and the Virgin Mary had come in, riding upon an ass, her meek hands folded over her big belly. . . .

That's rather nice, don't you think, that bit about the Virgin? It comes from the pen so gently; it has such a "dying fall." I thought so at the time and decided to make a note of it. One never knows when a little tag like that may come in useful to round off a paragraph. So, taking care to move as little as possible because the "spell" was still unbroken (you know that?), I reached over to the next table for a writing pad.

No paper or envelopes, of course. Only a morsel of pink blotting-paper, incredibly soft and limp and almost moist, like the tongue of a little dead kitten, which I've never felt.

I sat—but always underneath, in this state of expectation, rolling the little dead kitten's tongue round my finger and rolling the soft phrase round my mind while my eyes took in the girls' names and dirty jokes and drawings of bottles and cups that would not sit in the saucers, scattered over the writing pad.

They are always the same, you know. The girls always have the same names, the cups never sit in the saucers; all the hearts are stuck and tied up with ribbons.

But then, quite suddenly, at the bottom of the page, written in green ink, I fell on to that stupid, stale little phrase: *Je ne parle pas français.*

There! it had come—the moment—the *geste!* And although I was so ready, it caught me, it tumbled me over; I was simply overwhelmed. And the physical feeling was so curious, so particular. It was as if all of me, except my head and arms, all of me that was under the table, had simply dissolved, melted, turned into water. Just my head remained and two sticks of arms pressing on to the table. But, ah! the agony of that moment! How can I describe it? I didn't think of anything. I didn't even cry out to myself. Just for one moment I was not. I was Agony, Agony, Agony.

Then it passed, and the very second after I was thinking: "Good God! Am I capable of feeling as strongly as that? But I was absolutely unconscious! I hadn't a phrase to meet it with! I was overcome! I was swept off my feet! I didn't even try, in the dimmest way, to put it down!"

And up I puffed and puffed, blowing off finally with: "After

all I must be first-rate. No second-rate mind could have experienced such an intensity of feeling so . . . purely."

The waiter has touched a spill at the red stove and lighted a
bubble of gas under a spreading shade. It is no use looking out
of the window, Madame; it is quite dark now. Your white hands
hover over your dark shawl. They are like two birds that have
come home to roost. They are restless, restless. . . . You tuck them,
finally, under your warm little armpits.

Now the waiter has taken a long pole and clashed the curtains
together. "All gone," as children say.

And besides, I've no patience with people who can't let go
of things, who will follow after and cry out. When a thing's gone,
it's gone. It's over and done with. Let it go then! Ignore it, and
comfort yourself, if you do want comforting, with the thought
that you never do recover the same thing that you lose. It's always
a new thing. The moment it leaves you it's changed. Why, that's
even true of a hat you chase after; and I don't mean superficially—
I mean profoundly speaking . . . I have made it a rule of my life
never to regret and never to look back. Regret is an appalling
waste of energy, and no one who intends to be a writer can afford
to indulge in it. You can't get it into shape; you can't build on
it; it's only good for wallowing in. Looking back, of course, is
equally fatal to Art. It's keeping yourself poor. Art can't and won't
stand poverty.

Je ne parle pas français. Je ne parle pas français. All the while
I wrote that last page my other self has been chasing up and down
out in the dark there. It left me just when I began to analyse my
grand moment, dashed off distracted, like a lost dog who thinks
at last, at last, he hears the familiar step again.

"Mouse! Mouse! Where are you? Are you near? Is that you
leaning from the high window and stretching our your arms for
the wings of the shutters? Are you this soft bundle moving towards
me through the feathery snow? Are you this little girl pressing
through the swing-doors of the restaurant? Is that your dark
shadow bending forward in the cab? Where are you? Where are

you? Which way must I turn? Which way shall I run? And every moment I stand here hesitating you are farther away again. Mouse! Mouse!"

Now the poor dog has come back into the café, his tail between his legs, quite exhausted.

"It was a . . . false . . . alarm. She's nowhere . . . to . . . be seen."

"Lie down then! Lie down! Lie down!"

My name is Raoul Duquette. I am twenty-six years old and a Parisian, a true Parisian. About my family—it really doesn't matter. I have no family; I don't want any. I never think about my childhood. I've forgotten it.

In fact, there's only one memory that stands out at all. That is rather interesting because it seems to me now so very significant as regards myself from the literary point of view. It is this.

When I was about ten our laundress was an African woman, very big, very dark, with a check handkerchief over her frizzy hair. When she came to our house she always took particular notice of me, and after the clothes had been taken out of the basket she would lift me up into it and give me a rock while I held tight to the handles and screamed for joy and fright. I was tiny for my age, and pale, with a lovely little half-open mouth—I feel sure of that.

One day when I was standing at the door, watching her go, she turned round and beckoned to me, nodding and smiling in a strange secret way. I never thought of not following. She took me into a little outhouse at the end of the passage, caught me up in her arms and began kissing me. Ah, those kisses! Especially those kisses inside my ears that nearly deafened me.

When she set me down she took from her pocket a little round fried cake covered with sugar, and I reeled along the passage back to our door.

As this performance was repeated once a week it is no wonder that I remember it so vividly. Besides, from that very first afternoon, my childhood was, to put it prettily, "kissed away." I became very languid, very caressing, and greedy beyond measure. And so quickened, so sharpened, I seemed to understand everybody and be able to do what I liked with everybody.

I suppose I was in a state of more or less physical excitement, and that was what appealed to them. For all Parisians are more than half—oh, well, enough of that. And enough of my childhood, too. Bury it under a laundry basket instead of a shower of roses and *passons outre*.

I date myself from the moment that I became the tenant of a small bachelor flat on the fifth floor of a tall, not too shabby house, in a street that might or might not be discreet. Very useful, that. . . . There I emerged, came out into the light and put out my two horns with a study and a bedroom and a kitchen on my back. And real furniture planted in the rooms. In the bedroom a wardrobe with a long glass, a big bed covered with a yellow puffed-up quilt, a bed table with a marbled top and a toilet set sprinkled with tiny apples. In my study—English writing table with drawers, writing chair with leather cushions, books, armchair, side table with paper-knife and lamp on it and some nude studies on the walls. I didn't use the kitchen except to throw old papers into.

Ah, I can see myself that first evening, after the furniture men had gone and I'd managed to get rid of my atrocious old concierge—walking about on tip-toe, arranging and standing in front of the glass with my hands in my pockets and saying to that radiant vision: "I am a young man who has his own flat. I write for two newspapers. I am going in for serious literature. I am starting a career. The book that I shall bring out will simply stagger the critics. I am going to write about things that have never been touched before. I am going to make a name for myself as a writer about the submerged world. But not as others have done before me. Oh, no! Very naively, with a sort of tender humour and from the inside, as though it were all quite simple, quite natural. I see my way quite perfectly. Nobody has ever done it as I shall do it because none of the others have lived my experiences. I'm rich—I'm rich."

All the same I had no more money than I have now. It's extraordinary how one can live without money. . . . I have quantities of good clothes, silk underwear, two evening suits, four pairs of patent leather boots with light uppers, all sorts of little things, like gloves and powder boxes and a manicure set, perfumes, very good soap, and nothing is paid for. If I find myself in need of right-down cash—well, there's always an African laundress and an outhouse, and I am very frank and *bon enfant* about plenty of sugar on the little fried cake afterwards. . . .

And here I should like to put something on record. Not from any strutting conceit, but rather with a mild sense of wonder. I've never yet made the first advances to any woman. It isn't as though I've known only one class of woman—not by any means. But from little prostitutes and kept women and elderly widows and shop girls and wives of respectable men, and even advanced modern literary ladies at the most select dinners and soirées (I've been there), I've met invariably with not only the same readiness, but with the same positive invitation. It surprised me at first. I used to look across the table and think "Is that very distinguished young lady, discussing *le Kipling* with the gentleman with the brown beard, really pressing my foot?" And I was never really certain until I had pressed hers.

Curious, isn't it? I don't look at all like a maiden's dream. . . .

I am little and light with an olive skin, black eyes with long lashes, black silky hair cut short, tiny square teeth that show when I smile. My hands are supple and small. A woman in a bread shop once said to me: "You have the hands for making fine little pastries." I confess, without my clothes I am rather charming. Plump, almost like a girl, with smooth shoulders, and I wear a thin gold bracelet above my left elbow.

But, wait! Isn't it strange I should have written all that about my body and so on? It's the result of my bad life, my submerged life. I am like a little woman in a café who has to introduce herself with a handful of photographs. "Me in my chemise, coming out of an eggshell. . . . Me upside down in a swing, with a frilly behind like a cauliflower. . . ." You know the things.

If you think what I've written is merely superficial and impudent and cheap you're wrong. I'll admit it does sound so, but then it is not all. If it were, how could I have experienced what

I did when I read that stale little phrase written in green ink, in the writing-pad? That proves there's more in me and that I really am important, doesn't it? Anything a fraction less than that moment of anguish I might have put on. But no! That was real.

"Waiter, a whisky."

I hate whisky. Every time I take it into my mouth my stomach rises against it, and the stuff they keep here is sure to be particularly vile. I only ordered it because I am going to write about an Englishman. We French are incredibly old-fashioned and out of date still in some ways. I wonder I didn't ask him at the same time for a pair of tweed knickerbockers, a pipe, some long teeth and a set of ginger whiskers.

"Thanks, *mon vieux*. You haven't got perhaps a set of ginger whiskers?"

"No, monsieur," he answers sadly. "We don't sell American drinks."

And having smeared a corner of the table he goes back to have another couple of dozen taken by artificial light.

Ugh! The smell of it! And the sickly sensation when one's throat contracts.

"It's bad stuff to get drunk on," says Dick Harmon, turning his little glass in his fingers and smiling his slow, dreaming smile. So he gets drunk on it slowly and dreamily and at a certain moment begins to sing very low, very low, about a man who walks up and down trying to find a place where he can get some dinner.

Ah! how I loved that song, and how I loved the way he sang it, slowly, slowly, in a dark, soft voice:

> There was man
> Walked up and down
> To get a dinner in the town. . . .

It seemed to hold, in its gravity and muffled measure, all those tall grey buildings, those fogs, those endless streets, those sharp shadows of policemen that mean England.

And then—the subject! The lean, starved creature walking up and down with every house barred against him because he had no "home." How extraordinarily English that is. . . . I remember that it ended where he did at last "find a place" and ordered a little cake of fish, but when he asked for bread the waiter cried contemptuously, in a loud voice: "We don't serve bread with one fish ball."

What more do you want? How profound those songs are! There is the whole psychology of a people; and how un-French— how un-French!

"Once more, Deeck, once more!" I would plead, clasping my hands and making a pretty mouth at him. He was perfectly content to sing it for ever.

There again. Even with Dick. It was he who made the first advances.

I met him at an evening party given by the editor of a new review. It was a very select, very fashionable affair. One or two of the older men were there and the ladies were extremely *comme il faut*. They sat on cubist sofas in full evening dress and allowed us to hand them thimbles of cherry brandy and to talk to them about their poetry. For, as far as I can remember, they were all poetesses.

It was impossible not to notice Dick. He was the only Englishman present, and instead of circulating gracefully around the room as we all did he stayed in one place leaning against the wall, his hands in his pockets, that dreamy half smile on his lips, and replying in excellent French in his low, soft voice to anybody who spoke to him.

"Who is he?"

"An Englishman. From London. A writer. And he is making a special study of modern French literature."

That was enough for me. My little book, *False Coins*, had just been published. I was a young, serious writer who was making a special study of modern English literature.

But I really had not time to fling my line before he said, giving himself a soft shake, coming right out of the water after the bait, as it were: "Won't you come and see me at my hotel? Come about five o'clock and we can have a talk before going out to dinner."

"Enchanted!"

I was so deeply, deeply flattered that I had to leave him then and there to preen and preen myself before the cubist sofas. What a catch! An Englishman, reserved, serious, making a special study of French literature. . . .

That same night a copy of *False Coins* with a carefully cordial inscription was posted off, and a day or two later we did dine together and spent the evening talking.

Talking—but not only of literature. I discovered to my relief that it wasn't necessary to keep to the tendency of the modern novel, the need of a new form, or the reason why our young men appeared to be just missing it. Now and again, as if by accident, I threw in a card that seemed to have nothing to do with the game, just to see how he'd take it. But each time he gathered it into his hands with his dreamy look and smile unchanged. Perhaps he murmured: "That's very curious." But not as if it were curious at all.

That calm acceptance went to my head at last. It fascinated me. It led me on and on till I threw every card that I possessed at him and sat back and watched him arrange them in his hand.

"Very curious and interesting. . . ."

By that time we were both fairly drunk, and he began to sing his song very soft, very low, about the man who walked up and down seeking his dinner.

But I was quite breathless at the thought of what I had done. I had shown somebody both sides of my life. Told him everything as sincerely and truthfully as I could. Taken immense pains to explain things about my submerged life that really were disgusting and never could possibly see the light of literary day. On the whole I had made myself out far worse than I was—more boastful, more cynical, more calculating.

And there sat the man I had confided in, singing to himself and smiling. . . . It moved me so that real tears came into my eyes. I saw them glittering on my long silky lashes—so charming.

After that I took Dick about with me everywhere, and he came to my flat, and sat in the arm-chair, very indolent, playing with the paper-knife. I cannot think why his indolence and dreaminess always gave me the impression he had been to sea. And all his leisurely slow ways seemed to be allowing for the movement of the ship. This impression was so strong that often when we were together and he got up and left a little woman just when she did not expect him to get up and leave her, but quite the contrary, I would explain: "He can't help it, Baby. He has to go back to his ship." And I believed it far more than she did.

All the while we were together Dick never went with a woman. I sometimes wondered whether he wasn't completely innocent. Why didn't I ask him? Because I never did ask him anything about himself. But late one night he took out his pocket-book and a photograph dropped out of it. I picked it up and glanced at it before I gave it to him. It was of a woman. Not quite young. Dark, handsome, wild-looking, but so full in every line of a kind of haggard pride that even if Dick had not stretched out so quickly I wouldn't have looked longer.

"Out of my sight, you little perfumed fox-terrier of a Frenchman," said she.

(In my very worst moments my nose reminds me of a fox-terrier's.)

"That is my Mother," said Dick, putting up the pocketbook.

But if he had not been Dick I should have been tempted to cross myself, just for fun.

This is how we parted. As we stood outside his hotel one night waiting for the concierge to release the catch of the outer door, he said, looking up at the sky: "I hope it will be fine to-morrow. I am leaving for England in the morning."

"You're not serious."

"Perfectly. I have to get back. I've some work to do that I can't manage here."

"But—but have you made all your preparations?"

"Preparations?" He almost grinned. "I've none to make."

"But—*enfin,* Dick, England is not the other side of the boulevard."

"It isn't much farther off," said he. "Only a few hours, you know." The door cracked open.

"Ah, I wish I'd known at the beginning of the evening!"

I felt hurt. I felt as a woman must feel when a man takes out his watch and remembers an appointment that cannot possibly concern her, except that its claim is the stronger. "Why didn't you tell me?"

He put out his hand and stood, lightly swaying upon the step as though the whole hotel were his ship, and the anchor weighed.

"I forgot. Truly I did. But you'll write, won't you? Good night, old chap. I'll be over again one of these days."

And then I stood on the shore alone, more like a little fox-terrier than ever. . . .

"But after all it was you who whistled to me, you who asked me to come! What a spectacle I've cut wagging my tail and leaping round you, only to be left like this while the boat sails off in its slow, dreamy way. . . . Curse these English! No, this is too insolent altogether. Who do you imagine I am? A little paid guide to the night pleasures of Paris? . . . No, monsieur. I am a young writer, very serious, and extremely interested in modern English literature. And I have been insulted—insulted."

Two days after came a long, charming letter from him, written in French that was a shade too French, but saying how he missed me and counted on our friendship, on keeping in touch.

I read it standing in front of the (unpaid for) wardrobe mirror. It was early morning. I wore a blue kimono embroidered with white birds and my hair was still wet; it lay on my forehead, wet and gleaming.

"Portrait of Madame Butterfly," said I, "on hearing of the arrival of *ce cher Pinkerton*."

According to the books I should have felt immensely relieved and delighted. ". . . Going over to the window he drew apart the curtains and looked out at the Paris trees, just breaking into buds and green. . . . Dick! Dick! My English friend!"

I didn't. I merely felt a little sick. Having been up for my first ride in an aeroplane I didn't want to go up again, just now.

*   *   *

That passed, and months after, in the winter, Dick wrote that he was coming back to Paris to stay indefinitely. Would I take rooms for him? He was bringing a woman friend with him.

Of course I would. Away the little fox-terrier flew. It happened most usefully, too; for I owed much money at the hotel where I took my meals, and two English people requiring rooms for an indefinite time was an excellent sum on account.

Perhaps I did rather wonder, as I stood in the larger of the two rooms with Madame, saying "Admirable," what the woman friend would be like, but only vaguely. Either she would be very severe, flat back and front, or she would be tall, fair, dressed in mignonette green, name—Daisy, and smelling of rather sweetish lavender water.

You see, by this time, according to my rule of not looking back, I had almost forgotten Dick. I even got the tune of his song about the unfortunate man a little bit wrong when I tried to hum it. . . .

I very nearly did not turn up at the station after all. I had arranged to, and had, in fact, dressed with particular care for the occasion. For I intended to take a new line with Dick this time. No more confidences and tears on eyelashes. No, thank you!

"Since you left Paris," said I, knotting my black silver-spotted tie in the (also unpaid for) mirror over the mantelpiece, "I have been very successful, you know. I have two more books in preparation, and then I have written a serial story, 'Wrong Doors,' which is just on the point of publication and will bring me in a lot of money. And then my little book of poems," I cried, seizing the clothesbrush and brushing the velvet collar of my new indigo-blue overcoat, "my little book—*Left Umbrellas*—really did create," and I laughed and waved the brush, "an immense sensation!"

It was impossible not to believe this of the person who surveyed himself finally, from top to toe, drawing on his soft grey gloves. He was looking the part; he was the part.

That gave me an idea. I took out my notebook, and still in

full view, jotted down a note or two. . . . How can one look the part and not be the part? Or be the part and not look it? Isn't looking—being? Or being—looking? At any rate who is to say that it is not? . . .

This seemed to be extraordinarily profound at the time, and quite new. But I confess that something did whisper as, smiling, I put up the notebook: "You—literary? you look as though you've taken down a bet on a racecourse!" But I didn't listen. I went out, shutting the door of the flat with a soft, quick pull so as not to warn the concierge of my departure, and ran down the stairs quick as a rabbit for the same reason.

But ah! the old spider. She was too quick for me. She let me run down the last little ladder of the web and then she pounced. "One moment. One little moment, Monsieur," she whispered, odiously confidential. "Come in. Come in." And she beckoned with a dripping soup ladle. I went to the door, but that was not good enough. Right inside and the door shut before she would speak.

There are two ways of managing your concierge if you haven't any money. One is—to take the high hand, make her your enemy, bluster, refuse to discuss anything; the other is—to keep in with her, butter her up to the two knots of the black rag tying up her jaws, pretend to confide in her, and rely on her to arrange with the gas man and to put off the landlord.

I had tried the second. But both are equally detestable and unsuccessful. At any rate whichever you're trying is the worse, the impossible one.

It was the landlord this time. . . . Imitation of the landlord by the concierge threatening to toss me out. . . . Imitation of the concierge by the concierge taming the wild bull. . . . Imitation of the landlord rampant again, breathing in the concierge's face. I was the concierge. No, it was too nauseous. And all the while the black pot on the gas ring babbling away, stewing out the hearts and livers of every tenant in the place.

"Ah!" I cried, staring at the clock on the mantelpiece, and then, realizing that it didn't go, striking my forehead as though the idea had nothing to do with it. "Madame, I have a very important appointment with the director of my newspaper at nine-thirty. Perhaps to-morrow I shall be able to give you . . ."

Out, out. And down the métro and squeezed into a full carriage. The more the better. Everybody was one bolster the more between me and the concierge. I was radiant.

"Ah! pardon, Monsieur!" said the tall charming creature in black with a big full bosom and a great bunch of violets dropping from it. As the train swayed it thrust the bouquet right into my eyes. "Ah! pardon, Monsieur!"

But I looked up at her, smiling mischievously.

"There is nothing I love more, Madame, than flowers on a balcony."

At the very moment of speaking I caught sight of the huge man in a fur coat against whom my charmer was leaning. He poked his head over her shoulder and he went white to the nose; in fact his nose stood out a sort of cheese green.

"What was that you said to my wife?"

Gare Saint Lazare saved me. But you'll own that even as the author of *False Coins,* 'Wrong Doors,' *Left Umbrellas,* and two in preparation, it was not too easy to go on my triumphant way.

At length, after countless trains had steamed into my mind, and countless Dick Harmons had come rolling towards me, the real train came. The little knot of us waiting at the barrier moved up close, craned forward, and broke into cries as though we were some kind of many-headed monster, and Paris behind us nothing but a great trap we had set to catch these sleepy innocents.

Into the trap they walked and were snatched and taken off to be devoured. Where was my prey?

"Good God!" My smile and my lifted hand fell together. For one terrible moment I thought this was the woman of the photograph, Dick's mother, walking towards me in Dick's coat and hat. In the effort—and you saw what an effort it was—to smile, his lips curled in just the same way and he made for me, haggard and wild and proud.

What had happened? What could have changed him like this? Should I mention it?

I waited for him and was even conscious of venturing a fox-terrier wag or two to see if he could possibly respond, in the way I said: "Good evening, Dick! How are you, old chap? All right?"

"All right. All right." He almost gasped. "You've got the rooms?"

Twenty times, good God! I saw it all. Light broke on the dark waters and my sailor hadn't been drowned. I almost turned a somersault with amusement.

It was nervousness, of course. It was embarrassment. It was the famous English seriousness. What fun I was going to have! I could have hugged him.

"Yes, I've got the rooms," I nearly shouted. "But where is Madame?"

"She's been looking after the luggage," he panted. "Here she comes, now."

Not this baby walking beside the old porter as though he were her nurse and had just lifted her out of her ugly perambulator while he trundled the boxes on it.

"And she's not Madame," said Dick, drawling suddenly.

At that moment she caught sight of him and hailed him with her minute muff. She broke away for her nurse and ran up and said something, very quick, in English; but he replied in French: "Oh, very well. I'll manage."

But before he turned to the porter he indicated me with a vague wave and muttered something. We were introduced. She held out her hand in that strange boyish way Englishwomen do, and standing very straight in front of me with her chin raised and making—she too—the effort of her life to control her preposterous excitement, she said, wringing my hand (I'm sure she didn't know it was mine), *Je ne parle pas français*.

"But I'm sure you do," I answered, so tender, so reassuring, I might have been a dentist about to draw her first little milk tooth.

"Of course she does." Dick swerved back to us. "Here, can't we get a cab or taxi or something? We don't want to stay in this cursed station all night. Do we?"

This was so rude that it took me a moment to recover; and he must have noticed, for he flung his arm round my shoulder in the old way, saying: "Ah, forgive me, old chap. But we've had such a loathsome, hideous journey. We've taken years to come. Haven't we?" To her. But she did not answer. She bent her head and began stroking her grey muff; she walked beside us stroking her gray muff all the way.

"Have I been wrong?" thought I. "Is this simply a case of frenzied impatience on their part? Are they merely 'in need of a bed,' as we say? Have they been suffering agonies on the journey? Sitting, perhaps, very close and warm under the same travelling rug?" and so on and so on while the driver strapped on the boxes. That done—

"Look here, Dick. I go home by métro. Here is the address of your hotel. Everything is arranged. Come and see me as soon as you can."

Upon my life I thought he was going to faint. He went white to the lips.

"But you're coming back with us," he cried. "I thought it was all settled. Of course you're coming back. You're not going to leave us." No, I gave it up. It was too difficult, too English for me.

"Certainly, certainly. Delighted. I only thought, perhaps . . ."

"You must come!" said Dick to the little fox-terrier. And again he made that big awkward turn towards her.

"Get in, Mouse."

And Mouse got in the black hole and sat stroking Mouse II and not saying a word.

Away we jolted and rattled like three little dice that life had decided to have a fling with.

I had insisted on taking the flap seat facing them because I would not have missed for anything those occasional flashing glimpses I had as we broke through the white circles of lamplight.

They revealed Dick, sitting far back in his corner, his coat collar turned up, his hands thrust in his pockets, and his broad dark hat shading him as if it were a part of him—a sort of wing he hid under. They showed her, sitting up very straight, her lovely little face more like a drawing than a real face—every line was so full of meaning and so sharp cut against the swimming dark.

For Mouse was beautiful. She was exquisite, but so fragile and fine that each time I looked at her it was as if for the first time. She came upon you with the same kind of shock that you feel when you have been drinking tea out of a thin innocent cup and suddenly, at the bottom, you see a tiny creature, half butterfly, half woman, bowing to you with her hands in her sleeves.

As far as I could make out she had dark hair and blue or black eyes. Her long lashes and the two little feathers traced above were most important.

She wore a long dark cloak such as one sees in old-fashioned pictures of Englishwomen abroad. Where her arms came out of it there was grey fur—fur round her neck, too, and her close-fitting cap was furry.

"Carrying out the mouse idea," I decided.

Ah, but how intriguing it was—how intriguing! Their excitement came nearer and nearer to me, while I ran out to meet it, bathed in it, flung myself far out of my depth, until at last I was as hard put to it to keep control as they.

But what I wanted to do was to behave in the most extraordinary fashion—like a clown. To start singing, with large extravagant gestures, to point out of the window and cry: "We are now passing, ladies and gentlemen, one of the sights for which *notre Paris* is justly famous," to jump out of the taxi while it was going, climb over the roof and dive in by another door; to hang out of the window and look for the hotel through the wrong end of a broken telescope, which was also a peculiarly ear-splitting trumpet.

I watched myself do all this, you understand, and even managed to applaud in a private way by putting my gloved hands gently together, while I said to Mouse: "And is this your first visit to Paris?"

"Yes, I've not been here before."

"Ah, then you have a great deal to see."

175

And I was just going to touch lightly upon the objects of interest and the museums when we wrenched to a stop.

Do you know—it's very absurd—but as I pushed open the door for them and followed up the stairs to the bureau on the landing I felt somehow that this hotel was mine.

There was a vase of flowers on the window sill of the bureau and I even went so far as to re-arrange a bud or two and to stand off and note the effect while the manageress welcomed them. And when she turned to me and handed me the keys (the *garçon* was hauling up the boxes) and said: "Monsieur Duquette will show you your rooms"—I had a longing to tap Dick on the arm with a key and say, very confidentially: "Look here, old chap. As a friend of mine I'll be only too willing to make a slight reduction . . ."

Up and up we climbed. Round and round. Past an occasional pair of boots (why is it one never sees an attractive pair of boots outside a door?). Higher and higher.

"I'm afraid they're rather high up," I murmured idiotically. "But I chose them because . . ."

They so obviously did not care why I chose them that I went no further. They accepted everything. They did not expect anything to be different. This was just part of what they were going through—that was how I analysed it.

"Arrived at last." I ran from one side of the passage to the other, turning on the lights, explaining.

"This one I thought for you, Dick. The other is larger and it has a little dressing-room in the alcove."

My "proprietary" eye noted the clean towels and covers, and the bed linen embroidered in red cotton. I thought them rather charming rooms, sloping, full of angles, just the sort of rooms one would expect to find if one had not been to Paris before.

Dick dashed his hat down on the bed.

"Oughtn't I to help that chap with the boxes?" he asked—nobody.

"Yes, you ought," replied Mouse, "they're dreadfully heavy."

And she turned to me with the first glimmer of a smile: "Books, you know." Oh, he darted such a strange look at her before he rushed out. And he not only helped, he must have torn the box off the *garçon's* back, for he staggered back, carrying one, dumped it down and then fetched in the other.

"That's yours, Dick," said she.

"Well, you don't mind it standing here for the present, do you?" he asked, breathless, breathing hard (the box must have been tremendously heavy). He pulled out a handful of money. "I suppose I ought to pay this chap."

The *garçon*, standing by, seemed to think so too.

"And will you require anything further, Monsieur?"

"No! No!" said Dick impatiently.

But at that Mouse stepped forward. She said, too deliberately, not looking at Dick, with her quaint clipped English accent: "Yes, I'd like some tea. Tea for three."

And suddenly she raised her muff as though her hands were clasped inside it, and she was telling the pale, sweaty *garçon* by that action that she was at the end of her resources, that she cried out to him to save her with "Tea. Immediately!"

This seemed to me so amazingly in the picture, so exactly the gesture and cry that one would expect (though I couldn't have imagined it) to be wrung out of an Englishwoman faced with a great crisis, that I was almost tempted to hold up my hand and protest.

"No! No! Enough. Enough. Let us leave off there. At the word—tea. For really, really, you've filled your greediest subscriber so full that he will burst if he has to swallow another word."

It even pulled Dick up. Like someone who has been unconscious for a long long time he turned slowly to Mouse and slowly looked at her with his tired, haggard eyes, and murmured with the echo of his dreamy voice: "Yes. That's a good idea." And then: "You must be tired, Mouse. Sit down."

She sat down in a chair with lace tabs on the arms; he leaned against the bed, and I established myself on a straight-backed chair, crossed my legs and brushed some imaginary dust off the knees of my trousers. (The Parisian at his ease.)

There came a tiny pause. Then he said: "Won't you take off your coat, Mouse?"

"No, thanks. Not just now."

Were they going to ask me? Or should I hold up my hand and call out in a baby voice: "It's my turn to be asked."

No, I shouldn't. They didn't ask me.

The pause became a silence. A real silence.

". . . Come, my Parisian fox-terrier! Amuse these sad English! It's no wonder they are such a nation for dogs."

But, after all—why should I? It was not my "job," as they would say. Nevertheless, I made a vivacious little bound at Mouse.

"What a pity it is that you did not arrive by daylight. There is such a charming view from these two windows. You know, the hotel is on a corner and each window looks down an immensely long, straight street."

"Yes," said she.

"Not that that sounds very charming," I laughed. "But there is so much animation—so many absurd little boys on bicycles and people hanging out of windows and—oh, well, you'll see for yourself in the morning. . . . Very amusing. Very animated."

"Oh, yes," said she.

If the pale, sweaty *garçon* had not come in at that moment, carrying the tea-tray high on one hand as if the cups were cannonballs and he a heavy weight lifter on the cinema. . . .

He managed to lower it on to a round table.

"Bring the table over here," said Mouse. The waiter seemed to be the only person she cared to speak to. She took her hands out of her muff, drew off her gloves and flung back the old-fashioned cape.

"Do you take milk and sugar?"

"No milk, thank you, and no sugar."

I went over for mine like a little gentleman. She poured out another cup.

"That's for Dick."

And the faithful fox-terrier carried it across to him and laid it at his feet, as it were.

"Oh, thanks," said Dick.

And then I went back to my chair and she sank back in hers.

But Dick was off again. He stared wildly at the cup of tea for a moment, glanced round him, put it down on the bed-table, caught up his hat and stammered at full gallop: "Oh, by the way, do you mind posting a letter for me? I want to get it off by to-night's post. I must. It's very urgent. . . ." Feeling her eyes on him, he flung: "It's to my mother." To me: "I won't be long. I've got everything I want. But it must go off to-night. You don't mind? It . . . it won't take any time."

"Of course I'll post it. Delighted."

"Won't you drink your tea first?" suggested Mouse softly.

. . . Tea? Tea? Yes, of course. Tea. . . . A cup of tea on the bed-table. . . . In his racing dream he flashed the brightest, most charming smile at his little hostess.

"No, thanks. Not just now."

And still hoping it would not be any trouble to me he went out of the room and closed the door, and we heard him cross the passage.

I scalded myself with mine in my hurry to take the cup back to the table and to say as I stood there: "You must forgive me if I am impertinent . . . if I am too frank. But Dick hasn't tried to disguise it—has he? There is something the matter. Can I help?"

(Soft music. Mouse gets up, walks the stage for a moment or so before she returns to her chair and pours him out, oh, such a brimming, such a burning cup that the tears come into the friend's eyes while he sips—while he drains it to the bitter dregs. . . .)

I had time to do all this before she replied. First she looked in the teapot, filled it with hot water, and stirred it with a spoon.

"Yes, there is something the matter. No, I'm afraid you can't help, thank you." Again I got that glimmer of a smile. "I'm awfully sorry. It must be horrid for you."

Horrid, indeed! Ah, why couldn't I tell her that it was months and months since I had been so entertained?

"But you are suffering," I ventured softly, as though that was what I could not bear to see.

She didn't deny it. She nodded and bit her under-lip and I thought I saw her chin tremble.

"And there is really nothing I can do?' More softly still.

She shook her head, pushed back the table and jumped up.

"Oh, it will be all right soon," she breathed, walking over to the dressing table and standing with her back towards me. "It will be all right. It can't go on like this."

"But of course it can't," I agreed, wondering whether it would look heartless if I lit a cigarette; I had a sudden longing to smoke.

In some way she saw my hand move to my breast pocket, half draw out my cigarette case and put it back again, for the next thing she said was: "Matches . . . in . . . candlestick. I noticed them."

And I heard from her voice that she was crying.

"Ah! thank you. Yes. Yes. I've found them." I lighted my cigarette and walked up and down, smoking.

It was so quiet it might have been two o'clock in the morning. It was so quiet you heard the boards creak and pop as one does in a house in the country. I smoked the whole cigarette and stabbed the end into my saucer before Mouse turned round and came back to the table.

"Isn't Dick being rather a long time?"

"You are very tired. I expect you want to go to bed," I said kindly. (And pray don't mind me if you do, said my mind.)

"But isn't he being a very long time?" she insisted.

I shrugged. "He is, rather."

Then I saw she looked at me strangely. She was listening.

"He's been gone ages," she said, and she went with little light steps to the door, opened it, and crossed the passage into his room.

I waited. I listened too, now. I couldn't have borne to miss a word. She had left the door open. I stole across the room and looked after her. Dick's door was open, too. But—there wasn't a word to miss.

You know I had the mad idea that they were kissing in that quiet room—a long comfortable kiss. One of those kisses that not only puts one's grief to bed, but nurses it and warms it and tucks it up and keeps it fast enfolded until it is sleeping sound. Ah! how good that is.

It was over at last. I heard some one move and tip-toed away.

It was Mouse. She came back. She felt her way into the room carrying the letter for me. But it wasn't in an envelope; it was just a sheet of paper and she held it by the corner as though it was still wet.

Her head was bent so low—so tucked in her furry collar that I hadn't a notion—until she let the paper fall and almost fell herself on to the floor by the side of the bed, leaned her cheek against it, flung out her hands as though the last of her poor little weapons was gone and now she let herself be carried away, washed out into the deep water.

Flash! went my mind. Dick has shot himself, and then a succession of flashes while I rushed in, saw the body, head unharmed, small blue hole over temple, roused hotel, arranged funeral, attended funeral, closed cab, new morning coat. . . .

I stooped down and picked up the paper and would you believe it—so ingrained is my Parisian sense of *comme il faut*—I murmured "pardon" before I read it.

"Mouse, my little Mouse,

It's no good. It's impossible. I can't see it through. Oh, I do love you. I do love you, Mouse, but I can't hurt her. People have been hurting her all her life. I simply dare not give her this final blow. You see, though she's stronger than both of us, she's so frail and proud. It would kill her—kill her, Mouse. And, oh God, I can't kill my mother! Not even for you. Not even for us. You do see that—don't you?

It all seemed so possible when we talked and planned, but the very moment the train started it was all over. I felt her drag me back to her—calling. I can hear her now as I write. And she's alone and she doesn't know. A man would have to be a devil to tell her and I'm not a devil, Mouse. She mustn't know. Oh, Mouse, somewhere, somewhere in you don't you agree? It's all so unspeakably awful that I don't know if I want to go or not. Do I? Or is Mother just dragging me? I don't know. My head is too tired. Mouse, Mouse—what will you do? But I can't think of that either. I dare not. I'd break down. And I must not break down. All I've got to do is—just to tell you this and go. I couldn't have gone off without telling you. You'd have been frightened. And you must not be frightened. You won't—will you? I can't bear— but no more of that. And don't write. I should not have the courage to answer your letters and the sight of your spidery hand- writing—

Forgive me. Don't love me any more. Yes. Love me. Love me. Dick."

What do you think of that? Wasn't that a rare find? My relief at his not having shot himself was mixed with a wonderful sense of elation. I was even—more than even with my "that's very curious and interesting" Englishman. . . .

She wept so strangely. With her eyes shut, with her face quite calm except for the quivering eyelids. The tears pearled down her cheeks and she let them fall.

But feeling my glance upon her she opened her eyes and saw me holding the letter.

"You've read it?"

Her voice was quite calm, but it was not her voice any more. It was like the voice you might imagine coming out of a tiny, cold sea-shell swept high and dry at last by the salt tide. . . .

I nodded, quite overcome, you understand, and laid the letter down.

"It's incredible! incredible!" I whispered.

At that she got up from the floor, walked over to the wash- stand, dipped her handkerchief into the jug and sponged her eyes, saying: "Oh, no. It's not incredible at all." And still pressing the wet ball to her eyes she came back to me, to her chair with the lace tabs, and sank into it.

"I knew all along, of course," said the cold, salty little voice. "From the very moment that we started. I felt it all through me, but I still went on hoping—" and here she took the handkerchief down and gave me a final glimmer—"as one so stupidly does, you know."

"As one does."

Silence.

"But what will you do? You'll go back? You'll see him?"

That made her sit right up and stare across at me.

"What an extraordinary idea!" she said, more coldly than ever. "Of course I shall not dream of seeing him. As for going back—that is quite out of the question. I can't go back."

"But . . ."

"It's impossible. For one thing all my friends think I am married."

I put out my hand—"Ah, my poor little friend."

But she shrank away. (False move.)

Of course there was one question that had been at the back of my mind all this time. I hated it.

"Have you any money?"

"Yes, I have twenty pounds—here," and she put her hand on her breast. I bowed. It was a great deal more than I had expected.

"And what are your plans?"

Yes, I know. My question was the most clumsy, the most idiotic one I could have put. She had been so tame, so confiding, letting me, at any rate spiritually speaking, hold her tiny quivering body in one hand and stroke her furry head—and now, I'd thrown her away. Oh, I could have kicked myself.

She stood up. "I have no plans. But—it's very late. You must go now, please."

How could I get her back? I wanted her back. I swear I was not acting then.

"Do feel that I am your friend," I cried. "You will let me come to-morrow, early? You will let me look after you a little—take care of you a little? You'll use me just as you think fit?"

I succeeded. She came out of her hole . . . timid . . . but she came out.

"Yes, you're very kind. Yes. Do come to-morrow. I shall be glad. It makes things rather difficult because—" and again I clasped her boyish hand—*"je ne parle pas français."*

Not until I was half-way down the boulevard did it come over me—the full force of it.

Why, they were suffering . . . those two . . . really suffering. I have seen two people suffer as I don't suppose I ever shall again. . . .

Of course you know what to expect. You anticipate, fully, what I am going to write. It wouldn't be me, otherwise.

I never went near the place again.

Yes, I still owe that considerable amount for lunches and dinners, but that's beside the mark. It's vulgar to mention it in the same breath with the fact that I never saw Mouse again.

Naturally, I intended to. Started out—got to the door—wrote and tore up letters—did all those things. But I simply could not make the final effort.

Even now I don't fully understand why. Of course I knew that I couldn't have kept it up. That had a great deal to do with it. But you would have thought, putting it at its lowest, curiosity couldn't have kept my fox-terrier nose away . . .

Je ne parle pas français. That was her swan song for me.

But how she makes me break my rule. Oh, you've seen for yourself, but I could give you countless examples.

. . . Evenings, when I sit in some gloomy café, and an automatic piano starts playing a "mouse" tune (there are dozens of tunes that evoke just her) I begin to dream things like . . .

A little house on the edge of the sea, somewhere far, far away. A girl outside in a frock rather like Red Indian women wear, hailing a light, barefoot boy who runs up from the beach.

"What have you got?"

"A fish." I smile and give it to her.

. . . The same girl, the same boy, different costumes—sitting at an open window, eating fruit and leaning out and laughing.

"All the wild strawberries are for you, Mouse. I won't touch one."

. . . A wet night. They are going home together under an umbrella. They stop on the door to press their wet cheeks together.

And so on and so on until some dirty old gallant comes up to my table and sits opposite and begins to grimace and yap. Until I hear myself saying: "But I've got the little girl for you, *mon vieux*. So little . . . so tiny." I kiss the tips of my fingers and lay them upon my heart. "I give you my word of honour as a gentleman, a writer, serious, young, and extremely interested in modern English literature."

I must go. I must go. I reach down my coat and hat. Madame knows me. "You haven't dined yet?" she smiles.

"No, not yet, Madame."

Sun and Moon

IN THE AFTERNOON the chairs came, a whole big cart full of little gold ones with their legs in the air. And then the flowers came. When you stared down from the balcony at the people carrying them the flower pots looked like funny awfully nice hats nodding up the path.

Moon thought they were hats. She said: "Look. There's a man wearing a palm on his head." But she never knew the difference between real things and not real ones.

There was nobody to look after Sun and Moon. Nurse was helping Annie alter Mother's dress which was much-too-long-and-tight-under-the-arms and Mother was running all over the house and telephoning Father to be sure not to forget things. She only had time to say: "Out of my way, children!"

They kept out of her way—at any rate Sun did. He did so hate being sent stumping back to the nursery. It didn't matter about Moon. If she got tangled in people's legs they only threw her up and shook her till she squeaked. But Sun was too heavy for that. He was so heavy that the fat man who came to dinner on Sundays used to say: "Now, young man, let's try to lift you." And then he'd put his thumbs under Sun's arms and groan and try and give it up at last saying: "He's a perfect little ton of bricks!"

Nearly all the furniture was taken out of the dining-room. The big piano was put in a corner and then there came a row of flower pots and then there came the goldy chairs. That was for the concert. When Sun looked in a white faced man sat at the piano—not playing, but banging at it and then looking inside. He had a bag of tools on the piano and he had stuck his hat on a statue against the wall. Sometimes he just started to play and then he jumped up again and looked inside. Sun hoped he wasn't the concert.

But of course the place to be in was the kitchen. There was a man helping in a cap like a blancmange, and their real cook, Minnie, was all red in the face and laughing. Not cross at all. She gave them each an almond finger and lifted them up on to the flour bin so that they could watch the wonderful things she and the man were making for supper. Cook brought in the things and he put them on dishes and trimmed them. Whole fishes, with their heads and eyes and tails still on, he sprinkled with red and green and yellow bits; he made squiggles all over the jellies, he stuck a collar on a ham and put a very thin sort of a fork in it; he dotted almonds and tiny round biscuits on the creams. And more and more things kept coming.

"Ah, but you haven't seen the ice pudding," said Cook. "Come along." Why was she being so nice, thought Sun as she gave them each a hand. And they looked into the refrigerator.

Oh! Oh! Oh! It was a little house. It was a little pink house with white snow on the roof and green windows and a brown door and stuck in the door there was a nut for a handle.

When Sun saw the nut he felt quite tired and had to lean against Cook.

"Let me touch it. Just let me put my finger on the roof," said Moon, dancing. She always wanted to touch all the food. Sun didn't.

"Now, my girl, look sharp with the table," said Cook as the housemaid came in.

"It's a picture, Min," said Nellie. "Come along and have a look." So they all went into the dining-room. Sun and Moon were almost frightened. They wouldn't go up to the table at first; they just stood at the door and made eyes at it.

It wasn't real night yet but the blinds were down in the dining-room and the lights turned on—and all the lights were red roses. Red ribbons and bunches of roses tied up the table at the corners. In the middle was a lake with rose petals floating on it.

"That's where the ice pudding is to be," said Cook.

Two silver lions with wings had fruit on their backs, and the salt cellars were tiny birds drinking out of basins.

And all the winking glasses and shining plates and sparkling knives and forks—and all the food. And the little red table napkins made into roses. . . .

"Are people going to eat the food?" asked Sun.

"I should just think they were," laughed Cook, laughing with Nellie. Moon laughed, too; she always did the same as other people. But Sun didn't want to laugh. Round and round he walked with his hands behind his back. Perhaps he never would have stopped if Nurse hadn't called suddenly: "Now then, children. It's high time you were washed and dressed." And they were marched off to the nursery.

While they were being unbuttoned Mother looked in with a white thing over her shoulders; she was rubbing stuff on her face.

"I'll ring for them when I want them, Nurse, and then they can just come down and be seen and go back again," said she.

Sun was undressed, first nearly to his skin, and dressed again in a white shirt with red and white daisies speckled on it, breeches with strings at the sides and braces that came over, white socks and red shoes.

"Now you're in your Russian costume," said Nurse, flattening down his fringe.

"Am I?" said Sun.

"Yes. Sit quiet in that chair and watch your little sister."

Moon took ages. When she had her socks put on she pretended to fall back on the bed and waved her legs at Nurse as she always did, and every time Nurse tried to make her curls with a finger and a wet brush she turned round and asked Nurse to show her the photo on her brooch or something like that. But at last she was finished too. Her dress stuck out, with fur on it, all white; there was even fluffy stuff on the legs of her drawers. Her shoes were white with big blobs on them.

"There you are, my lamb," said Nurse. "And you look like a sweet little cherub of a picture of a powder-puff." Nurse rushed to the door. "Ma'am, one moment."

Mother came in again with half her hair down.

"Oh," she cried. "What a picture!"

"Isn't she," said Nurse.

And Moon held out her skirts by the tips and dragged one of her feet. Sun didn't mind people not noticing him—much. . . .

After that they played clean tidy games up at the table while Nurse stood at the door, and when the carriages began to come and the sound of laughter and voices and soft rustlings came from down below she whispered: "Now then, children, stay where you are." Moon kept jerking the table cloth so that it all hung down her side and Sun hadn't any—and then she pretended she didn't do it on purpose.

At last the bell rang. Nurse pounced at them with the hair brush, flattened his fringe, made her bow stand on end and joined their hands together.

"Down you go!" she whispered.

And down they went. Sun did feel silly holding Moon's hand like that but Moon seemed to like it. She swung her arm and the bell on her coral bracelet jingled.

At the drawing-room door stood Mother fanning herself with a black fan. The drawing-room was full of sweet smelling, silky, rustling ladies and men in black with funny tails on their coats—like beetles. Father was among them, talking very loud, and rattling something in his pocket.

"What a picture!" cried the ladies. "Oh, the ducks! Oh, the lambs! Oh, the sweets! Oh, the pets!"

All the people who couldn't get at Moon kissed Sun, and a skinny old lady with teeth that clicked said: "Such a serious little poppet," and rapped him on the head with something hard.

Sun looked to see if the same concert was there, but he was gone. Instead, a fat man with a pink head leaned over the piano talking to a girl who held a violin at her ear.

There was only one man that Sun really liked. He was a little grey man, with long grey whiskers, who walked about by himself. He came up to Sun and rolled his eyes in a very nice way and said: "Hullo, my lad." Then he went away. But soon he came back again and said: "Fond of dogs?" Sun said: "Yes." But then he went away again, and though Sun looked for him everywhere he couldn't find him. He thought perhaps he'd gone outside to fetch in a puppy.

"Good night, my precious babies," said Mother, folding them up in her bare arms. "Fly up to your little nest."

Then Moon went and made a silly of herself again. She put up her arms in front of everybody and said: "My Daddy must carry me."

But they seemed to like it, and Daddy swooped down and picked her up as he always did.

Nurse was in such a hurry to get them to bed that she even interrupted Sun over his prayers and said: "Get on with them, child, *do*." And the moment after they were in bed and in the dark except for the nightlight in its little saucer.

"Are you asleep?" asked Moon.

"No," said Sun. "Are you?"

"No," said Moon.

A long while after Sun woke up again. There was a loud, loud noise of clapping from downstairs, like when it rains. He heard Moon turn over.

"Moon, are you awake?"

"Yes, are you?"

"Yes. Well, let's go and look over the stairs."

They had just got settled on the top step when the drawing-room door opened and they heard the party cross over the hall into the dining-room. Then that door was shut; there was a noise of "pops" and laughing. Then that stopped and Sun saw them all walking round and round the lovely table with their hands behind their backs like he had done. . . . Round and round they walked, looking and staring. The man with the grey whiskers liked the little house best. When he saw the nut for a handle he rolled his eyes like he did before and said to Sun: "Seen the nut?"

"Don't nod your head like that, Moon."

"I'm not nodding. It's you."

"It is not. I never nod my head."

"O-oh, you do. You're nodding it now."

"I'm not. I'm only showing you how not to do it."

When they woke up again they could only hear Father's voice

very loud, and Mother, laughing away. Father came out of the dining-room, bounded up the stairs, and nearly fell over them.

"Hullo!" he said. "By Jove, Kitty, come and look at this."

Mother came out. "Oh, you naughty children," said she from the hall.

"Let's have 'em down and give 'em a bone," said Father. Sun had never seen him so jolly.

"No, certainly not," said Mother.

"Oh, my Daddy, do! Do have us down," said Moon.

"I'm hanged if I won't," cried Father. "I won't be bullied. Kitty—way there." And he caught them up, one under each arm.

Sun thought Mother would have been dreadfully cross. But she wasn't. She kept on laughing at Father.

"Oh, you dreadful boy!" said she. But she didn't mean Sun.

"Come on, kiddies. Come and have some pickings," said this jolly Father. But Moon stopped a minute.

"Mother—your dress is right off one side."

"Is it?' said Mother. And Father said "Yes" and pretended to bite her white shoulder, but she pushed him away.

And so they went back to the beautiful dining-room.

But—oh! oh! what had happened? The ribbons and the roses were all pulled untied. The little red table napkins lay on the floor, all the shining plates were dirty and all the winking glasses. The lovely food that the man had trimmed was all thrown about, and there were bones and bits and fruit peels and shells everywhere. There was even a bottle lying down with stuff coming out of it on to the cloth and nobody stood it up again.

And the little pink house with the snow roof and the green windows was broken—broken—half melted away in the centre of the table.

"Come on, Sun," said Father, pretending not to notice.

Moon lifted up her pyjama legs and shuffled up to the table and stood on a chair, squeaking away.

"Have a bit of this ice," said Father, smashing in some more of the roof.

Mother took a little plate and held it for him; she put her other arm round his neck.

"Daddy. Daddy," shrieked Moon. "The little handle's left.

The little nut. Kin I eat it?" And she reached across and picked it out of the door and scrunched it up, biting hard and blinking.

"Here, my lad," said Father.

But Sun did not move from the door. Suddenly he put up his head and gave a loud wail.

"I think it's horrid—horrid—horrid!" he sobbed.

"There, you see!" said Mother. "You see!"

"Off with you," said Father, no longer jolly. "This moment. Off you go!"

And wailing loudly, Sun stumped off to the nursery.

This Flower

"B UT I TELL YOU, my lord fool, out of this nettle danger, we pluck this flower, safety."

As she lay there, looking up at the ceiling, she had her moment—yes, she had her moment! And it was not connected with anything she had thought or felt before, not even with those words the doctor had scarcely ceased speaking. It was single, glowing, perfect; it was like—a pearl, too flawless to match with another . . . Could she describe what happened? Impossible. It was as though, even if she had not been conscious (and she certainly had not been conscious all the time) that she was fighting against the stream of life—the stream of life indeed!—she had suddenly ceased to struggle. Oh, more than that! She had yielded, yielded absolutely, down to every minutest pulse and nerve, and she had fallen into the bright bosom of the stream and it had borne her . . . She was part of her room—part of the great bouquet of southern anemones, of the white net curtains that blew in stiff against the light breeze, of the mirrors, the white silky rugs; she was part of the high, shaking, quivering clamour, broken with little bells and crying voices that went streaming by outside,—part of the leaves and the light.

Over. She sat up. The doctor had reappeared. This strange little figure with his stethoscope still strung round his neck—for she had asked him to examine her heart—squeezing and kneading his freshly washed hands, had told her . . .

It was the first time she had ever seen him. Roy, unable, of course, to miss the smallest dramatic opportunity, had obtained his rather shady Bloomsbury address from the man in whom he always confided everything, who, although he'd never met her, knew "all about them."

"My darling," Roy had said, "we'd better have an absolutely unknown man just in case it's—well, what we don't either of us want it to be. One can't be too careful in affairs of this sort. Doctors *do* talk. It's all damned rot to say they don't." Then, "Not that I care a straw who on earth knows. Not that I wouldn't—if you'd have me—blazon it on the skies, or take the front page of the *Daily Mirror* and have our two names on it, in a heart, you know—pierced by an arrow."

Nevertheless, of course, his love of mystery and intrigue, his passion for "keeping our secret beautifully" (his phrase!) had won the day, and off he'd gone in a taxi to fetch this rather sodden-looking little man.

She heard her untroubled voice saying, "Do you mind not mentioning anything of this to Mr. King? If you'd tell him that I'm a little run down and that my heart wants a rest. For I've been complaining about my heart."

Roy had been really *too* right about the kind of man the doctor was. He gave her a strange, quick, leering look, and taking off the stethoscope with shaking fingers he folded it into his bag that looked somehow like a broken old canvas shoe.

"Don't you worry, my dear," he said huskily. "I'll see you through."

Odious little toad to have asked a favour of! She sprang to her feet, and picking up her purple cloth jacket, went over to the mirror. There was a soft knock at the door, and Roy—he really did look pale, smiling his half-smile—came in and asked the doctor what he had to say.

"Well," said the doctor, taking up his hat, holding it against his chest and beating a tattoo on it, "all I've got to say is that Mrs.—h'm—Madam wants a bit of a rest. She's a bit run down. Her heart's a bit strained. Nothing else wrong."

In the street a barrel-organ struck up something gay, laughing, mocking, gushing, with little trills, shakes, jumbles of notes.

> That's *all* I got to say, to say,
> That's *all* I got to say,

it mocked. It sounded so near she wouldn't have been surprised if the doctor were turning the handle.

She saw Roy's smile deepen; his eyes took fire. He gave a little "Ah!" of relief and happiness. And just for one moment he allowed himself to gaze at her without caring a jot whether the doctor saw or not, drinking her up with that gaze she knew so well, as she stood tying the pale ribbons of her camisole and drawing on the little purple cloth jacket. He jerked back to the doctor, "She shall go away. She shall go away to the sea at once," said he, and then, terribly anxious, "What about her food?" At that, buttoning her jacket in the long mirror, she couldn't help laughing at him.

"That's all very well," he protested, laughing back delightedly at her and at the doctor. "But if I didn't manage her food, doctor, she'd never eat anything but caviare sandwiches and—and white grapes. About wine—oughtn't she to have wine?"

Wine would do her no harm.

"Champagne," pleaded Roy. How he was enjoying himself!

"Oh, as much champagne as she likes," said the doctor, "and a brandy and soda with her lunch if she fancies it."

Roy loved that; it tickled him immensely.

"Do you hear that?" he asked solemnly, blinking and sucking in his cheeks to keep from laughing. "Do you fancy a brandy and soda?"

And, in the distance, faint and exhausted, the barrel-organ:

> A brandy and so-da,
> A brandy and soda, please!
> A brandy and soda, please!

The doctor seemed to hear that, too. He shook hands with her and Roy went with him into the passage to settle his fee.

She heard the front door close and then . . . rapid, rapid steps along the passage. This time he simply burst into her room, and she was in his arms, crushed up small while he kissed her with warm quick kisses, murmuring between them, "My darling, my beauty, my delight. You're mine, you're safe." And then three soft groans. "Oh! Oh! Oh! the relief!" Still keeping his arms round her he leant his head against her shoulder as though exhausted. "If you knew how frightened I've been," he murmured. "I thought we were in for it this time. I really did. And it would have been so—fatal—so fatal!"

The Man Without a
Temperament

H E S T O O D at the hall door turning the ring, turning the
heavy signet ring upon his little finger while his glance travelled
coolly, deliberately, over the round tables and basket chairs scattered about the glassed-in verandah. He pursed his lips—he might
have been going to whistle—but he did not whistle—only turned
the ring—turned the ring on his pink, freshly washed hands.

Over in the corner sat The Two Topknots, drinking a de-
coction they always drank at this hour—something whitish, grey-
ish, in glasses, with little husks floating on the top—and rooting
in a tin full of paper shavings for pieces of speckled biscuit, which
they broke, dropped into the glasses and fished for with spoons.
Their two coils of knitting, like two snakes, slumbered beside the
tray.

The American Woman sat where she always sat against the
glass wall, in the shadow of a great creeping thing with wide open
purple eyes that pressed—that flattened itself against the glass,
hungrily watching her. And she knoo it was there—she knoo it
was looking at her just that way. She played up to it; she gave
herself little airs. Sometimes she even pointed at it, crying: "Isn't
that the most terrible thing you've ever seen! Isn't that ghoulish!"
It was on the other side of the verandah, after all . . . and besides
it couldn't touch her, could it, Klaymongso? She was an American
Woman, wasn't she Klaymongso, and she'd just go right away to
her Consul. Klaymongso, curled in her lap, with her torn antique
brocade bag, a grubby handkerchief, and a pile of letters from
home on top of him, sneezed for reply.

The other tables were empty. A glance passed between the

American and the Topknots. She gave a foreign little shrug; they waved an understanding biscuit. But he saw nothing. Now he was still, now from his eyes you saw he listened. "Hoo-e-zip-zoo-oo!" sounded the lift. The iron cage clanged open. Light dragging steps sounded across the hall, coming towards him. A hand, like a leaf, fell on his shoulder. A soft voice said: "Let's go and sit over there—where we can see the drive. The trees are so lovely." And he moved forward with the hand still on his shoulder, and the light, dragging steps beside his. He pulled out a chair and she sank into it, slowly, leaning her head against the back, her arms falling along the sides.

"Won't you bring the other up closer? It's such miles away." But he did not move.

"Where's your shawl?" he asked.

"Oh!" She gave a little groan of dismay. "How silly I am, I've left it upstairs on the bed. Never mind. Please don't go for it. I shan't want it, I know I shan't."

"You'd better have it." And he turned and swiftly crossed the verandah into the dim hall with its scarlet plush and gilt furniture—conjuror's furniture—its Notice of Services at the English Church, its green baize board with the unclaimed letters climbing the black lattice, huge "Presentation" clock that struck the hours at the half-hours, bundles of sticks and umbrellas and sunshades in the clasp of a brown wooden bear, past the two crippled palms, two ancient beggars at the foot of the staircase, up the marble stairs three at a time, past the life-size group on the landing of two stout peasant children with their marble pinnies full of marble grapes, and along the corridor, with its piled-up wreckage of old tin boxes, leather trunks, canvas hold-alls, to their room.

The servant girl was in their room, singing loudly while she emptied soapy water into a pail. The windows were open wide, the shutters put back, and the light glared in. She had thrown the carpets and the big white pillows over the balcony rails; the nets were looped up from the beds; on the writing table there stood a pan of fluff and match-ends. When she saw him her small impudent eyes snapped and her singing changed to humming.

But he gave no sign. His eyes searched the glaring room. Where the devil was the shawl!

"*Vous desirez, Monsieur?*" mocked the servant girl.

No answer. He had seen it. He strode across the room, grabbed the grey cobweb and went out, banging the door. The servant girl's voice at its loudest and shrillest followed him along the corridor.

"Oh, there you are. What happened? What kept you? The tea's here, you see. I've just sent Antonio off for the hot water. Isn't it extraordinary? I must have told him about it sixty times at least, and still he doesn't bring it. Thank you. That's very nice. One does just feel the air when one bends forward."

"Thanks." He took his tea and sat down in the other chair. "No, nothing to eat."

"Oh do! Just one, you had so little at lunch and it's hours before dinner."

Her shawl dropped off as she bent forward to hand him the biscuits. He took one and put it in his saucer.

"Oh, those trees along the drive," she cried, "I could look at them for ever. They are like the most exquisite huge ferns. And you see that one with the grey-silver bark and the clusters of cream coloured flowers, I pulled down a head of them yesterday to smell and the scent"—she shut her eyes at the memory and her voice thinned away, faint, airy—"was like freshly ground nutmegs." A little pause. She turned to him and smiled. "You do know what nutmegs smell like—do you, Robert?"

And he smiled back at her. "Now how am I going to prove to you that I do?"

Back came Antonio with not only the hot water—with letters on a salver and three rolls of paper.

"Oh, the post! Oh, how lovely! Oh, Robert, they mustn't be all for you! Have they just come, Antonio?" Her thin hands flew up and hovered over the letters that Antonio offered her, bending forward.

"Just this moment, Signora," grinned Antonio. "I took-a them from the postman myself. I made-a the postman give them for me."

"Noble Antonio!" laughed she. "There—those are mine, Robert; the rest are yours."

Antonio wheeled sharply, stiffened, the grin went out of his face. His striped linen jacket and his flat gleaming fringe made him look like a wooden doll.

Mr. Salesby put the letters into his pocket; the papers lay on the table. He turned the ring, turned the signet ring on his little finger and stared in front of him, blinking, vacant.

But she—with her teacup in one hand, the sheets of thin paper in the other, her head tilted back, her lips open, a brush of bright colour on her cheek-bones, sipped, sipped, drank . . . drank. . . .

"From Lottie," came her soft murmur. "Poor dear . . . such trouble . . . left foot. She thought . . . neuritis . . . Doctor Blyth . . . flat foot . . . massage. So many robins this year . . . maid most satisfactory . . . Indian Colonel . . . every grain of rice separate . . . very heavy fall of snow." And her wide lighted eyes looked up from the letter. "Snow, Robert! Think of it!" And she touched the little dark violets pinned on her thin bosom and went back to the letter.

. . . Snow. Snow in London. Millie with the early morning cup of tea. "There's been a terrible fall of snow in the night, Sir." "Oh, has there, Millie?" The curtains ring apart, letting in the pale, reluctant light. He raises himself in the bed; he catches a glimpse of the solid houses opposite framed in white, of their window boxes full of great sprays of white coral. . . . In the bathroom—overlooking the back garden. Snow—heavy snow over everything. The lawn is covered with a wavy pattern of cat's paws; there is a thick, thick icing on the garden table; the withered pods of the laburnum tree are white tassels; only here and there in the ivy is a dark leaf showing. . . . Warming his back at the dining-room fire, the paper drying over a chair. Millie with the bacon. "Oh, if you please, Sir, there's two little boys come as will do the steps and front for a shilling, shall I let them?" . . . And then flying lightly, lightly down the stairs—Jinnie. "Oh, Robert, isn't it wonderful! Oh, what a pity it has to melt. Where's the pussy-wee?"

"I'll get him from Millie" . . . "Millie, you might just hand me up the kitten if you've got him down there." "Very good, Sir." He feels the little beating heart under his hand. "Come on old chap, your Missus wants you." "Oh, Robert, do show him the snow—his first snow. Shall I open the window and give him a little piece on his paw to hold? . . ."

"Well, that's very satisfactory on the whole—very. Poor Lottie! Darling Anne! How I only wish I could send them something of this," she cried, waving her letters at the brilliant, dazzling garden. "More tea, Robert? Robert dear, more tea."

"No, thanks, no. It was very good," he drawled.

"Well mine wasn't. Mine was just like chopped hay. Oh, here comes the Honeymoon Couple."

Half striding, half running, carrying a basket between them and rods and lines, they came up the drive, up the shallow steps.

"My! Have you been out fishing?" cried the American Woman.

They were out of breath, they panted: "Yes, yes, we have been out in a little boat all day. We have caught seven. Four are good to eat. But three we shall give away. To the children."

Mrs. Salesby turned her chair to look; the Topknots laid the snakes down. They were a very dark young couple—black hair, olive skin, brilliant eyes and teeth. He was dressed "English fashion" in a flannel jacket, white trousers and shoes. Round his neck he wore a silk scarf; his head, with his hair brushed back, was bare. And he kept mopping his forehead, rubbing his hands with a brilliant handkerchief. Her white skirt had a patch of wet; her neck and throat were stained a deep pink. When she lifted her arms big half-hoops of perspiration showed under her armpits; her hair clung in wet curls to her cheeks. She looked as though her young husband had been dipping her in the sea, and fishing her out again to dry in the sun and then—in with her again—all day.

"Would Klaymongso like a fish?" they cried. Their laughing voices charged with excitement beat against the glassed-in verandah like birds, and a strange saltish smell came from the basket.

"You will sleep well to-night," said a Topknot, picking her ear with a knitting needle while the other Topknot smiled and nodded.

The Honeymoon Couple looked at each other. A great wave seemed to go over them. They gasped, gulped, staggered a little and then came up laughing—laughing.

"We cannot go upstairs, we are too tired. We must have tea just as we are. Here—coffee. No—tea. No—coffee. Tea—coffee, Antonio!" Mrs. Salesby turned.

"Robert! Robert!" Where was he? He wasn't there. Oh, there he was at the other end of the verandah, with his back turned, smoking a cigarette. "Robert, shall we go for our little turn?"

"Right." He stumped the cigarette into an ash-tray and sauntered over, his eyes on the ground. "Will you be warm enough?"

"Oh, quite."

"Sure?"

"Well," she put her hand on his arm, "perhaps"—and gave his arm the faintest pressure—"it's not upstairs, it's only in the hall—perhaps you'd get me my cape. Hanging up."

He came back with it and she bent her small head while he dropped it on her shoulders. Then, very stiff, he offered her his arm. She bowed sweetly to the people on the verandah while he just covered a yawn, and they went down the steps together.

"*Vous aves voo ça!*" said the American Woman.

"He is not a man," said the Two Topknots, "he is an ox. I say to my sister in the morning and at night when we are in bed, I tell her—*No* man is he, but an ox!"

Wheeling, tumbling, swooping, the laughter of the Honeymoon Couple dashed against the glass of the verandah.

The sun was still high. Every leaf, every flower in the garden lay open, motionless, as if exhausted, and a sweet, rich, rank smell filled the quivering air. Out of the thick, fleshy leaves of a cactus there rose an aloe stem loaded with pale flowers that looked as though they had been cut out of butter; light flashed upon the lifted spears of the palms; over a bed of scarlet waxen flowers some big black insects "zoom-zoomed"; a great, gaudy creeper, orange splashed with jet, sprawled against a wall.

"I don't need my cape after all," said she. "It's really too warm." So he took it off and carried it over his arm. "Let us go down this path here. I feel so well to-day—marvellously better. Good heavens—look at those children! And to think it's November!"

In a corner of the garden there were two brimming tubs of water. Three little girls, having thoughtfully taken off their drawers and hung them on a bush, their skirts clasped to their waists, were standing in the tubs and tramping up and down. They screamed, their hair fell over their faces, they splashed one another. But suddenly, the smallest, who had a tub to herself, glanced up and saw who was looking. For a moment she seemed overcome with terror, then clumsily she struggled and strained out of her tub, and still holding her clothes above her waist. "The Englishman! The Englishman!" she shrieked and fled away to hide. Shrieking and screaming, the other two followed her. In a moment they were gone; in a moment there was nothing but the two brimming tubs and their little drawers on the bush.

"How—very—extraordinary!" said she. "What made them so frightened? Surely they were much too young to . . ." She looked up at him. She thought he looked pale—but wonderfully handsome with that great tropical tree behind him with its long, spiked thorns.

For a moment he did not answer. Then he met her glance, and smiling his slow smile, "*Très* rum!" said he.

Très rum! Oh, she felt quite faint. Oh, why should she love him so much just because he said a thing like that. *Très* rum! That was Robert all over. Nobody else but Robert could ever say such a thing. To be so wonderful, so brilliant, so learned, and then to say in that queer, boyish voice. . . . She could have wept.

"You know you're very absurd, sometimes," said she.

"I am," he answered. And they walked on.

But she was tired. She had had enough. She did not want to walk any more.

"Leave me here and go for a little constitutional, won't you? I'll be in one of these long chairs. What a good thing you've got my cape; you won't have to go upstairs for a rug. Thank you,

Robert, I shall look at that delicious heliotrope. . . . You won't
be gone long?"

"No—no. You don't mind being left?"

"Silly! I want you to go. I can't expect you to drag after your
invalid wife every minute. . . . How long will you be?"

He took out his watch. "It's just after half past four. I'll be
back at a quarter past five."

"Back at a quarter past five," she repeated, and she lay still
in the long chair and folded her hands.

He turned away. Suddenly he was back again. "Look here,
would you like my watch?" And he dangled it before her.

"Oh!" She caught her breath. "Very, very much." And she
clasped the watch, the warm watch, the darling watch in her
fingers. "Now go quickly."

The gates of the Pension Villa Excelsior were open wide,
jammed open against some bold geraniums. Stooping a little,
staring straight ahead, walking swiftly, he passed through them
and began climbing the hill that wound behind the town like a
great rope looping the villas together. The dust lay thick. A carriage came bowling along driving towards the Excelsior. In it sat
the General and the Countess; they had been for his daily airing.
Mr. Salesby stepped to one side but the dust beat up, thick, white,
stifling like wool. The Countess just had time to nudge the General.

"There he goes," she said spitefully.

But the General gave a loud caw and refused to look.

"It is the Englishman," said the driver, turning round and
smiling. And the Countess threw up her hands and nodded so
amiably that he spat with satisfaction and gave the stumbling horse
a cut.

On—on—past the finest villas in the town, magnificent palaces, palaces worth coming any distance to see, past the public
gardens with the carved grottoes and statues and stone animals
drinking at the fountain, into a poorer quarter. Here the road ran
narrow and foul between high lean houses, the ground floors of
which were scooped and hollowed into stables and carpenters'
shops. At a fountain ahead of him two old hags were beating
linen. As he passed them they squatted back on their haunches,

stared, and then their "A-hak-kak-kak!" with the slap, slap, of the stone on the linen sounded after him.

He reached the top of the hill; he turned a corner and the town was hidden. Down he looked into a deep valley with a dried up river bed at the bottom. This side and that was covered with small dilapidated houses that had broken stone verandahs where the fruit lay drying, tomato lanes in the garden, and from the gates to the doors a trellis of vines. The late sunlight, deep, golden, lay in the cup of the valley; there was a smell of charcoal in the air. In the gardens the men were cutting grapes. He watched a man standing in the greenish shade, raising up, holding a black cluster in one hand, taking the knife from his belt, cutting, laying the bunch in a flat boat-shaped basket. The man worked leisurely, silently, taking hundreds of years over the job. On the hedges on the other side of the road there were grapes small as berries, growing wild, growing among the stones. He leaned against a wall, filled his pipe, put a match to it. . . .

Leaned across a gate, turned up the collar of his mackintosh. It was going to rain. It didn't matter, he was prepared for it. You didn't expect anything else in November. He looked over the bare field. From the corner by the gate there came the smell of swedes, a great stack of them, wet, rank coloured. Two men passed walking towards the straggling village. "Good day!" "Good day!" By Jove! he had to hurry if he was going to catch that train home. Over the gate, across a field, over the stile, into the lane, swinging along in the drifting rain and dusk. . . . Just home in time for a bath and a change before supper. . . . In the drawing-room; Jinnie is sitting pretty nearly in the fire. "Oh, Robert, I didn't hear you come in. Did you have a good time? How nice you smell! A present?" "Some bits of blackberry I picked for you. Pretty colour." "Oh, lovely, Robert! Dennis and Beaty are coming to supper." Supper—cold beef, potatoes in their jackets, claret, household bread. They are gay—everybody's laughing. "Oh, we all know Robert," says Dennis, breathing on his eye-glasses and polishing them. "By the way, Dennis, I picked up a very jolly little edition of . . ."

*   *   *

A clock struck. He wheeled sharply. What time was it. Five?
A quarter past? Back, back the way he came. As he passed through
the gates he saw her on the look-out. She got up, waved and
slowly she came to meet him, dragging the heavy cape. In her
hand she carried a spray of heliotrope.

"You're late," she cried gaily. "You're three minutes late.
Here's your watch, it's been very good while you were away. Did
you have a nice time? Was it lovely? Tell me. Where did you go?"

"I say—put this *on*," he said, taking the cape from her.

"Yes, I will. Yes, it's getting chilly. Shall we go up to our
room?"

When they reached the lift she was coughing. He frowned.

"It's nothing. I haven't been out too late. Don't be cross."
She sat down on one of the red plush chairs while he rang and
rang, and then, getting no answer, kept his finger on the bell.

"Oh, Robert, do you think you ought to?"

"Ought to what?"

The door of the *salon* opened. "What is that? Who is making
that noise?" sounded from within. Klaymongso began to yelp.
"Caw! Caw! Caw!" came from the General. A Topknot darted
out with one hand to her ear, opened the staff door, "Mr. Queet!
Mr. Queet!" she bawled. That brought the manager up at a run.

"Is that you ringing the bell, Mr. Salesby? Do you want the
lift? Very good, Sir. I'll take you up myself. Antonio wouldn't
have been a minute, he was just taking off his apron—" And
having ushered them in, the oily manager went to the door of
the *salon*. "Very sorry you should have been troubled, ladies and
gentlemen." Salesby stood in the cage, sucking in his cheeks,
staring at the ceiling and turning the ring, turning the signet ring
on his little finger. . . .

Arrived in their room he went swiftly over to the washstand,
shook the bottle, poured her out a dose and brought it across.

"Sit down. Drink it. And don't talk." And he stood over her
while she obeyed. Then he took the glass, rinsed it and put it
back in its case. "Would you like a cushion?"

"No, I'm quite all right. Come over here. Sit down by me just a minute, will you, Robert? Ah, that's very nice." She turned and thrust the piece of heliotrope in the lapel of his coat. "That," she said, "is most becoming." And then she leaned her head against his shoulder, and he put his arm round her.

"Robert—" her voice like a sigh—like a breath.

"Yes—"

They sat there for a long while. The sky flamed, paled; the two white beds were like two ships. . . . At last he heard the servant girl running along the corridor with the hot water cans, and gently he released her and turned on the light.

"Oh, what time is it? Oh, what a heavenly evening. Oh, Robert, I was thinking while you were away this afternoon . . ."

They were the last couple to enter the dining-room. The Countess was there with her lorgnette and her fan, the General was there with his special chair and air cushion and the small rug over his knees. The American Woman was there showing Klaymongso a copy of the *Saturday Evening Post.* . . . "We're having a feast of reason and a flow of soul." The Two Topknots were there feeling over the peaches and the pears in their dish of fruit, and putting aside all they considered unripe or overripe to show to the manager, and the Honeymoon Couple leaned across the table, whispering, trying not to burst out laughing.

Mr. Queet, in everyday clothes and white canvas shoes, served the soup, and Antonio, in full evening dress, handed it round.

"No," said the American Woman, "take it away, Antonio. We can't eat soup. We can't eat anything mushy, can we, Klaymongso?"

"Take them back and fill them to the rim!" said the Topknots, and they turned and watched while Antonio delivered the message.

"What is it? Rice? Is it cooked?" The Countess peered through her lorgnette. "Mr. Queet, the General can have some of this soup if it is cooked."

"Very good, Countess."

The Honeymoon Couple had their fish instead.

"Give me that one. That's the one I caught. No it's not. Yes, it is. No it's not. Well, it's looking at me with its eye so it must be. Tee! Hee! Hee!" Their feet were locked together under the table.

"Robert, you're not eating again. Is anything the matter?"

"No. Off food, that's all."

"Oh, what a bother. There are eggs and spinach coming. You don't like spinach, do you. I must tell them in future . . ."

An egg and mashed potatoes for the General.

"Mr. Queet! Mr. Queet!"

"Yes, Countess."

"The General's egg's too hard again."

"Caw! Caw! Caw!"

"Very sorry, Countess. Shall I have you another cooked, General?"

. . . They are the first to leave the dining-room. She rises, gathering her shawl and he stands aside waiting for her to pass, turning the ring, turning the signet ring on his little finger. In the hall Mr. Queet hovers. "I thought you might not want to wait for the lift. Antonio's just serving the finger bowls. And I'm sorry the bell won't ring, it's out of order. I can't think what's happened."

"Oh, I do hope . . ." from her.

"Get in," says he.

Mr. Queet steps after them and slams the door. . . .

. . . "Robert, do you mind if I go to bed very soon? Won't you go down to the *salon* or out into the garden? Or perhaps you might smoke a cigar on the balcony. It's lovely out there. And I like cigar smoke. I always did. But if you'd rather . . ."

"No, I'll sit here."

He takes a chair and sits on the balcony. He hears her moving about in the room, lightly, lightly, moving and rustling. Then she comes over to him. "Good night, Robert."

"Good night." He takes her hand and kisses the palm. "Don't catch cold."

The sky is the colour of jade. There are a great many stars; an enormous white moon hangs over the garden. Far away lightning flutters—flutters like a wing—flutters like a broken bird that tries to fly and sinks again and again struggles.

The lights from the *salon* shine across the garden path and there is the sound of a piano. And once the American Woman, opening the French window to let Klaymongso into the garden, cries: "Have you seen this moon?" But nobody answers.

He gets very cold sitting there, staring at the balcony rail. Finally he comes inside. The moon—the room is painted white with moonlight. The light trembles in the mirrors; the two beds seem to float. She is asleep. He sees her through the nets, half sitting, banked up with pillows, her white hands crossed on the sheet. Her white cheeks, her fair hair pressed against the pillow, are silvered over. He undresses quickly, stealthily and gets into bed. Lying there, his hands clasped behind his head. . . .

. . . In his study. Late summer. The virginia creeper just on the turn. . . .

"Well, my dear chap, that's the whole story. That's the long and the short of it. If she can't cut away for the next two years and give a decent climate a chance she don't stand a dog's—h'm—show. Better be frank about these things." "Oh, certainly. . . ." "And hang it all, old man, what's to prevent you going with her? It isn't as though you've got a regular job like us wage earners. You can do what you do wherever you are—" "Two years." "Yes, I should give it two years. You'll have no trouble about letting this house you know. As a matter of fact . . ."

. . . He is with her. "Robert, the awful thing is—I suppose it's my illness—I simply feel I could not go alone. You see—you're everything. You're bread and wine, Robert, bread and wine. Oh, my darling—what am I saying? Of course I could, of course I won't take you away. . . ."

He hears her stirring. Does she want something?

"Boogles?"

Good Lord! She is talking in her sleep. They haven't used that name for years.

"Boogles. Are you awake?"

"Yes, do you want anything?"

"Oh, I'm going to be a bother. I'm so sorry. Do you mind? There's a wretched mosquito inside my net—I can hear him singing. Would you catch him? I don't want to move because of my heart."

"No, don't move. Stay where you are." He switches on the light, lifts the net. "Where is the little beggar? Have you spotted him?"

"Yes, there, over by the corner. Oh, I do feel such a fiend to have dragged you out of bed. Do you mind dreadfully?"

"No, of course not." For a moment he hovers in his blue and white pyjamas. Then, "got him," he said.

"Oh, good. Was he a juicy one?"

"Beastly." He went over to the washstand and dipped his fingers in water. "Are you all right now? Shall I switch off the light?"

"Yes, please. No. Boogles! Come back here a moment. Sit down by me. Give me your hand." She turns his signet ring. "Why weren't you asleep? Boogles, listen. Come closer. I sometimes wonder—do you mind awfully being out here with me?"

He bends down. He kisses her. He tucks her in, he smoothes the pillow.

"Rot!" he whispers.

Revelations

FROM EIGHT O'CLOCK in the morning until about half past eleven Monica Tyrell suffered from her nerves, and suffered so terribly that these hours were —agonizing, simply. It was not as though she could control them. "Perhaps if I were ten years younger . . ." she would say. For now that she was thirty-three she had a queer little way of referring to her age on all occasions, of looking at her friends with grave, childish eyes and saying: "Yes, I remember how twenty years ago . . ." or of drawing Ralph's attention to the girls—real girls—with lovely youthful arms and throats and swift hesitating movements who sat near them in restaurants. "Perhaps if I were ten years younger . . ."

"Why don't you get Marie to sit outside your door and absolutely forbid anybody to come near your room until you ring your bell?"

"Oh, if it were as simple as that!" She threw her little gloves down and pressed her eyelids with her fingers in the way he knew so well. "But in the first place I'd be so conscious of Marie sitting there, Marie shaking her finger at Rudd and Mrs. Moon, Marie as a kind of cross between a wardress and a nurse for mental cases! And then, there's the post. One can't get over the fact that the post comes, and once it has come, who—who—could wait until eleven for the letters?"

His eyes grew bright; he quickly, lightly clasped her. "*My* letters, darling?"

"Perhaps," she drawled, softly, and she drew her hand over her reddish hair, smiling too, but thinking: "Heavens! What a stupid thing to say!"

But this morning she had been awakened by one great slam of the front door. Bang. The flat shook. What was it? She jerked up in bed, clutching the eiderdown; her heart beat. What could it be? Then she heard voices in the passage. Marie knocked, and, as the door opened, with a sharp tearing rip out flew the blind and the curtains, stiffening, flapping, jerking. The tassel of the blind knocked—knocked against the window. "Eh-h, *voilà!*" cried Marie, setting down the tray and running. *"C'est le vent, Madame. C'est un vent insupportable."*

Up rolled the blind; the window went up with a jerk; a whitey-greyish light filled the room. Monica caught a glimpse of a huge pale sky and a cloud like a torn shirt dragging across before she hid her eyes with her sleeve.

"Marie! the curtains! Quick, the curtains!" Monica fell back into bed and then "Ring-ting-a-ping-ping, ring-ting-a-ping-ping." It was the telephone. The limit of her suffering was reached; she grew quite calm. "Go and see, Marie."

"It is Monsieur. To know if Madame will lunch at Princes' at one-thirty to-day." Yes, it was Monsieur himself. Yes, he had asked that the message be given to Madame immediately. Instead of replying, Monica put her cup down and asked Marie in a small wondering voice what time it was. It was half past nine. She lay still and half closed her eyes. "Tell Monsieur I cannot come," she said gently. But as the door shut, anger—anger suddenly gripped her close, close, violent, half strangling her. How dared he? How dared Ralph do such a thing when he knew how agonizing her nerves were in the morning! Hadn't she explained and described and even—though lightly, of course; she couldn't say such a thing directly—given him to understand that this was the one unforgivable thing?

And then to choose this frightful windy morning. Did he think it was just a fad of hers, a little feminine folly to be laughed at and tossed aside? Why, only last night she had said: "Ah, but you must take me seriously, too." And he had replied: "My darling, you'll not believe me, but I know you infinitely better than you know yourself. Every delicate thought and feeling I bow to, I treasure. Yes, laugh! I love the way your lip lifts"—and he had leaned across the table—"I don't care who sees that I adore all of you. I'd be with you on mountain-top and have all the search-lights of the world play upon us."

"Heavens!" Monica almost clutched her head. Was it possible he had really said that? How incredible men were! And she had loved him—how could she have loved a man who talked like that. What had she been doing ever since that dinner party months ago, when he had seen her home and asked if he might come and "see again that slow Arabian smile"? Oh, what nonsense—what utter nonsense—and yet she remembered at the time a strange deep thrill unlike anything she had ever felt before.

"Coal! Coal! Coal! Old iron! Old iron! Old iron!" sounded from below. It was all over. Understand her? He had understood nothing. That ringing her up on a windy morning was immensely significant. Would he understand that? She could almost have laughed. "You rang me up when the person who understood me simply couldn't have." It was the end. And when Marie said: "Monsieur replied he would be in the vestibule in case Madame changed her mind," Monica said: "No, not verbena, Marie. Carnations. Two handfuls."

A wild white morning, a tearing, rocking wind. Monica sat down before the mirror. She was pale. The maid combed back her dark hair—combed it all back—and her face was like a mask, with pointed eyelids and dark red lips. As she stared at herself in the blueish shadowy glass she suddenly felt—oh, the strangest, most tremendous excitement filling her slowly, slowly, until she wanted to fling out her arms, to laugh, to scatter everything, to shock Marie, to cry: "I'm free. I'm free. I'm free as the wind." And now all this vibrating, trembling, exciting, flying world was hers. It was her kingdom. No, no, she belonged to nobody but Life.

"That will do, Marie," she stammered. "My hat, my coat, my bag. And now get me a taxi." Where was she going? Oh, any-where. She could not stand this silent flat, noiseless Marie, this ghostly, quiet, feminine interior. She must be out; she must be driving quickly—anywhere, anywhere.

"The taxi is there, Madame." As she pressed open the big outer doors of the flats the wild wind caught her and floated her across the pavement. Where to? She got in, and smiling radiantly at the cross, cold-looking driver, she told him to take her to her hairdresser's. What would she have done without her hairdresser? Whenever Monica had nowhere else to go to or nothing on earth to do she drove there. She might just have her hair waved, and by that time she'd have thought out a plan. The cross, cold driver drove at a tremendous pace, and she let herself be hurled from side to side. She wished he would go faster and faster. Oh, to be free of Princes' at one-thirty, of being the tiny kitten in the swansdown basket, of being the Arabian, and the grave, delighted child and the little wild creature. . . . "Never again," she cried aloud, clenching her small fist. But the cab had stopped, and the driver was standing holding the door open for her.

The hairdresser's shop was warm and glittering. It smelled of soap and burnt paper and wallflower brilliantine. There was Madame behind the counter, round, fat, white, her head like a powder-puff rolling on a black satin pin-cushion. Monica always had the feeling that they loved her in this shop and understood her—the real her—far better than many of her friends did. She was her real self here, and she and Madame had often talked—quite strangely—together. Then there was George who did her hair, young, dark, slender George. She was really fond of him.

But to-day—how curious! Madame hardly greeted her. Her face was whiter than ever, but rims of bright red showed round her blue bead eyes, and even the rings on her pudgy fingers did not flash. They were cold, dead, like chips of glass. When she called through the wall-telephone to George there was a note in her voice that had never been there before. But Monica would not believe this. No, she refused to. It was just her imagination. She sniffed greedily the warm, scented air, and passed behind the velvet curtain into the small cubicle.

Her hat and jacket were off and hanging from the peg, and still George did not come. This was the first time he had ever not been there to hold the chair for her, to take her hat and hang up her bag, dangling it in his fingers as though it were something he'd never seen before—something fairy. And how quiet the shop was! There was not a sound even from Madame. Only the wind blew, shaking the old house; the wind hooted, and the portraits of Ladies of the Pompadour Period looked down and smiled, cunning and sly. Monica wished she hadn't come. Oh, what a mistake to have come! Fatal. Fatal. Where was George? If he didn't appear the next moment she would go away. She took off the white kimono. She didn't want to look at herself any more. When she opened a big pot of cream on the glass shelf her fingers trembled. There was a tugging feeling at her heart as though her happiness—her marvellous happiness—were trying to get free.

"I'll go. I'll not stay." She took down her hat. But just at that moment steps sounded, and, looking in the mirror, she saw George bowing in the doorway. How queerly he smiled! It was the mirror of course. She turned round quickly. His lips curled back in a sort of grin, and—wasn't he unshaved?—he looked almost green in the face.

"Very sorry to have kept you waiting," he mumbled, sliding, gliding forward.

Oh, no, she wasn't going to stay. "I'm afraid," she began. But he had lighted the gas and laid the tongs across, and was holding out the kimono.

"It's a wind," he said. Monica submitted. She smelled his fresh young fingers pinning the jacket under her chin. "Yes, there is a wind," said she, sinking back into the chair. And silence fell. George took out the pins in his expert way. Her hair tumbled back, but he didn't hold it as he usually did, as though to feel how fine and soft and heavy it was. He didn't say it "was in a lovely condition." He let it fall, and, taking a brush out of a drawer, he coughed faintly, cleared his throat and said dully: "Yes, it's a pretty strong one, I should say it was."

She had no reply to make. The brush fell on her hair. Oh, oh, how mournful, how mournful! It fell quick and light, it fell like leaves; and then it fell heavy, tugging like the tugging at her heart. "That's enough," she cried, shaking herself free.

"Did I do it too much?" asked George. He crouched over the tongs. "I'm sorry." There came the smell of burnt paper—the smell she loved—and he swung the hot tongs round in his hand, staring before him. "I shouldn't be surprised if it rained." He took up a piece of her hair, when—she couldn't bear it any longer—she stopped him. She looked at him; she saw herself looking at him in the white kimono like a nun. "Is there something the matter here? Has something happened?" But George gave a half shrug and a grimace. "Oh, no, Madame. Just a little occurrence." And he took up the piece of hair again. But, oh, she wasn't deceived. That was it. Something awful had happened. The silence—really, the silence seemed to come drifting down like flakes of snow. She shivered. It was cold in the little cubicle, all cold and glittering. The nickel taps and jets and sprays looked somehow almost malignant. The wind rattled the window-frame; a piece of iron banged, and the young man went on changing the tongs, crouching over her. Oh, how terrifying Life was, thought Monica. How dreadful. It is the loneliness which is so appalling. We whirl along like leaves, and nobody knows—nobody cares where we fall, in what black river we float away. The tugging feeling seemed to rise into her throat. It ached, ached; she longed to cry. "That will do," she whispered. "Give me the pins." As he stood beside her, so submissive, so silent, she nearly dropped her arms and sobbed. She couldn't bear any more. Like a wooden man the gay young George still slid, glided, handed her her hat and veil, took the note, and brought back the change. She stuffed it into her bag. Where was she going now?

George took a brush. "There is a little powder on your coat," he murmured. He brushed it away. And then suddenly he raised himself and, looking at Monica, gave a strange wave with the brush and said: "The truth is, Madame, since you are an old customer—my little daughter died this morning. A first child"— and then his white face crumpled like paper, and he turned his back on her and began brushing the cotton kimono. "Oh, oh," Monica began to cry. She ran out of the shop into the taxi. The driver, looking furious, swung off the seat and slammed the door again. "Where to?"

"Princes'," she sobbed. And all the way there she saw nothing but a tiny wax doll with a feather of gold hair, lying meek, its tiny hands and feet crossed. And then just before she came to Princes' she saw a flower shop full of white flowers. Oh, what a perfect thought. Lilies-of-the-valley, and white pansies, double white violets and white velvet ribbon. . . . From an unknown friend. . . . From one who understands. . . . For a Little Girl. . . . She tapped against the window, but the driver did not hear; and, anyway, they were at Princes' already.

The Young Girl

I N H E R B L U E D R E S S with her cheeks lightly flushed, her blue, blue eyes, and her gold curls pinned up as though for the first time—pinned up to be out of the way for her flight—Mrs. Raddick's daughter might have just dropped from this radiant heaven. Mrs. Raddick's timid, faintly astonished, but deeply admiring glance looked as if she believed it, too; but the daughter didn't appear any too pleased—why should she?—to have alighted on the steps of the Casino. Indeed, she was bored—bored as though Heaven had been full of casinos with snuffy old saints for *croupiers* and crowns to play with.

"You don't mind taking Hennie?" said Mrs. Raddick. "Sure you don't? There's the car, and you'll have tea and we'll be back here on this step—right here—in an hour. You see, I want her to go in. She's not been before, and it's worth seeing. I feel it wouldn't be fair to her."

"Oh, shut up, mother," said she wearily. "Come along. Don't talk so much. And your bag's open; you'll be losing all your money again."

"I'm sorry, darling," said Mrs. Raddick.

"Oh, *do* come in! I want to make money," said the impatient voice. "It's all jolly well for you—but I'm broke!"

"Here—take fifty francs, darling, take a hundred!" I saw Mrs. Raddick pressing notes into her hand as they passed through the swing doors.

Hennie and I stood on the steps a minute, watching the people. He had a very broad, delighted smile.

"I say," he cried, "there's an English bulldog. Are they allowed to take dogs in there?"

"No, they're not."

"He's a ripping chap, isn't he? I wish I had one. They're such fun. They frighten people so, and they're never fierce with their—the people they belong to." Suddenly he squeezed my arm. "I say, *do* look at that old woman. Who is she? Why does she look like that? Is she a gambler?"

The ancient, withered creature, wearing a green satin dress, a black velvet cloak and a white hat with purple feathers, jerked slowly, slowly up the steps as though she were being drawn up on wires. She stared in front of her, she was laughing and nodding and cackling to herself; her claws clutched round what looked like a dirty bootbag.

But just at that moment there was Mrs. Raddick again with—*her*—and another lady hovering in the background. Mrs. Raddick rushed at me. She was brightly flushed, gay, a different creature. She was like a woman who is saying "good-bye" to her friends on the station platform, with not a minute to spare before the train starts.

"Oh, you're here, still. Isn't that lucky! You've not gone. Isn't that fine! I've had the most dreadful time with—her," and she waved to her daughter, who stood absolutely still, disdainful, looking down, twiddling her foot on the step, miles away. "They won't let her in. I swore she was twenty-one. But they won't believe me. I showed the man my purse; I didn't dare to do more. But it was no use. He simply scoffed. . . . And now I've just met Mrs. MacEwen from New York, and she just won thirteen thousand in the *Salle Privée*—and she wants me to go back with her while the luck lasts. Of course I can't leave—her. But if you'd—"

At that "she" looked up; she simply withered her mother. "Why can't you leave me?" she said furiously. "What utter rot! How dare you make a scene like this? This is the last time I'll come out with you. You really are too awful for words." She looked her mother up and down. "Calm yourself," she said superbly.

Mrs. Raddick was desperate, just desperate. She was "wild" to go back with Mrs. MacEwen, but at the same time . . .

I seized my courage. "Would you—do you care to come to tea with—us?"

"Yes, yes, she'll be delighted. That's just what I wanted, isn't it, darling? Mrs. MacEwen . . . I'll be back here in an hour . . . or less . . . I'll—"

Mrs. R. dashed up the steps. I saw her bag was open again. So we three were left. But really it wasn't my fault. Hennie looked crushed to the earth, too. When the car was there she wrapped her dark coat round her—to escape contamination. Even her little feet looked as though they scorned to carry her down the steps to us.

"I am so awfully sorry," I murmured as the car started.

"Oh, I don't *mind*," said she. "I don't *want* to look twenty-one. Who would—if they were seventeen! It's"—and she gave a faint shudder—"the stupidity I loathe, and being stared at by old fat men. Beasts!"

Hennie gave her a quick look and then peered out of the window.

We drew up before an immense palace of pink-and-white marble with orange trees outside the doors in gold-and-black tubs.

"Would you care to go in?" I suggested.

She hesitated, glanced, bit her lip, and resigned herself. "Oh well, there seems nowhere else," said she. "Get out, Hennie."

I went first—to find the table, of course—she followed. But the worst of it was having her little brother, who was only twelve, with us. That was the last, final straw—having that child, trailing at her heels.

There was one table. It had pink carnations and pink plates with little blue tea-napkins for sails.

"Shall we sit here?"

She put her hand wearily on the back of a white wicker chair.

"We may as well. Why not?" said she.

Hennie squeezed past her and wriggled on to a stool at the end. He felt awfully out of it. She didn't even take her gloves off. She lowered her eyes and drummed on the table. When a faint violin sounded she winced and bit her lip again. Silence.

The waitress appeared. I hardly dared to ask her. "Tea—coffee? China tea—or iced tea with lemon?"

Really she didn't mind. It was all the same to her. She didn't really want anything. Hennie whispered, "Chocolate!"

But just as the waitress turned away she cried out carelessly, "Oh, you may as well bring me a chocolate, too."

While we waited she took out a little, gold powder-box with a mirror in the lid, shook the poor little puff as though she loathed it, and dabbed her lovely nose.

"Hennie," she said, "take those flowers away." She pointed with her puff to the carnations, and I heard her murmur, "I can't bear flowers on a table." They had evidently been giving her intense pain, for she positively closed her eyes as I moved them away.

The waitress came back with the chocolate and the tea. She put the big, frothing cups before them and pushed across my clear glass. Hennie buried his nose, emerged, with, for one dreadful moment, a little trembling blob of cream on the tip. But he hastily wiped it off like a little gentleman. I wondered if I should dare draw her attention to her cup. She didn't notice it—didn't see it—until suddenly, quite by chance, she took a sip. I watched anxiously; she faintly shuddered.

"Dreadfully sweet!" said she.

A tiny boy with a head like a raisin and a chocolate body came round with a tray of pastries—row upon row of little freaks, little inspirations, little melting dreams. He offered them to her. "Oh, I'm not at all hungry. Take them away."

He offered them to Hennie. Hennie gave me a swift look—it must have been satisfactory—for he took a chocolate cream, a coffee éclair, a meringue stuffed with chestnut and a tiny horn filled with fresh strawberries. She could hardly bear to watch him. But just as the boy swerved away she held up her plate.

"Oh well, give me *one*," said she.

The silver tongs dropped one, two, three—and a cherry tart-let. "I don't know why you're giving me all these," she said, and nearly smiled. "I shan't eat them; I couldn't!"

I felt much more comfortable. I sipped my tea, leaned back, and even asked if I might smoke. At that she paused, the fork in her hand, opened her eyes and really did smile. "Of course," said she. "I always expect people to."

But at that moment a tragedy happened to Hennie. He speared his pastry horn too hard, and it flew in two, and one half spilled on the table. Ghastly affair! He turned crimson. Even his ears flared, and one ashamed hand crept across the table to take what was left of the body away.

"You *utter* little beast!" said she.

Good heavens! I had to fly to the rescue. I cried hastily, "Will you be abroad long?"

But she had already forgotten Hennie. I was forgotten, too. She was trying to remember something. . . . She was miles away.

"I—don't—know," she said slowly, from that far place.

"I suppose you prefer it to London. It's more—more—"

When I didn't go on she came back and looked at me, very puzzled. "More—?"

"*Enfin*—gayer," I cried, waving my cigarette.

But that took a whole cake to consider. Even then, "Oh well, that depends!" was all she could safely say.

Hennie had finished. He was still very warm.

I seized the butterfly list off the table. "I say—what about an ice, Hennie? What about tangerine and ginger? No, something cooler. What about a fresh pineapple cream?"

Hennie strongly approved. The waitress had her eye on us. The order was taken when she looked up from her crumbs.

"Did you say tangerine and ginger? I like ginger. You can bring me one." And then quickly, "I wish that orchestra wouldn't play things from the year One. We were dancing to that all last Christmas. It's too sickening!"

But it was a charming air. Now that I noticed it, it warmed me.

"I think this is rather a nice place, don't you, Hennie?" I said.

Hennie said: "Ripping!" He meant to say it very low, but it came out very high in a kind of squeak.

Nice? This place? Nice? For the first time she stared about her, trying to see what there was. . . . She blinked; her lovely eyes wondered. A very good-looking elderly man stared back at her through a monocle on a black ribbon. But him she simply couldn't see. There was a hole in the air where he was. She looked through and through him.

Finally the little flat spoons lay still on the glass plates. Hennie looked rather exhausted, but she pulled on her white gloves again. She had some trouble with her diamond wrist-watch; it got in her way. She tugged at it—tried to break the stupid little thing—it wouldn't break. Finally, she had to drag her glove over. I saw, after that, she couldn't stand this place a moment longer, and, indeed, she jumped up and turned away while I went through the vulgar act of paying for the tea.

And then we were outside again. It had grown dusky. The sky was sprinkled with small stars; the big lamps glowed. While we waited for the car to come up she stood on the step, just as before, twiddling her foot, looking down.

Hennie bounded forward to open the door and she got in and sank back with—oh—such a sigh!

"Tell him," she gasped, "to drive as fast as he can."

Hennie grinned at his friend the chauffeur. *"Allie veet!"* said he. Then he composed himself and sat on the small seat facing us.

The gold powder-box came out again. Again the poor little puff was shaken; again there was that swift, deadly-secret glance between her and the mirror.

We tore through the black-and-gold town like a pair of scissors tearing through brocade. Hennie had great difficulty not to look as though he were hanging on to something.

And when we reached the Casino, of course Mrs. Raddick wasn't there. There wasn't a sign of her on the steps—not a sign.

"Will you stay in the car while I go and look?"

But no—she wouldn't do that. Good heavens, no! Hennie could stay. She couldn't bear sitting in a car. She'd wait on the steps.

"But I scarcely like to leave you," I murmured. "I'd very much rather not leave you here."

At that she threw back her coat; she turned and faced me; her lips parted. "Good heavens—why! I—I don't mind it a bit. I—I like waiting." And suddenly her cheeks crimsoned, her eyes grew dark—for a moment I thought she was going to cry. "L—

let me, please," she stammered, in a warm, eager voice. "I like it. I love waiting! Really—really I do! I'm always waiting—in all kinds of places. . . ."

Her dark coat fell open, and her white throat—all her soft young body in the blue dress—was like a flower that is just emerging from its dark bud.

The Stranger

I T S E E M E D to the little crowd on the wharf that she was never going to move again. There she lay, immense, motionless on the grey crinkled water, a loop of smoke above her, an immense flock of gulls screaming and diving after the galley droppings at the stern. You could just see little couples parading—little flies walking up and down the dish on the grey crinkled tablecloth. Other flies clustered and swarmed at the edge. Now there was a gleam of white on the lower deck—the cook's apron or the stewardess perhaps. Now a tiny black spider raced up the ladder on to the bridge.

In the front of the crowd a strong-looking, middle-aged man, dressed very well, very snugly in a grey overcoat, grey silk scarf, thick gloves and dark felt hat, marched up and down, twirling his folded umbrella. He seemed to be the leader of the little crowd on the wharf and at the same time to keep them together. He was something between the sheep-dog and the shepherd.

But what a fool—what a fool he had been not to bring any glasses! There wasn't a pair of glasses between the whole lot of them.

"Curious thing, Mr. Scott, that none of us thought of glasses. We might have been able to stir 'em up a bit. We might have managed a little signalling. *Don't hesitate to land. Natives harmless.* Or: *A welcome awaits you. All is forgiven.* What? Eh?"

Mr. Hammond's quick, eager glance, so nervous and yet so friendly and confiding, took in everybody on the wharf, roped in even those old chaps lounging against the gangways. They knew, every man-jack of them, that Mrs. Hammond was on that boat, and he was so tremendously excited it never entered his head not to believe that this marvellous fact meant something to them too. It warmed his heart towards them. They were, he decided, as decent a crowd of people—Those old chaps over by the gangways, too—fine, solid old chaps. What chests—by Jove! And he squared his own, plunged his thick-gloved hands into his pockets, rocked from heel to toe.

"Yes, my wife's been in Europe for the last ten months. On a visit to our eldest girl, who was married last year. I brought her up here, as far as Salisbury, myself. So I thought I'd better come and fetch her back. Yes, yes, yes." The shrewd grey eyes narrowed again and searched anxiously, quickly, the motionless liner. Again his overcoat was unbuttoned. Out came the thin, butter-yellow watch again, and for the twentieth—fiftieth—hundredth time he made the calculation.

"Let me see, now. It was two-fifteen when the doctor's launch went off. Two-fifteen. It is now exactly twenty-eight minutes past four. That is to say, the doctor's been gone two hours and thirteen minutes. Two hours and thirteen minutes! Whee-ooh!" He gave a queer little half-whistle and snapped his watch to again. "But I think we should have been told if there was anything up—don't you, Mr. Gaven?"

"Oh, yes, Mr. Hammond! I don't think there's anything to—anything to worry about," said Mr. Gaven, knocking out his pipe against the heel of his shoe. "At the same time—"

"Quite so! Quite so!" cried Mr. Hammond. "Dashed annoying!" He paced quickly up and down and came back again to his stand between Mr. and Mrs. Scott and Mr. Gaven. "It's getting quite dark, too," and he waved his folded umbrella as though the dusk at least might have had the decency to keep off for a bit. But the dusk came slowly, spreading like a slow stain over the water. Little Jean Scott dragged at her mother's hand.

"I wan' my tea, mammy!" she wailed.

"I expect you do," said Mr. Hammond. "I expect all these ladies want their tea." And his kind, flushed, almost pitiful glance roped them all in again. He wondered whether Janey was having a final cup of tea in the saloon out there. He hoped so; he thought not. It would be just like her not to leave the deck. In that case perhaps the deck steward would bring her up a cup. If he'd been there he'd have got it for her—somehow. And for a moment he was on deck, standing over her, watching her little hand fold round the cup in the way she had, while she drank the only cup of tea to be got on board. . . . But now he was back here, and the Lord only knew when that cursed Captain would stop hanging about in the stream. He took another turn, up and down, up and down. He walked as far as the cab-stand to make sure his driver hadn't disappeared; back he swerved again to the little flock huddled in the shelter of the banana crates. Little Jean Scott was still wanting her tea. Poor little beggar! He wished he had a bit of chocolate on him.

"Here, Jean!" he said. "Like a lift up?" And easily, gently, he swung the little girl on to a higher barrel. The movement of holding her, steadying her, relieved him wonderfully, lightened his heart.

"Hold on," he said, keeping an arm round her.

"Oh, don't worry about *Jean,* Mr. Hammond!" said Mrs. Scott.

"That's all right, Mrs. Scott. No trouble. It's a pleasure. Jean's a little pal of mine, aren't you, Jean?"

"Yes, Mr. Hammond," said Jean, and she ran her finger down the dent of his felt hat.

But suddenly she caught him by the ear and gave a loud scream. "Lo-ok, Mr. Hammond! She's moving! Look, she's coming in!"

By Jove! So she was. At last! She was slowly, slowly turning round. A bell sounded far over the water and a great spout of steam gushed into the air. The gulls rose; they fluttered away like bits of white paper. And whether that deep throbbing was her engines or his heart Mr. Hammond couldn't say. He had to nerve himself to bear it, whatever it was. At that moment old Captain Johnson, the harbour-master, came striding down the wharf, a leather portfolio under his arm.

"Jean'll be all right," said Mr. Scott. "I'll hold her." He was just in time. Mr. Hammond had forgotten about Jean. He sprang away to greet old Captain Johnson.

"Well, Captain," the eager, nervous voice rang out again, "you've taken pity on us at last."

"It's no good blaming me, Mr. Hammond," wheezed old Captain Johnson, staring at the liner. "You got Mrs. Hammond on board, ain't yer?"

"Yes, yes!" said Hammond, and he kept by the harbour-master's side. "Mrs. Hammond's there. Hul-lo! We shan't be long now!"

With her telephone ring-ringing, the thrum of her screw filling the air, the big liner bore down on them, cutting sharp through the dark water so that big white shavings curled to either side. Hammond and the harbour-master kept in front of the rest. Hammond took off his hat; he raked the decks—they were crammed with passengers; he waved his hat and bawled a loud, strange "Hul-lo!" across the water; and then turned round and burst out laughing and said something—nothing—to old Captain Johnson.

"Seen her?" asked the harbour-master.

"No, not yet. Steady—wait a bit!" And suddenly, between two great clumsy idiots—"Get out of the way there!" he signed with his umbrella—he saw a hand raised—a white glove shaking a handkerchief. Another moment, and—thank God, thank God!—there she was. There was Janey. There was Mrs. Hammond, yes, yes, yes—standing by the rail and smiling and nodding and waving her handkerchief.

"Well, that's first class—first class! Well, well, well!" He positively stamped. Like lightning he drew out his cigar-case and offered it to old Captain Johnson. "Have a cigar, Captain! They're pretty good. Have a couple! Here"—and he pressed all the cigars in the case on the harbour-master—"I've a couple of boxes up at the hotel."

"Thanks, Mr. Hammond!" wheezed old Captain Johnson.

Hammond stuffed the cigar-case back. His hands were shaking, but he'd got hold of himself again. He was able to face Janey. There she was, leaning on the rail, talking to some woman and at the same time watching him, ready for him. It struck him, as the gulf of water closed, how small she looked on that huge ship.

His heart was wrung with such a spasm that he could have cried out. How little she looked to have come all that long way and back by herself! Just like her, though. Just like Janey. She had the courage of a— And now the crew had come forward and parted the passengers; they had lowered the rails for the gangways.

The voices on shore and the voices on board flew to greet each other.

"All well?"

"All well."

"How's mother?"

"Much better."

"Hullo, Jean!"

"Hillo, Aun' Emily!"

"Had a good voyage?"

"Splendid!"

"Shan't be long now!"

"Not long now."

The engines stopped. Slowly she edged to the wharfside.

"Make way there—make way—make way!" And the wharf hands brought the heavy gangways along at a sweeping run. Hammond signed to Janey to stay where she was. The old harbourmaster stepped forward; he followed. As to "ladies first," or any rot like that, it never entered his head.

"After you, Captain!" he cried genially. And, treading on the old man's heels, he strode up the gangway on to the deck in a bee-line to Janey, and Janey was clasped in his arms.

"Well, well, well! Yes, yes! Here we are at last!" he stammered. It was all he could say. And Janey emerged, and her cool little voice—the only voice in the world for him—said,

"Well, darling! Have you been waiting long?"

No; not long. Or, at any rate, it didn't matter. It was over now. But the point was, he had a cab waiting at the end of the wharf. Was she ready to go off. Was her luggage ready? In that case they could get off sharp with her cabin luggage and let the rest go hang until tomorrow. He bent over her and she looked up with her familiar half-smile. She was just the same. Not a day changed. Just as he'd always known her. She laid her small hand on his sleeve.

"How are the children, John?" she asked.

(Hang the children!) "Perfectly well. Never better in their lives."

"Haven't they sent me letters?"

"Yes, yes—of course! I've left them at the hotel for you to digest later on."

"We can't go quite so fast," said she. "I've got people to say good-bye to—and then there's the Captain." As his face fell she gave his arm a small understanding squeeze. "If the Captain comes off the bridge I want you to thank him for having looked after your wife so beautifully." Well, he'd got her. If she wanted another ten minutes— As he gave way she was surrounded. The whole first-cabin seemed to want to say good-bye to Janey.

"Good-bye, *dear* Mrs. Hammond! And next time you're in Sydney I'll *expect* you."

"Darling Mrs. Hammond! You won't forget to write to me, will you?"

"Well, Mrs. Hammond, what this boat would have been without you!"

It was as plain as a pikestaff that she was by far the most popular woman on board. And she took it all—just as usual. Absolutely composed. Just her little self—just Janey all over; standing there with her veil thrown back. Hammond never noticed what his wife had on. It was all the same to him whatever she wore. But to-day he did notice that she wore a black "costume"—didn't they call it?—with white frills, trimmings he supposed they were, at the neck and sleeves. All this while Janey handed him round.

"John, dear!" And then: "I want to introduce you to—"

Finally they did escape, and she led the way to her stateroom. To follow Janey down the passage that she knew so well—that was so strange to him; to part the green curtains after her and to step into the cabin that had been hers gave him exquisite happiness. But—confound it!—the stewardess was there on the floor, strapping up the rugs.

"That's the last, Mrs. Hammond," said the stewardess, rising and pulling down her cuffs.

He was introduced again, and then Janey and the stewardess

disappeared into the passage. He heard whisperings. She was
getting the tipping business over, he supposed. He sat down on
the striped sofa and took his hat off. There were the rugs she had
taken with her; they looked good as new. All her luggage looked
fresh, perfect. The labels were written in her beautiful little clear
hand—"Mrs. John Hammond."

"Mrs. John Hammond!" He gave a long sigh of content and
leaned back, crossing his arms. The strain was over. He felt he
could have sat there for ever sighing his relief—the relief at being
rid of that horrible tug, pull, grip on his heart. The danger was
over. That was the feeling. They were on dry land again.

But at that moment Janey's head came round the corner.

"Darling—do you mind? I just want to go and say good-bye
to the doctor."

Hammond started up. "I'll come with you."

"No, no!" she said. "Don't bother. I'd rather not. I'll not be
a minute."

And before he could answer she was gone. He had half a
mind to run after her; but instead he sat down again.

Would she really not be long? What was the time now? Out
came the watch; he stared at nothing. That was rather queer of
Janey, wasn't it? Why couldn't she have told the stewardess to
say good-bye for her? Why did she have to go chasing after the
ship's doctor? She could have sent a note from the hotel even if
the affair had been urgent. Urgent? Did it—could it mean that
she had been ill on the voyage—she was keeping something from
him? That was it! He seized his hat. He was going off to find
that fellow and to wring the truth out of him at all costs. He
thought he'd noticed just something. She was just a touch too
calm—too steady. From the very first moment—

The curtains rang. Janey was back. He jumped to his feet.

"Janey, have you been ill on this voyage? You have!"

"Ill?" Her airy little voice mocked him. She stepped over the
rugs, and came up close, touched his breast, and looked up at
him.

"Darling," she said, "don't frighten me. Of course I haven't!
Whatever makes you think I have? Do I look ill?"

But Hammond didn't see her. He only felt that she was

looking at him and that there was no need to worry about anything. She was here to look after things. It was all right. Everything
was.

The gentle pressure of her hand was so calming that he put
his over hers to hold it there. And she said:

"Stand still. I want to look at you. I haven't seen you yet.
You've had your beard beautifully trimmed, and you look—
younger, I think, and decidedly thinner! Bachelor life agrees with
you."

"Agrees with me!" He groaned for love and caught her close
again. And again, as always, he had the feeling he was holding
something that never was quite his—his. Something too delicate,
too precious, that would fly away once he let go.

"For God's sake let's get off to the hotel so that we can be
by ourselves!" And he rang the bell hard for some one to look
sharp with the luggage.

Walking down the wharf together she took his arm. He had
her on his arm again. And the difference it made to get into the
cab after Janey—to throw the red-and-yellow striped blanket
round them both—to tell the driver to hurry because neither of
them had had any tea. No more going without his tea or pouring
out his own. She was back. He turned to her, squeezed her hand,
and said gently, teasingly, in the "special" voice he had for her:
"Glad to be home again, dearie?" She smiled; she didn't even
bother to answer, but gently she drew his hand away as they came
to the brighter streets.

"We've got the best room in the hotel," he said. "I wouldn't
be put off with another. And I asked the chambermaid to put in
a bit of a fire in case you felt chilly. She's a nice, attentive girl.
And I thought now we were here we wouldn't bother to go home
to-morrow, but spend the day looking round and leave the morning after. Does that suit you? There's no hurry, is there? The
children will have you soon enough. . . . I thought a day's sight-
seeing might make a nice break in your journey—eh, Janey?"

"Have you taken the tickets for the day after?" she asked.

"I should think I have!" He unbuttoned his overcoat and

took out his bulging pocket-book. "Here we are! I reserved a first-class carriage to Cooktown. There it is—'Mr. *and* Mrs. John Hammond.' I thought we might as well do ourselves comfortably, and we don't want other people butting in, do we? But if you'd like to stop here a bit longer—?"

"Oh, no!" said Janey quickly. "Not for the world! The day after to-morrow, then. And the children—"

But they had reached the hotel. The manager was standing in the broad, brilliantly-lighted porch. He came down to greet them. A porter ran from the hall for their boxes.

"Well, Mr. Arnold, here's Mrs. Hammond at last!"

The manager led them through the hall himself and pressed the elevator-bell. Hammond knew there were business pals of his sitting at the little hall tables having a drink before dinner. But he wasn't going to risk interruption; he looked neither to the right nor the left. They could think what they pleased. If they didn't understand, the more fools they—and he stepped out of the lift, unlocked the door of their room, and shepherded Janey in. The door shut. Now, at last, they were alone together. He turned up the light. The curtains were drawn; the fire blazed. He flung his hat on to the huge bed and went towards her.

But—would you believe it!—again they were interrupted. This time it was the porter with the luggage. He made two journeys of it, leaving the door open in between, taking his time, whistling through his teeth in the corridor. Hammond paced up and down the room, tearing off his gloves, tearing off his scarf. Finally he flung his overcoat on to the bedside.

At last the fool was gone. The door clicked. Now they *were* alone. Said Hammond: "I feel I'll never have you to myself again. These cursed people! Janey"—and he bent his flushed, eager gaze upon her—"let's have dinner up here. If we go down to the restaurant we'll be interrupted, and then there's the confounded music" (the music he'd praised so highly, applauded so loudly last night!). "We shan't be able to hear each other speak. Let's have something up here in front of the fire. It's too late for tea. I'll order a little supper, shall I? How does that idea strike you?"

"Do, darling!" said Janey. "And while you're away—the children's letters—"

"Oh, later on will do!" said Hammond.

"But then we'd get it over," said Janey. "And I'd first have time to—"

"Oh, I needn't go down!" explained Hammond. "I'll just ring and give the order . . . you don't want to send me away, do you?"

Janey shook her head and smiled.

"But you're thinking of something else. You're worrying about something," said Hammond. "What is it? Come and sit here—come and sit on my knee before the fire."

"I'll just unpin my hat," said Janey, and she went over to the dressing table. "A-ah!" She gave a little cry.

"What is it?"

"Nothing, darling. I've just found the children's letters. That's all right! They will keep. No hurry now!" She turned to him, clasping them. She tucked them into her frilled blouse. She cried quickly, gaily: "Oh, how typical this dressing table is of you!"

"Why? What's the matter with it?" said Hammond.

"If it were floating in eternity I should say 'John!'" laughed Janey, staring at the big bottle of hair tonic, the wicker bottle of eau-de-Cologne, the two hair-brushes, and a dozen new collars tied with pink tape. "Is this all your luggage?"

"Hang my luggage!" said Hammond; but all the same he liked being laughed at by Janey. "Let's talk. Let's get down to things. Tell me"—and as Janey perched on his knees he leaned back and drew her into the deep, ugly chair—"tell me you're really glad to be back, Janey."

"Yes, darling, I am glad," she said.

But just as when he embraced her he felt she would fly away, so Hammond never knew—never knew for dead certain that she was as glad as he was. How could he know? Would he ever know? Would he always have this craving—this pang like hunger, somehow, to make Janey so much part of him that there wasn't any of her to escape? He wanted to blot out everbody, everything. He wished now he'd turned off the light. That might have brought her nearer. And now those letters from the children rustled in her blouse. He could have chucked them into the fire.

"Janey," he whispered.

233

"Yes, dear?" She lay on his breast, but so lightly, so remotely. Their breathing rose and fell together.

"Janey!"

"What is it?"

"Turn to me," he whispered. A slow, deep flush flowed into his forehead. "Kiss me, Janey! You kiss me!"

It seemed to him there was a tiny pause—but long enough for him to suffer torture—before her lips touched his, firmly, lightly—kissing them as she always kissed him, as though the kiss—how could he describe it?—confirmed what they were saying, signed the contract. But that wasn't what he wanted; that wasn't at all what he thirsted for. He felt suddenly, horribly tired.

"If you knew," he said, opening his eyes, "what it's been like—waiting to-day. I thought the boat never would come in. There we were, hanging about. What kept you so long?"

She made no answer. She was looking away from him at the fire. The flames hurried—hurried over the coals, flickered, fell.

"Not asleep, are you?" said Hammond, and he jumped her up and down.

"No," she said. And then: "Don't do that, dear. No, I was thinking. As a matter of fact," she said, "one of the passengers died last night—a man. That's what held us up. We brought him in—I mean, he wasn't buried at sea. So, of course, the ship's doctor and the shore doctor—"

"What was it?" asked Hammond uneasily. He hated to hear of death. He hated this to have happened. It was, in some queer way, as though he and Janey had met a funeral on their way to the hotel.

"Oh, it wasn't anything in the least infectious!" said Janey. She was speaking scarcely above her breath. "It was *heart*." A pause. "Poor fellow!" she said. "Quite young." And she watched the fire flicker and fall. "He died in my arms," said Janey.

The blow was so sudden that Hammond thought he would faint. He couldn't move; he couldn't breathe. He felt all his strength flowing—flowing into the big dark chair, and the big dark chair held him fast, gripped him, forced him to bear it.

"What?" he said dully. "What's that you say?"

"The end was quite peaceful," said the small voice. "He just"—and Hammond saw her lift her gentle hand—"breathed his life away at the end." And her hand fell.

"Who—else was there?" Hammond managed to ask.

"Nobody. I was alone with him."

Ah, my God, what was she saying! What was she doing to him! This would kill him! And all the while she spoke:

"I saw the change coming and I sent the steward for the doctor, but the doctor was too late. He couldn't have done anything, anyway."

"But—why *you*, why *you*?" moaned Hammond.

At that Janey turned quickly, quickly searched his face.

"You don't *mind*, John, do you?" she asked. "You don't—It's nothing to do with you and me."

Somehow or other he managed to shake some sort of smile at her. Somehow or other he stammered: "No—go—on, go on! I want you to tell me."

"But, John darling—"

"Tell me, Janey!"

"There's nothing to tell," she said, wondering. "He was one of the first-class passengers. I saw he was very ill when he came on board. . . . But he seemed to be so much better until yesterday. He had a severe attack in the afternoon—excitement—nervousness, I think, about arriving. And after that he never recovered."

"But why didn't the stewardess—"

"Oh, my dear—the stewardess!" said Janey. "What would he have felt? And besides . . . he might have wanted to leave a message . . . to—"

"Didn't he?" muttered Hammon. "Didn't he say anything?"

"No, darling, not a word!" She shook her head softly. "All the time I was with him he was too weak . . . he was too weak even to move a finger. . . ."

Janey was silent. But her words, so light, so soft, so chill, seemed to hover in the air, to rain into his breast like snow.

The fire had gone red. Now it fell in with a sharp sound and the room was colder. Cold crept up his arms. The room was huge, immense, glittering. It filled his whole world. There was the great

blind bed, with his coat flung across it like some headless man
saying his prayers. There was the luggage, ready to be carried
away again, anywhere, tossed into trains, carted on to boats.

. . . "He was too weak. He was too weak to move a finger."
And yet he died in Janey's arms. She—who'd never—never once
in all these years—never on one single solitary occasion—

No; he mustn't think of it. Madness lay in thinking of it.
No, he wouldn't face it. He couldn't stand it. It was too much
to bear!

And now Janey touched his tie with her fingers. She pinched
the edges of the tie together.

"You're not—sorry I told you, John darling? It hasn't made
you sad? It hasn't spoilt our evening—our being alone together?"

But at that he had to hide his face. He put his face into her
bosom and his arms enfolded her.

Spoilt their evening! Spoilt their being alone together! They
would never be alone together again.

I can't bear thought

Result

The Daughters of the
Late Colonel

I

THE WEEK AFTER was one of the busiest weeks of their
lives. Even when they went to bed it was only their bodies that
lay down and rested; their minds went on, thinking things out,
talking things over, wondering, deciding, trying to remember
where . . .

Constantia lay like a statue, her hands by her sides, her feet
just overlapping each other, the sheet up to her chin. She stared
at the ceiling.

"Do you think father would mind if we gave his top-hat to
the porter?"

"The porter?" snapped Josephine. "Why ever the porter?
What a very extraordinary idea!"

"Because," said Constantia slowly, "he must often have to
go to funerals. And I noticed at—at the cemetery that he only
had a bowler." She paused. "I thought then how very much he'd
appreciate a top-hat. We ought to give him a present, too. He
was always very nice to father."

"But," cried Josephine, flouncing on her pillow and staring
across the dark at Constantia, "father's head!" And suddenly, for
one awful moment, she nearly giggled. Not, of course, that she
felt in the least like giggling. It must have been habit. Years ago,
when they had stayed awake at night talking, their beds had simply
heaved. And now the porter's head, disappearing, popped out,
like a candle, under father's hat. . . . The giggle mounted,

mounted; she clenched her hands; she fought it down; she frowned fiercely at the dark and said "Remember" terribly sternly.

"We can decide to-morrow," she sighed.

Constantia had noticed nothing; she sighed.

"Do you think we ought to have our dressing-gowns dyed as well?"

"Black?" almost shrieked Josephine.

"Well, what else?" said Constantia. "I was thinking—it doesn't seem quite sincere, in a way, to wear black out of doors and when we're fully dressed, and then when we're at home—"

"But nobody sees us," said Josephine. She gave the bedclothes such a twitch that both her feet became uncovered, and she had to creep up the pillows to get them well under again.

"Kate does," said Constantia. "And the postman very well might."

Josephine thought of her dark-red slippers, which matched her dressing-gown, and of Constantia's favourite indefinite green ones which went with hers. Black! Two black dressing-gowns and two pairs of black woolly slippers, creeping off to the bathroom like black cats.

"I don't think it's absolutely necessary," said she.

Silence. Then Constantia said, "We shall have to post the papers with the notice in them to-morrow to catch the Ceylon mail. . . . How many letters have we had up till now?"

"Twenty-three."

Josephine had replied to them all, and twenty-three times when she came to "We miss our dear father so much" she had broken down and had to use her handkerchief, and on some of them even to soak up a very light-blue tear with an edge of blotting-paper. Strange! She couldn't have put it on—but twenty-three times. Even now, though, when she said over to herself sadly, "We miss our dear father *so* much," she could have cried if she'd wanted to.

"Have you got enough stamps?" came from Constantia.

"Oh, how can I tell?" said Josephine crossly. "What's the good of asking me that now?"

"I was just wondering," said Constantia mildly.

Silence again. There came a little rustle, a scurry, a hop.

"A mouse," said Constantia.

"It can't be a mouse because there aren't any crumbs," said Josephine.

"But it doesn't know there aren't," said Constantia.

A spasm of pity squeezed her heart. Poor little thing! She wished she'd left a tiny piece of biscuit on the dressing table. It was awful to think of it not finding anything. What would it do?

"I can't think how they manage to live at all," she said slowly.

"Who?" demanded Jospehine.

And Constantia said more loudly than she meant to, "Mice."

Josephine was furious. "Oh, what nonsense, Con!" she said. "What have mice got to do with it? You're asleep."

"I don't think I am," said Constantia. She shut her eyes to make sure. She was.

Josephine arched her spine, pulled up her knees, folded her arms so that her fists came under her ears, and pressed her cheek hard against the pillow.

2

Another thing which complicated matters was they had Nurse Andrews staying on with them that week. It was their own fault; they had asked her. It was Josephine's idea. On the morning—well, on the last morning, when the doctor had gone, Josephine had said to Constantia, "Don't you think it would be rather nice if we asked Nurse Andrews to stay on for a week as our guest?"

"Very nice," said Constantia.

"I thought," went on Josephine quickly, "I should just say this afternoon, after I've paid her, 'My sister and I would be very pleased, after all you've done for us, Nurse Andrews, if you would stay on for a week as our guest.' I'd have to put that in about being our guest in case—"

"Oh, but she could hardly expect to be paid!" cried Constantia.

"One never knows," said Josephine sagely.

Nurse Andrews had, of course, jumped at the idea. But it was a bother. It meant they had to have regular sit-down meals at the proper times, whereas if they'd been alone they could just have asked Kate if she wouldn't have minded bringing them a tray wherever they were. And meal-times now that the strain was over were rather a trial.

Nurse Andrews was simply fearful about butter. Really they couldn't help feeling that about butter, at least, she took advantage of their kindness. And she had that maddening habit of asking for just an inch more bread to finish what she had on her plate, and then, at the last mouthful, absent-mindedly—of course it wasn't absent-mindedly—taking another helping. Josephine got very red when this happened, and she fastened her small, bead-like eyes on the tablecloth as if she saw a minute strange insect creeping through the web of it. But Constantia's long, pale face lengthened and set, and she gazed away—away—far over the desert, to where that line of camels unwound like a thread of wool. . . .

"When I was with Lady Tukes," said Nurse Andrews, "she had such a dainty little contrayvance for the buttah. It was a silvah Cupid balanced on the—on the bordah of a glass dish, holding a tayny fork. And when you wanted some buttah you simply pressed his foot and he bent down and speared you a piece. It was quite a gayme."

Josephine could hardly bear that. But "I think those things are very extravagant" was all she said.

"But whey?" asked Nurse Andrews, beaming through her eye-glasses. "No one, surely, would take more buttah than one wanted—would one?"

"Ring, Con," cried Josephine. She couldn't trust herself to reply.

And proud young Kate, the enchanted princess, came in to see what the old tabbies wanted now. She snatched away their plates of mock something or other and slapped down a white, terrified blancmange.

"Jam, please, Kate," said Josephine kindly.

Kate knelt and burst open the sideboard, lifted the lid of the jam-pot, saw it was empty, put it on the table, and stalked off.

"I'm afraid," said Nurse Andrews a moment later, "there isn't any."

"Oh, what a bother!" said Josephine. She bit her lip. "What had we better do?"

Constantia looked dubious. "We can't disturb Kate again," she said softly.

Nurse Andrews waited, smiling at them both. Her eyes wandered, spying at everything behind her eye-glasses. Constantia in despair went back to her camels. Josephine frowned heavily—concentrated. If it hadn't been for this idiotic woman she and Con would, of course, have eaten their blancmange without. Suddenly the idea came.

"I know," she said. "Marmalade. There's some marmalade in the sideboard. Get it, Con."

"I hope," laughed Nurse Andrews, and her laugh was like a spoon tinkling against a medicine-glass—"I hope it's not very bittah marmalayde."

3

But, after all, it was not long now, and then she'd be gone for good. And there was no getting over the fact that she had been very kind to father. She had nursed him day and night at the end. Indeed, both Constantia and Josephine felt privately she had rather overdone the not leaving him at the very last. For when they had gone in to say good-bye Nurse Andrews had sat beside his bed the whole time, holding his wrist and pretending to look at her watch. It couldn't have been necessary. It was so tactless, too. Supposing father had wanted to say something—something private to them. Not that he had. Oh, far from it! He lay there, purple, a dark, angry purple in the face, and never even looked at them when they came in. Then, as they were standing there, wondering what to do, he had suddenly opened one eye. Oh, what a difference it would have made, what a difference to their memory of him, how much easier to tell people about it, if he had only opened both! But no—one eye only. It glared at them a moment and then . . . went out.

4

It had made it very awkward for them when Mr. Farolles, of St. John's, called the same afternoon.

"The end was quite peaceful, I trust?" were the first words he said as he glided towards them through the dark drawing-room.

"Quite," said Josephine faintly. They both hung their heads. Both of them felt certain that eye wasn't at all a peaceful eye.

"Won't you sit down?" said Josephine.

"Thank you, Miss Pinner," said Mr. Farolles gratefully. He folded his coat-tails and began to lower himself into father's arm-chair, but just as he touched it he almost sprang up and slid into the next chair instead.

He coughed. Josephine clasped her hands; Constantia looked vague.

"I want you to feel, Miss Pinner," said Mr. Farolles, "and you, Miss Constantia, that I'm trying to be helpful. I want to be helpful to you both, if you will let me. These are the times," said Mr. Farolles, very simply and earnestly, "when God means us to be helpful to one another."

"Thank you very much, Mr. Farolles," said Josephine and Constantia.

"Not at all," said Mr. Farolles gently. He drew his kid gloves through his fingers and leaned forward. "And if either of you would like a little Communion, either or both of you, here *and* now, you have only to tell me. A little Communion is often very help—a great comfort," he added tenderly.

But the idea of a little Communion terrified them. What! In the drawing-room by themselves—with no—no altar or anything! The piano would be much too high, thought Constantia, and Mr.

Farolles could not possibly lean over it with the chalice. And Kate would be sure to come bursting in and interrupt them, thought Josephine. And supposing the bell rang in the middle? It might be somebody important—about their mourning. Would they get up reverently and go out, or would they have to wait . . . in torture?

"Perhaps you will send round a note by your good Kate if you would care for it later," said Mr. Farolles.

"Oh yes, thank you very much!" they both said.

Mr. Farolles got up and took his black straw hat from the round table.

"And about the funeral," he said softly. "I may arrange that—as your dear father's old friend and yours, Miss Pinner—and Miss Constantia?"

Josephine and Constantia got up too.

"I should like it to be quite simple," said Josephine firmly, "and not too expensive. At the same time, I should like—"

"A good one that will last," thought dreamy Constantia, as if Josephine were buying a nightgown. But of course Josephine didn't say that. "One suitable to our father's position." She was very nervous.

"I'll run round to our good friend Mr. Knight," said Mr. Farolles soothingly. "I will ask him to come and see you. I am sure you will find him very helpful indeed."

5

Well, at any rate, all that part of it was over, though neither of them could possibly believe that father was never coming back. Josephine had had a moment of absolute terror at the cemetery, while the coffin was lowered, to think that she and Constantia had done this thing without asking his permission. What would father say when he found out? For he was bound to find out sooner or later. He always did. "Buried. You two girls had me *buried*!" She heard his stick thumping. Oh, what would they say?

What possible excuse could they make? It sounded such an appallingly heartless thing to do. Such a wicked advantage to take of a person because he happened to be helpless at the moment. The other people seemed to treat it all as a matter of course. They were strangers; they couldn't be expected to understand that father was the very last person for such a thing to happen to. No, the entire blame for it all would fall on her and Constantia. And the expense, she thought, stepping into the tight-buttoned cab. When she had to show him the bills. What would he say then?

She heard him absolutely roaring, "And do you expect me to pay for this gimcrack excursion of yours?"

"Oh," groaned poor Josephine aloud, "we shouldn't have done it, Con!"

And Constantia, pale as a lemon in all that blackness, said in a frightened whisper, "Done what, Jug?"

"Let them bu-bury father like that," said Josephine, breaking down and crying into her new, queer-smelling mourning handkerchief.

"But what else could we have done?" asked Constantia wonderingly. "We couldn't have kept him, Jug—we couldn't have kept him unburied. At any rate, not in a flat that size."

Josephine blew her nose; the cab was dreadfully stuffy.

"I don't know," she said forlornly. "It is all so dreadful. I feel we ought to have tried to, just for a time at least. To make perfectly sure. One things' certain"—and her tears sprang out again—"father will never forgive us for this—never!"

6

Father would never forgive them. That was what they felt more than ever when, two mornings later, they went into his room to go through his things. They had discussed it quite calmly. It was even down on Josephine's list of things to be done. *Go through father's things and settle about them.* But that was a very different matter from saying after breakfast:

"Well, are you ready, Con?"

"Yes, Jug—when you are."

"Then I think we'd better get it over."

It was dark in the hall. It had been a rule for years never to disturb father in the morning, whatever happened. And now they were going to open the door without knocking even. . . . Constantia's eyes were enormous at the idea; Josephine felt weak in the knees.

"You—you go first," she gasped, pushing Constantia.

But Constantia said, as she always had said on those occasions, "No, Jug, that's not fair. You're eldest."

Josephine was just going to say—what at other times she wouldn't have owned to for the world—what she kept for her very last weapon, "But you're tallest," when they noticed that the kitchen door was open, and there stood Kate. . . .

"Very stiff," said Josephine, grasping the door-handle and doing her best to turn it. As if anything ever deceived Kate!

It couldn't be helped. That girl was . . . Then the door was shut behind them, but—but they weren't in father's room at all. They might have suddenly walked through the wall by mistake into a different flat altogether. Was the door just behind them? They were too frightened to look. Josephine knew that if it was it was holding itself tight shut; Constantia felt that, like the doors in dreams, it hadn't any handle at all. It was the coldness which made it so awful. Or the whiteness—which? Everything was covered. The blinds were down, a cloth hung over the mirror, a sheet hid the bed; a huge fan of white paper filled the fireplace. Constantia timidly put out her hand; she almost expected a snowflake to fall. Josephine felt a queer tingling in her nose, as if her nose was freezing. Then a cab klop-klopped over the cobbles below, and the quiet seemed to shake into little pieces.

"I had better pull up a blind," said Josephine bravely.

"Yes, it might be a good idea," whispered Constantia.

They only gave the blind a touch, but it flew up and the cord flew after, rolling round the blindstick, and the little tassel tapped as if trying to get free. That was too much for Constantia.

"Don't you think—don't you think we might put it off for another day?" she whispered.

"Why?" snapped Josephine, feeling, as usual, much better now that she knew for certain that Constantia was terrified. "It's got to be done. But I do wish you wouldn't whisper, Con."

"I didn't know I was whispering," whispered Constantia.

"And why do you keep on staring at the bed?" said Josephine, raising her voice almost defiantly. "There's nothing *on* the bed."

"Oh, Jug, don't say so!" said poor Connie. "At any rate, not so loudly."

Josephine felt herself that she had gone too far. She took a wide swerve over to the chest of drawers, put out her hand, but quickly drew it back again.

"Connie!" she gasped, and she wheeled round and leaned with her back against the chest of drawers.

"Oh, Jug—what?"

Josephine could only glare. She had the most extraordinary feeling that she had just escaped something simply awful. But how could she explain to Constantia that father was in the chest of drawers? He was in the top drawer with his handkerchiefs and neckties, or in the next with his shirts and pyjamas, or in the lowest of all with his suits. He was watching there, hidden away—just behind the door-handle—ready to spring.

She pulled a funny old-fashioned face at Constantia, just as she used to in the old days when she was going to cry.

"I can't open," she nearly wailed.

"No, don't, Jug," whispered Constantia earnestly. "It's much better not to. Don't let's open anything. At any rate, not for a long time."

"But—but it seems so weak," said Josephine, breaking down.

"But why not be weak for once, Jug?" argued Constantia, whispering quite fiercely. "If it is weak." And her pale stare flew from the locked writing-table—so safe—to the huge glittering wardrobe, and she began to breathe in a queer, panting way. "Why shouldn't we be weak for once in our lives, Jug? It's quite excusable. Let's be weak—be weak, Jug. It's much nicer to be weak than to be strong."

And then she did one of those amazingly bold things that she'd done about twice before in their lives; she marched over to the wardrobe, turned the key, and took it out of the lock. Took it out of the lock and held it up to Josephine, showing Josephine by her extraordinary smile that she knew what she'd done, she'd risked deliberately father being in there among his overcoats.

If the huge wardrobe had lurched forward, had crashed down on Constantia, Josephine wouldn't have been surprised. On the contrary, she would have thought it the only suitable thing to happen. But nothing happened. Only the room seemed quieter than ever, and bigger flakes of cold air fell on Josephine's shoulders and knees. She began to shiver.

"Come, Jug," said Constantia, still with that awful callous smile, and Josephine followed just as she had that last time, when Constantia had pushed Benny into the round pond.

7

But the strain told on them when they were back in the dining-room. They sat down, very shaky, and looked at each other.

"I don't feel I can settle to anything," said Josephine, "until I've had something. Do you think we could ask Kate for two cups of hot water?"

"I really don't see why we shouldn't," said Constantia carefully. She was quite normal again. "I won't ring. I'll go to the kitchen door and ask her."

"Yes, do," said Josephine, sinking down into a chair. "Tell her, just two cups, Con, nothing else—on a tray."

"She needn't even put the jug on, need she?" said Constantia, as though Kate might very well complain if the jug had been there.

"Oh no, certainly not! The jug's not at all necessary. She can pour it direct out of the kettle," cried Josephine, feeling that would be a labour-saving indeed.

Their cold lips quivered at the greenish brims. Josephine curved her small red hands round the cup; Constantia sat up and blew on the wavy stream, making it flutter from one side to the other.

"Speaking of Benny," said Josephine.

And though Benny hadn't been mentioned Constantia immediately looked as though he had.

"He'll expect us to send him something of father's, of course. But it's so difficult to know what to send to Ceylon."

"You mean things get unstuck so on the voyage," murmured Constantia.

"No, lost," said Josephine sharply. "You know there's no post. Only runners."

Both paused to watch a black man in which linen drawers running through the pale fields for dear life, with a large brown-paper parcel in his hands. Josephine's black man was tiny; he scurried along glistening like an ant. But there was something blind and tireless about Constantia's tall, thin fellow, which made him, she decided, a very unpleasant person indeed. . . . On the verandah, dressed all in white and wearing a cork helmet, stood Benny. His right hand shook up and down, as father's did when he was impatient. And behind him, not in the least interested, sat Hilda, the unknown sister-in-law. She swung in a cane rocker and flicked over the leaves of the *Tatler*.

"I think his watch would be the most suitable present," said Josephine.

Constantia looked up; she seemed surprised.

"Oh, would you trust a gold watch to a native?"

"But of course I'd disguise it," said Josephine. "No one would know it was a watch." She liked the idea of having to make a parcel such a curious shape that no one could possibly guess what it was. She even thought for a moment of hiding the watch in a narrow cardboard corset-box that she'd kept by her for a long time, waiting for it to come in for something. It was such beautiful firm cardboard. But, no, it wouldn't be appropriate for this occasion. It had lettering on it: *Medium Women's 28. Extra Firm Busks*. It would be almost too much of a surprise for Benny to open that and find father's watch inside.

"And of course it isn't as though it would be going—ticking, I mean," said Constantia, who was still thinking of the native love of jewellery. "At least," she added, "it would be very strange if after all that time it was."

8

Josephine made no reply. She had flown off on one of her tangents. She had suddenly thought of Cyril. Wasn't it more usual for the only grandson to have the watch? And then dear Cyril was so appreciative, and a gold watch meant so much to a young man. Benny, in all probability, had quite got out of the habit of watches; men so seldom wore waistcoats in those hot climates. Whereas Cyril in London wore them from year's end to year's end. And it would be so nice for her and Constantia, when he came to tea, to know it was there. "I see you've got on grandfather's watch, Cyril." It would be somehow so satis-factory.

Dear boy! What a blow his sweet, sympathetic little note had been! Of course they quite understood; but it was most unfor-tunate.

"It would have been such a point, having him," said Jose-phine.

"And he would have enjoyed it so," said Constantia, not thinking what she was saying.

However, as soon as he got back he was coming to tea with his aunties. Cyril to tea was one of their rare treats.

"Now, Cyril, you mustn't be frightened of our cakes. Your Auntie Con and I bought them at Buszard's this morning. We know what a man's appetite is. So don't be ashamed of making a good tea."

Josephine cut recklessly into the rich dark cake that stood for her winter gloves or the soling and heeling of Constantia's only respectable shoes. But Cyril was most unmanlike in appetite.

"I say, Aunt Josephine, I simply can't. I've only just had lunch, you know."

"Oh, Cyril, that can't be true! It's after four," cried Josephine. Constantia sat with her knife poised over the chocolate-roll.

"It is, all the same," said Cyril. "I had to meet a man at Victoria, and he kept me hanging about till . . . there was only

time to get lunch and to come on here. And he gave me—phew"—
Cyril put his hand to his forehead—"a terrific blow-out," he said.

It was disappointing—to-day of all days. But still he couldn't
be expected to know.

"But you'll have a meringue, won't you, Cyril?" said Aunt
Josephine. "These meringues were bought specially for you. Your
dear father was so fond of them. We were sure you are, too."

"I *am*, Aunt Josephine," cried Cyril ardently. "Do you mind
if I take half to begin with?"

"Not at all, dear boy; but we mustn't let you off with
that."

"Is your dear father still so fond of meringues?" asked Auntie
Con gently. She winced faintly as she broke through the shell of
hers.

"Well, I don't quite know, Auntie Con," said Cyril breezily.

At that they both looked up.

"Don't know?" almost snapped Josephine. "Don't know a
thing like that about your own father, Cyril?"

"Surely," said Auntie Con softly.

Cyril tried to laugh it off. "Oh, well," he said, "it's such a
long time since—" He faltered. He stopped. Their faces were too
much for him.

"Even *so*," said Josephine.

And Auntie Con looked.

Cyril put down his teacup. "Wait a bit," he cried. "Wait a
bit, Aunt Josephine. What am I thinking of?"

He looked up. They were beginning to brighten. Cyril
slapped his knee.

"Of course," he said, "it was meringues. How could I have
forgotten? Yes, Aunt Josephine, you're perfectly right. Father's
most frightfully keen on meringues."

They didn't only beam. Aunt Josephine went scarlet with
pleasure; Auntie Con gave a deep, deep sigh.

"And now, Cyril, you must come and see father," said Josephine. "He knows you were coming to-day."

"Right," said Cyril, very firmly and heartily. He got up from
his chair; suddenly he glanced at the clock.

"I say, Auntie Con, isn't your clock a bit slow? I've got to meet a man at—at Paddington just after five. I'm afraid I shan't be able to stay very long with grandfather."

"Oh, he won't expect you to stay *very* long!" said Aunt Josephine.

Constantia was still gazing at the clock. She couldn't make up her mind if it was fast or slow. It was one or the other, she felt almost certain of that. At any rate, it had been.

Cyril still lingered. "Aren't you coming along, Auntie Con?"

"Of course," said Josephine, "we shall all go. Come on, Con."

9

They knocked at the door, and Cyril followed his aunts into grandfather's hot, sweetish room.

"Come on," said Grandfather Pinner. "Don't hang about. What is it? What've you been up to?"

He was sitting in front of a roaring fire, clasping his stick. He had a thick rug over his knees. On his lap there lay a beautiful pale yellow silk handkerchief.

"It's Cyril, father," said Josephine shyly. And she took Cyril's hand and led him forward.

"Good afternoon, grandfather," said Cyril, trying to take his hand out of Aunt Josephine's. Grandfather Pinner shot his eyes at Cyril in the way he was famous for. Where was Auntie Con? She stood on the other side of Aunt Josephine; her long arms hung down in front of her; her hands were clasped. She never took her eyes off grandfather.

"Well," said Grandfather Pinner, beginning to thump, "what have you got to tell me?"

What had he, what had he got to tell him? Cyril felt himself smiling like a perfect imbecile. The room was stifling, too.

But Aunt Josephine came to his rescue. She cried brightly, "Cyril says his father is still very fond of meringues, father dear."

"Eh?" said Grandfather Pinner, curving his hand like a purple meringue-shell over one ear.

Josephine repeated, "Cyril says his father is still very fond of meringues."

"Can't hear," said old Colonel Pinner. And he waved Josephine away with his stick, then pointed with his stick to Cyril. "Tell me what she's trying to say," he said.

(My God) "Must I?" said Cyril, blushing and staring at Aunt Josephine.

"Do, dear," she smiled. "It will please him so much."

"Come on, out with it!" cried Colonel Pinner testily, beginning to thump again.

And Cyril leaned forward and yelled, "Father's still very fond of meringues."

At that Grandfather Pinner jumped as though he had been shot.

"Don't shout!" he cried. "What's the matter with the boy? *Meringues!* What about 'em?"

"Oh, Aunt Josephine, must we go on?" groaned Cyril desperately.

"It's quite all right, dear boy," said Aunt Josephine, as though he and she were at the dentist's together. "He'll understand in a minute." And she whispered to Cyril, "He's getting a bit deaf, you know." Then she leaned forward and really bawled at Grandfather Pinner, "Cyril only wanted to tell you, father dear, that *his* father is still very fond of meringues."

Colonel Pinner heard that time, heard and brooded, looking Cyril up and down.

"What an esstrordinary thing!" said old Grandfather Pinner. "What an esstrordinary thing to come all this way here to tell me!"

And Cyril felt it *was*.

"Yes, I shall send Cyril the watch," said Josephine.

"That would be very nice," said Constantia. "I seem to remember last time he came there was some little trouble about the time."

They were interrupted by Kate bursting through the door in her usual fashion, as though she had discovered some secret panel in the wall.

"Fried or boiled?" asked the bold voice.

Fried or boiled? Josephine and Constantia were quite bewildered for the moment. They could hardly take it in.

"Fried or boiled what, Kate?" asked Josephine, trying to begin to concentrate.

Kate gave a loud sniff. "Fish."

"Well, why didn't you say so immediately?" Josephine reproached her gently. "How could you expect us to understand, Kate? There are a great many things in this world, you know, which are fried or boiled." And after such a display of courage she said quite brightly to Constantia, "Which do you prefer, Con?"

"I think it might be nice to have it fried," said Constantia. "On the other hand, of course boiled fish is very nice. I think I prefer both equally well . . . Unless you . . . In that case—"

"I shall fry it," said Kate, and she bounced back, leaving their door open and slamming the door of her kitchen.

Josephine gazed at Constantia; she raised her pale eyebrows until they rippled away into her pale hair. She got up. She said in a very lofty, imposing way, "Do you mind following me into the drawing-room, Constantia? I've something of great importance to discuss with you."

For it was always to the drawing-room they retired when they wanted to talk over Kate.

Josephine closed the door meaningly. "Sit down, Constantia," she said, still very grand. She might have been receiving Constantia for the first time. And Con looked round vaguely for a chair, as though she felt indeed quite a stranger.

"Now the question is," said Josephine, bending forward, "whether we shall keep her or not."

"That is the question," agreed Constantia.

"And this time," said Josephine firmly, "we must come to a definite decision."

Constantia looked for a moment as though she might begin going over all the other times, but she pulled herself together and said, "Yes, Jug."

"You see, Con," explained Josephine, "everything is so changed now." Constantia looked up quickly. "I mean," went on Josephine, "we're not dependent on Kate as we were." And she blushed faintly. "There's not father to cook for."

"That is perfectly true," agreed Constantia. "Father certainly doesn't want any cooking now, whatever else—"

Josephine broke in sharply. "You're not sleepy, are you, Con?"

"Sleepy, Jug?" Constantia was wide-eyed.

"Well, concentrate more," said Josephine sharply, and she returned to the subject. "What it comes to is, if we did"—and this she barely breathed, glancing at the door—"give Kate notice"—she raised her voice again—"we could manage our own food."

"Why not?" cried Constantia. She couldn't help smiling. The idea was so exciting. She clasped her hands. "What should we live on, Jug?"

"Oh, eggs in various forms!" said Jug, lofty again. "And, besides, there are all the cooked foods."

"But I've always heard," said Constantia, "they are considered so very expensive."

"Not if one buys them in moderation," said Josephine. But she tore herself away from this fascinating bypath and dragged Constantia after her.

"What we've got to decide now, however, is whether we really do trust Kate or not."

Constantia leaned back. Her flat little laugh flew from her lips. "Isn't it curious, Jug," said she, "that just on this subject I've never been able to quite make up my mind?"

II

She never had. The whole difficulty was to prove anything. How did one prove things, how could one? Suppose Kate had stood in front of her and deliberately made a face. Mightn't she very well have been in pain? Wasn't it impossible, at any rate, to ask Kate if she was making a face at her? If Kate answered "No"—and of course she would say "No"—what a position! How undignified! Then again Constantia suspected, she was almost certain that Kate went to her chest of drawers when she and Josephine were out, not to take things but to spy. Many times she had come back to find her amethyst cross in the most unlikely places, under her lace ties or on top of her evening Bertha. More than once she had laid a trap for Kate. She had arranged things in a special order and then called Josephine to witness.

"You see, Jug?"

"Quite, Con."

"Now we shall be able to tell."

But, oh dear, when she did go to look, she was as far off from a proof as ever! If anything was displaced, it might so very well have happened as she closed the drawer; a jolt might have done it so easily.

"You come, Jug, and decide. I really can't. It's too difficult."

But after a pause and a long glare Josephine would sigh, "Now you've put the doubt into my mind, Con, I'm sure I can't tell myself."

"Well, we can't postpone it again," said Josephine. "If we postpone it this time—"

But at that moment in the steet below a barrel-organ struck up. Josephine and Constantia sprang to their feet together.

"Run, Con," said Josephine. "Run quickly. There's six-pence on the—"

Then they remembered. It didn't matter. They would never have to stop the organ-grinder again. Never again would she and Constantia be told to make that monkey take his noise somewhere else. Never would sound that loud, strange bellow when father thought they were not hurrying enough. The organ-grinder might play there all day and the stick would not thump.

> It never will thump again,
> It never will thump again,

played the barrel-organ.

What was Constantia thinking? She had such a strange smile; she looked different. She couldn't be going to cry.

"Jug, Jug," said Constantia softly, pressing her hands together. "Do you know what day it is? It's Saturday. It's a week to-day, a whole week."

> A week since father died,
> A week since father died,

cried the barrel-organ. And Josephine, too, forgot to be practical and sensible; she smiled faintly, strangely. On the Indian carpet there fell a square of sunlight, pale red; it came and went and came—and stayed, deepened—until it shone almost golden.

"The sun's out," said Josephine, as though it really mattered.

A perfect fountain of bubbling notes shook from the barrel-organ, round, bright notes, carelessly scattered.

Constantia lifted her big, cold hands as if to catch them, and then her hands fell again. She walked over to the mantelpiece to her favourite Buddha. And the stone and gilt image, whose smile always gave her such a queer feeling, almost a pain and yet a pleasant pain, seemed today to be more than smiling. He knew something; he had a secret. "I know something that you don't know," said her Buddha. Oh, what was it, what could it be? And yet she had always felt there was . . . something.

The sunlight pressed through the windows, thieved its way in, flashed its light over the furniture and the photographs. Josephine watched it. When it came to mother's photograph, the enlargement over the piano, it lingered as though puzzled to find so little remained of mother, except the earrings shaped like tiny pagodas and a black feather boa. Why did the photographs of dead people always fade so? wondered Josephine. As soon as a person was dead their photograph died too. But, of course, this one of mother was very old. It was thirty-five years old. Josephine remembered standing on a chair and pointing out that feather boa to Constantia and telling her that it was a snake that had killed their mother in Ceylon. . . . Would everything have been different if mother hadn't died? She didn't see why. Aunt Florence had lived with them until they had left school, and they had moved three times and had their yearly holiday and . . . and there'd been changes of servants, of course.

Some little sparrows, young sparrows they sounded, chirped on the window-ledge. *Yeep—eyeep—yeep.* But Josephine felt they were not sparrows, not on the window-ledge. It was inside her, that queer little crying noise. *Yeep—eyeep—yeep.* Ah, what was it crying, so weak and forlorn?

If mother had lived, might they have married? But there had been nobody for them to marry. There had been father's Anglo-Indian friends before he quarrelled with them. But after that she and Constantia never met a single man except clergymen. How did one meet men? Or even if they'd met them, how could they have got to know men well enough to be more than strangers? One read of people having adventures, being followed, and so on. But nobody had ever followed Constantia and her. Oh yes, there had been one year at Eastbourne a mysterious man at their boarding-house who had put a note on the jug of hot water outside their bedroom door! But by the time Connie had found it the steam had made the writing too faint to read; they couldn't even make out to which of them it was addressed. And he had left next day. And that was all. The rest had been looking after father, and at the same time keeping out of father's way. But now? But now? The thieving sun touched Josephine gently. She lifted her face. She was drawn over to the window by gentle beams. . . .

Until the barrel-organ stopped playing Constantia stayed before the Buddha, wondering, but not as usual, not vaguely. This time her wonder was like longing. She remembered the times she had come in here, crept out of bed in her nightgown when the moon was full, and lain on the floor with her arms outstretched, as though she was crucified. Why? The big, pale moon had made her do it. The horrible dancing figures on the carved screen had leered at her and she hadn't minded. She remembered too how, whenever they were at the seaside, she had gone off by herself and got as close to the sea as the could, and sung something, something she had made up, while she gazed all over that restless water. There had been this other life, running out, bringing things home in bags, getting things on approval, discussing them with Jug, and taking them back to get more things on approval, and arranging father's trays and trying not to annoy father. But it all seemed to have happened in a kind of tunnel. It wasn't real. It was only when she came out of the tunnel into the moonlight or by the sea or into a thunderstorm that she really felt herself. What did it mean? What was it she was always wanting? What did it all lead to? Now? Now?

She turned away from the Buddha with one of her vague gestures. She went over to where Josephine was standing. She wanted to say something to Josephine, something frightfully important, about—about the future and what . . .

"Don't you think perhaps—" she began.

But Josephine interrupted her. "I was wondering if now—" she murmured. They stopped; they waited for each other.

"Go on, Con," said Josephine.

"No, no, Jug; after you," said Constantia.

"No, say what you were going to say. You began," said Josephine.

"I . . . I'd rather hear what you were going to say first," said Constantia.

"Don't be absurd, Con."

"Really, Jug."

"Connie!"

"Oh, *Jug!*"

A pause. Then Constantia said faintly, "I can't say what I was going to say, Jug, because I've forgotten what it was . . . that I was going to say."

Josephine was silent for a moment. She stared at a big cloud where the sun had been. Then she replied shortly, "I've forgotten too."

Life of Ma Parker

WHEN THE LITERARY GENTLEMAN, whose flat old Ma Parker cleaned every Tuesday, opened the door to her that morning, he asked after her grandson. Ma Parker stood on the doormat inside the dark little hall, and she stretched out her hand to help her gentleman shut the door before she replied. "We buried 'im yesterday, sir," she said quietly.

"Oh, dear me! I'm sorry to hear that," said the literary gentleman in a shocked tone. He was in the middle of his breakfast. He wore a very shabby dressing-gown and carried a crumpled newspaper in one hand. But he felt awkward. He could hardly go back to the warm sitting-room without saying something— something more. Then because these people set such store by funerals he said kindly, "I hope the funeral went off all right."

"Beg parding, sir?" said old Ma Parker huskily.

Poor old bird! She did look dashed. "I hope the funeral was a—a—success," said he. Ma Parker gave no answer. She bent her head and hobbled off to the kitchen, clasping the old fish bag that held her cleaning things and an apron and a pair of felt shoes. The literary gentleman raised his eyebrows and went back to his breakfast.

"Overcome, I suppose," he said aloud, helping himself to the marmalade.

Ma Parker drew the two jetty spears out of her toque and hung it behind the door. She unhooked her worn jacket and hung that up too. Then she tied her apron and sat down to take off her boots. To take off her boots or to put them on was an agony to her, but it had been an agony for years. In fact, she was so

260

accustomed to the pain that her face was drawn and screwed up ready for the twinge before she'd so much as untied the laces. That over, she sat back with a sigh and softly rubbed her knees. . . .

"Gran! Gran!" Her little grandson stood on her lap in his button boots. He'd just come in from playing in the street.

"Look what a state you've made your gran's skirt into—you wicked boy!"

But he put his arms round her neck and rubbed his cheek against hers.

"Gran, gi' us a penny!" he coaxed.

"Be off with you; Gran ain't got no pennies."

"Yes, you 'ave."

"No, I ain't."

"Yes, you 'ave. Gi' us one!"

Already she was feeling for the old, squashed, black leather purse.

"Well, what'll you give your gran?"

He gave a shy little laugh and pressed closer. She felt his eyelid quivering against her check. "I ain't got nothing," he murmured. . . .

The old woman sprang up, seized the iron kettle off the gas stove and took it over to the sink. The noise of the water drumming in the kettle deadened her pain, it seemed. She filled the pail, too, and the washing-up bowl.

It would take a whole book to describe the state of that kitchen. During the week the literary gentleman "did" for himself. That is to say, he emptied the tea leaves now and again into a jam jar set aside for that purpose, and if he ran out of clean forks he wiped over one or two on the roller towel. Otherwise, as he explained to his friends, his "system" was quite simple, and he couldn't understand why people made all this fuss about house-keeping.

"You simply dirty everything you've got, get a hag in once a week to clean up, and the thing's done."

The result looked like a gigantic dustbin. Even the floor was littered with toast crusts, envelopes, cigarette ends. But Ma Parker bore him no grudge. She pitied the poor young gentleman for having no one to look after him. Out of the smudgy little window you could see an immense expanse of sad-looking sky, and whenever there were clouds they looked very worn, old clouds, frayed at the edges, with holes in them, or dark stains like tea.

While the water was heating, Ma Parker began sweeping the floor. "Yes," she thought, as the broom knocked, "what with one thing and another I've had my share. I've had a hard life."

Even the neighbours said that of her. Many a time, hobbling home with her fish bag she heard them, waiting at the corner, or leaning over the area railings, say among themselves, "She's had a hard life, has Ma Parker." And it was so true she wasn't in the least proud of it. It was just as if you were to say she lived in the basement-back at Number 27. A hard life! . . .

At sixteen she'd left Stratford and come up to London as kitching-maid. Yes, she was born in Stratford-on-Avon. Shakespeare, sir? No, people were always asking her about him. But she'd never heard his name until she saw it on the theatres.

Nothing remained of Stratford except that "sitting in the fireplace of a evening you could see the stars through the chimley," and "Mother always 'ad 'er side of bacon 'anging from the ceiling." And there was something—a bush, there was—at the front door, that smelt ever so nice. But the bush was very vague. She'd only remembered it once or twice in the hospital, when she'd been taken bad.

That was a dreadful place—her first place. She was never allowed out. She never went upstairs except for prayers morning and evening. It was a fair cellar. And the cook was a cruel woman. She used to snatch away her letters from home before she'd read them, and throw them in the range because they made her dreamy. . . . And the beedles! Would you believe it?—until she came to London she'd never seen a black beedle. Here Ma always gave a little laugh, as though—not to have seen a black beedle! Well! It was as if to say you'd never seen your own feet.

When that family was sold up she went as "help" to a doctor's house, and after two years there, on the run from morning till night, she married her husband. He was a baker.

"A baker, Mrs. Parker!" the literary gentleman would say. For occasionally he laid aside his tomes and lent an ear, at least, to this product called Life. "It must be rather nice to be married to a baker!"

Mrs. Parker didn't look so sure.

"Such a clean trade," said the gentleman.

Mrs. Parker didn't look convinced.

"And didn't you like handing the new loaves to the customers?"

"Well, sir," said Mrs. Parker, "I wasn't in the shop above a great deal. We had thirteen little ones and buried seven of them. If it wasn't the 'ospital it was the infirmary, you might say!"

"You might, *indeed,* Mrs. Parker!" said the gentleman, shuddering, and taking up his pen again.

Yes, seven had gone, and while the six were still small her husband was taken ill with consumption. It was flour on the lungs, the doctor told her at the time. . . . Her husband sat up in bed with his shirt pulled over his head, and the doctor's finger drew a circle on his back.

"Now, if we were to cut him open *here,* Mrs. Parker," said the doctor, "you'd find his lungs chock-a-block with white powder. Breathe, my good fellow!" And Mrs. Parker never knew for certain whether she saw or whether she fancied she saw a great fan of white dust come out of her poor dead husband's lips. . . .

But the struggle she'd had to bring up those six little children and keep herself to herself. Terrible it had been! Then, just when they were old enough to go to school her husband's sister came to stop with them to help things along, and she hadn't been there more than two months when she fell down a flight of steps and hurt her spine. And for five years Ma Parker had another baby— and such a one for crying!—to look after. Then young Maudie went wrong and took her sister Alice with her; the two boys emigrated, and young Jim went to India with the army, and Ethel,

263

the youngest, married a good-for-nothing little waiter who died of ulcers the year little Lennie was born. And now little Lennie—my grandson. . . .

The piles of dirty cups, dirty dishes, were washed and dried. The ink-black knives were cleaned with a piece of potato and finished off with a piece of cork. The table was scrubbed, and the dresser and the sink that had sardine tails swimming in it. . . .

He'd never been a strong child—never from the first. He'd been one of those fair babies that everybody took for a girl. Silvery fair curls he had, blue eyes, and a little freckle like a diamond on one side of his nose. The trouble she and Ethel had had to rear that child! The things out of the newspapers they tried him with! Every Sunday morning Ethel would read aloud while Ma Parker did her washing.

"Dear Sir,—Just a line to let you know my little Myrtil was laid out for dead. . . . After four bottils . . . gained 8 lbs. in 9 weeks, *and is still putting it on.*"

And then the egg-cup of ink would come off the dresser and the letter would be written, and Ma would buy a postal order on her way to work next morning. But it was no use. Nothing made little Lennie put it on. Taking him to the cemetery, even, never gave him a colour; a nice shake-up in the bus never improved his appetite.

But he was gran's boy from the first. . . .

"Whose boy are you?" said old Ma Parker, straightening up from the stove and going over to the smudgy window. And a little voice, so warm, so close, it half stifled her—it seemed to be in her breast under her heart—laughed out, and said, "I'm gran's boy!"

At that moment there was a sound of steps, and the literary gentleman appeared, dressed for walking.

"Oh, Mrs. Parker, I'm going out."

"Very good, sir."

"And you'll find your half-crown in the tray of the ink-stand."

"Thank you, sir."

"Oh, by the way, Mrs. Parker," said the literary gentleman

quickly, "you didn't throw away any cocoa last time you were here—did you?"

"No, sir."

"*Very* strange. I could have sworn I left a teaspoonful of cocoa in the tin." He broke off. He said softly and firmly, "You'll always tell me when you throw things away—won't you, Mrs. Parker?" And he walked off very well pleased with himself, convinced, in fact, he'd shown Mrs. Parker that under his apparent carelessness he was as vigilant as a woman.

The door banged. She took her brushes and cloths into the bedroom. But when she began to make the bed, smoothing, tucking, patting, the thought of little Lennie was unbearable. Why did he have to suffer so? That's what she couldn't understand. Why should a little angel child have to arsk for his breath and fight for it? There was no sense in making a child suffer like that.

. . . From Lennie's little box of a chest there came a sound as though something was boiling. There was a great lump of something bubbling in his chest that he couldn't get rid of. When he coughed the sweat sprang out on his head; his eyes bulged, his hands waved, and the great lump bubbled as a potato knocks in a saucepan. But what was more awful than all was when he didn't cough he sat against the pillow and never spoke or answered, or even made as if he heard. Only he looked offended.

"It's not your poor old gran's doing it, my lovey," said old Ma Parker, patting back the damp hair from his little scarlet ears. But Lennie moved his head and edged away. Dreadfully offended with her he looked—and solemn. He bent his head and looked at her sideways as though he couldn't have believed it of his gran.

But at the last . . . Ma Parker threw the counterpane over the bed. No, she simply couldn't think about it. It was too much— she'd had too much in her life to bear. She'd born it up till now, she'd kept herself to herself, and never once had she been seen to cry. Never by a living soul. Not even her own children had seen Ma break down. She'd kept a proud face always. But now! Lennie gone—what had she? She had nothing. He was all she'd got from life, and now he was took too. Why must it all have happened to me? she wondered. "What have I done?" said old Ma Parker. "What have I done?"

As she said those words she suddenly let fall her brush. She found herself in the kitchen. Her misery was so terrible that she pinned on her hat, put on her jacket and walked out of the flat like a person in a dream. She did not know what she was doing. She was like a person so dazed by the horror of what has happened that he walks away—anywhere, as though by walking away he could escape. . . .

It was cold in the street. There was a wind like ice. People went flitting by, very fast; the men walked like scissors; the women trod like cats. And nobody knew—nobody cared. Even if she broke down, if at last, after all these years, she were to cry, she'd find herself in the lock-up as like as not.

But at the thought of crying it was as though little Lennie leapt in his gran's arms. Ah, that's what she wants to do, my dove. Gran wants to cry. If she could only cry now, cry for a long time, over everything, beginning with her first place and the cruel cook, going on to the doctor's, and then the seven little ones, death of her husband, the children's leaving her, and all the years of misery that led up to Lennie. But to have a proper cry over all these things would take a long time. All the same, the time for it had come. She must do it. She couldn't put it off any longer; she couldn't wait any more. . . . Where could she go?

"She's had a hard life, has Ma Parker." Yes, a hard life, indeed! Her chin began to tremble; there was no time to lose. But where? Where?

She couldn't go home; Ethel was there. It would frighten Ethel out of her life. She couldn't sit on a bench anywhere; people would come arsking her questions. She couldn't possibly go back to the gentleman's flat; she had no right to cry in strangers' houses. If she sat on some steps a policeman would speak to her.

Oh, wasn't there anywhere where she could hide and keep herself to herself and stay as long as she liked, not disturbing anybody, and nobody worrying her? Wasn't there anywhere in the world where she could have her cry out—at last?

Ma Parker stood, looking up and down. The icy wind blew out her apron into a balloon. And now it began to rain. There was nowhere.

The Singing Lesson

WITH DESPAIR—cold, sharp despair—buried deep in her heart like a wicked knife, Miss Meadows, in cap and gown and carrying a little baton, trod the cold corridors that led to the music hall. Girls of all ages, rosy from the air, and bubbling over with that gleeful excitement that comes from running to school on a fine autumn morning, hurried, skipped, fluttered by; from the hollow classrooms came a quick drumming of voices; a bell rang; a voice like a bird cried, "Muriel." And then there came from the staircase a tremendous knock-knock-knocking. Some one had dropped her dumbbells.

The Science Mistress stopped Miss Meadows.

"Good mor-ning," she cried, in her sweet, affected drawl. "Isn't it cold? It might be win-ter."

Miss Meadows, hugging the knife, stared in hatred at the Science Mistress. Everything about her was sweet, pale, like honey. You would not have been surprised to see a bee caught in the tangles of that yellow hair.

"It is rather sharp," said Miss Meadows, grimly.

The other smiled her sugary smile.

"You look fro-zen," said she. Her blue eyes opened wide; there came a mocking light in them. (Had she noticed anything?)

"Oh, not quite as bad as that," said Miss Meadows, and she gave the Science Mistress, in exchange for her smile, a quick grimace and passed on. . . .

Forms Four, Five, and Six were assembled in the music hall. The noise was deafening. On the platform, by the piano, stood Mary Beazley, Miss Meadows' favourite, who played accompaniments. She was turning the music stool. When she saw Miss Meadows she gave a loud, warning "Sh-sh! girls!" and Miss Meadows, her hands thrust in her sleeves, the baton under her arm, strode down the centre aisle, mounted the steps, turned sharply, seized the brass music stand, planted it in front of her, and gave two sharp taps with her baton for silence.

"Silence, please! Immediately!" and, looking at nobody, her glance swept over that sea of coloured flannel blouses, with bobbing pink faces and hands, quivering butterfly hair-bows, and music-books outspread. She knew perfectly well what they were thinking. "Meady is in a wax." Well, let them think it! Her eyelids quivered; she tossed her head, defying them. What could the thoughts of those creatures matter to some one who stood there bleeding to death, pierced to the heart, to the heart, by such a letter—

. . ."I feel more and more strongly that our marriage would be a mistake. Not that I do not love you. I love you as much as it is possible for me to love any woman, but, truth to tell, I have come to the conclusion that I am not a marrying man, and the idea of settling down fills me with nothing but—" and the word "disgust" was scratched out lightly and "regret" written over the top.

Basil! Miss Meadows stalked over to the piano. And Mary Beazley, who was waiting for this moment, bent forward; her curls fell over her cheeks while she breathed, "Good morning, Miss Meadows," and she motioned towards rather than handed to her mistress a beautiful yellow chrysanthemum. This little ritual of the flower had been gone through for ages and ages, quite a term and a half. It was as much part of the lesson as opening the piano. But this morning, instead of taking it up, instead of tucking it into her belt while she leant over Mary and said, "Thank you, Mary. How very nice! Turn to page thirty-two," what was Mary's horror when Miss Meadows totally ignored the chrysanthemum, made no reply to her greeeting, but said in a voice of ice, "Page fourteen, please, and mark the accents well."

Staggering moment! Mary blushed until the tears stood in her eyes, but Miss Meadows was gone back to the music stand; her voice rang through the music hall.

"Page fourteen. We will begin with page fourteen. 'A Lament.' Now, girls, you ought to know it by this time. We shall take it all together; not in parts, all together. And without expression. Sing it, though, quite simply, beating time with the left hand."

She raised the baton; she tapped the music stand twice. Down came Mary on the opening chord; down came all those left hands, beating the air, and in chimed those young, mournful voices:

Fast! Ah, too Fast Fade the Ro-o-ses of Pleasure;
Soon Autumn yields unto Wi-i-nter Drear.
Fleetly! Ah, Fleetly Mu-u-sic's Gay Measure
Passes away from the Listening Ear.

Good Heavens, what could be more tragic than that lament! Every note was a sigh, a sob, a groan of awful mournfulness. Miss Meadows lifted her arms in the wide gown and began conducting with both hands. ". . . I feel more and more strongly that our marriage would be a mistake. . . ." she beat. And the voices cried: *Fleetly! Ah, Fleetly.* What could have possessed him to write such a letter! What could have led up to it! It came out of nothing. His last letter had been all about a fumed-oak bookcase he had bought for "our" books, and a "natty little hall-stand" he had seen, "a very neat affair with a carved owl on a bracket, holding three hat-brushes in its claws." How she had smiled at that! So like a man to think one needed three hat-brushes! *From the Listening Ear,* sang the voices.

"Once again," said Miss Meadows. "But this time in parts. Still without expression." *Fast! Ah, too Fast.* With the gloom of the contraltos added, one could scarcely help shuddering. *Fade the Roses of Pleasure.* Last time he had come to see her, Basil had worn a rose in his buttonhole. How handsome he had looked in that bright blue suit, with that dark red rose! And he knew it, too. He couldn't help knowing it. First he stroked his hair, then his moustache; his teeth gleamed when he smiled.

"The headmaster's wife keeps on asking me to dinner. It's a perfect nuisance. I never get an evening to myself in that place."

"But can't you refuse?"

"Oh, well, it doesn't do for a man in my position to be unpopular."

Music's Gay Measure, wailed the voices. The willow trees, outside the high, narrow windows, waved in the wind. They had lost half their leaves. The tiny ones that clung wriggled like fishes caught on a line. ". . . I am not a marrying man. . . ." The voices were silent; the piano waited.

"Quite good," said Miss Meadows, but still in such a strange, stony tone that the younger girls began to feel positively frightened. "But now that we know it, we shall take it with expression. As much expression as you can put into it. Think of the words, girls. Use your imaginations. *Fast! Ah, too Fast,*" cried Miss Meadows. "That ought to break out—a loud, strong *forte*—a lament. And then in the second line, *Winter Drear,* make that *Drear* sound as if a cold wind were blowing through it. *Dre-ear!*" said she so awfully that Mary Beazley, on the music stool, wriggled her spine. "The third line should be one crescendo. *Fleetly! Ah, Fleetly Music's Gay Measure.* Breaking on the first word of the last line, *Passes.* And then on the word, *Away,* you must begin to die . . . to fade . . . until *The Listening Ear* is nothing more than a faint whisper. . . . You can slow down as much as you like almost on the last line. Now, please."

Again the two light taps; she lifted her arms again. *Fast! Ah, too Fast.* ". . . and the idea of settling down fills me with nothing but disgust—" Disgust was what he had written. That was as good as to say their engagement was definitely broken off. Broken off! Their engagement! People had been surprised enough that she had got engaged. The Science Mistress would not believe it at first. But nobody had been as surprised as she. She was thirty. Basil was twenty-five. It had been a miracle, simply a miracle, to hear him say, as they walked home from church that very dark night, "You know, somehow or other, I've got fond of you." And he had taken hold of the end of her ostrich feather boa. *Passes away from the Listening Ear.*

"Repeat! Repeat!" said Miss Meadows. "More expression, girls! Once more!"

Fast! Ah, too Fast. The older girls were crimson; some of the younger ones began to cry. Big spots of rain blew against the

windows, and one could hear the willows whispering, ". . . not
that I do not love you. . . ."

"But, my darling, if you love me," thought Miss Meadows,
"I don't mind how much it is. Love me as little as you like." But
she knew he didn't love her. Not to have cared enough to scratch
out that word "disgust," so that she couldn't read it! *Soon Autumn
yields unto Winter Drear*. She would have to leave the school, too.
She could never face the Science Mistress or the girls after it got
known. She would have to disappear somewhere. *Passes away*. The
voices began to die, to fade, to whisper . . . to vanish. . . .

Suddenly the door opened. A little girl in blue walked fussily
up the aisle, hanging her head, biting her lips, and twisting the
silver bangle on her red little wrist. She came up the steps and
stood before Miss Meadows.

"Well, Monica, what is it?"

"Oh, if you please, Miss Meadows," said the little girl, gasping, "Miss Wyatt wants to see you in the mistress's room."

"Very well," said Miss Meadows. And she called to the girls,
"I shall put you on your honour to talk quietly while I am away."
But they were too subdued to do anything else. Most of them
were blowing their noses.

The corridors were silent and cold; they echoed to Miss
Meadows' steps. The head mistress sat at her desk. For a moment
she did not look up. She was as usual disentangling her eye-glasses,
which had got caught in her lace tie. "Sit down, Miss Meadows,"
she said very kindly. And then she picked up a pink envelope
from the blotting-pad. "I sent for you just now because this telegram has come for you."

"A telegram for me, Miss Wyatt?"

Basil! He had committed suicide, decided Miss Meadows.
Her hand flew out, but Miss Wyatt held the telegram back a
moment. "I hope it's not bad news," she said, so more than kindly.
And Miss Meadows tore it open.

"Pay no attention to letter, must have been mad, bought hatstand to-day—Basil," she read. She couldn't take her eyes off the
telegram.

"I do hope it's nothing very serious," said Miss Wyatt, leaning
forward.

271

"Oh, no, thank you, Miss Wyatt," blushed Miss Meadows. "It's nothing bad at all. It's"—and she gave an apologetic little laugh—"it's from my *fiancé* saying that . . . saying that—" There was a pause. "I *see*," said Miss Wyatt. And another pause. Then—"You've fifteen minutes more of your class, Miss Meadows, haven't you?"

"Yes, Miss Wyatt." She got up. She half ran towards the door.

"Oh, just one minute, Miss Meadows," said Miss Wyatt. "I must say I don't approve of my teachers having telegrams sent to them in school hours, unless in case of very bad news, such as death," explained Miss Wyatt, "or a very serious accident, or something to that effect. Good news, Miss Meadows, will always keep, you know."

On the wings of hope, of love, of joy, Miss Meadows sped back to the music hall, up the aisle, up the steps, over to the piano.

"Page thirty-two, Mary," she said, "page thirty-two," and, picking up the yellow chrysanthemum, she held it to her lips to hide her smile. Then she turned to the girls, rapped with her baton: "Page thirty-two, girls. Page thirty-two."

> We come here To-day with Flowers o'erladen,
> With Baskets of Fruit and Ribbons to boot,
> To-oo Congratulate. . . .

"Stop! Stop!" cried Miss Meadows. "This is awful. This is dreadful." And she beamed at her girls. "What's the matter with you all? Think, girls, think of what you're singing. Use your imaginations. *With Flowers o'erladen. Baskets of Fruit and Ribbons to boot.* And *Congratulate.*" Miss Meadows broke off. "Don't look so doleful, girls. It ought to sound warm, joyful, eager. *Congratulate.* Once more. Quickly. All together. Now then!"

And this time Miss Meadows' voice sounded over all the other voices—full, deep, glowing with expression.

She's right about feeling possibility about what women will think of her.

272

— Chooses to take content (blame as little as you like)

The Voyage

THE PICTON boat was due to leave at half-past eleven. It was a beautiful night, mild, starry, only when they got out of the cab and started to walk down the Old Wharf that jutted out into the harbour, a faint wind blowing off the water ruffled under Fenella's hat, and she put up her hand to keep it on. It was dark on the Old Wharf, very dark; the wool sheds, the cattle trucks, the cranes standing up so high, the little squat railway engine, all seemed carved out of solid darkness. Here and there on a rounded woodpile that was like the stalk of a huge black mushroom, there hung a lantern, but it seemed afraid to unfurl its timid, quivering light in all that blackness; it burned softly, as if for itself.

Fenella's father pushed on with quick, nervous strides. Beside him her grandma bustled along in her crackling black ulster; they went so fast that she had now and again to give an undignified little skip to keep up with them. As well as her luggage strapped into a neat sausage, Fenella carried clasped to her her grandma's umbrella, and the handle, which was a swan's head, kept giving her shoulder a sharp little peck as if it too wanted her to hurry. . . . Men, their caps pulled down, their collars turned up, swung by; a few women all muffled scurried along; and one tiny boy, only his little black arms and legs showing out of a white woolly shawl, was jerked along angrily between his father and mother; he looked like a baby fly that had fallen into the cream.

Then suddenly, so suddenly that Fenella and her grandma both leapt, there sounded from behind the largest wool shed, that had a trail of smoke hanging over it, *Mia-oo-oo-O-O!*

"First whistle," said her father briefly, and at that moment they came in sight of the Picton boat. Lying beside the dark wharf, all strung, all beaded with round golden lights, the Picton boat looked as if she was more ready to sail among stars than out into the cold sea. People pressed along the gangway. First went her grandma, then her father, then Fenella. There was a high step down on to the deck, and an old sailor in a jersey standing by gave her his dry, hard hand. They were there; they stepped out of the way of the hurrying people, and standing under a little iron stairway that led to the upper deck they began to say good-bye.

"There, mother, there's your luggage!" said Fenella's father, giving grandma another strapped-up sausage.

"Thank you, Frank."

"And you've got your cabin tickets safe?"

"Yes, dear."

"And your other tickets?"

Grandma felt for them inside her glove and showed him the tips.

"That's right."

He sounded stern, but Fenella, eagerly watching him, saw that he looked tired and sad. *Mia-oo-oo-O-O!* The second whistle blared just above their heads, and a voice like a cry shouted, "Any more for the gangway?"

"You'll give my love to father," Fenella saw her father's lips say. And her grandma, very agitated, answered, "Of course I will, dear. Go now. You'll be left. Go now, Frank. Go now."

"It's all right, mother. I've got another three minutes." To her surprise Fenella saw her father take off his hat. He clasped grandma in her arms and pressed her to him. "God bless you, mother!" she heard him say.

And grandma put her hand, with the black thread glove that was worn through on her ring finger, against his cheek, and she sobbed, "God bless you, my own brave son!"

This was so awful that Fenella quickly turned her back on them, swallowed once, twice, and frowned terribly at a little green star on a mast head. But she had to turn round again; her father was going.

"Good-bye, Fenella. Be a good girl." His cold, wet moustache brushed her cheek. But Fenella caught hold of the lapels of his coat.

"How long am I going to stay?" she whispered anxiously. He wouldn't look at her. He shook her off gently, and gently said, "We'll see about that. Here! Where's your hand?" He pressed something into her palm. "Here's a shilling in case you should need it."

A shilling! She must be going away for ever! "Father!" cried Fenella. But he was gone. He was the last off the ship. The sailors put their shoulders to the gangway. A huge coil of dark rope went flying through the air and fell "thump" on the wharf. A bell rang; a whistle shrilled. Silently the dark wharf began to slip, to slide, to edge away from them. Now there was a rush of water between. Fenella strained to see with all her might. "Was that father turning round?"—or waving?—or standing alone?—or walking off by himself? The strip of water grew broader, darker. Now the Picton boat began to swing round steady, pointing out to sea. It was no good looking any longer. There was nothing to be seen but a few lights, the face of the town clock hanging in the air, and more lights, little patches of them, on the dark hills.

The freshening wind tugged at Fenella's skirts; she went back to her grandma. To her relief grandma seemed no longer sad. She had put the two sausages of luggage one on top of the other, and she was sitting on them, her hands folded, her head a little on one side. There was an intent, bright look on her face. Then Fenella saw that her lips were moving and guessed that she was praying. But the old woman gave her a bright nod as if to say the prayer was nearly over. She unclasped her hands, sighed, clasped them again, bent forward, and at last gave herself a soft shake.

"And now, child," she said, fingering the bow of her bonnet-strings, "I think we ought to see about our cabins. Keep close to me, and mind you don't slip."

"Yes, grandma!"

"And be careful the umbrellas aren't caught in the stair rail. I saw a beautiful umbrella broken in half like that on my way over."

"Yes, grandma."

Dark figures of men lounged against the rails. In the glow of their pipes a nose shone out, or the peak of a cap, or a pair of surprised-looking eyebrows. Fenella glanced up. High in the air, a little figure, his hands thrust in his short jacket pockets, stood staring out to sea. The ship rocked ever so little, and she thought the stars rocked too. And now a pale steward in a linen coat, holding a tray high in the palm of his hand, stepped out of a lighted doorway and skimmed past them. They went through the doorway. Carefully over the high brass-bound step on to the rubber mat and then down such a terribly steep flight of stairs that grandma had to put both feet on each step, and Fenella clutched the clammy brass rail and forgot all about the swan-necked umbrella.

At the bottom grandma stopped; Fenella was rather afraid she was going to pray again. But no, it was only to get out the cabin tickets. They were in the saloon. It was glaring bright and stifling; the air smelled of paint and burnt chop-bones and india-rubber. Fenella wished her grandma would go on, but the old woman was not to be hurried. An immense basket of ham sand-wiches caught her eye. She went up to them and touched the top one delicately with her finger.

"How much are the sandwiches?" she asked.

"Tuppence!" bawled a rude steward, slamming down a knife and fork.

Grandma could hardly believe it.

"Twopence *each*?" she asked.

"That's right," said the steward, and he winked at his companion.

Grandma made a small, astonished face. Then she whispered primly to Fenella. "What wickedness!" And they sailed out at the further door and along a passage that had cabins on either side. Such a very nice stewardess came to meet them. She was dressed all in blue, and her collar and cuffs were fastened with large brass buttons. She seemed to know grandma well.

"Well, Mrs. Crane," said she, unlocking their washstand. "We've got you back again. It's not often you give yourself a cabin."

"No," said grandma. "But this time my dear son's thought-fulness—"

"I hope—" began the stewardess. Then she turned round and took a long mournful look at grandma's blackness and at Fenella's black coat and skirt, black blouse, and hat with a crape rose.

Grandma nodded. "It was God's will," said she.

The stewardess shut her lips and, taking a deep breath, she seemed to expand.

"What I always say is," she said, as though it was her own discovery, "sooner or later each of us has to go, and that's a certingty." She paused. "Now, can I bring you anything, Mrs. Crane? A cup of tea? I know it's no good offering you a little something to keep the cold out."

Grandma shook her head. "Nothing, thank you. We've got a few wine biscuits, and Fenella has a very nice banana."

"Then I'll give you a look later on," said the stewardess, and she went out, shutting the door.

What a very small cabin it was! It was like being shut up in a box with grandma. The dark round eye above the washstand gleamed at them dully. Fenella felt shy. She stood against the door, still clasping her luggage and the umbrella. Were they going to get undressed in here? Already her grandma had taken off her bonnet, and, rolling up the strings, she fixed each with a pin to the lining before she hung the bonnet up. Her white hair shone like silk; the little bun at the back was covered with a black net. Fenella hardly ever saw her grandma with her head uncovered; she looked strange.

"I shall put on the woollen fascinator your dear mother cro-cheted for me," said grandma, and, unstrapping the sausage, she took it out and wound it round her head; the fringe of grey bobbles danced at her eyebrows as she smiled tenderly and mourn-fully at Fenella. Then she undid her bodice, and something under that, and something else underneath that. Then there seemed a short, sharp tussle, and grandma flushed faintly. Snip! Snap! She had undone her stays. She breathed a sigh of relief, and sitting on the plush couch, she slowly and carefully pulled off her elastic-sided boots and stood them side by side.

By the time Fenella had taken off her coat and skirt and put on her flannel dressing-gown grandma was quite ready.

"Must I take off my boots, grandma? They're lace."

Grandma gave them a moment's deep consideration. "You'd feel a great deal more comfortable if you did, child," said she. She kissed Fenella. "Don't forget to say your prayers. Our dear Lord is with us when we are at sea even more than when we are on dry land. And because I am an experienced traveller," said grandma briskly, "I shall take the upper berth."

"But, grandma, however will you get up there?"

Three little spider-like steps were all Fenella saw. The old woman gave a small silent laugh before she mounted them nimbly, and she peered over the high bunk at the astonished Fenella.

"You didn't think your grandma could do that, did you?" said she. And as she sank back Fenella heard her light laugh again.

The hard square of brown soap would not lather, and the water in the bottle was like a kind of blue jelly. How hard it was, too, to turn down those stiff sheets; you simply had to tear your way in. If everything had been different, Fenella might have got the giggles. . . . At last she was inside, and while she lay there panting, there sounded from above a long, soft whispering, as though some one was gently, gently rustling among tissue paper to find something. It was grandma saying her prayers. . . .

A long time passed. Then the stewardess came in; she trod softly and leaned her hand on grandma's bunk.

"We're just entering the Straits," she said.

"Oh!"

"It's a fine night, but we're rather empty. We may pitch a little."

And indeed at that moment the Picton boat rose and rose and hung in the air just long enough to give a shiver before she swung down again, and there was the sound of heavy water slapping against her sides. Fenella remembered she had left that swan-necked umbrella standing up on the little couch. If it fell over, would it break? But grandma remembered too, at the same time.

"I wonder if you'd mind, stewardess, laying down my umbrella," she whispered.

"Not at all, Mrs. Crane." And the stewardess, coming back

to grandma, breathed, "Your little granddaughter's in such a beautiful sleep."

"God be praised for that!" said grandma.

"Poor little motherless mite!" said the stewardess. And grandma was still telling the stewardess all about what happened when Fenella fell asleep.

But she hadn't been asleep long enough to dream before she woke up again to see something waving in the air above her head. What was it? What could it be? It was a small grey foot. Now another joined it. They seemed to be feeling about for something; there came a sigh.

"I'm awake, grandma," said Fenella.

"Oh, dear, am I near the ladder?" asked grandma. "I thought it was this end."

"No, grandma, it's the other. I'll put your foot on it. Are we there?" asked Fenella.

"In the harbour," said grandma. "We must get up, child. You'd better have a biscuit to steady yourself before you move."

But Fenella had hopped out of her bunk. The lamp was still burning, but night was over, and it was cold. Peering through that round eye, she could see far off some rocks. Now they were scattered over with foam; now a gull flipped by; and now there came a long piece of real land.

"It's land, grandma," said Fenella, wonderingly, as though they had been at sea for weeks together. She hugged herself; she stood on one leg and rubbed it with the toes of the other foot; she was trembling. Oh, it had all been so sad lately. Was it going to change? But all her grandma said was, "Make haste, child. I should leave your nice banana for the stewardess as you haven't eaten it." And Fenella put on her black clothes again, and a button sprang off one of her gloves and rolled to where she couldn't reach it. They went up on deck.

But if it had been cold in the cabin, on deck it was like ice. The sun was not up yet, but the stars were dim, and the cold pale sky was the same colour as the cold pale sea. On the land, a white mist rose and fell. Now they could see quite plainly dark bush. Even the shapes of the umbrella ferns showed, and those strange silvery withered trees that are like skeletons. . . . Now they could see the landing-stage and some little houses, pale too, clustered together, like shells on the lid of a box. The other passengers tramped up and down, but more slowly than they had the night before, and they looked gloomy.

And now the landing-stage came out to meet them. Slowly it swam towards the Picton boat, and a man holding a coil of rope, and a cart with a small drooping horse and another man sitting on the step, came too.

"It's Mr. Penreddy, Fenella, come for us," said grandma. She sounded pleased. Her white waxen cheeks were blue with cold, her chin trembled, and she had to keep wiping her eyes and her little pink nose.

"You've got my—"

"Yes, grandma." Fenella showed it to her.

The rope came flying through the air, and "smack" it fell on to the deck. The gangway was lowered. Again Fenella followed her grandma on to the wharf over to the little cart, and a moment later they were bowling away. The hooves of the little horse drummed over the wooden piles, then sank softly into the sandy road. Not a soul was to be seen; there was not even a feather of smoke. The mist rose and fell, and the sea still sounded asleep as slowly it turned on the beach.

"I seen Mr. Crane yestiddy," said Mr. Penreddy. "He looked himself then. Missus knocked him up a batch of scones last week."

And now the little horse pulled up before one of the shell-like houses. They got down. Fenella put her hand on the gate, and the big, trembling dewdrops soaked through her glove-tips. Up a little path of round white pebbles they went, with drenched sleeping flowers on either side. Grandma's delicate white picotees were so heavy with dew that they were fallen, but their sweet smell was part of the cold morning. The blinds were down in the little house; they mounted the steps on to the verandah. A pair of old Bluchers was on one side of the door, and a large red watering-can on the other.

"Tut! tut! Your grandpa," said grandma. She turned the handle. Not a sound. She called, "Walter!" And immediately a deep voice that sounded half stifled called back, "Is that you, Mary?"

"Wait, dear," said grandma. "Go in there." She pushed Fenella gently into a small dusky sitting-room.

On the table a white cat, that had been folded up like a camel, rose, stretched itself, yawned, and then sprang on to the tips of its toes. Fenella buried one cold little hand in the white, warm fur, and smiled timidly while she stroked and listened to grandma's gentle voice and the rolling tones of grandpa.

A door creaked. "Come in, dear." The old woman beckoned, Fenella followed. There, lying to one side of an immense bed, lay grandpa. Just his head with a white tuft, and his rosy face and long silver beard showed over the quilt. He was like a very old wide-awake bird.

"Well, my girl!" said grandpa. "Give us a kiss!" Fenella kissed him. "Ugh!" said grandpa. "Her little nose is as cold as a button. What's that she's holding? Her grandma's umbrella?"

Fenella smiled again, and crooked the swan neck over the bed-rail. Above the bed there was a big text in a deep-black frame:

> Lost! One Golden Hour
> Set with Sixty Diamond Minutes.
> No Reward Is Offered
> For It Is Gone For Ever!

"Yer grandma painted that," said grandpa. And he ruffled his white tuft and looked at Fenella so merrily she almost thought he winked at her.

The Garden-Party

AND AFTER ALL the weather was ideal. They could not have had a more perfect day for a garden-party if they had ordered it. Windless, warm, the sky without a cloud. Only the blue was veiled with a haze of light gold, as it is sometimes in early summer. The gardener had been up since dawn, mowing the lawns and sweeping them, until the grass and the dark flat rosettes where the daisy plants had been seemed to shine. As for the roses, you could not help feeling they understood that roses are the only flowers that impress people at garden-parties; the only flowers that everybody is certain of knowing. Hundreds, yes, literally hundreds, had come out in a single night; the green bushes bowed down as though they had been visited by archangels.

Breakfast was not yet over before the men came to put up the marquee.

"Where do you want the marquee put, mother?"

"My dear child, it's no use asking me. I'm determined to leave everything to you children this year. Forget I am your mother. Treat me as an honoured guest."

But Meg could not possibly go and supervise the men. She had washed her hair before breakfast, and she sat drinking her coffee in a green turban, with a dark wet curl stamped on each cheek. Jose, the butterfly, always came down in a silk petticoat and a kimono jacket.

"You'll have to go, Laura; you're the artistic one."

Away Laura flew, still holding her piece of bread-and-butter. It's so delicious to have an excuse for eating out of doors, and besides, she loved having to arrange things; she always felt she could do it so much better than anybody else.

Four men in their shirt-sleeves stood grouped together on the garden path. They carried staves covered with rolls of canvas, and they had big tool-bags slung on their backs. They looked impressive. Laura wished now that she had not got the bread-and-butter, but there was nowhere to put it, and she couldn't possibly throw it away. She blushed and tried to look severe and even a little bit short-sighted as she came up to them.

"Good morning," she said, copying her mother's voice. But that sounded so fearfully affected that she was ashamed, and stammered like a little girl, "Oh—er—have you come—is it about the marquee?"

"That's right, miss," said the tallest of the men, a lanky, freckled fellow, and he shifted his tool-bag, knocked back his straw hat and smiled down at her. "That's about it."

His smile was so easy, so friendly that Laura recovered. What nice eyes he had, small, but such a dark blue! And now she looked at the others, they were smiling too. "Cheer up, we won't bite," their smile seemed to say. How very nice workmen were! And what a beautiful morning! She mustn't mention the morning; she must be businesslike. The marquee.

"Well, what about the lily-lawn? Would that do?"

And she pointed to the lily-lawn with the hand that didn't hold the bread-and-butter. They turned, they stared in the direction. A little fat chap thrust out his under-lip, and the tall fellow frowned.

"I don't fancy it," said he. "Not conspicuous enough. You see, with a thing like a marquee," and he turned to Laura in his easy way, "you want to put it somewhere where it'll give you a bang slap in the eye, if you follow me."

Laura's upbringing made her wonder for a moment whether it was quite respectful of a workman to talk to her of bangs slap in the eye. But she did quite follow him.

"A corner of the tennis-court," she suggested. "But the band's going to be in the corner."

"H'm, going to have a band, are you?" said another of the

workmen. He was pale. He had a haggard look as his dark eyes scanned the tennis-court. What was he thinking?

"Only a very small band," said Laura gently. Perhaps he wouldn't mind so much if the band was quite small. But the tall fellow interrupted.

"Look here, miss, that's the place. Against those trees. Over there. That'll do fine."

Against the karakas. Then the karaka trees would be hidden. And they were so lovely, with their broad, gleaming leaves, and their clusters of yellow fruit. They were like trees you imagined growing on a desert island, proud, solitary, lifting their leaves and fruits to the sun in a kind of silent splendour. Must they be hidden by a marquee?

They must. Already the men had shouldered their staves and were making for the place. Only the tall fellow was left. He bent down, pinched a sprig of lavender, put his thumb and forefinger to his nose and snuffed up the smell. When Laura saw that gesture she forgot all about the karakas in her wonder at him caring for things like that—caring for the smell of lavender. How many men that she knew would have done such a thing? Oh, how extraordinarily nice workmen were, she thought. Why couldn't she have workmen for friends rather than the silly boys she danced with and who came to Sunday night supper? She would get on much better with men like these.

It's all the fault, she decided, as the tall fellow drew something on the back of an envelope, something that was to be looped up or left to hang, of these absurd class distinctions. Well, for her part, she didn't feel them. Not a bit, not an atom. . . . And now there came the chock-chock of wooden hammers. Some one whistled, some one sang out, "Are you right there, matey?" "Matey!" The friendliness of it, the—the— Just to prove how happy she was, just to show the tall fellow how at home she felt, and how she despised stupid conventions, Laura took a big bite of her bread-and-butter as she stared at the little drawing. She felt just like a work-girl.

"Laura, Laura, where are you? Telephone, Laura!" a voice cried from the house.

"Coming!" Away she skimmed, over the lawn, up the path,

up the steps, across the verandah, and into the porch. In the hall her father and Laurie were brushing their hats ready to go to the office.

"I say, Laura," said Laurie very fast, "you might just give a squiz at my coat before this afternoon. See if it wants pressing."

"I will," said she. Suddenly she couldn't stop herself. She ran at Laurie and gave him a small, quick squeeze. "Oh, I do love parties, don't you?" gasped Laura.

"Ra-ther," said Laurie's warm, boyish voice, and he squeezed his sister too, and gave her a gentle push. "Dash off to the telephone, old girl."

The telephone. "Yes, yes; oh yes. Kitty? Good morning, dear. Come to lunch? Do, dear. Delighted of course. It will only be a very scratch meal—just the sandwich crusts and broken meringue-shells and what's left over. Yes, isn't it a perfect morning? Your white? Oh, I certainly should. One moment—hold the line. Mother's calling." And Laura sat back. "What, mother? Can't hear."

Mrs. Sheridan's voice floated down the stairs. "Tell her to wear that sweet hat she had on last Sunday."

"Mother says you're to wear that *sweet* hat you had on last Sunday. Good. One o'clock. Bye-bye."

Laura put back the receiver, flung her arms over her head, took a deep breath, stretched and let them fall. "Huh," she sighed, and the moment after the sigh she sat up quickly. She was still, listening. All the doors in the house seemed to be open. The house was alive with soft, quick steps and running voices. The green baize door that led to the kitchen regions swung open and shut with a muffled thud. And now there came a long, chuckling absurd sound. It was the heavy piano being moved on its stiff castors. But the air! If you stopped to notice, was the air always like this? Little faint winds were playing chase, in at the tops of the windows, out at the doors. And there were two tiny spots of sun, one on the inkpot, one on a silver photograph frame, playing too. Darling little spots. Especially the one on the inkpot lid. It was quite warm. A warm little silver star. She could have kissed it.

The front door bell pealed, and there sounded the rustle of Sadie's print skirt on the stairs. A man's voice murmured; Sadie answered, careless, "I'm sure I don't know. Wait. I'll ask Mrs. Sheridan."

"What is it, Sadie?" Laura came into the hall.

"It's the florist, Miss Laura."

It was, indeed. There, just inside the door, stood a wide, shallow tray full of pots of pink lilies. No other kind. Nothing but lilies—canna lilies, big pink flowers, wide open, radiant, almost frighteningly alive on bright crimson stems.

"O-oh, Sadie!" said Laura, and the sound was like a little moan. She crouched down as if to warm herself at that blaze of lilies; she felt they were in her fingers, on her lips, growing in her breast.

"It's some mistake," she said faintly. "Nobody ever ordered so many. Sadie, go and find mother."

But at that moment Mrs. Sheridan joined them.

"It's quite right," she said calmly. "Yes, I ordered them. Aren't they lovely?" She pressed Laura's arm. "I was passing the shop yesterday, and I saw them in the window. And I suddenly thought for once in my life I shall have enough canna lilies. The garden-party will be a good excuse."

"But I thought you said you didn't mean to interfere," said Laura. Sadie had gone. The florist's man was still outside at his van. She put her arm round her mother's neck and gently, very gently, she bit her mother's ear.

"My darling child, you wouldn't like a logical mother, would you? Don't do that. Here's the man."

He carried more lilies still, another whole tray.

"Bank them up, just inside the door, on both sides of the porch, please," said Mrs. Sheridan. "Don't you agree, Laura?"

"Oh, I *do* mother."

In the drawing-room Meg, Jose and good little Hans had at last succeeded in moving the piano.

"Now, if we put this chesterfield against the wall and move everything out of the room except the chairs, don't you think?"

"Quite."

"Hans, move these tables into the smoking-room, and bring a sweeper to take these marks off the carpet and—one moment, Hans—" Jose loved giving orders to the servants, and they loved obeying her. She always made them feel they were taking part in some drama. "Tell mother and Miss Laura to come here at once."

"Very good, Miss Jose."

She turned to Meg. "I want to hear what the piano sounds like, just in case I'm asked to sing this afternoon. Let's try over 'This life is Weary.'"

Pom! Ta-ta-ta *Tee*-ta! The piano burst out so passionately that Jose's face changed. She clasped her hands. She looked mournfully and enigmatically at her mother and Laura as they came in.

> This Life is *Wee*-ary,
> A Tear—a Sigh.
> A Love that *Chan*-ges,
> This Life is *Wee*-ary,
> A Tear—a Sigh.
> A Love that *Chan*-ges,
> And then . . . Good-bye!

But at the word "Good-bye," and although the piano sounded more desperate than ever, her face broke into a brilliant, dreadfully unsympathetic smile.

"Aren't I in good voice, mummy?" she beamed.

> This Life is *Wee*-ary,
> Hope comes to Die.
> A Dream—a *Wa*-kening.

But now Sadie interrupted them. "What is it, Sadie?"

"If you please, m'm, cook says have you got the flags for the sandwiches?"

"The flags for the sandwiches, Sadie?" echoed Mrs. Sheridan dreamily. And the children knew by her face that she hadn't got them. "Let me see." And she said to Sadie firmly, "Tell cook I'll let her have them in ten minutes."

Sadie went.

"Now, Laura," said her mother quickly. "Come with me into the smoking-room. I've got the names somewhere on the back of an envelope. You'll have to write them out for me. Meg, go upstairs this minute and take that wet thing off your head. Jose, run and finish dressing this instant. Do you hear me, children, or shall I have to tell your father when he comes home to-night? And—and, Jose, pacify cook if you do go into the kitchen, will you? I'm terrified of her this morning."

The envelope was found at last behind the dining-room clock, though how it had got there Mrs. Sheridan could not imagine.

"One of you children must have stolen it out of my bag, because I remember vividly—cream cheese and lemon-curd. Have you done that?"

"Yes."

"Egg and—" Mrs. Sheridan held the envelope away from her. "It looks like mice. It can't be mice, can it?"

"Olive, pet," said Laura, looking over her shoulder.

"Yes, of course, olive. What a horrible combination it sounds. Egg and olive."

They were finished at last, and Laura took them off to the kitchen. She found Jose there pacifying the cook, who did not look at all terrifying.

"I have never seen such exquisite sandwiches," said Jose's rapturous voice. "How many kinds did you say there were, cook? Fifteen?"

"Fifteen, Miss Jose."

"Well, cook, I congratulate you."

Cook swept up crusts with the long sandwich knife, and smiled broadly.

"Godber's has come," announced Sadie, issuing out of the pantry. She had seen the man pass the window.

That meant the cream puffs had come. Godber's were famous for their cream puffs. Nobody ever thought of making them at home.

"Bring them in and put them on the table, my girl," ordered cook.

Sadie brought them in and went back to the door. Of course Laura and Jose were far too grown-up to really care about such things. All the same, they couldn't help agreeing that the puffs looked very attractive. Very. Cook began arranging them, shaking off the extra icing sugar.

"Don't they carry one back to all one's parties?" said Laura.

"I suppose they do," said practical Jose, who never liked to be carried back. "They look beautifully light and feathery, I must say."

"Have one each, my dears," said cook in her comfortable voice. "Yer ma won't know."

Oh, impossible. Fancy cream puffs so soon after breakfast. The very idea made one shudder. All the same, two minutes later Jose and Laura were licking their fingers with that absorbed inward look that only comes from whipped cream.

"Let's go into the garden, out by the back way," suggested Laura. "I want to see how the men are getting on with the marquee. They're such awfully nice men."

But the back door was blocked by cook, Sadie, Godber's man and Hans.

Something had happened.

"Tuk-tuk-tuk," clucked cook like an agitated hen. Sadie had her hand clapped to her cheek as though she had toothache. Hans's face was screwed up in the effort to understand. Only Godber's man seemed to be enjoying himself; it was his story.

"What's the matter? What's happened?"

"There's been a horrible accident," said cook. "A man killed."

"A man killed! Where? How? When?"

But Godber's man wasn't going to have his story snatched from under his very nose.

"Know those little cottages just below here, miss?" Know them? Of course, she knew them. "Well, there's a young chap living there, name of Scott, a carter. His horse shied at a traction-engine, corner of Hawke Street this morning, and he was thrown out on the back of his head. Killed."

"Dead!" Laura stared at Godber's man.

"Dead when they picked him up," said Godber's man with relish. "They were taking the body home as I come up here." And he said to the cook, "He's left a wife and five little ones."

"Jose, come here." Laura caught hold of her sister's sleeve and dragged her through the kitchen to the other side of the green baize door. There she paused and leaned against it. "Jose!" she said, horrified, "however are we going to stop everything?"

"Stop everything, Laura!" cried Jose in astonishment. "What do you mean?"

"Stop the garden-party, of course." Why did Jose pretend?

But Jose was still more amazed. "Stop the garden-party? My dear Laura, don't be so absurd. Of course we can't do anything of the kind. Nobody expects us to. Don't be so extravagant."

"But we can't possibly have a garden-party with a man dead just outside the front gate."

That really was extravagant, for the little cottages were in a lane to themselves at the very bottom of a steep rise that led up to the house. A broad road ran between. True, they were far too near. They were the greatest possible eyesore, and they had no right to be in that neighbourhood at all. They were little mean dwellings painted a chocolate brown. In the garden patches there was nothing but cabbage stalks, sick hens and tomato cans. The very smoke coming out of their chimneys was poverty-stricken. Little rags and shreds of smoke, so unlike the great silvery plumes that uncurled from the Sheridans' chimneys. Washerwomen lived in the lane and sweeps and a cobbler, and a man whose house-front was studded all over with minute bird-cages. Children swarmed. When the Sheridans were little they were forbidden to set foot there because of the revolting language and of what they might catch. But since they were grown up, Laura and Laurie on their prowls sometimes walked through. It was disgusting and sordid. They came out with a shudder. But still one must go everywhere; one must see everything. So through they went.

"And just think of what the band would sound like to that poor woman," said Laura.

"Oh, Laura!" Jose began to be seriously annoyed. "If you're going to stop a band playing every time some one has an accident, you'll lead a very strenuous life. I'm every bit as sorry about it as you. I feel just as sympathetic." Her eyes hardened. She looked at her sister just as she used to when they were little and fighting together. "You won't bring a drunken workman back to life by being sentimental," she said softly.

"Drunk! Who said he was drunk?" Laura turned furiously on Jose. She said, just as they had used to say on those occasions, "I'm going straight up to tell mother."

"Do, dear," cooed Jose.

"Mother, can I come into your room?" Laura turned the big glass door-knob.

"Of course, child. Why, what's the matter? What's given you such a colour?" And Mrs. Sheridan turned round from her dressing table. She was trying on a new hat.

"Mother, a man's been killed," began Laura.

"*Not* in the garden?" interrupted her mother.

"No, no!"

"Oh, what a fright you gave me!" Mrs. Sheridan sighed with relief, and took off the big hat and held it on her knees.

"But listen, mother," said Laura. Breathless, half-choking, she told the dreadful story. "Of course, we can't have our party, can we?" she pleaded. "The band and everybody arriving. They'd hear us, mother; they're nearly neighbours!"

To Laura's astonishment her mother behaved just like Jose, it was harder to bear because she seemed amused. She refused to take Laura seriously.

"But, my dear child, use your common sense. It's only by accident we've heard of it. If some one had died there normally—and I can't understand how they keep alive in those poky little holes—we should still be having our party, shouldn't we?"

Laura had to say "yes" to that, but she felt it was all wrong. She sat down on her mother's sofa and pinched the cushion frill.

"Mother, isn't it really terribly heartless of us?" she asked.

"Darling!" Mrs. Sheridan got up and came over to her, carrying the hat. Before Laura could stop her she had popped it on. "My child!" said her mother, "the hat is yours. It's made for you. It's much too young for me. I have never seen you look such a picture. Look at yourself!" And she held up her hand-mirror.

"But, mother," Laura began again. She couldn't look at herself; she turned aside.

This time Mrs. Sheridan lost patience just as Jose had done.

"You are being very absurd, Laura," she said coldly. "People like that don't expect sacrifices from us. And it's not very sympathetic to spoil everybody's enjoyment as you're doing now."

"I don't understand," said Laura, and she walked quickly out of the room into her own bedroom. There, quite by chance, the first thing she saw was this charming girl in the mirror, in her black hat trimmed with gold daisies, and a long black velvet ribbon. Never had she imagined she could look like that. Is mother right? she thought. And now she hoped her mother was right. Am I being extravagant? Perhaps it was extravagant. Just for a moment she had another glimpse of that poor woman and those little children, and the body being carried into the house. But it all seemed blurred, unreal, like a picture in the newspaper. I'll remember it again after the party's over, she decided. And somehow that seemed quite the best plan. . . .

Lunch was over by half past one. By half past two they were all ready for the fray. The green-coated band had arrived and was established in a corner of the tennis-court.

"My dear!" trilled Kitty Maitland, "aren't they too like frogs for words? You ought to have arranged them round the pond with the conductor in the middle on a leaf."

Laurie arrived and hailed them on his way to dress. At the sight of him Laura remembered the accident again. She wanted to tell him. If Laurie agreed with the others, then it was bound to be all right. And she followed him into the hall.

"Laurie!"

"Hallo!" He was half-way upstairs, but when he turned round and saw Laura he suddenly puffed out his cheeks and goggled his eyes at her. "My word, Laura; you do look stunning," said Laurie. "What an absolutely topping hat!"

Laura said faintly "Is it?" and smiled up at Laurie, and didn't tell him after all.

Soon after that people began coming in streams. The band struck up; the hired waiters ran from the house to the marquee. Wherever you looked there were couples strolling, bending to the flowers, greeting, moving on over the lawn. They were like bright birds that had alighted in the Sheridans' garden for this one afternoon, on their way to—where? Ah, what happiness it is to be with people who all are happy, to press hands, press cheeks, smile into eyes.

"Darling Laura, how well you look!"

"What a becoming hat, child!"

"Laura, you look quite Spanish. I've never seen you look so striking."

And Laura, glowing, answered softly, "Have you had tea? Won't you have an ice? The passion-fruit ices really are rather special." She ran to her father and begged him. "Daddy darling, can't the band have something to drink?"

And the perfect afternoon slowly ripened, slowly faded, slowly its petals closed.

"Never a more delightful garden-party . . ." "The greatest success . . ." "Quite the most . . ."

Laura helped her mother with the good-byes. They stood side by side in the porch till it was all over.

"All over, all over, thank heaven," said Mrs. Sheridan. "Round up the others, Laura. Let's go and have some fresh coffee. I'm exhausted. Yes, it's been very successful. But oh, these parties, these parties! Why will you children insist on giving parties!" And they all of them sat down in the deserted marquee.

"Have a sandwich, daddy dear. I wrote the flag."

"Thanks." Mr. Sheridan took a bite and the sandwich was gone. He took another. "I suppose you didn't hear of a beastly accident that happened to-day?" he said.

"My dear," said Mrs. Sheridan, holding up her hand, "we did. It nearly ruined the party. Laura insisted we should put it off."

"Oh, mother!" Laura didn't want to be teased about it.

"It was a horrible affair all the same," said Mr. Sheridan. "The chap was married too. Lived just below in the lane, and leaves a wife and half a dozen kiddies, so they say."

An awkward little silence fell. Mrs. Sheriden fidgeted with her cup. Really, it was very tactless of father . . .

Suddenly she looked up. There on the table were all those sandwiches, cakes, puffs, all uneaten, all going to be wasted. She had one of her brilliant ideas.

"I know," she said. "Let's make up a basket. Let's send that poor creature some of this perfectly good food. At any rate, it will be the greatest treat for the children. Don't you agree? And she's sure to have neighbours calling in and so on. What a point to have it all ready prepared. Laura!" She jumped up. "Get me the big basket out of the stairs cupboard."

"But, mother, do you really think it's a good idea?" said Laura.

Again, how curious, she seemed to be different from them all. To take scraps from their party. Would the poor woman really like that?

"Of course! What's the matter with you to-day? An hour or two ago you were insisting on us being sympathetic, and now—"

Oh, well! Laura ran for the basket. It was filled, it was heaped by her mother.

"Take it yourself, darling," said she. "Run down just as you are. No, wait, take the arum lilies too. People of that class are so impressed by arum lilies."

"The stems will ruin her lace frock," said practical Jose.

So they would. Just in time. "Only the basket, then. And, Laura!"—her mother followed her out of the marquee—"don't on any account—"

"What, mother?"

No, better not put such ideas into the child's head! "Nothing! Run along."

It was just growing dusky as Laura shut their garden gates. A big dog ran by like a shadow. The road gleamed white, and down below in the hollow the little cottages were in deep shade. How quiet it seemed after the afternoon. Here she was going down the hill to somewhere where a man lay dead, and she couldn't realize it. Why couldn't she? She stopped a minute. And it seemed to her that kisses, voices, tinkling spoons, laughter, the smell of crushed grass were somehow inside her. She had no room for anything else. How strange! She looked up at the pale sky, and all she thought was, "Yes, it was the most successful party."

Now the broad road was crossed. The lane began, smoky and dark. Women in shawls and men's tweed caps hurried by. Men hung over the palings; the children played in the doorways. A low hum came from the mean little cottages. In some of them there was a flicker of light, and a shadow, crab-like, moved across the window. Laura bent her head and hurried on. She wished now she had put on a coat. How her frock shone! And the big hat with the velvet streamer—if only it was another hat! Were the people looking at her? They must be. It was a mistake to have come; she knew all along it was a mistake. Should she go back even now?

No, too late. This was the house. It must be. A dark knot of people stood outside. Beside the gate an old, old woman with a crutch sat in a chair, watching. She had her feet on a newspaper. The voices stopped as Laura drew near. The group parted. It was as though she was expected, as though they had known she was coming here.

Laura was terribly nervous. Tossing the velvet ribbon over her shoulder, she said to a woman standing by, "Is this Mrs. Scott's house?" and the woman, smiling queerly, said, "It is, my lass."

Oh, to be away from this! She actually said, "Help me, God," as she walked up the tiny path and knocked. To be away from those staring eyes, or to be covered up in anything, one of those women's shawls even. I'll just leave the basket and go, she decided. I shan't even wait for it to be emptied.

Then the door opened. A little woman in black showed in the gloom.

Laura said, "Are you Mrs. Scott?" But to her horror the woman answered, "Walk in please, miss," and she was shut in the passage.

"No," said Laura, "I don't want to come in. I only want to leave this basket. Mother sent—"

The little woman in the gloomy passage seemed not to have heard her. "Step this way, please, miss," she said in an oily voice, and Laura followed her.

She found herself in a wretched little low kitchen lighted by a smoky lamp. There was a woman sitting before the fire.

"Em," said the little creature who had let her in. "Em! It's a young lady." She turned to Laura. She said meaningly, "I'm 'er sister, miss. You'll excuse 'er, won't you?"

"Oh, but of course!" said Laura. "Please, please don't disturb her. I—I only want to leave—"

But at that moment the woman at the fire turned round. Her

face, puffed up, red, with swollen eyes and swollen lips, looked terrible. She seemed as though she couldn't understand why Laura was there. What did it mean? Why was this stranger standing in the kitchen with a basket? What was it all about? And the poor face puckered up again.

"All right, my dear," said the other. "I'll thenk the young lady."

And again she began, "You'll excuse her, miss, I'm sure," and her face, swollen too, tried an oily smile.

Laura only wanted to get out, to get away. She was back in the passage. The door opened. She walked straight through into the bedroom, where the dead man was lying.

"You'd like a look at 'im, wouldn't you?" said Em's sister, and she brushed past Laura over to the bed. "Don't be afraid, my lass,—" and now her voice sounded fond and sly, and fondly she drew down the sheet—" 'e looks a picture. There's nothing to show. Come along, my dear."

Laura came.

There lay a young man, fast asleep—sleeping so soundly, so deeply, that he was far, far away from them both. Oh, so remote, so peaceful. He was dreaming. Never wake him up again. His head was sunk in the pillow, his eyes were closed; they were blind under the closed eyelids. He was given up to his dream. What did garden-parties and baskets and lace frocks matter to him? He was far from all those things. He was wonderful, beautiful. While they were laughing and while the band was playing, this marvel had come to the lane. Happy . . . happy. . . . All is well, said that sleeping face. This is just as it should be. I am content.

But all the same you had to cry, and she couldn't go out of the room without saying something to him. Laura gave a loud childish sob.

"Forgive my hat," she said.

And this time she didn't wait for Em's sister. She found her way out of the door, down the path, past all those dark people. At the corner of the lane she met Laurie.

He stepped out of the shadow. "Is that you, Laura?"

"Yes."

"Mother was getting anxious. Was it all right?"

"Yes, quite. Oh, Laurie!" She took his arm, she pressed up against him.

"I say, you're not crying, are you?" asked her brother.

Laura shook her head. She was.

Laurie put his arm round her shoulder. "Don't cry," he said in his warm, loving voice. "Was it awful?"

"No," sobbed Laura. "It was simply marvellous. But, Laurie—" She stopped, she looked at her brother. "Isn't life," she stammered, "isn't life—" But what life was she couldn't explain. No matter. He quite understood.

"*Isn't* it, darling?" said Laurie.

Miss Brill

ALTHOUGH it was so brilliantly fine—the blue sky powdered with gold and great spots of light like white wine splashed
over the Jardins Publiques—Miss Brill was glad that she had
decided on her fur. The air was motionless, but when you opened
your mouth there was just a faint chill, like a chill from a glass
of iced water before you sip, and now and again a leaf came
drifting—from nowhere, from the sky. Miss Brill put up her hand
and touched her fur. Dear little thing! It was nice to feel it again.
She had taken it out of its box that afternoon, shaken out the
moth-powder, given it a good brush, and rubbed the life back
into the dim little eyes. "What has been happening to me?" said
the sad little eyes. Oh, how sweet it was to see them snap at her
again from the red eiderdown! . . . But the nose, which was of
some black composition, wasn't at all firm. It must have had a
knock, somehow. Never mind—a little dab of black sealing-wax
when the time came—when it was absolutely necessary. . . . Little
rogue! Yes, she really felt like that about it. Little rogue biting
its tail just by her left ear. She could have taken it off and laid it
on her lap and stroked it. She felt a tingling in her hands and
arms, but that came from walking, she supposed. And when she
breathed, something light and sad—no, not sad, exactly—something gentle seemed to move in her bosom.

There were a number of people out this afternoon, far more
than last Sunday. And the band sounded louder and gayer. That
was because the Season had begun. For although the band played
all the year round on Sundays, out of season it was never the
same. It was like some one playing with only the family to listen;

298

it didn't care how it played if there weren't any strangers present. Wasn't the conductor wearing a new coat, too? She was sure it was new. He scraped with his foot and flapped his arms like a rooster about to crow, and the bandsmen sitting in the green rotunda blew out their cheeks and glared at the music. Now there came a little "flutey" bit—very pretty!—a little chain of bright drops. She was sure it would be repeated. It was; she lifted her head and smiled.

Only two people shared her "special" seat: a fine old man in a velvet coat, his hands clasped over a huge carved walking-stick, and a big old woman, sitting upright, with a roll of knitting on her embroidered apron. They did not speak. This was disappointing, for Miss Brill always looked forward to the conversation. She had become really quite expert, she thought, at listening as though she didn't listen, at sitting in other people's lives just for a minute while they talked round her.

She glanced, sideways, at the old couple. Perhaps they would go soon. Last Sunday, too, hadn't been as interesting as usual. An Englishman and his wife, he wearing a dreadful Panama hat and she button boots. And she'd gone on the whole time about how she ought to wear spectacles; she knew she needed them; but that it was no good getting any; they'd be sure to break and they'd never keep on. And he'd been so patient. He'd suggested everything—gold rims, the kind that curved round your ears, little pads inside the bridge. No, nothing would please her. "They'll always be sliding down my nose!" Miss Brill had wanted to shake her.

The old people sat on the bench, still as statues. Never mind, there was always the crowd to watch. To and fro, in front of the flower-beds and the band rotunda, the couples and groups paraded, stopped to talk, to greet, to buy a handful of flowers from the old beggar who had his tray fixed to the railings. Little children ran among them, swooping and laughing; little boys with big white silk bows under their chins, little girls, little French dolls, dressed up in velvet and lace. And sometimes a tiny staggerer came suddenly rocking into the open from under the trees, stopped, stared, as suddenly sat down "flop," until its small high-stepping mother, like a young hen, rushed scolding to its rescue.

Other people sat on the benches and green chairs, but they were nearly always the same, Sunday after Sunday, and—Miss Brill had often noticed—there was something funny about nearly all of them. They were odd, silent, nearly all old, and from the way they stared they looked as though they'd just come from dark little rooms or even—even cupboards!

Behind the rotunda the slender trees with yellow leaves down drooping, and through them just a line of sea, and beyond the blue sky with gold-veined clouds.

Tum-tum-tum tiddle-um! tiddle-um! tum tiddley-um tum ta! blew the band.

Two young girls in red came by and two young soldiers in blue met them, and they laughed and paired and went off arm-in-arm. Two peasant women with funny straw hats passed, gravely, leading beautiful smoke-coloured donkeys. A cold, pale nun hurried by. A beautiful woman came along and dropped her bunch of violets, and a little boy ran after to hand them to her, and she took them and threw them away as if they'd been poisoned. Dear me! Miss Brill didn't know whether to admire that or not! And now an ermine toque and a gentleman in grey met just in front of her. He was tall, stiff, dignified, and she was wearing the ermine toque she'd bought when her hair was yellow. Now everything, her hair, her face, even her eyes, was the same colour as the shabby ermine, and her hand, in its cleaned glove, lifted to dab her lips, was a tiny yellowish paw. Oh, she was so pleased to see him—delighted! She rather thought they were going to meet that afternoon. She described where she'd been—everywhere, here, there, along by the sea. The day was so charming—didn't he agree? And wouldn't he, perhaps? . . . But he shook his head, lighted a cigarette, slowly breathed a great deep puff into her face, and, even while she was still talking and laughing, flicked the match away and walked on. The ermine toque was alone; she smiled more brightly than ever. But even the band seemed to know what she was feeling and played more softly, played tenderly, and the drum beat, "The Brute! The Brute!" over and over. What would she do? What was going to happen now? But as Miss Brill wondered, the ermine toque turned, raised her hand as though she'd seen some one else, much nicer, just over there, and pattered away. And the band changed again and played more quickly, more gaily than ever, and the old couple on Miss Brill's seat got up and marched away, and such a funny old man with long whiskers hobbled along in time to the music and was nearly knocked over by four girls walking abreast.

Oh, how fascinating it was! How she enjoyed it! How she loved sitting here, watching it all! It was like a play. It was exactly like a play. Who could believe the sky at the back wasn't painted? But it wasn't till a little brown dog trotted on solemn and then slowly trotted off, like a little "theatre" dog, a little dog that had been drugged, that Miss Bill discovered what it was that made it so exciting. They were all on the stage. They weren't only the audience, not only looking on; they were acting. Even she had a part and came every Sunday. No doubt somebody would have noticed if she hadn't been there; she was part of the performance after all. How strange she'd never thought of it like that before! And yet it explained why she made such a point of starting from home at just the same time each week—so as not to be late for the performance—and it also explained why she had quite a queer, shy feeling at telling her English pupils how she spent her Sunday afternoons. No wonder! Miss Brill nearly laughed out loud. She was on the stage. She thought of the old invalid gentleman to whom she read the newspaper four afternoons a week while he slept in the garden. She had got quite used to the frail head on the cotton pillow, the hollowed eyes, the open mouth and the high pinched nose. If he'd been dead she mightn't have noticed for weeks; she wouldn't have minded. But suddenly he knew he was having the paper read to him by an actress! "An actress!" The old head lifted; two points of light quivered in the old eyes. "An actress—are ye?" And Miss Brill smoothed the newspaper as though it were the manuscript of her part and said gently: "Yes, I have been an actress for a long time."

The band had been having a rest. Now they started again. And what they played was warm, sunny, yet there was just a faint chill—a something, what was it?—not sadness—no, not sadness—a something that made you want to sing. The tune lifted, lifted, the light shone; and it seemed to Miss Brill that in another moment all of them, all the whole company, would begin singing.

The young ones, the laughing ones who were moving together, they would begin, and the men's voices, very resolute and brave, would join them. And then she too, she too, and the others on the benches—they would come in with a kind of accompaniment—something low, that scarcely rose or fell, something so beautiful—moving. . . . And Miss Brill's eyes filled with tears and she looked smiling at all the other members of the company. Yes, we understand, we understand, she thought—though what they understood she didn't know.

Just at that moment a boy and a girl came and sat down where the old couple had been. They were beautifully dressed; they were in love. The hero and heroine, of course, just arrived from his father's yacht. And still soundlessly singing, still with that trembling smile, Miss Brill prepared to listen.

"No, not now," said the girl. "Not here, I can't."

"But why? Because of that stupid old thing at the end there?" asked the boy. "Why does she come here at all—who wants her? Why doesn't she keep her silly old mug at home?"

"It's her fu-fur which is so funny," giggled the girl. "It's exactly like a fried whiting."

"Ah, be off with you!" said the boy in an angry whisper. Then: "Tell me, ma petite chérie—"

"No, not here," said the girl. "Not *yet*."

On her way home she usually bought a slice of honeycake at the baker's. It was her Sunday treat. Sometimes there was an almond in her slice, sometimes not. It made a great difference. If there was an almond it was like carrying home a tiny present—a surprise—something that might very well not have been there. She hurried on the almond Sundays and struck the match for the kettle in quite a dashing way.

But to-day she passed the baker's by, climbed the stairs, went into the little dark room—her room like a cupboard—and sat down on the red eiderdown. She sat there for a long time. The box that the fur came out of was on the bed. She unclasped the necklet quickly; quickly, without looking, laid it inside. But when she put the lid on she thought she heard something crying.

302

Marriage à la Mode

O N H I S W A Y to the station William remembered with a
fresh pang of disappointment that he was taking nothing down
to the kiddies. Poor little chaps! It was hard lines on them. Their
first words always were as they ran to greet him, "What have you
got for me, daddy?" and he had nothing. He would have to buy
them some sweets at the station. But that was what he had done
for the past four Saturdays; their faces had fallen last time when
they saw the same old boxes produced again.

And Paddy had said, "I had red ribbing on mine *bee*-fore!"

And Johnny had said, "It's always pink on mine. I hate pink."

But what was William to do? The affair wasn't so easily
settled. In the old days, of course, he would have taken a taxi off
to a decent toyshop and chosen them something in five minutes.
But nowadays they had Russian toys, French toys, Serbian toys—
toys from God knows where. It was over a year since Isabel had
scrapped the old donkeys and engines and so on because they
were so "dreadfully sentimental" and "so appallingly bad for the
babies' sense of form."

"It's so important," the new Isabel had explained, "that they
should like the right things from the very beginning. It saves so
much time later on. Really, if the poor pets have to spend their
infant years staring at these horrors, one can imagine them growing up and asking to be taken to the Royal Academy."

And she spoke as though a visit to the Royal Academy was
certain immediate death to any one. . . .

"Well, I don't know," said William slowly. "When I was

their age I used to go to bed hugging an old towel with a knot in it."

The new Isabel looked at him, her eyes narrowed, her lips apart.

"*Dear* William! I'm sure you did!" She laughed in the new way.

Sweets it would have to be, however, thought William gloomily, fishing in his pocket for change for the taxi-man. And he saw the kiddies handing the boxes round—they were awfully generous little chaps—while Isabel's precious friends didn't hesitate to help themselves. . . .

What about fruit? William hovered before a stall just inside the station. What about a melon each? Would they have to share that, too? Or a pineapple for Pad, and a melon for Johnny? Isabel's friends could hardly go sneaking up to the nursery at the children's meal-times. All the same, as he bought the melon William had a horrible vision of one of Isabel's young poets lapping up a slice, for some reason, behind the nursery door.

With his two very awkward parcels he strode off to his train. The platform was crowded, the train was in. Doors banged open and shut. There came such a loud hissing from the engine that people looked dazed as they scurried to and fro. William made straight for a first-class smoker, stowed away his suit-case and parcels, and taking a huge wad of papers out of his inner pocket, he flung down in the corner and began to read.

"Our client moreover is positive. . . . We are inclined to reconsider . . . in the event of—" Ah, that was better. William pressed back his flattened hair and stretched his legs across the carriage floor. The familiar dull gnawing in his breast quietened down. "With regard to our decision—" He took out a blue pencil and scored a paragraph slowly.

Two men came in, stepped across him, and made for the farther corner. A young fellow swung his golf clubs into the rack and sat down opposite. The train gave a gentle lurch, they were off. William glanced up and saw the hot, bright station slipping away. A red-faced girl raced along by the carriages, there was something strained and almost desperate in the way she waved and called. "Hysterical!" thought William dully. Then a greasy, black-faced workman at the end of the platform grinned at the passing train. And William thought, "A filthy life!" and went back to his papers.

When he looked up again there were fields, and beasts standing for shelter under the dark trees. A wide river, with naked children splashing in the shallows, glided into sight and was gone again. The sky shone pale, and one bird drifted high like a dark fleck in a jewel.

"We have examined our client's correspondence files. . . ." The last sentence he had read echoed in his mind. "We have examined . . ." William hung on to that sentence, but it was no good; it snapped in the middle, and the fields, the sky, the sailing bird, the water, all said, "Isabel." The same thing happened every Saturday afternoon. When he was on his way to meet Isabel there began those countless imaginary meetings. She was at the station, standing just a little apart from everybody else; she was sitting in the open taxi outside; she was at the garden gate; walking across the parched grass; at the door, or just inside the hall.

And her clear, light voice said, "It's William," or "Hillo, William!" or "So William has come!" He touched her cool hand, her cool cheek.

The exquisite freshness of Isabel! When he had been a little boy, it was his delight to run into the garden after a shower of rain and shake the rose-bush over him. Isabel was that rose-bush, petal-soft, sparkling and cool. And he was still that little boy. But there was no running into the garden now, no laughing and shaking. The dull, persistent gnawing in his breast started again. He drew up his legs, tossed the papers aside, and shut his eyes.

"What is it, Isabel? What is it?" he said tenderly. They were in their bedroom in the new house. Isabel sat on a painted stool before the dressing table that was strewn with little black and green boxes.

"What is what, William?" And she bent forward, and her fine light hair fell over her cheeks.

"Ah, you know!" He stood in the middle of the strange room and he felt a stranger. At that Isabel wheeled round quickly and faced him.

"Oh, William!" she cried imploringly, and she held up the

305

hair-brush: "Please! Please don't be so dreadfully stuffy and—tragic. You're always saying or looking or hinting that I've changed. Just because I've got to know really congenial people, and go about more, and am frightfully keen on—on everything, you behave as though I'd—" Isabel tossed back her hair and laughed—"killed our love or something. It's so awfully absurd"—she bit her lip—"and it's so maddening, William. Even this new house and the servants you grudge me."

"Isabel!"

"Yes, yes, it's true in a way," said Isabel quickly. "You think they are another bad sign. Oh, I know you do. I feel it," she said softly, "every time you come up the stairs. But we couldn't have gone on living in that other poky little hole, William. Be practical, at least! Why, there wasn't enough room for the babies even."

No, it was true. Every morning when he came back from chambers it was to find the babies with Isabel in the back drawing-room. They were having rides on the leopard skin thrown over the sofa back, or they were playing shops with Isabel's desk for a counter, or Pad was sitting on the hearthrug rowing away for dear life with a little brass fire shovel, while Johnny shot at pirates with the tongs. Every evening they each had a pick-a-back up the narrow stairs to their fat old Nanny.

Yes, he supposed it was a poky little house. A little white house with blue curtains and a window-box of petunias. William met their friends at the door with "Seen our petunias? Pretty terrific for London, don't you think?"

But the imbecile thing, the absolutely extraordinary thing was that he hadn't the slightest idea that Isabel wasn't as happy as he. God, what blindness! He hadn't the remotest notion in those days that she really hated that inconvenient little house, that she thought the fat Nanny was ruining the babies, that she was desperately lonely, pining for new people and new music and pictures and so on. If they hadn't gone to that studio party at Moira Morrison's—if Moira Morrison hadn't said as they were leaving, "I'm going to rescue your wife, selfish man. She's like an exquisite little Titania"—if Isabel hadn't gone with Moira to Paris—if—if . . .

The train stopped at another station. Bettingford. Good

heavens! They'd be there in ten minutes. William stuffed the papers back into his pockets; the young man opposite had long since disappeared. Now the other two got out. The late afternoon sun shone on women in cotton frocks and little sunburnt, barefoot children. It blazed on a silky yellow flower with coarse leaves which sprawled over a bank of rock. The air ruffling through the window smelled of the sea. Had Isabel the same crowd with her this week-end, wondered William?

And he remembered the holidays they used to have, the four of them, with a little farm girl, Rose, to look after the babies. Isabel wore a jersey and her hair in a plait; she looked about fourteen. Lord! how his nose used to peel! And the amount they ate, and the amount they slept in that immense feather bed with their feet locked together. . . . . William couldn't help a grim smile as he thought of Isabel's horror if she knew the full extent of his sentimentality. *She doesn't know him*

"Hillo, William!" She was at the station after all, standing just as he had imagined, apart from the others, and—William's heart leapt—she was alone.

"Hallo, Isabel!" William stared. He thought she looked so beautiful that he had to say something. "You look very cool."

"Do I?" said Isabel. "I don't feel very cool. Come along, your horrid old train is late. The taxi's outside." She put her hand lightly on his arm as they passed the ticket collector. "We've all come to meet you," she said. "But we've left Bobby Kane at the sweet shop, to be called for."

"Oh!" said William. It was all he could say for the moment.

There in the glare waited the taxi, with Bill Hunt and Dennis Green sprawling on one side, their hats tilted over their faces, while on the other, Moira Morrison, in a bonnet like a huge strawberry, jumped up and down.

"No ice! No ice! No ice!" she shouted gaily.

And Dennis chimed in from under his hat. "*Only* to be had from the fishmonger's."

And Bill Hunt, emerging, added, "With *whole* fish in it."

"Oh, what a bore!" wailed Isabel. And she explained to William how they had been chasing round the town for ice while she waited for him. "Simply everything is running down the steep cliffs into the sea, beginning with the butter."

"We shall have to anoint ourselves with the butter," said Dennis. "May thy head, William, lack not ointment."

"Look here," said William, "how are we going to sit? I'd better get up by the driver."

"No, Bobby Kane's by the driver," said Isabel. "You're to sit between Moira and me." The taxi started. "What have you got in those mysterious parcels?"

"De-cap-it-ated heads!" said Bill Hunt, shuddering beneath his hat.

"Oh, fruit!" Isabel sounded very pleased. "Wise William! A melon and a pineapple. How too nice!"

"No, wait a bit," said William, smiling. But he really was anxious. "I brought them down for the kiddies."

"Oh, my dear!" Isabel laughed, and slipped her hand through his arm. "They'd be rolling in agonies if they were to eat them. No"—she patted his hand—"you must bring them something next time. I refuse to part with my pineapple."

"Cruel Isabel! Do let me smell it!" said Moira. She flung her arms across William appealingly. "Oh!" The strawberry bonnet fell forward: she sounded quite faint.

"A Lady in Love with a Pineapple," said Dennis, as the taxi drew up before a little shop with a striped blind. Out came Bobby Kane, his arms full of little packets.

"I do hope they'll be good. I've chosen them because of the colours. There are some round things which really look too divine. And just look at this nougat," he cried ecstatically, "just look at it! It's a perfect little ballet."

But at that moment the shopman appeared. "Oh, I forgot. They're none of them paid for," said Bobby, looking frightened. Isabel gave the shopman a note, and Bobby was radiant again. "Hallo, William! I'm sitting by the driver." And bareheaded, all in white, with his sleeves rolled up to the shoulders, he leapt into his place. "Avanti!" he cried. . . .

After tea the others went off to bathe, while William stayed and made his peace with the kiddies. But Johnny and Paddy were asleep, the rose-red glow had paled, bats were flying, and still the bathers had not returned. As William wandered downstairs, the maid crossed the hall carrying a lamp. He followed her into the sitting-room. It was a long room, coloured yellow. On the wall opposite William some one had painted a young man, over life-size, with very wobbly legs, offering a wide-eyed daisy to a young woman who had one very short arm and one very long, thin one. Over the chairs and sofa there hung strips of black material, covered with big splashes like broken eggs, and every-where one looked there seemed to be an ash-tray full of cigarette ends. William sat down in one of the arm-chairs. Nowadays, when one felt with one hand down the sides, it wasn't to come upon a sheep with three legs or a cow that had lost one horn, or a very fat dove out of the Noah's Ark. One fished up yet another little paper-covered book of smudged-looking poems. . . . He thought of the wad of papers in his pocket, but he was too hungry and tired to read. The door was open; sounds came from the kitchen. The servants were talking as if they were alone in the house. Suddenly there came a loud screech of laughter and an equally loud "Sh!" They had remembered him. William got up and went through the French windows into the garden, and as he stood there in the shadow he heard the bathers coming up the sandy road; their voices rang through the quiet.

"I think it's up to Moira to use her little arts and wiles."

A tragic moan from Moira.

"We ought to have a gramophone for the week-ends that played 'The Maid of the Mountains.' "

"Oh no! Oh no!" cried Isabel's voice. "That's not fair to William. Be nice to him, my children! He's only staying until to-morrow evening."

"Leave him to me," cried Bobby Kane. "I'm awfully good at looking after people."

The gate swung open and shut. William moved on the ter-race; they had seen him. "Hallo, William!" And Bobby Kane, flapping his towel, began to leap and pirouette on the parched lawn. "Pity you didn't come, William. The water was divine. And we all went to a little pub afterwards and had sloe gin."

The others had reached the house. "I say, Isabel," called

Bobby, "would you like me to wear my Nijinsky dress to-night?"

"No," said Isabel, "nobody's going to dress. We're all starving. William's starving, too. Come along, *mes amis,* let's begin with sardines."

"I've found the sardines," said Moira, and she ran into the hall, holding a box high in the air.

"A Lady with a Box of Sardines," said Dennis gravely.

"Well, William, and how's London?" asked Bill Hunt, drawing the cork out of a bottle of whisky.

"Oh, London's not much changed," answered William.

"Good old London," said Bobby, very hearty, spearing a sardine.

But a moment later William was forgotten. Moira Morrison began wondering what colour one's legs really were under water.

"Mine are the palest, palest mushroom colour."

Bill and Dennis ate enormously. And Isabel filled glasses, and changed plates, and found matches, smiling blissfully. At one moment she said, "I do wish, Bill, you'd paint it."

"Paint what?"" said Bill loudly, stuffing his mouth with bread.

"Us," said Isabel, "round the table. It would be so fascinating in twenty years' time."

Bill screwed up his eyes and chewed. "Light's wrong," he said rudely, "far too much yellow"; and went on eating. And that seemed to charm Isabel, too.

But after supper they were all so tired they could do nothing but yawn until it was late enough to go to bed. . . .

It was not until William was waiting for his taxi the next afternoon that he found himself alone with Isabel. When he brought his suit-case down into the hall, Isabel left the others and went over to him. She stooped down and picked up the suit-case. "What a weight!" she said, and she gave a little awkward laugh. "Let me carry it! To the gate."

"No, why should you?" said William. "Of course not. Give it to me."

"Oh, please do let me," said Isabel. "I want to, really." They walked together silently. William felt there was nothing to say now.

"There," said Isabel triumphantly, setting the suit-case down, and she looked anxiously along the sandy road. "I hardly seem to have seen you this time," she said breathlessly. "It's so short, isn't it? I feel you've only just come. Next time—" The taxi came into sight. "I hope they look after you properly in London. I'm so sorry the babies have been out all day, but Miss Neil had arranged it. They'll hate missing you. Poor William, going back to London." The taxi turned. "Good-bye!" She gave him a little hurried kiss; she was gone.

Fields, trees, hedges streamed by. They shook through the empty, blind-looking little town, ground up the steep pull to the station.

The train was in. William made straight for a first-class smoker, flung back into the corner, but this time he let the papers alone. He folded his arms against the dull, persistent gnawing, and began in his mind to write a letter to Isabel.

The post was late as usual. They sat outside the house in long chairs under coloured parasols. Only Bobby Kane lay on the turf at Isabel's feet. It was dull, stifling; the day drooped like a flag.

"Do you think there will be Mondays in Heaven?" asked Bobby childishly.

And Dennis murmured, "Heaven will be one long Monday."

But Isabel couldn't help wondering what had happened to the salmon they had for supper last night. She had meant to have fish mayonnaise for lunch and now . . .

Moira was asleep. Sleeping was her latest discovery. "It's *so* wonderful. One simply shuts one's eyes, that's all. It's *so* delicious."

When the old ruddy postman came beating along the sandy road on his tricycle one felt the handlebars ought to have been oars.

Bill Hunt put down his book. "Letters," he said complacently, and they all waited. But, heartless postman—O malignant world! There was only one, a fat one for Isabel. Not even a paper.

"And mine's only from William," said Isabel mournfully.

"From William—already?"

"He's sending you back your marriage lines as a gentle reminder."

"Does everybody have marriage lines? I thought they were only for servants."

"Pages and pages! Look at her! A Lady reading a Letter," said Dennis.

My darling, precious Isabel. Pages and pages there were. As Isabel read on her feeling of astonishment changed to a stifled feeling. What on earth had induced William . . . ? How extraordinary it was. . . . What could have made him . . . ? She felt confused, more and more excited, even frightened. It was just like William. Was it? It was absurd, of course, it must be absurd, ridiculous. "Ha, ha, ha! Oh dear!" What was she to do? Isabel flung back in her chair and laughed till she couldn't stop laughing.

"Do, do tell us," said the others. "You must tell us."

"I'm longing to," gurgled Isabel. She sat up, gathered the letter, and waved it at them. "Gather round," she said. "Listen, it's too marvellous. A love-letter!"

"A love-letter! But how divine!" *Darling, precious Isabel.* But she had hardly begun before their laughter interrupted her.

"Go on, Isabel, it's perfect."

"It's the most marvellous find."

"Oh, do go on, Isabel!"

God forbid, my darling, that I should be a drag on your happiness.

"Oh! oh! oh!"

"Sh! sh! sh!"

And Isabel went on. When she reached the end they were hysterical: Bobby rolled on the turf and almost sobbed.

"You must let me have it just as it is, entire, for my new book," said Dennis firmly. "I shall give it a whole chapter."

"Oh, Isabel," moaned Moira, "that wonderful bit about holding you in his arms!"

"I always thought those letters in divorce cases were made up. But they pale before this."

"Let me hold it. Let me read it, mine own self," said Bobby Kane.

But, to their surprise, Isabel crushed the letter in her hand. She was laughing no longer. She glanced quickly at them all; she looked exhausted. "No, not just now. Not just now," she stammered.

And before they could recover she had run into the house, through the hall, up the stairs into her bedroom. Down she sat on the side of the bed. "How vile, odious, abominable, vulgar," muttered Isabel. She pressed her eyes with her knuckles and rocked to and fro. And again she saw them, but not four, more like forty, laughing, sneering, jeering, stretching out their hands while she read them William's letter. Oh, what a loathsome thing to have done. How could she have done it! *God forbid, my darling, that I should be a drag on your happiness.* William! Isabel pressed her face into the pillow. But she felt that even the grave bedroom knew her for what she was, shallow, tinkling, vain. . . .

Presently from the garden below there came voices.

"Isabel, we're all going for a bathe. Do come!"

"Come, thou wife of William!"

"Call her once before you go, call once yet!"

Isabel sat up. Now was the moment, now she must decide. Would she go with them, or stay here and write to William. Which, which should it be? "I must make up my mind." Oh, but how could there be any question? Of course she would stay here and write.

"Titania!" piped Moira.

"Isa-bel?"

No, it was too difficult. "I'll—I'll go with them, and write to William later. Some other time. Later. Not now. But I shall *certainly* write," thought Isabel hurriedly.

And, laughing in the new way, she ran down the stairs.

The Doll's House

W HEN DEAR OLD MRS. HAY went back to town after
staying with the Burnells she sent the children a doll's house. It
was so big that the carter and Pat carried it into the courtyard,
and there it stayed, propped up on two wooden boxes beside the
feed-room door. No harm could come of it; it was summer. And
perhaps the smell of paint would have gone off by the time it had
to be taken in. For, really, the smell of paint coming from that
doll's house ("Sweet of old Mrs. Hay, of course; most sweet and
generous!")—but the smell of paint was quite enough to make
any one seriously ill, in Aunt Beryl's opinion. Even before the
sacking was taken off. And when it was. . . .

There stood the doll's house, a dark, oily, spinach green,
picked out with bright yellow. Its two solid little chimneys, glued
on to the roof, were painted red and white, and the door, gleaming
with yellow varnish, was like a little slab of toffee. Four windows,
real windows, were divided into panes by a broad streak of green.
There was actually a tiny porch, too, painted yellow, with big
lumps of congealed paint hanging along the edge.

But perfect, perfect little house! Who could possibly mind
the smell? It was part of the joy, part of the newness.

"Open it quickly, some one!"

The hook at the side was stuck fast. Pat pried it open with
his penknife, and the whole house-front swung back, and—there
you were, gazing at one and the same moment into the drawing-
room and dining-room, the kitchen and two bedrooms. That is
the way for a house to open! Why don't all houses open like that?
How much more exciting than peering through the slit of a door

into a mean little hall with a hatstand and two umbrellas! That is—isn't it?—what you long to know about a house when you put your hand on the knocker. Perhaps it is the way God opens houses at dead of night when He is taking a quiet turn with an angel. . . .

"O-oh!" The Burnell children sounded as though they were in despair. It was too marvellous; it was too much for them. They had never seen anything like it in their lives. All the rooms were papered. There were pictures on the walls, painted on the paper, with gold frames complete. Red carpet covered all the floors except the kitchen; red plush chairs in the drawing-room, green in the dining-room; tables, beds with real bedclothes, a cradle, a stove, a dresser with tiny plates and one big jug. But what Kezia liked more than anything, what she liked frightfully, was the lamp. It stood in the middle of the dining-room table, an exquisite little amber lamp with a white globe. It was even filled all ready for lighting, though, of course, you couldn't light it. But there was something inside that looked like oil, and that moved when you shook it.

The father and mother dolls, who sprawled very stiff as though they had fainted in the drawing-room, and their two little children asleep upstairs, were really too big for the doll's house. They didn't look as though they belonged. But the lamp was perfect. It seemed to smile at Kezia, to say, "I live here." The lamp was real.

The Burnell children could hardly walk to school fast enough the next morning. They burned to tell everybody, to describe, to—well—to boast about their doll's house before the school-bell rang.

"I'm to tell," said Isabel, "because I'm the eldest. And you two can join in after. But I'm to tell first."

There was nothing to answer. Isabel was bossy, but she was always right, and Lottie and Kezia knew too well the powers that went with being eldest. They brushed through the thick butter-cups at the road edge and said nothing.

"And I'm to choose who's to come and see it first. Mother said I might."

For it had been arranged that while the doll's house stood

in the courtyard they might ask the girls at school, two at a time, to come and look. Not to stay to tea, of course, or to come traipsing through the house. But just to stand quietly in the court-yard while Isabel pointed out the beauties, and Lottie and Kezia looked pleased. . . .

But hurry as they might, by the time they had reached the tarred palings of the boys' playground the bell had begun to jangle. They only just had time to whip off their hats and fall into line before the roll was called. Never mind. Isabel tried to make up for it by looking very important and mysterious and by whispering behind her hand to the girls near her, "Got something to tell you at playtime."

Playtime came and Isabel was surrounded. The girls of her class nearly fought to put their arms round her, to walk away with her, to beam flatteringly, to be her special friend. She held quite a court under the huge pine trees at the side of the playground. Nudging, giggling together, the little girls pressed up close. And the only two who stayed outside the ring were the two who were always outside, the little Kelveys. They knew better than to come anywhere near the Burnells.

For the fact was, the school the Burnell children went to was not at all the kind of place their parents would have chosen if there had been any choice. But there was none. It was the only school for miles. And the consequence was all the children in the neighbourhood, the Judge's little girls, the doctor's daughters, the storekeeper's children, the milkman's, were forced to mix together. Not to speak of there being an equal number of rude, rough little boys as well. But the line had to be drawn somewhere. It was drawn at the Kelveys. Many of the children, including the Bur-nells, were not allowed even to speak to them. They walked past the Kelveys with their heads in the air, and as they set the fashion in all matters of behaviour, the Kelveys were shunned by every-body. Even the teacher had a special voice for them, and a special smile for the other children when Lil Kelvey came up to her desk with a bunch of dreadfully common-looking flowers.

They were the daughters of a spry, hardworking little wash-erwoman, who went about from house to house by the day. This was awful enough. But where was Mr. Kelvey? Nobody knew for certain. But everybody said he was in prison. So they were the daughters of a washerwoman and a gaolbird. Very nice company for other people's children! And they looked it. Why Mrs. Kelvey made them so conspicuous was hard to understand. The truth was they were dressed in "bits" given to her by the people for whom she worked. Lil, for instance, who was a stout, plain child, with big freckles, came to school in a dress made from a green art-serge table-cloth of the Burnells', with red plush sleeves from the Logans' curtains. Her hat, perched on top of her high forehead, was a grown-up woman's hat, once the property of Miss Lecky, the postmistress. It was turned up at the back and trimmed with a large scarlet quill. What a little guy she looked! It was impossible not to laugh. And her little sister, our Else, wore a long white dress, rather like a nightgown, and a pair of little boy's boots. But whatever our Else wore she would have looked strange. She was a tiny wishbone of a child, with cropped hair and enormous solemn eyes—a little white owl. Nobody had ever seen her smile; she scarcely ever spoke. She went through life holding on to Lil, with a piece of Lil's skirt screwed up in her hand. Where Lil went our Else followed. In the playground, on the road going to and from school, there was Lil marching in front and our Else holding on behind. Only when she wanted anything, or when she was out of breath, our Else gave Lil a tug, a twitch, and Lil stopped and turned round. The Kelveys never failed to understand each other.

Now they hovered at the edge; you couldn't stop them listening. When the little girls turned round and sneered, Lil, as usual, gave her silly, shamefaced smile, but our Else only looked.

And Isabel's voice, so very proud, went on telling. The carpet made a great sensation, but so did the beds with real bedclothes, and the stove with an oven door.

When she finished Kezia broke in. "You've forgotten the lamp, Isabel."

"Oh, yes," said Isabel, "and there's a teeny little lamp, all made of yellow glass, with a white globe that stands on the dining-room table. You couldn't tell it from a real one."

"The lamp's best of all," cried Kezia. She thought Isabel wasn't making half enough of the little lamp. But nobody paid any attention. Isabel was choosing the two who were to come back with them that afternoon and see it. She chose Emmie Cole and Lena Logan. But when the others knew they were all to have a chance, they couldn't be nice enough to Isabel. One by one they put their arms round Isabel's waist and walked her off. They had something to whisper to her, a secret. "Isabel's *my* friend."

Only the little Kelveys moved away forgotten; there was nothing more for them to hear.

Days passed, and as more children saw the doll's house, the fame of it spread. It became the one subject, the rage. The one question was, "Have you seen Burnells' doll's house? Oh, ain't it lovely!" "Haven't you seen it? Oh, I say!"

Even the dinner hour was given up to talking about it. The little girls sat under the pines eating their thick mutton sandwiches and big slabs of johnny cake spread with butter. While always, as near as they could get, sat the Kelveys, our Else holding on to Lil, listening too, while they chewed their jam sandwiches out of a newspaper soaked with large red blobs. . . .

"Mother," said Kezia, "can't I ask the Kelveys just once?"

"Certainly not, Kezia."

"But why not?"

"Run away, Kezia; you know quite well why not."

At last everybody had seen it except them. On that day the subject rather flagged. It was the dinner hour. The children stood together under the pine trees, and suddenly, as they looked at the Kelveys eating out of their paper, always by themselves, always listening, they wanted to be horrid to them. Emmie Cole started the whisper.

"Lil Kelvey's going to be a servant when she grows up."

"O-oh, how awful!" said Isabel Burnell, and she made eyes at Emmie.

Emmie swallowed in a very meaning way and nodded to Isabel as she'd seen her mother do on those occasions.

"It's true—it's true—it's true," she said.

Then Lena Logan's little eyes snapped. "Shall I ask her?" she whispered.

"Bet you don't," said Jessie May.

"Pooh, I'm not frightened," said Lena. Suddenly she gave a little squeal and danced in front of the other girls. "Watch! Watch me! Watch me now!" said Lena. And sliding, gliding, dragging one foot, giggling behind her hand, Lena went over to the Kelveys.

Lil looked up from her dinner. She wrapped the rest quickly away. Our Else stopped chewing. What was coming now?

"Is it true you're going to be a servant when you grow up, Lil Kelvey?" shrilled Lena.

Dead silence. But instead of answering, Lil only gave her silly, shamefaced smile. She didn't seem to mind the question at all. What a sell for Lena! The girls began to titter.

Lena couldn't stand that. She put her hands on her hips; she shot forward. "Yah, yer father's in prison!" she hissed, spitefully.

This was such a marvellous thing to have said that the little girls rushed away in a body, deeply, deeply excited, wild with joy. Some one found a long rope, and they began skipping. And never did they skip so high, run in and out so fast, or do such daring things as on that morning.

In the afternoon Pat called for the Burnell children with the buggy and they drove home. There were visitors. Isabel and Lottie, who liked visitors, went upstairs to change their pinafores. But Kezia thieved out at the back. Nobody was about; she began to swing on the big white gates of the courtyard. Presently, looking along the road, she saw two little dots. They grew bigger, they were coming towards her. Now she could see that one was in front and one close behind. Now she could see that they were the Kelveys. Kezia stopped swinging. She slipped off the gate as if she was going to run away. Then she hesitated. The Kelveys came nearer, and beside them walked their shadows, very long, stretching right across the road with their heads in the buttercups. Kezia clambered back on the gate; she had made up her mind; she swung out.

"Hullo," she said to the passing Kelveys.

They were so astounded that they stopped. Lil gave her silly smile. Our Else stared.

"You can come and see our doll's house if you want to," said

Kezia, and she dragged one toe on the ground. But at that Lil turned red and shook her head quickly.

"Why not?" asked Kezia.

Lil gasped, then she said, "Your ma told our ma you wasn't to speak to us."

"Oh, well," said Kezia. She didn't know what to reply. "It doesn't matter. You can come and see our doll's house all the same. Come on. Nobody's looking."

But Lil shook her head still harder.

"Don't you want to?" asked Kezia.

Suddenly there was a twitch, a tug at Lil's skirt. She turned round. Our Else was looking at her with big, imploring eyes; she was frowning; she wanted to go. For a moment Lil looked at our Else very doubtfully. But then our Else twitched her skirt again. She started forward. Kezia led the way. Like two little stray cats they followed across the courtyard to where the doll's house stood.

"There it is," said Kezia.

There was a pause. Lil breathed loudly, almost snorted; our Else was still as a stone.

"I'll open it for you," said Kezia kindly. She undid the hook and they looked inside.

"There's the drawing-room and the dining-room, and that's the—"

"Kezia!"

Oh, what a start they gave!

"Kezia!"

It was Aunt Beryl's voice. They turned round. At the back door stood Aunt Beryl, staring as if she couldn't believe what she saw.

"How dare you ask the little Kelveys into the courtyard?" said her cold, furious voice. "You know as well as I do, you're not allowed to talk to them. Run away, children, run away at once. And don't come back again," said Aunt Beryl. And she stepped into the yard and shooed them out as if they were chickens.

"Off you go immediately!" she called, cold and proud.

They did not need telling twice. Burning with shame, shrinking together, Lil huddling along like her mother, our Else dazed, somehow they crossed the big courtyard and squeezed through the white gate.

"Wicked, disobedient little girl!" said Aunt Beryl bitterly to Kezia, and she slammed the doll's house to.

The afternoon had been awful. A letter had come from Willie Brent, a terrifying, threatening letter, saying if she did not meet him that evening in Pulman's Bush, he'd come to the front door and ask the reason why! But now that she had frightened those little rats of Kelveys and given Kezia a good scolding, her heart felt lighter. That ghastly pressure was gone. She went back to the house humming.

When the Kelveys were well out of sight of Burnells', they sat down to rest on a big red drain-pipe by the side of the road. Lil's cheeks were still burning; she took off the hat with the quill and held it on her knee. Dreamily they looked over the hay paddocks, past the creek, to the group of wattles where Logan's cows stood waiting to be milked. What were their thoughts?

Presently our Else nudged up close to her sister. But now she had forgotten the cross lady. She put out a finger and stroked her sister's quill; she smiled her rare smile.

"I seen the little lamp," she said, softly.

Then both were silent once more.

The Doves' Nest

AFTER LUNCH Milly and her mother were sitting as usual on the balcony beyond the salon, admiring for the five hundredth time the stocks, the roses, the small, bright grass beneath the palms, and the oranges against a wavy line of blue, when a card was brought them by Marie. Visitors at the Villa Martin were very rare. True, the English clergyman, Mr. Sandiman, had called, and he had come a second time with his wife to tea. But an awful thing had happened on that second occasion. Mother had made a mistake. She had said "More tea, Mr. Sandybags?" Oh, what a frightful thing to have happened! How could she have done it? Milly still flamed at the thought. And he had evidently not forgiven them; he'd never come again. So this card put them both into a flutter.

Mr. Walter Prodger, they read. And then an American address, so very much abbreviated that neither of them understood it. Walter Prodger? But they'd never heard of him. Mother looked from the card to Milly.

"Prodger, dear?" she asked mildly, as though helping Milly to a slice of a never-before-tasted pudding.

And Milly seemed to be holding her plate back in the way she answered "I—don't—know, Mother."

"These are the occasions," said Mother, becoming a little flustered, "when one does so feel the need of our dear English servants. Now if I could just say, 'What is he like, Annie?' I should know whether to see him or not. But he may be some common man, selling something—one of those American inventions for peeling things, you know, dear. Or he may even be some kind of foreign sharper." Mother winced at the hard, bright little word as though she had given herself a dig with her embroidery scissors.

But here Marie smiled at Milly and murmured "C'est un très beau Monsieur."

"What does she say, dear?"

"She says he looks very nice, Mother."

"Well, we'd better—" began Mother. "Where is he now I wonder."

Marie answered "In the vestibule, Madame."

In the hall! Mother jumped up, seriously alarmed. In the hall, with all those valuable little foreign things that didn't belong to them scattered over the tables.

"Show him in, Marie. Come, Milly, come dear. We will see him in the salon. Oh, why isn't Miss Anderson here?" almost wailed Mother.

But Miss Anderson, Mother's new companion, never was on the spot when she was wanted. She had been engaged to be a comfort, a support to them both. Fond of travelling, a cheerful disposition, a good packer and so on. And then, when they had come all this way and taken the Villa Martin and moved in, she had turned out to be a Roman Catholic. Half her time, more than half, was spent wearing out the knees of her skirts in cold churches. It was really too . . .

The door opened. A middle-aged clean-shaven, very well dressed stranger stood bowing before them. His bow was stately. Milly saw it pleased Mother very much; she bowed her Queen Alexandra bow back. As for Milly, she never could bow. She smiled, feeling shy, but deeply interested.

"Have I the pleasure," said the stranger very courteously, with a strong American accent, "of speaking with Mrs. Wyndham Fawcett?"

"I am Mrs. Fawcett," said Mother, graciously, "and this is my daughter, Mildred."

"Pleased to meet you, Miss Fawcett." And the stranger shot a fresh, chill hand at Milly, who grasped it just in time before it was gone again.

"Won't you sit down?" said Mother, and she waved faintly at all the gilt chairs.

"Thank you, I will," said the stranger.

Down he sat, still solemn, crossing his legs, and, most surprisingly, his arms as well. His face looked at them over his dark arms as over a gate.

"Milly, sit down, dear."

So Milly sat down, too, on the Madame Recamier couch, and traced a filet lace flower with her finger. There was a little pause. She saw the stranger swallow; Mother's fan opened and shut.

Then he said, "I took the liberty of calling, Mrs. Fawcett, because I had the pleasure of your husband's acquaintance in the States when he was lecturing there some years ago. I should like very much to renoo our—well—I venture to hope we might call it friendship. Is he with you at present? Are you expecting him out? I noticed his name was not mentioned in the local paper. But I put that down to a foreign custom, perhaps—giving precedence to the lady."

And here the stranger looked as though he might be going to smile.

But as a matter of fact it was extremely awkward. Mother's mouth shook. Milly squeezed her hands between her knees, but she watched hard from under her eyebrows. Good, noble little Mummy! How Milly admired her as she heard her say, gently and quite simply, "I am sorry to say my husband died two years ago."

Mr. Prodger gave a great start. "Did he?" He thrust out his under-lip, frowned, pondered. "I am truly sorry to hear that, Mrs. Fawcett. I hope you'll believe me when I say I had no idea your husband had . . . passed over."

"Of course." Mother softly stroked her skirt.

"I do trust," said Mr. Prodger, more seriously still, "that my inquiry didn't give you too much pain."

"No, no. It's quite all right," said the gentle voice.

But Mr. Podger insisted. "You're sure? You're positive?"

At that Mother raised her head and gave him one of her still, bright, exalted glances that Milly knew so well. "I'm not in the least hurt," she said, as one might say it from the midst of the fiery furnace.

Mr. Prodger looked relieved. He changed his attitude and continued. "I hope this regrettable circumstance will not deprive me of your—"

"Oh, certainly not. We shall be delighted. We are always so pleased to know any one who—" Mother gave a little bound, a little flutter. She flew from her shadowy branch on to a sunny one. "Is this your first visit to the Riviera?"

"It is," said Mr. Prodger. "The fact is I was in Florence until recently. But I took a heavy cold there—"

"Florence so damp," cooed Mother.

"And the doctor recommended I should come here for the sunshine before I started for home."

"The sun is so very lovely here," agreed Mother, enthusiastically.

"Well, I don't think we get too much of it," said Mr. Prodger, dubiously, and two lines showed at his lips. "I seem to have been sitting around in my hotel more days than I care to count."

"Ah, hotels are so very trying," said Mother, and she drooped sympathetically at the thought of a lonely man in an hotel. . . . "You are alone here?" she asked, gently, just in case . . . one never knew . . . it was better to be on the safe, the tactful side.

But her fears were groundless.

"Oh, yes, I'm alone," cried Mr. Prodger, more heartily than he had spoken yet, and he took a speck of thread off his immaculate trouser leg. Something in his voice puzzled Milly. What was it?

"Still, the scenery is so very beautiful," said Mother, "that one really does not feel the need of friends. I was only saying to my daughter yesterday I could live here for years without going outside the garden gate. It is all so beautiful."

"Is that so?" said Mr. Prodger, soberly. He added, "You have a very charming villa." And he glanced round the salon. "Is all this antique furniture genuine, may I ask?"

"I believe so," said Mother. "I was certainly given to understand it was. Yes, we love our villa. But of course it is very large for two, that is to say three, ladies. My companion, Miss Anderson, is with us. But unfortunately she is a Roman Catholic, and so she is out most of the time."

325

Mr. Prodger bowed as one who agreed that Roman Catholics were very seldom in.

"But I am so fond of space," continued Mother, "and so is my daughter. We both love large rooms and plenty of them—don't we, Milly?"

This time Mr. Prodger looked at Milly quite cordially and remarked, "Yes, young people like plenty of room to run about."

He got up, put one hand behind his back, slapped the other upon it and went over to the balcony.

"You've a view of the sea from here," he observed.

The ladies might well have noticed it; the whole Mediterranean swung before the windows.

"We are so fond of the sea," said Mother, getting up, too.

Mr. Prodger looked towards Milly. "Do you see those yachts, Miss Fawcett?"

Milly saw them.

"Do you happen to know what they're doing?" asked Mr. Prodger.

What they were doing? What a funny question! Milly stared and bit her lip.

"They're racing!" said Mr. Prodger, and this time he did actually smile at her.

"Oh, yes, of course," stammered Milly. "Of course they are." She knew that.

"Well, they're not always at it," said Mr. Prodger, good-humoredly. And he turned to Mother and began to take a ceremonious farewell.

"I wonder," hesitated Mother, folding her little hands and eyeing him, "if you would care to lunch with us—if you would not be too dull with two ladies. We should be so very pleased."

Mr. Prodger became intensely serious again. He seemed to brace himself to meet the luncheon invitation. "Thank you very much, Mrs. Fawcett. I should be delighted."

"That will be very nice," said Mother, warmly. "Let me see. Today is Monday—isn't it, Milly? Would Wednesday suit you?"

Mr. Prodger replied, "It would suit me excellently to lunch with you on Wednesday, Mrs. Fawcett. At *meedee,* I presume, as they call it here."

"Oh, no! We keep our English times. At one o'clock," said Mother.

And that being arranged, Mr. Prodger became more and more ceremonious and bowed himself out of the room.

Mother rang for Marie to look after him, and a moment later the big glass hall-door shut.

"Well!" said Mother. She was all smiles. Little smiles like butterflies, alighting on her lips and gone again. "That was an adventure, Milly, wasn't it, dear! And I thought he was such a very charming man, didn't you?"

Milly made a little face at Mother and rubbed her eye.

"Of course you did. You must have, dear. And his appearance was so satisfactory—wasn't it?" Mother was obviously enraptured. "I mean he looked so very well kept. Did you notice his hands? Every nail shone like a diamond. I must say I do like to see . . ."

She broke off. She came over to Milly and patted her big collar staight.

"You do think it was right of me to ask him to lunch—don't you, dear?" said Mother pathetically.

Mother made her feel so big, so tall. But she was tall. She could pick Mother up in her arms. Sometimes, rare moods came when she did. Swooped on Mother who squeaked like a mouse and even kicked. But not lately. Very seldom now. . . .

"It was so strange," said Mother. There was the still, bright, exalted glance again. "I suddenly seemed to hear Father say to me 'Ask him to lunch.' And then there was some—warning. . . . I think it was about the wine. But that I didn't catch—very unfortunately," she added, mournfully. She put her hand on her breast; she bowed her head. "Father is still so near," she whispered.

Milly looked out of the window. She hated Mother going on like this. But of course she couldn't say anything. Out of the window there was the sea and the sunlight silver on the palms, like water dripping from silver oars. Milly felt a yearning—what was it?—it was like a yearning to fly.

But Mother's voice brought her back to the salon, to the gilt chairs, the gilt couches, sconces, cabinets, the tables with the heavy-sweet flowers, the faded brocade, the pink-spotted Chinese dragons on the mantelpiece and the two Turks' heads in the fireplace that supported the broad logs.

"I think a leg of lamb would be nice, don't you, dear?" said Mother. "The lamb is so very small and delicate just now. And men like nothing so much as plain roast meat. Yvonne prepares it so nicely, too, with that little frill of paper lace round the top of the leg. It always reminds me of something—I can't think what. But it certainly makes it look very attractive indeed."

Wednesday came. And the flutter that Mother and Milly had felt over the visiting card extended to the whole villa. Yes, it was not too much to say that the whole villa thrilled and fluttered at the idea of having a man to lunch. Old, flat-footed Yvonne came waddling back from market with a piece of gorgonzola in so perfect a condition that when she found Marie in the kitchen she flung down her great basket, snatched the morsel up and held it, rustling in its paper, to her quivering bosom.

"J'ai trouvé un morceau de gorgonzola," she panted, rolling up her eyes as though she invited the heavens themselves to look down upon it. "J'ai un morceau de gorgonzola ici pour un prince, ma fille." And hissing the word "prr-ince" like lightning, she thrust the morsel under Marie's nose. Marie, who was a delicate creature, almost swooned at the shock.

"Do you think," cried Yvonne, scornfully, "that I would ever buy such cheese *pour ces dames*? Never. Never. *Jamais de ma vie.*" Her sausage finger wagged before her nose, and she minced in a dreadful imitation of Mother's French, "We have none of us large appetites, Yvonne. We are very fond of boiled eggs and mashed potatoes and a nice, plain salad. Ah-Bah!" With a snort of contempt she flung away her shawl, rolled up her sleeves, and began unpacking the basket. At the bottom there was a flat bottle which, sighing, she laid aside.

"De quoi pour mes cors," said she.

And Marie, seizing a bottle of Sauterne and bearing it off to the dining-room murmured, as she shut the kitchen door behind her, "Et voilà pour les cors de Monsieur!"

The dining-room was a large room panelled in dark wood.

It had a massive mantelpiece and carved chairs covered in crimson damask. On the heavy, polished table stood an oval glass dish decorated with little gilt swags. This dish, which it was Marie's duty to keep filled with fresh flowers, fascinated her. The sight of it gave her a *frisson*. It reminded her always, as it lay solitary on the dark expanse, of a little tomb. And one day, passing through the long windows on to the stone terrace and down the steps into the garden she had the happy thought of so arranging the flowers that they would be appropriate to one of the ladies on a future tragic occasion. Her first creation had been terrible. *Tomb of Mademoiselle Anderson* in black pansies, lily-of-the-valley, and a frill of heliotrope. It gave her a most intense, curious pleasure to hand Miss Anderson the potatoes at lunch, and at the same time to gaze beyond her at her triumph. It was like (*O ciel!*), it was like handing potatoes to a corpse.

The *Tomb of Madame* was on the contrary almost gay. Foolish little flowers, half yellow, half blue, hung over the edge, wisps of green trailed across, and in the middle there was a large scarlet rose. *Coeur saignant,* Marie had called it. But it did not look in the least like a *coeur saignant*. It looked flushed and cheerful, like Mother emerging from the luxury of a warm bath.

Milly's, of course, was all white. White stocks, little white rosebuds, with a sprig or two of dark box edging. It was Mother's favourite.

Poor innocent! Marie, at the sideboard, had to turn her back when she heard Mother exclaim, "Isn't it pretty, Milly? Isn't it sweetly pretty? Most artistic. So original." And she had said to Marie, "C'est très joli, Marie. Très original."

Marie's smile was so remarkable that Milly, peeling a tangerine, remarked to Mother, "I don't think she likes you to admire them. It makes her uncomfortable."

But today—the glory of her opportunity made Marie feel quite faint as she seized her flower scissors. *Tombeau d'un beau Monsieur*. She was forbidden to cut the orchids that grew round the fountain basin. But what were orchids for if not for such an occasion? Her fingers trembled as the scissors snipped away. They were enough; Marie added two small sprays of palm. And back in the dining-room she had the happy idea of binding the palm together with a twist of gold thread deftly torn off the fringe of the dining-room curtains. The effect was superb. Marie almost seemed to see her *beau Monsieur,* very small, very small, at the bottom of the bowl, in full evening dress with a ribbon across his chest and his ears white as wax.

What surprised Milly, however, was that Miss Anderson should pay any attention to Mr. Prodger's coming. She rustled to breakfast in her best black silk blouse, her Sunday blouse, with the large, painful-looking crucifix dangling over the front. Milly was alone when Miss Anderson entered the dining-room. This was unfortunate, for she always tried to avoid being left alone with Miss Anderson. She could not say exactly why; it was a feeling. She had the feeling that Miss Anderson might say something about God, or something fearfully intimate. Oh, she would sink through the floor if such a thing happened; she would expire. Supposing she were to say "Milly, do you believe in our Lord?" Heavens! It simply didn't bear thinking about.

"Good-morning, my dear," said Miss Anderson, and her fingers, cold, pale, like church candles, touched Milly's cheeks.

"Good-morning, Miss Anderson. May I give you some coffee?" said Milly, trying to be natural.

"Thank you, dear child," said Miss Anderson, and laughing her light, nervous laugh, she hooked on her eye-glasses and stared at the basket of rolls. "And is it today that you expect your guest?" she asked.

Now why did she ask that? Why pretend when she knew perfectly well? That was all part of her strangeness. Or was it because she wanted to be friendly? Miss Anderson was more than friendly; she was genial. But there was always this something. Was she spying? People said at school that Roman Catholics spied. . . . Miss Anderson rustled, rustled about the house like a dead leaf. Now she was on the stairs, now in the upstairs passage. Sometimes, at night, when Milly was feverish, she woke up and heard that rustle outside her door. Was Miss Anderson looking through the keyhole? And one night she actually had the idea that Miss Anderson had bored two holes in the wall above her head and was watching her from there. The feeling was so strong that next time she went into Miss Anderson's room her eyes flew to the spot. To her horror a large picture hung there. Had it been there before? . . .

"Guest?" The crisp breakfast roll broke in half at the word.

"Yes, I think it is," said Milly, vaguely, and her blue, flower-like eyes were raised to Miss Anderson in a vague stare.

"It will make quite a little change in our little party," said the much-too-pleasant voice. "I confess I miss very much the society of men. I have had such a great deal of it in my life. I think that ladies by themselves are apt to get a little—h'm—h'm . . ." And helping herself to cherry jam, she spilt it on the cloth.

Milly took a large, childish bite out of her roll. There was nothing to reply to this. But how young Miss Anderson made her feel! She made her want to be naughty, to pour milk over her head or make a noise with a spoon.

"Ladies by themselves," went on Miss Anderson, who realized none of this, "are very apt to find their interests limited."

"Why?" said Milly, goaded to reply. People always said that; it sounded most unfair.

"I think," said Miss Anderson, taking off her eye-glasses and looking a little dim, "it is the absence of political discussion."

"Oh, politics!" cried Milly, airily. "I hate politics. Father always said—" but here she pulled up short. She crimsoned. She didn't want to talk about Father to Miss Anderson.

"Oh! Look! Look! A butterfly!" cried Miss Anderson, softly and hastily. "Look, what a darling!" Her own cheeks flushed a slow red at the sight of the darling butterfly fluttering so softly over the glittering table.

That was very nice of Miss Anderson—fearfully nice of her. She must have realized that Milly didn't want to talk about Father and so she had mentioned the butterfly on purpose. Milly smiled at Miss Anderson as she never had smiled at her before. And she said in her warm, youthful voice, "He is a duck, isn't he? I love butterflies. I think they are great lambs."

The morning whisked away as foreign mornings do. Mother had half decided to wear her hat at lunch.

"What do you think, Milly? Do you think as head of the house it might be appropriate? On the other hand one does not want to do anything at all extreme."

"Which do you mean, Mother? Your mushroom or the jam-pot?"

"Oh, not the jampot, dear." Mother was quite used to Milly's name for it. "I somehow don't feel myself in a hat without a brim. And to tell you the truth I am still not quite certain whether I was wise in buying the jampot. I cannot help the feeling that if I were to meet Father in it he would be a little too surprised. More than once lately," went on Mother quickly, "I have thought of taking off the trimming, turning it upside down, and making it into a nice little workbag. What do you think, dear? But we must not go into it now, Milly. This is not the moment for such schemes. Come on to the balcony. I have told Marie we shall have coffee there. What about bringing out that big chair with the nice, substantial legs for Mr. Prodger? Men are so fond of nice, substantial . . . No, not by yourself, love! Let me help you."

When the chair was carried out Milly thought it looked exactly like Mr. Prodger. It *was* Mr. Prodger admiring the view.

"No, don't sit down on it. You mustn't," she cried hastily, as Mother began to subside. She put her arm through Mother's and drew her back into the salon.

Happily, at that moment there was a rustle and Miss Anderson was upon them. In excellent time, for once. She carried a copy of the *Morning Post*.

"I have been trying to find out from this," said she, lightly tapping the newspaper with her eye-glasses, "whether Congress is sitting at present. But unfortunately, after reading my copy right through, I happened to glance at the heading and discovered it was five weeks old."

Congress! Would Mr. Prodger expect them to talk about Congress? The idea terrified Mother. Congress! The American parliament, of course, composed of senators—grey-bearded old men in frock coats and turn-down collars, rather like missionaries. But she did not feel at all competent to discuss them.

"I think we had better not be too intellectual," she suggested, timidly, fearful of disappointing Miss Anderson, but more fearful still of the alternative.

"Still, one likes to be prepared," said Miss Anderson. And after a pause she added softly, "One never knows."

Ah, how true that is! One never does. Miss Anderson and Mother seemed both to ponder this truth. They sat silent, with head bent, as though listening to the whisper of the words.

"One never knows," said the pink-spotted dragons on the mantelpiece and the Turks' heads pondered. Nothing is known— nothing. Everybody just waits for things to happen as they were waiting there for the stranger who came walking towards them through the sun and shadow under the budding plane trees, or driving, perhaps, in one of the small, cotton-covered cabs. . . . An angel passed over the Villa Martin. In that moment of hovering silence something beseeching seemed to lift, seemed to offer itself, as the flowers in the salon, uplifted, gave themselves to the light.

Then Mother said, "I hope Mr. Prodger will not find the scent of the mimosa too powerful. Men are not fond of flowers in a room as a rule. I have heard it causes actual hay-fever in some cases. What do you think, Milly? Ought we perhaps—" But there was no time to do anything. A long firm trill sounded from the hall door. It was a trill so calm and composed and unlike the tentative little push they gave the bell that it brought them back to the seriousness of the moment. They heard a man's voice; the door clicked and shut again. He was inside. A stick rattled on the table. There was a pause, and then the door handle of the salon turned and Marie, in frilled muslin cuffs and an apron shaped like a heart, ushered in Mr. Prodger.

Only Mr. Prodger after all? But whom had Milly expected to see? The feeling was there and gone again that she would not have been surprised to see somebody quite different, before she realized this wasn't quite the same Mr. Prodger as before. He was smarter than ever; all brushed, combed, shining. The ears that Marie had seen white as wax flashed as if they had been pink enamelled. Mother fluttered up in her pretty little way, so hoping he had not found the heat of the day too trying to be out in . . . but happily it was a little early in the year for dust. Then Miss Anderson was introduced. Milly was ready this time for that fresh hand, but she almost gasped; it was so very chill. It was like a hand stretched out to you from the water. Then together they all sat down.

"Is this your first visit to the Riviera?" asked Miss Anderson, graciously, dropping her handkerchief.

"It is," answered Mr. Prodger composedly, and he folded his arms as before. "I was in Florence until recently, but I caught a heavy cold—"

"Florence so—" began Mother, when the beautiful brass gong, that burned like a fallen sun in the shadows of the hall, began to throb. First it was a low muttering, then it swelled, it quickened, it burst into a clash of triumph under Marie's sympathetic fingers. Never had they been treated to such a performance before. Mr. Prodger was all attention.

"That's a very fine gong," he remarked approvingly.

"We think it is so very Oriental," said Mother. "It gives our little meals an Eastern flavour. Shall we . . ."

Their guest was at the door bowing.

"So many gentlemen and only one lady," fluttered Mother. "What I mean is the boot is on the other shoe. That is to say— come, Milly, come, dear." And she led the way to the dining-room.

Well, there they were. The cold, fresh napkins were shaken out of their charming shapes and Marie handed the omelette. Mr. Prodger sat on Mother's right, facing Milly, and Miss Anderson had her back to the long windows. But after all—why should the fact of their having a man with them make such a difference? It did; it made all the difference. Why should they feel so stirred at the sight of that large hand outspread, moving among the wine glasses? Why should the sound of that loud, confident "Ah-hm!" change the very look of the dining-room? It was not a favourite room of theirs as a rule; it was overpowering. They bobbed uncertainly at the pale table with a curious feeling of exposure. They were like those meek guests who arrive unexpectedly at the fashionable hotel, and are served with whatever may be ready, while the real luncheon, the real guests lurk important and contemptuous in the background. And although it was impossible for Marie to be other than deft, nimble and silent, what heart could she have in ministering to that most uninspiring of spectacles— three ladies dining alone?

Now all was changed. Marie filled their glasses to the brim as if to reward them for some marvellous feat of courage. These timid English ladies had captured a live lion, a real one, smelling faintly of eau de cologne, and with a tip of handkerchief showing, white as a flake of snow.

"He is worthy of it," decided Marie, eyeing her orchids and palms.

Mr. Prodger touched his hot plate with appreciative fingers.

"You'll hardly believe it, Mrs. Fawcett," he remarked, turning to Mother, "but this is the first hot plate I've happened on since I left the States. I had begun to believe there were two things that just weren't to be had in Europe. One was a hot plate and the other was a glass of cold water. Well, the cold water one can do without; but a hot plate is more difficult. I'd got so discouraged with the cold wet ones I encountered everywhere that when I was arranging with Cook's Agency about my room here I explained to them 'I don't care what the expense may be. But for mercy's sake find me an hotel where I can get a hot plate by ringing for it.' "

Mother, though outwardly all sympathy, found this a little bewildering. She had a momentary vision of Mr. Prodger ringing for hot plates to be brought to him at all hours. Such strange things to want in any numbers.

"I have always heard the American hotels are so very well equipped," said Miss Anderson. "Telephones in all the rooms and even tape machines."

Milly could see Miss Anderson reading that tape machine.

"I should like to go to America awfully," she cried, as Marie brought in the lamb and set it before Mother.

"There's certainly nothing wrong with America," said Mr. Prodger, soberly. "America's a great country. What are they? Peas? Well, I'll just take a few. I don't eat peas as a rule. No, no salad, thank you. Not with the hot meat."

"But what makes you want to go to America?" Miss Anderson ducked forward, smiling at Milly, and her eyeglasses fell into her plate, just escaping the gravy.

Because one wants to go everywhere, was the real answer. But Milly's flower-blue gaze rested thoughtfully on Miss Anderson as she said, "The ice-cream. I adore ice-cream."

"Do you?" said Mr. Prodger, and he put down his fork; he seemed moved. "So you're fond of ice-cream, are you, Miss Fawcett?"

Milly transferred her dazzling gaze to him. It said she was.

"Well," said Mr. Prodger quite playfully, and he began eating again, "I'd like to see you get it. I'm sorry we can't manage to ship some across. I like to see young people have just what they want. It seems right, somehow."

Kind man! Would he have any more lamb?

Lunch passed so pleasantly, so quickly, that the famous piece of gorgonzola was on the table in all its fatness and richness before there had been an awkward moment. The truth was that Mr. Prodger proved most easy to entertain, most ready to chat. As a rule men were not fond of chat as Mother understood it. They did not seem to understand that it does not matter very much what one says; the important thing is not to let the conversation drop. Strange! Even the best men ignored that simple rule. They refused to realize that conversation is like a dear little baby that is brought in to be handed round. You must rock it, nurse it, keep it on the move if you want it to keep smiling. What could be simpler? But even Father . . . Mother winced away from memories that were not as sweet as memories ought to be.

All the same she could not help hoping that Father saw what a successful little lunch party it was. He did so love to see Milly happy, and the child looked more animated than she had done for weeks. She had lost that dreamy expression, which, though very sweet, did not seem natural at her age. Perhaps what she wanted was not so much Easton's Syrup as taking out of herself.

"I have been very selfish," thought Mother, blaming herself as usual. She put her hand on Milly's arm; she pressed it gently as they rose from the table. And Marie held the door open for the white and grey figure; for Miss Anderson, who peered shortsightedly, as though looking for something; for Mr. Prodger who brought up the rear, walking stately, with the benign air of a Monsieur who had eaten well.

Beyond the balcony, the garden, the palms and the sea lay bathed in quivering brightness. Not a leaf moved; the oranges were little worlds of burning light. There was the sound of grass-hoppers ringing their tiny tambourines, and the hum of bees as they hovered, as though to taste their joy in advance, before burrowing close into the warm wide-open stocks and roses. The sound of the sea was like a breath, was like a sigh.

Did the little group on the balcony hear it? Mother's fingers moved among the black and gold coffee-cups; Miss Anderson brought the most uncomfortable chair out of the salon and sat down. Mr. Prodger put his large hand on to the yellow stone ledge of the balcony and remarked gravely, "This balcony rail is just as hot as it can be."

"They say," said Mother, "that the greatest heat of the day is at about half-past two. We have certainly noticed it is very hot then."

"Yes, it's lovely then," murmured Milly, and she stretched out her hand to the sun. "It's simply baking!"

"Then you're not afraid of the sunshine?" said Mr. Prodger, taking his coffee from Mother. "No, thank you. I won't take any cream. Just one lump of sugar." And he sat down balancing the little, chattering cup on his broad knee.

"No, I adore it," answered Milly, and she began to nibble the lump of sugar. . . .

Six Years After

IT WAS NOT the afternoon to be on deck—on the contrary. It was exactly the afternoon when there is no snugger place than a warm cabin, a warm bunk. Tucked up with a rug, a hot-water bottle and a piping hot cup of tea she would not have minded the weather in the least. But he—hated cabins, hated to be inside anywhere more than was absolutely necessary. He had a passion for keeping, as he called it, above board, especially when he was travelling. And it wasn't surprising, considering the enormous amount of time he spent cooped up in the office. So, when he rushed away from her as soon as they got on board and came back five minutes later to say he had secured two deck chairs on the lee side and the steward was undoing the rugs, her voice through the high sealskin collar murmured "Good"; and because he was looking at her, she smiled with bright eyes and blinked quickly, as if to say, "Yes, perfectly all right—absolutely," and she meant it.

"Then we'd better—" said he, and he tucked her hand inside his arm and began to rush her off to where the two chairs stood. But she just had time to breathe. "Not so fast, Daddy, please," when he remembered too and slowed down.

Strange! They had been married twenty-eight years, and it was still an effort to him, each time, to adapt his pace to hers.

"Not cold, are you?" he asked, glancing sideways at her. Her little nose, geranium pink above the dark fur, was answer enough. But she thrust her free hand into the velvet pocket of her jacket and murmured gaily, "I shall be glad of my rug."

He pressed her tighter to his side—a quick, nervous pressure.

338

He knew, of course, that she ought to be down in the cabin; he knew that it was no afternoon for her to be sitting on deck, in this cold and raw mist, lee side or no lee side, rugs or no rugs, and he realized how she must be hating it. But he had come to believe that it really was easier for her to make these sacrifices than it was for him. Take their present case, for instance. If he had gone down to the cabin with her, he would have been miserable the whole time, and he couldn't have helped showing it. At any rate, she would have found him out. Whereas, having made up her mind to fall in with his ideas, he would have betted anybody she would even go so far as to enjoy the experience. Not because she was without personality of her own. Good Lord! She was absolutely brimming with it. But because . . . but here his thoughts always stopped. Here they always felt the need of a cigar, as it were. And, looking at the cigar-tip, his fine blue eyes narrowed. It was a law of marriage, he supposed. . . . All the same, he always felt guilty when he asked these sacrifices of her. That was what the quick pressure meant. His being said to her being: "You do understand, don't you?" and there was an answering tremor of her fingers, "I *understand*."

Certainly, the steward—good little chap—had done all in his power to make them comfortable. He had put up their chairs in whatever warmth there was and out of the smell. She did hope he would be tipped adequately. It was on occasions like these (and her life seemed to be full of such occasions) that she wished it was the woman who controlled the purse.

"Thank you, steward. That will do beautifully."

"Why are stewards so often delicate-looking?" she wondered, as her feet were tucked under. "This poor little chap looks as though he'd got a chest, and yet one would have thought . . . the sea air. . . ."

The button of the pigskin purse was undone. The tray was tilted. She saw sixpences, shillings, half-crowns.

"I should give him five shillings," she decided, "and tell him to buy himself a good nourishing—"

He was given a shilling, and he touched his cap and seemed genuinely grateful.

Well, it might have been worse. It might have been sixpence.

339

It might, indeed. For at that moment Father turned towards her and said, half-apologetically, stuffing the purse back, "I gave him a shilling. I think it was worth it, don't you?"

"Oh, quite! Every bit!" said she.

It is extraordinary how peaceful it feels on a little steamer once the bustle of leaving port is over. In a quarter of an hour one might have been at sea for days. There is something almost touching, childish, in the way people submit themselves to the new conditions. They go to bed in the early afternoon, they shut their eyes and "it's night" like little children who turn the table upside down and cover themselves with the table-cloth. And those who remain on deck—they seem to be always the same, those few hardened men travellers—pause, light their pipes, stamp softly, gaze out to sea, and their voices are subdued as they walk up and down. The long-legged little girl chases after the red-cheeked boy, but soon both are captured; and the old sailor, swinging an unlighted lantern, passes and disappears. . . .

He lay back, the rug up to his chin and she saw he was breathing deeply. Sea air! If anyone believed in sea air, it was he. He had the strongest faith in its tonic qualities. But the great thing was, according to him, to fill the lungs with it the moment you came on board. Otherwise, the sheer strength of it was enough to give you a chill. . . .

She gave a small chuckle, and he turned to her quickly. "What is it?"

"It's your cap," she said. "I never can get used to you in a cap. You look such a thorough burglar."

"Well, what the deuce am I to wear?" He shot up one grey eyebrow and wrinkled his nose. "It's a very good cap, too. Very fine specimen of its kind. It's got a very rich white satin lining." He paused. He declaimed, as he had hundreds of times before at this stage, "Rich and rare were the gems she wore."

But she was thinking he really was childishly proud of the white satin lining. He would like to have taken off his cap and made her feel it. "Feel the quality!" How often had she rubbed between finger and thumb his coat, his shirt cuff, tie, sock, linen handkerchief, while he said that.

She slipped down more deeply into her chair.

And the little steamer pressed on, pitching gently, over the grey, unbroken, gently-moving water, that was veiled with slanting rain.

Far out, as though idly, listlessly, gulls were flying. Now they settled on the waves, now they beat up into the rainy air, and shone against the pale sky like the lights within a pearl. They looked cold and lonely. How lonely it will be when we have passed by, she thought. There will be nothing but the waves and those birds and rain falling.

She gazed through the rust-spotted railing along which big drops trembled, until suddenly she shut her lips. It was as if a warning voice inside her had said, "Don't look!"

"No, I won't," she decided. "It's too depressing, much too depressing."

But immediately, she opened her eyes and looked again. Lonely birds, water lifting, white pale sky—how were they changed?

And it seemed to her there was a presence far out there, between the sky and the water; someone very desolate and longing watched them pass and cried as if to stop them—but cried to her alone.

"Mother!"

"Don't leave me," sounded the cry. "Don't forget me! You are forgetting me, you know you are!" And it was as though from her own breast there came the sound of childish weeping.

"My son—my precious child—it isn't true!"

Sh! How was it possible that she was sitting there on that quiet steamer beside Father and at the same time she was hushing and holding a little slender boy—so pale—who had just waked out of a dreadful dream?

"I dreamed I was in a wood—somewhere far away from everybody,—and I was lying down and a great blackberry vine grew over me. And I called and called to you—and you wouldn't come—you wouldn't come—so I had to lie there for ever."

What a terrible dream! He had always had terrible dreams. How often, years ago, when he was small, she had made some excuse and escaped from their friends in the dining-room or the drawing-room to come to the foot of the stairs and listen.

"Mother!" And when he was asleep, his dream had journeyed with her back into the circle of lamplight; it had taken its place there like a ghost. And now—

Far more often—at all times—in all places—like now, for instance—she never settled down, she was never off her guard for a moment but she heard him. He wanted her. "I am coming as fast as I can! As fast as I can!" But the dark stairs have no ending, and the worst dream of all—the one that is always the same—goes for ever and ever uncomforted.

This is anguish! How is it to be borne? Still, it is not the idea of her suffering which is unbearable—it is his. Can one do nothing for the dead? And for a long time the answer had been—Nothing!

. . . But softly without a sound the dark curtain has rolled down. There is no more to come. That is the end of the play. But it can't end like that—so suddenly. There must be more. No, it's cold, it's still. There is nothing to be gained by waiting.

But—did he go back again? Or, when the war was over, did he come home for good? Surely, he will marry—later on—not for several years. Surely, one day I shall remember his wedding and my first grandchild—a beautiful dark-haired boy born in the early morning—a lovely morning—spring!

"Oh, Mother, it's not fair to me to put these ideas into my head! Stop, Mother, stop! When I think of all I have missed, I can't bear it."

"I can't bear it!" She sits up breathing the words and tosses the dark rug away. It is colder than ever, and now the dusk is falling, falling like ash upon the pallid water.

And the little steamer, growing determined, throbbed on, pressed on, as if at the end of the journey there waited. . . .

The Fly

Y'ARE VERY SNUG in here," piped old Mr. Woodifield, and he peered out of the great, green-leather arm-chair by his friend the boss's desk as a baby peers out of its pram. His talk was over; it was time for him to be off. But he did not want to go. Since he had retired, since his . . . stroke, the wife and the girls kept him boxed up in the house every day of the week except Tuesday. On Tuesday he was dressed and brushed and allowed to cut back to the City for the day. Though what he did there the wife and girls couldn't imagine. Made a nuisance of himself to his friends, they supposed. . . . Well, perhaps so. All the same, we cling to our last pleasures as the tree clings to its last leaves. So there sat old Woodifield, smoking a cigar and staring almost greedily at the boss, who rolled in his office chair, stout, rosy, five years older than he, and still going strong, still at the helm. It did one good to see him.

Wistfully, admiringly, the old voice added, "It's snug in here, upon my word!"

"Yes, it's comfortable enough," agreed the boss, and he flipped the *Financial Times* with a paper-knife. As a matter of fact he was proud of his room; he liked to have it admired, especially by old Woodifield. It gave him a feeling of deep, solid satisfaction to be planted there in the midst of it in full view of that frail old figure in the muffler.

"I've had it done up lately," he explained, as he had explained for the past—how many?—weeks. "New carpet," and he pointed to the bright red carpet with a pattern of large white rings. "New furniture," and he nodded towards the massive bookcase and the table with legs like twisted treacle. "Electric heating!" He waved almost exultantly towards the five transparent, pearly sausages glowing so softly in the tilted copper pan.

But he did not draw old Woodifield's attention to the photograph over the table of a grave-looking boy in uniform standing in one of those spectral photographers' parks with photographers' storm-clouds behind him. It was not new. It had been there for over six years.

"There was something I wanted to tell you," said old Woodifield, and his eyes grew dim remembering. "Now what was it? I had it in my mind when I started out this morning." His hands began to tremble, and patches of red showed above his beard.

Poor old chap, he's on his last pins, thought the boss. And, feeling kindly, he winked at the old man, and said jokingly, "I tell you what. I've got a little drop of something here that'll do you good before you go out into the cold again. It's beautiful stuff. It wouldn't hurt a child." He took a key off his watch-chain, unlocked a cupboard below his desk, and drew forth a dark, squat bottle. "That's the medicine," said he. "And the man from whom I got it told me on the strict Q.T. it came from the cellars at Windsor Castle."

Old Woodifield's mouth fell open at the sight. He couldn't have looked more surprised if the boss had produced a rabbit.

"It's whisky, ain't it?" he piped feebly.

The boss turned the bottle and lovingly showed him the label. Whisky it was.

"D'you know," said he, peering up at the boss wonderingly, "they won't let me touch it at home." And he looked as though he was going to cry.

"Ah, that's where we know a bit more than the ladies," cried the boss, swooping across for two tumblers that stood on the table with the water-bottle, and pouring a generous finger into each. "Drink it down. It'll do you good. And don't put any water with it. It's sacrilege to tamper with stuff like this. Ah!" He tossed off his, pulled out his handkerchief, hastily wiped his moustaches, and cocked an eye at old Woodifield, who was rolling his in his chaps.

The old man swallowed, was silent a moment, and then said faintly, "It's nutty!"

But it warmed him; it crept into his chill old brain—he remembered.

"That was it," he said, heaving himself out of his chair. "I thought you'd like to know. The girls were in Belgium last week having a look at poor Reggie's grave, and they happened to come across your boy's. They're quite near each other, it seems."

Old Woodifield paused, but the boss made no reply. Only a quiver in his eyelids showed that he heard.

"The girls were delighted with the way the place is kept," piped the old voice. "Beautifully looked after. Couldn't be better if they were at home. You've not been across, have yer?"

"No, no!" For various reasons the boss had not been across.

"There's miles of it," quavered old Woodifield, "and it's all as neat as a garden. Flowers growing on all the graves. Nice broad paths." It was plain from his voice how much he liked a nice broad path.

The pause came again. Then the old man brightened wonderfully.

"D'you know what the hotel made the girls pay for a pot of jam?" he piped. "Ten francs! Robbery, I call it. It was a little pot, so Gertrude says, no bigger than a half-crown. And she hadn't taken more than a spoonful when they charged her ten francs. Gertrude brought the pot away with her to teach 'em a lesson. Quite right, too; it's trading on our feelings. They think because we're over there having a look round we're ready to pay anything. That's what it is." And he turned towards the door.

"Quite right, quite right!" cried the boss, though what was quite right he hadn't the least idea. He came round by his desk, followed the shuffling footsteps to the door, and saw the old fellow out. Woodifield was gone.

For a long moment the boss stayed, staring at nothing, while the grey-haired office messenger, watching him, dodged in and out of his cubby-hole like a dog that expects to be taken for a run. Then: "I'll see nobody for half an hour, Macey," said the boss. "Understand? Nobody at all."

"Very good, sir."

The door shut, the firm heavy steps recrossed the bright carpet, the fat body plumped down in the spring chair, and leaning forward, the boss covered his face with his hands. He wanted, he intended, he had arranged to weep. . . .

It had been a terrible shock to him when old Woodifield sprang that remark upon him about the boy's grave. It was exactly as though the earth had opened and he had seen the boy lying there with Woodifield's girls staring down at him. For it was strange. Although over six years had passed away, the boss never thought of the boy except as lying unchanged, unblemished in his uniform, asleep for ever. "My son!" groaned the boss. But no tears came yet. In the past, in the first months and even years after the boy's death, he had only to say those words to be overcome by such grief that nothing short of a violent fit of weeping could relieve him. Time, he had declared then, he had told everybody, could make no difference. Other men perhaps might recover, might live their loss down, but not he. How was it possible? His boy was an only son. Ever since his birth the boss had worked at building up this business for him; it had no other meaning if it was not for the boy. Life itself had come to have no other meaning. How on earth could he have slaved, denied himself, kept going all those years without the promise for ever before him of the boy's stepping into his shoes and carrying on where he left off?

And that promise had been so near being fulfilled. The boy had been in the office learning the ropes for a year before the war. Every morning they had started off together; they had come back by the same train. And what congratulations he had received as the boy's father! No wonder; he had taken to it marvellously. As to his popularity with the staff, every man jack of them down to old Macey couldn't make enough of the boy. And he wasn't in the least spoilt. No, he was just his bright natural self, with the right word for everybody, with that boyish look and his habit of saying, "Simply splendid!"

But all that was over and done with as though it never had been. The day had come when Macey had handed him the telegram that brought the whole place crashing about his head.

346

"Deeply regret to inform you . . ." And he had left the office a broken man, with his life in ruins.

Six years ago, six years. . . . How quickly time passed! It might have happened yesterday. The boss took his hands from his face; he was puzzled. Something seemed to be wrong with him. He wasn't feeling as he wanted to feel. He decided to get up and have a look at the boy's photograph. But it wasn't a favourite photograph of his; the expression was unnatural. It was cold, even stern-looking. The boy had never looked like that.

At that moment the boss noticed that a fly had fallen into his broad inkpot, and was trying feebly but desperately to clamber out again. Help! help! said those struggling legs. But the sides of the inkpot were wet and slippery; it fell back again and began to swim. The boss took up a pen, picked the fly out of the ink, and shook it on to a piece of blotting-paper. For a fraction of a second it lay still on the dark patch that oozed round it. Then the front legs waved, took hold, and, pulling its small, sodden body up, it began the immense task of cleaning the ink from its wings. Over and under, over and under, went a leg along a wing as the stone goes over and under the scythe. Then there was a pause, while the fly, seeming to stand on the tips of its toes, tried to expand first one wing and then the other. It succeeded at last, and, sitting down, it began, like a minute cat, to clean its face. Now one could imagine that the little front legs rubbed against each other lightly, joyfully. The horrible danger was over; it had escaped; it was ready for life again.

But just then the boss had an idea. He plunged his pen back into the ink, leaned his thick wrist on the blotting-paper, and as the fly tried its wings down came a great heavy blot. What would it make of that? What indeed! The little beggar seemed absolutely cowed, stunned, and afraid to move because of what would happen next. But then, as if painfully, it dragged itself forward. The front legs waved, caught hold, and, more slowly this time, the task began from the beginning.

He's a plucky little devil, thought the boss, and he felt a real admiration for the fly's courage. That was the way to tackle things; that was the right spirit. Never say die; it was only a question of . . . But the fly had again finished its laborious task, and the boss had just time to refill his pen, to shake fair and square on the new-cleaned body yet another dark drop. What about it this time? A painful moment of suspense followed. But behold, the front legs were again waving; the boss felt a rush of relief. He leaned over the fly and said to it tenderly, "You artful little b . . ." And he actually had the brilliant notion of breathing on it to help the drying process. All the same, there was something timid and weak about its efforts now, and the boss decided that this time should be the last, as he dipped the pen deep into the inkpot.

It was. The last blot fell on the soaked blotting-paper, and the draggled fly lay in it and did not stir. The back legs were stuck to the body; the front legs were not to be seen.

"Come on," said the boss. "Look sharp!" And he stirred it with his pen—in vain. Nothing happened or was likely to happen. The fly was dead.

The boss lifted the corpse on the end of the paper-knife and flung it into the waste-paper basket. But such a grinding feeling of wretchedness seized him that he felt positively frightened. He started forward and pressed the bell for Macey.

"Bring me some fresh blotting-paper," he said sternly, "and look sharp about it." And while the old dog padded away he fell to wondering what it was he had been thinking about before. What was it? It was . . . He took out his handkerchief and passed it inside his collar. For the life of him he could not remember.

____ **A Lost Lady** by Willa Cather $8.95 679-72887-2

____ **Death Comes for the Archbishop** by Willa Cather $8.95 679-72889-9

____ **My Mortal Enemy** by Willa Cather $8.95 679-73179-2

____ **The Professor's House** by Willa Cather $9.95 679-73180-6

____ **Forty Stories** by Anton Chekhov, $11.00 679-73375-2
translated by Robert Payne

____ **A Tale of Two Cities** by Charles Dickens, $7.95 679-72965-8
with an introduction by Simon Schama

____ **The Aeneid**, translated by Robert Fitzgerald $7.95 679-72952-6

____ **The Odyssey**, translated by Robert Fitzgerald $7.95 679-72813-9

____ **Three Classic African-American Novels,**
edited and with an introduction $12.95 679-72742-6
by Henry Louis Gates, Jr.
Clotel by William Wells Brown,
Iola Leroy by Frances E.W. Harper,
The Marrow of Tradition by Charles W. Chestnutt

____ **The Sorrows of Young Werther** $8.95 679-72951-8
by Johann Wolfgang von Goethe
translated by Elizabeth Mayer and Louise Bogan,
with a foreword by W. H. Auden

____ **The Ink Dark Moon: Love Poems** $9.95 679-72958-5
by Ono No Komachi and Izumi Shikibu,
Women of the Ancient Court of Japan,
translated by Jane Hirshfield with Mariko Aratani

____ **Selected Poems of Langston Hughes** $9.95 679-72818-X
by Langston Hughes

____ **The Ways of White Folks** by Langston Hughes $8.95 679-72817-1

____ **Stories** by Katherine Mansfield, $11.00 679-73374-4
with an introduction by Jeffrey Meyers

____ **The Republic** by Plato, translated by B. Jowett $9.00 679-73387-6

____ **Cyrano de Bergerac** by Edmond Rostand, $9.95 679-73413-9
translated by Anthony Burgess

____ **The Tale of Genji** by Murasaki Shikibu, $9.95 679-72953-4
translated and abridged by Edward Seidensticker

____ **Dr. Jekyll and Mr. Hyde** by Robert Louis Stevenson, $7.00 679-73476-7
with an introduction by Joyce Carol Oates

____ **Democracy in America: Volume I** $8.95 679-72825-2
by Alexis de Tocqueville, translated by Phillips Bradley,
with an introduction by Daniel J. Boorstin

____ **Democracy in America: Volume II** $8.95 679-72826-0
by Alexis de Tocqueville, translated by Phillips Bradley

Available at your bookstore or call toll-free to order: 1-800-733-3000.
Credit cards only. Prices subject to change.

VINTAGE BOOKS/THE LIBRARY OF AMERICA

Available at your bookstore or call toll-free to order: 1-800-733-3000.
Credit cards only. Prices subject to change.